MARE INCOGNITO

WILLIAM W. STANARD

DEDICATION

To Mary who, as pilot, came aboard and, with love and skill,
guided me safely and surely out to the Sea Buoy

CHAPTER ONE

St. Louis, early morning

I lay on my back, the corner of the white and blue flower-patterned sheet across my ankles and put my hand on the pucker of the six-inch scar running from my waist down onto my thigh.

I opened my eyes and looked at the pattern of the single bedroom window projected onto the ceiling from the security light at the back of the family house on Old Bonhomme Road. The white, plastic globe of the ceiling light was unlit and empty, I knew. I had unscrewed the burnt-out bulb last week, and I had not replaced it. I turned my head to the right and looked at the luminous hands of the olive drab Baby Ben alarm clock. One-twenty. Monday? No, it was Tuesday night or Wednesday morning. I was alone in my old bedroom, home in the Midwest, no longer in the rivers of Vietnam.

I rolled first to a sitting position and then stood up at the right side of my bed. I felt the sway and tilt of nausea for a moment, but it cleared, leaving me standing unsteadily staring at the dark shape of the doorway leading to the short hallway and the living room.

I could sense the empty space of the bedroom in front of me, and I stood there and waited until I was sure that the floor stretched securely ahead of me. I closed my eyes and crossed

1

the room and stopped just as my thighs contacted the round oak table near the double windows that overlooked the back yard. My left hand and then my right found the small cassette recorder, its lid open, a tape still inside, just as I had left it yesterday morning when I had also been unable to sleep. Keeping my eyes closed, I pressed the REWIND button, the one to the left of the machine with two small dots above it. The sound of the cassette tape rewinding was a good sound, I thought, but I couldn't decide why. I stood in front of the table and listened to the whin of the tape and touched the scar.

After a minute, the cassette recorder snapped to a stop, and I pushed the right-hand PLAY button. The hiss of the tape was a good sound, too, I thought as I sat down on the smooth cotton fabric of the couch and pulled the wool serape over my legs and up across my chest. My head still, eyes closed, my arms at my sides outside of the serape, my hands tightly gripping the rough weave. I held my breath as I waited for the voice to begin. The hiss of the leader was suddenly replaced by a low, dull roar. My hands relaxed and I was back on my boat again, the twin diesel engines' comforting rumble enveloping and soothing me.

This tape was one of several my sister had returned to me. I had sent the tapes back to St. Louis from the rivers, and Sis had kept them, returning them to me after finding them as she cleaned out her living quarters at the back of her studio. She was a sculptress and, until our father died, lived and worked in a spacious studio on Delmar in the old business section of mid-town St. Louis, an area that had become the Mecca of the Bohemian set. The voice I heard was my own, as usual pitched slightly higher than I was used to hearing.

Sister, Sister. This is Abbey November nine three, over.

Location of this unit still classified, but it wasn't a dream. We really have left the rivers for good.

How are you, Sis? I can't believe that this might be my last tape to you all from in-country.

We're starting to hear a lot of stuff from on high about having won our part and now is the time for turning over this war to the rightful owners. But remember this... this war isn't over for any of us until we get home. If something should happen to me and I don't make it back, don't let the bastards tell you, and they sure as hell will try to tell you, that it was worth it. It wasn't. I'm sure we'll be in the record books as placing second in these Southeast Asia War Games for a damned good reason.

Seriously, Sis, we're about to leave Cam Rahn Bay, heading for Vung Tau. Our whole group over here is getting short, I'm sitting up and taking solid food, I still can't picture where your new apartment is, and we are all getting our jollies on a regular basis.

Yeah. Don't I wish! The closest any of us gets to a sex life is a long, muddy street of shacks covered with printed but uncut plates of steel and aluminum used to make beer cans. Each shack is about twelve by twelve and tastefully decorated with an Army cot and a white enamel wash basin.

I pushed and held the PAUSE button.

Good God, I thought. Did I really send her this adolescent crap? I felt embarrassed, but I was sure that she had heard shabbier stuff out of my mouth before. She could cuss like a Teamster, I knew, and that was one of the reasons I could still talk to her, why our childhood closeness had survived adolescence into adult friendship. She had probably shocked me more times as we had grown up together than I had shocked her. I released the PAUSE button.

I can't wait for the elegance of the massage parlors of Vung Tau.

It's so bad down the Row... that's what we call their street of heavenly bliss here in Cam Rahn... that I heard the Kid, one of my own crew for God's sake, talking to this... girl in the shack next to the one I was in.

"All I want is love." Just like that. "All I want is love." Jesus, Sis! What can you do in a place like that, huh?

Wonder if it was his first time.

Oh, yeah, before I forget, Thanks for the CARE package. The herbs and spices and A1 Sauce are great. Muchly appreciated. I liked the postcards from the Ozarks, too. How about Dad? Can't get him to write or send another tape, huh? Well, thanks for trying. Retally. How's he doing?

The driver I hang around with the most is Tim Barnes, but in the last weeks, since we came out of the rivers and left Sea Float, even he and I just seem to stare at the walls in the O Club and not say much. We've been on a lot of missions together, and I guess we've about talked it all out. Either that or there are some things we just won't get into.

We've been in it up to our asses together and all, but it's still not like we're close friends, really.

I need to hear your voices to help through the last weeks, so get the Crew together some night if you see them and send me a last tape. Maybe you could take a cassette recorder to Sir John's Den. *I've got this real hang-up about keeping in touch with you all. I'm afraid... or something... that I'll lose it.*

Love to Dad. I miss you, Sis. Tell the Crew, "Hi!" and send that tape soon.

This is Abbey November nine three.

Nothing further.

Out.

CHAPTER TWO

Vung Tau, 4 December, 2000 hours

The six American Swift boat skippers, all in their mid-twenties, sat at a round plywood table in the Officer's Club at the Navy base in Vung Tau, Republic of South Vietnam. For them the war was almost over. They were going home in three days, their fifty-foot aluminum hulled boats the last to be turned over to the South Vietnamese Navy. In front of each of them stood an empty glass and a brown bottle of Ba Mi Ba, a local beer, rich in formaldehyde. One of the skippers, the one with red hair, sat with his back to the screen door. He looked up at the turquoise plastic clock hanging over the rows of bottles and cracked mirror behind the white painted wood bar. He cleared his throat. The Vietnamese bartender smiled at him, showing two gold teeth, and nodded his head in agreement as though the red head had said something very clever.

"I give them twelve hours," the red headed driver, as the skippers liked to be called, said and slowly poured two inches of beer into his glass. The foam rushed up the inside and stood an inch high before slipping down the outside of the highball glass and making another small ring on the bare plywood. One more to go, he thought as he studied what appeared to be the Olympic symbol, two rows of interlocking rings. The stitched name on his shirt said O'Connor.

The blond to his left, aviator glasses pushed up on his forehead and the name Davis on his uniform, said, "Eighteen hours for the 12s and another six for the gen set." The blond pulled his beer bottle closer to him with two hands, ignoring the empty glass. He had sunken eyes, and they slowly blinked as he looked around the table.

"I'11 give them a week. My guy's pretty sharp and his crew's scared of him," said the curly black-haired driver in the broad, flat accent of Philadelphia. His eyes sparkled as he poured his beer slowly down the inside of his tilted glass. The beer did not foam, lying flat and oily in his glass. "Panther piss," he said, almost to himself. Marco was stitched in black over his left-hand breast pocket. "Ned?" he asked the one to his left.

"Warm panther piss, at that," answered Ned Taylor. His brown hair just touched his ears and was worn longer in the back, sweeping his collar as he looked to his right and then to his left around the table at the other five. "Make mine twenty-four hours for both. It'll all go at the same time. Nguyen will foul up the fuel tanks, and everything will go to hell at once." Ned poured his beer slowly up to the rim and centered the full glass carefully in front of him on the table. There was only one other ring in the space in front of him where the newly filled glass sat.

"I'll go short with an hour after the turn-over, but I can only go for one of the main engines." The speaker, Tim Barnes, was going bald. He had no name at all sewn on his fatigue shirt. He was the oldest of the group and everybody called him Dog, short for Sea Dog, even his boat crew. He touched the neck of his beer bottle and turned to his left. "You want to bet this one, Sleek-hood?"

Diego Acosta, known as Sleek-hood because of his South LA accented pronunciation of their old stateside radio call sign, smiled. "My left engine's still in pieces, gentlemen. No bets. I will pour in any case if it is all right?" Marco and Dog agreed aloud and there was no dissent. Sleek-hood poured and the entire group smiled as the beer foamed over and flushed out in a yellow rush across the plywood in front of the heavy-set, dark haired driver. He mopped up part of the mess with an already damp white handkerchief. He returned the damp cloth to the front thigh pocket of his untidy fatigues.

"All bets in?" asked the red-headed O'Connor.

"Go for it, Pat," answered Marco, raising his glass to eye level.

Each of them raised his glass or bottle and waited.

"I send in code," O'Connor said and turned to face the yellow and red striped South Vietnamese flag hanging limply to the right of the door. He held his glass just above his head. "Alfa. Mike. Foxtrot."

"Yeah," breathed Marco and Acosta together.

"You got my vote," said Davis.

"Adios, motherfucker," Ned said under his breath, his eyes closed.

"I have this awful feeling I'll miss the bitch," spoke Dog after a moment of silence and they all drank together.

Old Bonhomme Road, early morning

I stirred on the couch and tried to remember how many other tapes I had sent from Vietnam. I had made a lot of tapes at first, then fewer and fewer as the months went on.

The closest I had come to having a girl back home had been Margot, but I had left the States without writing to her. I had sent her a tape after I had listened to the one she had sent me, a long one with some great jazz and some oddball, raunchy beat poetry she'd written, but my tape had been returned to me in the river a month later, Addressee Unknown. I had kept the tape, never erasing it, finally bringing it back home with me. I looked at it through its cracked clear plastic case and then tossed it into the waste basket.

CHAPTER THREE

Ca Mau Peninsula, June 12, 1200 hours

It was late June when Ned went up to Vung Tau for the first time. Killian, the bow gunner he had never liked on the 93 boat, had been hit by a VC claymore mine, the cut-off end of a fifty- five gallon drum hung from a tree and packed with high explosives and glass and bits of metal. The flash and low thump seemed to come simultaneously, the boat running so close to the edge of the narrow canal and the mine. Most of the force of the blast was taken by the hull, one piece of rusty metal hitting the only crewman who had his flak jacket closed tight and sprawling him there on the bow, his helmet off on the deck to his left and his legs down in the peak tank all twisted under him, bleeding like that all the way out the canal.

As they were coming back out of the canal, Harris, up in the twin mount on top of the pilot house had shouted, "There's a wire! Back'er down!" and the boat continued to roll forward ahead of its own wake before the engines, now in reverse, could slow them.

Ned was standing next to the helmsman putting the mic back in the clip on the side of the radio from talking to *Sea Float* with a report that the canal was clear. He heard the shout and was searching ahead along the canal sides and at a point about two feet above the water for the wire as he heard the

9

scrape of the metal at the bow.

"You backing?" he asked the helmsman.

"I'm backing. Where's 127?"

He could see through the window in the back of the pilot house that the other boat was coming up behind them to starboard, backing also, slewing across the canal, its bow almost even with 93's stern.

"You're clear. Back it hard!" he was shouting now, the roar of the diesels filling the pilot house.

The thump and bright flash of the mine to port from somewhere in the trees blew leaves and twigs onto the deck and a coil of line spun off the bow and into the brown water. There was gray smoke and the acid taste of the explosion.

Killian had half-climbed out of the peak tank, a small compartment in the bow that the gunners hung their feet in when they sat on deck up forward. Killian was always bitching about something when they went on patrol, especially in the canals.

"Here we go again. For the glory of the Navy," Killian's pale pinched face would call up to the gunner each morning. Harris would shake his head and turn away and keep working on the two .50 calibers, cleaning and oiling and rubbing them, an unlit cigar clamped firmly in the side of his wide mouth, his black face glistening with sweat even in the early cool of the day. Harris had already been awarded a Bronze Star and Ned had put him in for a second one.

" 'Nother shot at a Bronze, eh, Harris?" Killian had brayed at Harris that morning, and Harris had looked at him hard, not smiling his usual wide and splendid smile.

"Know your problem, Harris?" Killian continued.

Harris stopped moving the oily cloth out along the length of the barrel of the machine gun on the right. His yellow shooting glasses winked in the sun as he looked down at Killian. "I have a problem?" he asked quietly. "Other than you, none of us has a problem."

"Yeah. You think getting a Bronze will make you white," Killian said with a thin grin. "That's your problem."

"Nothing will ever make you white, Killian," Harris spoke slowly and bent to work on his '50s, running the oily cloth out to the end of the barrel and back slowly, lovingly. Killian then barked his short, unhappy laugh and walked up to the bow.

He spent most patrols up on the bow where he was out of the way, and they wouldn't have to listen to his bitching. It had been better for everyone for Killian to be up there like that.

There was the claymore going off and the bow was then rising slowly into the air as the helmsman was pushing the throttles hard forward and there was the flat smashing answer of the heavy machine guns from the twin mount on top of the pilot house. Ned had the radio mic back off the clip in his hand again and was trying to speak calmly and clearly each word telling *Sea Float* of the mine and the canal and that there wasn't any firefight but just the mine when he saw Killian slowly roll to port and topple over, losing his helmet.

"Sea Float, this is nine three. We've got a man hit. Need a dust-off," Ned spoke carefully into the mic as he craned his neck to see Killian better on the bow.

"Roger, nine three. Stand by this push for traffic from Sea Wolf zero six."

"We're coming out fast. Be home soon. Standing by." He couldn't see the man on the bow very well, so he came down off his toes.

"Is Killian OK?" Tom, the helmsman, asked.

"He's down on his side. I can't tell. Come on, zero six, call in." He wanted to get out to the bow.

"He'll be OK. Always wears his flak jacket closed up tight. The guy's better protected than any of us," offered Tom who wore no shirt under his open flak jacket, cut off fatigue pants, and jungle boots without laces. His helmet sat on the back of his head, his red-blond hair hanging low over blue eyes and a boy's face full of freckles. His dog-tags flashed as he laughed. "Killian's a shit, Boss, and shits don't get hurt."

He knew that Killian was a shit, but he *was* hurt.

Ned held onto the edge of the chart table in front of him, standing on his tiptoes again. He held the mic in his right hand wanting to move out the door of the pilot house to get to him when he heard the first rounds of the firefight but this time from the right side as the canal widened to almost fifty yards and the helmsman swung the boat to port away from it. Ned hung on the doorjamb with his left hand as the deck tilted and they curved away from the shore and the smoke and tiny cracks of the small arms fire more toward the middle of the canal. Ned didn't notice if there were splashes in the water or not, but the fire would continue, he remembered later, almost to where the canal joined the river.

He remembered giving their position to Sea Wolf zero six, the lead helicopter gunship of the two which had been diverted from a SEAL op to support them, as the boat turned, and he could only hang on and talk to the pilot of the helicopter.

"Abbey November nine three, this is Sea Wolf zero six and wingman one eight. Heard you got some problems down there. Can we give you a hand?" said the voice of Tad Lawrence, a lanky Texan who continually chain-smoked Camels and showed everyone his collection of photographs of dead VC and NVA. The intel officer, Don Cherry, said that Tad carried a shriveled ear in his flight suit pocket for good luck, but Ned had never asked to see it.

"This is nine three. We took a claymore up forward and have one man down. We're coming out. Do you have us visually?"

"Affirmative. What's your partner's number?"

"One two seven."

"Roger," Tad said. He always sounded relaxed, in control. "Would you like us to hose down the banks up ahead of you?"

"Roger. Have at it."

"Any other of your guys in the arca? Ground troops? Other boats?"

"Negative. "

"Roger that. Standby."

"Standing by," Ned said and handed the mic to Tom.

He knelt next to Killian, noticing that the grey deck was

wet, but he could not see a wound. Ned sat on the deck, his feet hanging down through the peak tank hatch and took the bow gunner by the shoulders and rolled him over onto his back. Killian lay now in Ned's lap and Ned could feel the wetness of his blood but could still see no wound.

He listened as the two gunships came in low over the canal from behind them and then saw them overhead moving fast and low and then beginning to fire. The long burp of their mini-guns came to him over the sound of the bellowing diesels and the hiss of the water from their speed echoing from the green nipa palms and creepers of the walls of the jungle on either side of the canal.

He was holding the bow gunner and watching the helos precede them out the canal when he first noticed the piece of rusty metal like a pointing finger sticking out just above the top of Killian's flak jacket. Ned could feel the blood soaking into his clothes as he sat there with Killian in his lap.

He wondered about touching the rusty metal finger, but he couldn't do it. He wondered how he could stop the bleeding. He looked up at the helos as they began their second run and then looked down, seeing the metal in Killian's neck move as the boy breathed and Ned wished he liked Killian better since he knew he would not make it.

Killian died on an operating table late that night a hundred and fifty miles away after the two boats ran full-bore all the way out the six miles of the canal and back the four miles along the Cua Long to *Sea Float*, their base anchored in the middle of the river.

The dust-off to the Navy hospital at Can Tho took off from the barges with Killian inside still strapped to the boat's stretcher they had put him on once they were out of the canal and in the much wider river. Rocking gently in the river near the mouth of the canal, Ned had slowed the flow of blood with a field dressing, but Killian's pulse was by then very weak. Ned had sat with him the fifteen minutes it had taken to get out of the canal and the eight minutes it took them to run the river to get back to *Sea Float* and he had looked at the boy's eyelids and mouth and watched his nostrils move ever so slightly as he tried to breathe. He had let go of Killian's right hand only long enough to get him on the stretcher and to change the field dressings on his neck. Killian's eyes had opened only once as they were near the end of the canal, and he had looked up at Ned and there was hatred in his eyes. Ned tried but could not feel the same hatred.

"You've been hit," Ned said to the silent figure, "but you're going to be OK. You'll get a trip home out of this. You're lucky. "

"You never wanted me on board." Killian's voice was almost a whisper. Ned had to turn his head and put his right ear almost touching the thin, bloodless lips to hear the words, The eyes were closed again.

"You'll be OK, Killian," Ned promised. "Don't talk."

Don't make your last minutes any worse than they have to be. Shut up and let us remember something good of you, he thought.

The boy's pulse was almost gone as they handed him to the corpsmen on the barge stooping low under the slowly turning helicopter blades and watched as the dust-off lifted slightly, turning into the wind, gathering speed, its tail tilting up, heading up the river at fifty feet, spreading the troubled water ahead and beneath, rising a hundred feet into the air, turning to the north and disappearing in the bright distance toward the Navy Base and hospital at Can Tho.

Ned watched the helo disappear.

The kid might just make it, he thought. He had been on the verge of transferring Killian a half dozen times in the last month. The kid really soured the moral of the boat with his bitching all the time. At least up in the peak tank he had been out of the way, and he had been too scared to bitch very much. He thought Killian would pull through. He really did. They had good doctors up there in Can Tho.

CHAPTER FOUR

Cua Lon River, June 13, 0815 hours

Division told Ned the morning after Killian was hit to proceed, with the 127 boat, up the coast to Vung Tau for two weeks of engine and hull work and some time off.

"I don't need any time off," Ned answered the senior officer in charge of the Swift boat division. He came down to the side of the barge where the 93 and 127 boats were rafted. He wore no insignia, just his name and rank, LCDR FREDERICK, sewn in black on the pressed fatigues.

"How about your men, then?" said Frederick as he stood looking down at the stains on the bow of the 93 boat. "They could use some time out of the river, couldn't they?"

"Sure. Yes," said Ned after a pause. "Yes, Sir. They could use it. They've earned it. We're five for five, this last week. "

"Only got hit on this last one, right?"

"Yes, Sir. We've been lucky," Nick said. "And the guys are good, too," he added.

"Then take the one-twenty-seven boat with you and head up for Vung Tau," Frederick ordered. "Stand down for a week and relax. Have some fun." He paused. "You married, Ned?"

"No, Sir."

"Have some fun. Try the Saigon Hotel. They used to have a dance every night."

"A dance, Sir?" Ned wondered. "I'm really not much of a dancer."

"Oh, come on. You know what I mean," said Frederick as he walked away across the barge. "Not a real dance."

"Yes, Sir. I see," said Ned but he didn't.

On the way up the coast in the hot sun and bright noontime heat, as soon as they were clear of the Bo De river, Ned ignored the instructions on the quart can of Haze Gray flat enamel and painted the deck up on the bow where he could not clean away all of Killian's blood. As the helmsman, Tom, kept the northeasterly course, staying about a mile offshore, Ned tried hard to forget about putting Killian up in the bow and his bleeding like that during the run out the canal and along the river to the barges and the dust-off helo at *Sea Float*.

When he finished painting, he sat on the fold-down stool that was usually kept out of the way under the chart table and thought about a tape he had to record and send home to his father in St. Louis. He had sent one every two weeks as he had promised, but it had been four months and the only word he had had in return had been a single tape five minutes long.

He knew that his father was getting the tapes he had sent. He had learned that in a letter from his sister, who had written that his father was drinking a bit less after his latest trip out of town, though she didn't know where.

He switched on the tape recorder, turning his back to the helmsman and looking out the pilot house door. No one listened to anyone else's tapes, but he was always embarrassed to record when someone else was around. It was too wet with spray to go out on deck aft and the paint on the deck in the bow was still wet.

"Hi, Dad. How're you doing. I'm OK over here." He took a breath, holding the PAUSE button. Why do I say that? he thought. Nobody over here's OK. We're all just as screwed up as he is. But it would be mean to worry them back home. He held the tape recorder up in the air, aiming the mic out the door of the pilot house.

"Hear that?" he asked. *"We're headed up the coast to Vung Tau, an old French city on the coast, for some repairs and some R and R. It's a beautiful day. The water is calm. About two-foot rollers and almost no wind. We should be there in about eighteen hours or so. Can't wait. I'll be going to a dance at..."* he thumbed the pause button. *"The Saigon Hotel,"* he continued, letting the tape advance.

"Sis wrote me a letter. She said she left you a phone message the other week after she saw you at a party at the Country Club, and you looked happier than she'd seen you look in a while. What's happening that's good?... By the way, she'd like to hear some of the tapes I've sent back. Why don't the two of you get together? She said she hadn't seen you since... " Ned paused without holding down the button. He stopped the tape, ran it back, and pushed the play button.

"... your last trip out of town... She'd like to hear some of the tapes I've sent back." Ned stopped the tape. Dad hadn't told her where he'd been, his sister had written. Ned pressed the record button and continued, *"Give her a call, OK? I'll stop for now and get back to you in a while."* Ned put the tape recorder in the tray behind the chart table and rested his chin in his hand, staring out through the windshield at the blue sea and endless rolling waves.

"Course?" he asked Tom after a minute.

"Zero three eight. About eighteen hundred yards off the coast," the helmsman answered.

"Sounds good," said Ned. "Call me when we're off the mouth of the Bassac. When the water gets muddy. I'm going down below for a nap."

"See you, Boss. Sleep good," answered Tom, giving him the thumbs up.

"Yeah. Thanks, Tom," Ned said and ducked down the three steps into the cabin where Harris and CB were playing hearts. Harris looked up and smiled. Ned smiled back and went into the bunk area in the bow. He kicked his boots off as he climbed into the lower bunk to starboard and pulled the quilted poncho liner over his shoulders, turning his face away from the dim red cabin light and toward the rumble of the water along the hull.

He thought about how he would tell his father in St. Louis

17

about Killian and his being killed like that. He would talk about holding him in his lap on the bow and how he had really not liked him and about their putting his dying body in the helo to be flown up to the hospital in Can Tho. He would tell him the whole thing, leaving nothing out. He wouldn't even leave out the part about making him ride up there on the bow and having to hold him in his lap while he was dying like that. He would make sure he remembered to put in that part about how nobody liked him. His father would have to answer *that* tape, he thought, and then he slept.

Old Bonhomme Road, early morning

I sat hunched over at the table in the dining room in Warson Village, the serape pulled tightly around me. I put another tape in the cassette recorder and pushed PLAY.

Now hear this. Now hear this. The following will be a test of the one em cee. This is your captain speaking.

We're back from the dead, Sister of Mine, and I'm the proud possessor of important information. This puppy will not... I say again... I will not be taken alive. If there's anything they taught us at that awful survival school, it's save the last round for yourself. Jesus, those bastards scared the hell out of me! I thought I knew what I could take, but they brought me somewhere new in about two days' time, and they didn't even break into a sweat.

I told you that we were going up to Whidbey Island to learn some escape and evasion stuff in the woods. Well, that was just the start. After they had supposedly trained us... and I think that I knew more from going to Camp Minocqua as a kid for two years than I learned there... they turned us loose. After about four hours of running through the pucker brush and trying to catch chipmunks for lunch, we were easily picked up by a bunch of bit players dressed up like Mao's palace guard, pushed into the back of a gray Navy truck with a huge red star on each door, and told that we could not speak. We were not an impressive group by any stretch.

"The game is over, Yankee dogs," was all the one of them who would speak said when we asked him if we'd made it, if we'd successfully evaded

capture. It was pitiful. The Yankee dogs bit, I mean. Very Hollywood.

They drove us to a compound that looked like a Walt Disney fort on the outside, except it had a lot of concertina wire all over it, and made us pile out and stand around in the cold with bags over our heads. By this time, most of us were beginning to shiver because we just had fatigues on and the temperature was about forty. They then had us strip! Can you believe it? We are all standing there in our skivvies with canvas bags over our heads and our right hands on the shoulder of the guy in front of us. Just like hell night in a fraternity. Suddenly someone, one of the Hollywood Maoists I guess, douches me with a bucket of cold water.

Sis, my love, I've never been so instantly frozen or dumbstruck in my life.

The next thing I knew is that I'm standing in some tar-paper shack looking down at the boots of some really big clown, the bag is yanked off my head, and he's asking me how many boats we've got in our division, a piece of information we were told was a no-no to let out, especially to the Chairman's gorillas.

I did my thing, giving him name, rank, etcetera, and the bastard tosses a glass of cold water in my face. He let me stand there for about five minutes and shiver, asking me the same thing every fifteen seconds. When I wouldn't tell him, he finally let me go and gave me my clothes to put back on again.

The rest of the two days in what they kept calling a Re-Education Camp was truly mind expanding. I spent most of my time in a pitch-black box the size of a telephone booth but only five feet high. A coffee can was supposed to be the latrine, but I had eaten so little for the last couple of days that I didn't need to do anything more than pee, and that I did through a hole in the floor.

As I knelt there on the floor with my plumbing pointing toward that hole, I asked myself two things: Are there hungry animals under this box? and is command of a Swift boat really worth it?

Every two hours or so they'd take me outside the box and go through the strip down to the skivvies, the bucket of water routine, and the questions. At the end of the second day, I was really glad that these bad guys were only pretend. If it hadn't been so serious a game we were all playing, I began to suspect that I was closer than hell to telling the bastards something... anything.... just to get them off my back. What the hell could they do as punishment? Send me to Vietnam? I already had a first-class ticket and my seat chosen.

What finally clinched it was the barrel of water. Two of the big ones grabbed me by the legs as I was doing my firm but polite routine and refusing to give anything away. They turned me upside down and, before I could even tell them to perform miracles on themselves, they put me headfirst into a fifty-five-gallon steel barrel full of the world's coldest water.

I held my breath.

They held my legs.

The three of us waited.

I guess I held my breath for long enough because they hauled me out and asked their question again. I did my officer and a gentleman bit, and they called me a whole list of Maoist names. I must have impressed them with the Houdini imitation, though, because they let me put on my clothes. I was half-carried back to the box, but that was the last of the questions and water routine.

Later that day the camp was "liberated." We were told we had all behaved in the highest traditions and so on, and we were trucked back to the main base, drank entirely too many toddies at the O Club, and did hand to hand combat with a roast beef dinner that would have made Henry the Eighth envious.

The group I was with, Nash, Mitch, the Yalie, Barnes, and I didn't talk much about the camp, except to discover that we had each decided individually that being in the rivers in Vietnam would be a hell of a lot easier to deal with than Survival School in the State of Washington.

I didn't sleep very well that night, as well fed and as sloshed as I think I must have been. I kept running over in my head what happened inside of me when they pulled me out of the barrel that afternoon.

I knew that I would tell them whatever they wanted to know, game or no game, if they got me near that barrel again. I knew that a couple of pretend thugs had, in two days, brought me that close to letting it all go.

A hell of a way to start a tour in 'Nam.

South China Sea, June 13, 1930 hours

The land was gone now, replaced by a smudge of brown along the western sky where the big rivers emptied into the

South China Sea. Once during the afternoon, a slowly rising and falling speck had appeared on the horizon to their left as the 93 and the 127 boats worked their way along the low coast and below the speck had sprouted bright orange blossoms with oily black leaves, one blossom every minute or so. There had been eight blossoms, and Tom had reported to Ned about the first three, but the last five Tom watched alone after Ned had gone back down to his bunk. The radio was set to the Army frequency in the Bac Lieu area, and Tom had listened and watched as the controller called in the napalm strikes.

"Three-man rocket team working the main canal from Bac Lieu to the coast," the controller had reported explaining the bright blossoms, and Tom gave the coast another two hundred yards room using the radar's range rings to keep his distance. That had been two hours ago.

Now the open mouth of the Bassac was to their left, and the radar could find no land. Tom called Ned and the two of them sat in the early evening dimness of the pilot house. Ned sat on the folded down stool to the left of the helmsman's seat, his elbows resting on the clear plexiglas chart table cover. He enjoyed Tom's company.

"Been to Vung Tau, Tom?"

"Once. No good places to hang out except the EM club. The town was off limits. Got laid though. "

"When were you up there?" Ned asked.

"'We'd just come in country and had to get the injectors replaced. Mr. Kelley'd run a whole tank of turbine fuel, and the injector tips had all burned out."

Ned wondered how Kelley had made it out of the rivers in one piece. "We told him not to run so much turbine, but he wouldn't listen. Used to be on a carrier. Never listened to anyone below Chief," Tom said.

"Division tells me the town is open, Tom, so maybe you'll have more places to go." He'd paused and then asked, "How'd you do it, with the town closed and all?"

"Do what?"

"Get laid."

"Oh, that. Easy. The laundry girls at the EM Club. We went

to the laundry hootch."

"At least you didn't have to worry about clean sheets," Ned said with a smile.

"No sheets, Boss. She did me standing up," Tom said matter-of-factly.

In the lower right corner, someone had scratched FUCK THEM. Probably Killian, Ned thought. The shaky letters had filled with crayon from the grease pencils they used on the plastic. The words were easy to read, now. When they had first been written, the words had been an idle obscenity scratched into the clear plastic used to cover the maps and charts. A little time in the rivers changes everything, Ned thought. Makes everything easier to read.

"Running lights?" Tom asked and Ned reached up to the row of toggle switches. They weren't in the rivers and could follow standard Rules of the Road, navigation lights on one half hour after sunset until one half hour before sunrise. It was strange how pleasant such a routine gesture could be. For months, in the rivers, they had never used lights at night, driving the canals and main channels alike relying on radar and starlight scopes.

Ned stepped out onto the deck and looked up at the red light mounted on the gun tub. He hung onto the handrail against the ocean's gentle roll and made his way around to the green light on the starboard side, checking the reflection in their wake of the bright stern light. A hundred yards to the east was the red running light on the low silhouette of the 127 boat He went back inside the pilot house.

"All running lights are bright lights," he said to himself, mimicking the chief quartermaster from whom he had learned on his first ship. He wrote the time, 1815, in the log, a school child's black and white composition book. Next to the time he wrote, "Underway as before. Main channel entrance buoy (west branch, Bassac) bears 010°, 1000 yards."

Off to the southeast glowed the lights of an inbound freighter about two miles distant. Bound upriver to Phnom Penh Ned thought. Wonder what it feels like to go through a country at war. Like driving through the wrong part of town late on a Saturday night. He smiled and his finger traced up the river on the chart under the clear plexiglas past the medium sized dots of Can Tho and Long Xuyen to a much smaller dot of Chau Doc. Ned's finger stopped, and he stared at the small letters at the end of the Vinh Te Canal.

That's where Killian had joined them, Ned remembered. He had been sent there to join Pat O'Connor's boat, but they had left the day before, so the 93 inherited him for the next week while the two boats leapfrogged down river with both new and old partners through a series of one day or overnight missions until they returned to *Sea Float*. By the time the 93 got back to the Cua Lon, Killian's orders had been changed. He was scheduled to replace Ned's engineman, Tenney, who was due to go home in another two weeks.

An hour after Ned had told him about becoming part of the crew of the 93 boat, Killian had unloaded his sea bag and was playing his Country and Western tapes over the psy-ops speakers. Ned didn't say anything because he let the crew play their tapes over the speakers. He had thought back to when he was still a teenager in St. Louis. They had used to cruise around in his friend Dave's red Buick Skylark with the top down and the radio loud. The old ladies in their black Plymouths and the kids from The Priory or Saint A's used to stare at them, envious of the convertible and the music and that they were out there on the street, cruising. Music in the rivers reminded Ned of home.

Killian's music wasn't the same. They all liked Tom's acid rock, Harris' Stones or Creedence, and the Beatles and Crosby, Stills. No one really liked Killian's C & W, though, and everyone was quick to let him know it the first time some trucker's unrequited love twanged from the speakers. He then seemed to make it a point to play it often and at top volume.

"Killian, do you have to play that ugly music so loudly?" Harris asked the first time, his face empty of its usual good humor. Harris was driving as they approached the sea buoy at the mouth of the Bo De. They were to wait there for an escort into *Sea Float*.

"You guys play your tapes at 7 or 8, don't you? That's all

this is set at," came Killian's answer, missing the point. "Boss hasn't complained yet, has he?"

Ned hated Killian calling him Boss because he knew that he didn't mean it. For the other crew members Boss had become a term of acceptance and loyalty. When Killian said it, the word became a sneer.

"Hey, Boss. OK if I play my tape?" Killian's head looked down into the cabin from the pilot house. Even his voice had begun to irritate.

"If it's OK with the others," Ned answered flatly, looking up at the thin lips and small eyes. Ned didn't want to answer with a yes or a no. He disliked the question being asked. They all worked well together at a casual level. They just knew and didn't have to ask. Asking admitted that you didn't know that you weren't part of the group.

Once Killian's music became an everyday annoyance, he wished that he had said something to stop it earlier. The others seemed to understand when playing music was appropriate and when it was not. Killian even tried to play a tape just after the big firefight in the Duong Keo. Ned had smiled at Harris and what he had been thinking when the gunner had signaled Tom to kill the speakers by drawing his finger across his throat.

"We should be so lucky," had been all Tom had said as he killed the music.

The dark bulk of the inbound freighter was astern of them now. It was stopped, waiting at the sea buoy for the pilot to take it into the river.

CHAPTER FIVE

Old Bonhomme Road, early morning

The hum of the tape player straining at the end of the cassette woke me back in St. Louis again. The room was stuffy. The serape felt rough against my skin. The anxiety had not left entirely, but I felt calmer than I had in a week. I thought I might have caught another hour or so of sleep.

I spent that day doing the sort of mindless duties one performs while waiting for dinner that evening with Sis. We promised each other that every Wednesday would be our dinner date, and today was Wednesday. That meant that our father had been dead for a month, and I had been back in St. Louis for just about three weeks and a day.

His liver had seized up, as the doctor, an ex-Navy type whom our father trusted, had put it, even though he had, surprisingly, been drinking less over the last year. He went in for a test, had been admitted to ICU, and had died later that day. Sis had tried to get a hold of me, but I was, as near as I could reconstruct, with the date-line time warp and all, somewhere between the Evac hospital in Can Tho and the body-bag hangar at Tan So Nhut.

Sis tried to figure it out, and she swore that our father had died sometime during my last op, maybe just as it was going sour. I wasn't so sure; that sort of stuff was OK for college psych and religion classes, but... I had read all my college roommate, Trey's, papers on synchronicity and Jung and had fantasized about enough white goddesses in my college days, but the Navy and the rivers had weaned me away from the cosmic breast, the world center.

Our father died. I almost bought it. Sis and I were left. Simple. His ashes sat sealed in a cylindrical paper container on a bookshelf in the living room, and neither of us wanted to deal with them.

Sis had moved into the house on Old Bonhomme Road the week after his death. There had been no memorial service at our father's request, through his doctor. This happened the same week I had gone from in to out-patient in San Francisco, and Sis had met me at the airport in St. Louis three days later looking like the first normal thing I'd seen in a year.

"Welcome home, Nedgar!" she had shouted across the barrier as I came down the steps of the boarding ramp of the quietly whining TWA 707. "Hey, Sailor, you want someone show you the town, OK?" she joked in a stage whisper, and the middle-aged couple standing next to her turned away. She gave me a huge hug, and I felt as though I might really be home and safe, at last.

"I tried to get in touch with you when Dad went in for the tests, but even the Navy couldn't find you for about two days," she explained as we drove southeast toward the city. The car lots and fast-food places all looked older, but the highway was new, and we seemed to glide along in a twilight I had only dimly remembered for the past year.

"You said it was fast?" I asked.

"Yes. Very. He went into shock and a coma the day of the tests. He was gone that day." I heard no tears in her voice. I remembered feeling a nostalgia at his passing when she had told me about him over the 'phone when she'd reached me in San Francisco, but I hadn't cried for him yet. I wondered if she was the same. Had she loved him, our dad? I wasn't really sure that I had.

"How are you holding up?" I asked.

"Keeping busy, I guess. I'm all moved into the house. Got

your room all ready for you."

Outside the car, a middle-aged Ford station wagon, the bright neon of the area south of Lambert Field gave way to the thick trees and mellow darkness on both sides of what Sis explained was the new Inner Belt, an ugly, bare concrete ribbon connecting north to south.

"How's Jim?" Jim was Sis's steady boyfriend, an oil geologist who came and went, giving Sis what she called, in her tapes to me, latitude, something I didn't quite get, but there was a lot about my sister I didn't understand.

"He's off in the islands, Bahamas this time, looking for black goo to screw up even those beaches. He's on a ship called the *Glomar Explorer*. Said to tell you the name and see if you knew about it."

The name meant nothing to me.

Jim and Sis didn't live together, which was fine with me. I still didn't like the idea of Sis having sex, even if she was two years older.

I was installed in our father's house by that evening, had skipped the niceties of breakfast with Sis, called a cab, grabbed a grimy lunch in the White Tile Room at the RC Steak House across the street from Car Wash Charlie's, a small, square brick and granite building that used to house St. Louis' first mechanical car wash.

Charles Hansen, a pioneer with a poor sense of direction, had emigrated from California to St. Louis just before I went into the Navy and made a living wearing navy blazers and selling used sports cars to the local gentry for strictly cash. I spent two hours looking for a car to buy, a purchase I interpreted as the true token of my new-found freedom, and drove away in a Lotus Europa, a racy fiberglass two-seater with a high-strung Renault 4CV engine mounted in the middle. After five blocks in traffic, I purchased a box of ping pong balls from a 5 & 10 and jammed one on the tip of my car's radio antenna. Nobody seemed to see the low-slung white sports car, and I hoped that the ball would call attention to it. I headed home for my first meal.

As I drove into the circular drive in front of the house, Sis stood in the open door and waved. I hadn't noticed the night before how beautiful she had become. She was wearing her long blond hair in a heavy plait down her back. Her green eyes looked out at the world from below a high forehead with fine eyebrows that always seemed to be arched in questionable amusement. She had avoided the Taylor nose. Hers was so fine and straight that, after a trip to the Art Museum as teenagers, we had decided that she could be the Greek boy statue and I could be the Italian peasant in the corner of someone or another's Annunciation, the big-faced peasant who might start to sing at any moment. Her likeness to a Greek boy stopped at her nose, for she had a girl's full build, with high breasts, broad hips, and a small waist leading the eye toward long legs. A sun worshipper, Sis had a tan throughout the year, and I could see in the evening light that she looked as dark as any Vietnamese. She wore a man's white, button-down shirt, blue jeans, Mexican tire-soled sandals, and a blue bandana knotted around her hair.

"Nice wheels, Nedgar!" she said, sounding as if she meant it. "Come on in and we'll have a drink." She stood in the doorway, blocking the entrance.

"Have I forgotten the password or something?" I asked, standing in front of her.

"No hug, no drink."

We hugged and, even though she was my sister, I noticed that she had changed from a girl to a woman. "You're looking good, Miss Taylor. Life back at Old Bonhomme Road must be agreeing with you." She squeezed my hand in response.

"I hated giving up my apartment on Delmar. I'd spent a year getting rid of the cat smell, and I figured out how to make the bathroom into a kitchen," she explained as she led the way down the front hall, past the front stairs, toward the pantry and kitchen. The stairs were narrower than I remembered. In three years in the Navy, I had only been home twice, and one of those times I had stayed with Sis at her apartment. My memory of the house was four years old.

"*Dragonwyck* still smells the same," I noticed, using the

name our father had invented for the house. The name came from an old movie, I thought. "Pipe tobacco and bourbon, with a slight hint of moth balls... No, don't do it!" I quickly added, as Sis began.

"I didn't know they had balls!" she chanted, and I joined in, both of us laughing.

"You remember the storage room on the third floor? It must have been three years since Dad had been in there, but the place still burns your eyes when you walk in."

Our mother had put moth balls in everything. I can still remember wondering for a week about the vague burning sensation in my crotch one summer at camp before discovering that even my jockey shorts had spent time being pickled in camphor. Sis and I had joked about it often, but our father couldn't see the humor, the moth balls symbolizing, for him, the tyranny of the one woman he couldn't control. Mother and he had been divorced twenty-odd years ago, leaving *Dragonwyck* and her two children and the room full of moth-balled clothes for a dead end newspaper job and a short-lived second marriage in St. Louis followed by a new job and matching husband in New York City.

Our father never understood her but did not accuse her of anything.

She, however, would accuse him, usually in infrequent 'phone calls at Christmas and on birthdays, of such varied crimes as taking snuff to induce an orgasm during sneezing bouts and never having been really in love with any woman since his mother died. This latter opinion was perhaps an accurate observation but was delivered with such malice that Sis and I avoided thinking about it.

Mother had died suddenly five years ago in New York City. She had had a massive stroke while having lunch with her new husband, Ivor McLaren, a retired British RAF officer whom she was sure was sleeping with all of her friends, "But only the married ones, the bastard," she assured us. By the time Ivor returned from the bathroom and noticed the crowd of people surrounding their table in the corner at the Embassy Bridge Club, it was too late. She died on her way to Lennox Hill hospital.

I had been more stunned than Sis, who assured me that this was precisely the way that our mother wanted to go, out on the town, elegantly dressed. We went to the funeral together, carrying our father's single comment. "Your mother was a remarkable woman," he said simply when we announced her death to him. I had agreed with him.

Dragonwyck's kitchen hadn't changed at all in the past three years. The large white enameled stove still hulked at one end of the room, while, at the other, in an alcove containing the back door, stood the huge, four doored refrigerator which had been converted from an old ice box. The lower right-hand compartment could still be chilled using a block of ice. For some reason the milk was always kept in that compartment, and it always seemed to be on the verge of going sour. My imagination, Sis insisted.

We each poured a glass of white wine from the ever-present Portuguese pitcher kept in the coldest part of the 'fridge, and we sat across from each other at the scrubbed maple topped kitchen table.

"God bless," Sis saluted.

"Cheers," I answered. "To dad," I added.

"To our father," she echoed, and a single tear ran down her cheek. "Bustard had no right to die like that," she said with a snuffle, and I reached out and patted her hand. "I'm OK. I'm just not used to it yet. I had just gotten used to being on my own when this happens, and here I am back at the house. It's almost like I never left."

""Was it tough being here before you got your apartment," I asked.

"Oh, he was OK, but there were times. I'd hear him come in at night, late, and I'd tense up in bed listening for him to hit the garage or go too far into the garage and smack into the trash cans. And then he'd come up the stairs and I'd hear him standing outside my room, waiting. And he'd come in. I'd pretend to be asleep and could feel him bending over me, could smell the boozy breath, and he'd whisper my name. When I wouldn't answer, he'd kiss me on the forehead and go to his room, closing my bedroom door with a bump."

"Did it scare you, his being drunk?"

"No. He was OK. He'd never argue with me the way he'd fight with you. It was kind of nice, him wanting to say goodnight and all. I always felt good after he came in like that. Like he cared about me," Sis added with a sigh.

"You'll miss him," I said.

"Oh, yes, I will. He was a bastard at times, but he had a good heart and a good mind." We both drank, and then Sis added, "He must have been something when he was younger. Like you, maybe, Ned."

After pasta and vegetables (Sis was a vegetarian among her other virtues), the two of us sat in the sunroom, the French doors open onto the small back lawn, the oak tree, and the disheveled brick patio our father had constructed almost ten years before. The fireflies were out, we didn't say much to each other, and the sound of the train caught me by surprise.

"Jesus," I said as the clanging of the crossing bells started. "What the hell's that?"

"They just put it in about a year ago. Dad got Uncle Penny at the MoPac to have them do it."

I could feel the rumble of the approaching switch engine and its string of box cars from the Monsanto plant a mile or so to the west.

There had been an unguarded level crossing halfway down our driveway since the house was built. Mother always used to remind us and our friends to *Watch out for the trains!* whenever we'd leave the house, even though the only traffic on the line was four empty box cars each weekday morning and four full ones each evening. It had been that way for as long as I could remember.

"Loud thing, isn't it?" I commented as the clanging stopped and the rumble receded into the night. I went to the 'fridge and refilled my wine glass.

"I've already asked them to get rid of the bells," Sis said. "Uncle Penny said it would be about a month before they could get to it. He thought it would be easier to go along with Dad on this than fight him. The railroad's trying to be a good citizen these days."

Sis went over to the stereo cabinet in the corner of the sunroom and picked up a plastic tape box. "I found this," she said, "in that bunch of tapes you returned to me." This wasn't one of the ones you sent me. It's to Denny, I think. Part of that bunch of stuff he dropped off at my place before he took off." She took a sip of her wine.

Denny had been my best friend, had been a founding member of the Crew, and had recently left St. Louis for Mexico. He had taken a job as a yacht delivery skipper and would be away for at least a year. He had written to me in the rivers that he was leaving his advertising job at Seven-Up and that he thought he needed a little sun and fun and would try to forget his short, erotic marriage and long, mean divorce. Denny had kept the tapes I had sent him, returning them to Sis just before he left.

"What's on it?" I asked.

"Quien sabe? I don't read other people's mail, Nedgar."

"Go ahead. Let's play it. I'm almost used to hearing my voice on tape." I paused and tried to remember. "I don't think I said or suggested anything salacious about you in it," I said with a grin.

"Best not have, you little shit," Sis answered and inserted the tape. She was grinning. I was happy to be there with her and felt safe at home. "I like listening to your tapes. They give me a real sense of being there. Used to blow Dad away, though. He'd get all teary-eyed and couldn't have anybody else in the room with him when he'd listen to them." She pushed the PLAY button.

Hey, Denny. Thanks for the tape, man. I got it the other day and at first thought it was one from my father since it was from St. Louis. I haven't got one from him yet, but you know how he is. You see him at the Country Club at all? He's been going there on Thursday nights now that he's out of the hospital. Go up and say, Hi. He'd really like to see you...

I was surprised to hear your voice and Dave's. I didn't realize he was completely out of the Army already. Who the hell was that other stoned pony in the background? Sounds like you guys needed a place to land.

Anyway, can you guess where I'm recording this? Listen to the noises in the background...

Sis was holding her wine glass to her lips, and I could tell from the expression on her face that she couldn't identify the noise on the tape. I sure as hell could. I had heard it every day for over three hundred days, and it had become a soothing mantra: the drum of the twin diesel engines of the Swift boat blended with the hiss of the boat cutting through a calm sea.

It's the background sound of the boat engines. I'm up on the bow, recording. I knew that I could easily slip away and become part of the sound; even through a poor-quality tape recording, I could feel its calming embrace. It must have been what the World War Two bomber pilots felt as they trudged across the sky at ten thousand feet headed for...

I was sorry as hell about you and Anne, my voice on the tape broke in. *That first tape you sent me, the one I got at Cam Rahn Bay when I first got in country, sounded like it had been a long winter, but I thought that trip to the Bahamas would smooth things out. Guess not, huh? Did you see Roger down there? He's been living with his folks in Barbados and in New York with Nina. I heard they might get married.*

I had to open my mouth on that one, all right. Told him he ought to leave her alone, that she wasn't good enough for him. Some sort of crap like that. Jesus, I guess I was stoned when I said it, but you know the deal. "Say anything you like, as long as it's sincere." Bullshit...

Anyway, I'm on my way back to this island called An Thoi from a real hole called Ha Tien. You should see it out here. Thirty-five miles of beautiful flat ocean. This is the first good ride out on the big blue since that disaster at the end of training in Bodega Bay. I told you about that, didn't I? Six guys in the hospital, one dead, when a couple of them were on Swifts that rolled in the surf off San Francisco. One hell of a sudden storm. One of the guys lost all his fingers when the engine hatch slammed shut on it.

I've been putting a lot of miles on my new boat, the 93, a middle aged one that's working on its second pair of engines. She makes almost thirty knots flat out, though. Smooth as silk. She doesn't have all her ammo aboard right now, so she gets up on plane right off and stays there...

I'm sitting up forward of the pilot house, on the bow. There isn't anything for me to do, so I can just relax and enjoy the trip back to An Thoi. The whole scene's out of a 40's movie. I don't know if you'd call it

33

bad Bogart or good John Wayne. It's at the end of a big island. Phu Quoc. And we have a repair base and O Club on land at An Thoi and a barracks ship and repair ship anchored off the coast about a mile. We keep the boats rafted up out at the barracks ship. This barracks is something else. Imagine this: three stories high, built on a huge barge. Supposed to be air conditioned, but it only works part time. Two or three mess halls. A ship's store. I even bought a good camera. A Canon. I'll send you some pictures from here. There are maybe twelve different berthing compartments. It's like a floating hotel. Someone said they brought it out of mothballs from the Second World War. Doesn't seem much like being in the Navy, but it's comfortable. Its official Navy designation is an A P L and its painted olive drab, so, of course, they call it the big green apple. Clever, huh?

We get to spend another week or so here while they fix up the 93 boat. I took over for the skipper, a guy named Paul Kelley, who rotated home. He was an interesting guy. I'll tell you about him later when I've got a bit more privacy.

I'll bring you up to date on what I've been doing since getting here...

At Cam Rahn Bay, I spent flaming forever sitting in a series of air conditioned hootches (Quonset huts really, but they call everything over here a hootch) while they cut my orders, issued uniforms, and gave me my choice of side arm. I took a .38 because it's lighter than a .45 and doesn't have as much of a kick. I got pretty good with one in training. Got my Expert Pistol. Web belt and all. I'll send you guys a picture of me in uniform with it on.

Cam Rahn's the most beautiful harbor I've seen since I've been in the Navy. All the beaches are white sand, and they even have lifeguards who sit in those tall chairs. Their only problem is that Charlie is across the bay and sends 120-millimeter rockets into the base at night sometimes... Nice, huh?

It's a pretty good bunch of guys over here. Most of us came through the training school at Mare Island together. Tim Barnes's already going bald and is shorter than all of us, but he's smart as hell. Pete Mills's solid, real solid and would be good in a firefight, I think. Rowe Crosby is a flake, but knows boats. He wears yellow shooting glasses all the time and drinks immense quantities of beer. I like him. Laid back. They sent my roommate, Nash, to the Vinh Te Canal, so I haven't seen much of him since we got here. He was out on patrol when I was at Ha Tien...

You know what he did just before we left Valley Joe (that's Vallejo to the Navy folks)? He gave the pink slip for his Z-28 to a go-go dancer! Yeah. For real. He had been sleeping with her for about a month, I guess. She worked at a place in Vallejo called The Tide's Inn. Danced up on the bar under a blacklight. Nice looking, but she bleached her hair too much. Good figure, even though she's probably had a couple of kids.

Nash invited her back to the apartment once for dinner, and we had a good time. She cooked Mexican for us: tacos and beans and all that. Some good Tres Equis beer, too. Nash got into José Cuervo shooters, but Dawn, that's her name, was driving herself home in her old Valiant, a real beast with push button drive and the driver's window doesn't work, so the shooters were OK. Jesus, did Nash get wasted!

Anyhow, he gave her his year-old, fire-engine red Z-28! I told him he'd never see her again, that she'd meet someone else while he was over here, but he said he didn't care. He was really funny about it, too. Said he didn't want to leave it with his parents. Said they'd told him they didn't have room for it in their garage. Something like that. He hasn't lived at home since high school anyway, so she was going to keep it for him. She'd make the payments, and he'd keep the insurance up on it. Something to come home for, he said. I don't quite see it....

Sis stopped the tape, and the engine sound went away. "So, tell me," Sis said.

I looked at her blankly.

"Did the questionable dancer keep the nice officer's pretty car for him until he got back?" The sarcasm in Sis's voice surprised me.

"Almost," I answered.

"You guys can be such priggish bastards! You know that, don't you?" Sis was mad, and I had missed the point.

"What about?" I asked.

"About your goddamned toys and all." She was glaring at me. "It's OK for this girl to sign her body over to Nash, but it's not OK for Nash to sign his damned car over to her?"

"But it was a goddamned expensive car, Sis," I protested.

"You can be such a shit head, Ned Taylor. Really you can." She was mad, and even I could tell it was time to cut my losses and try to get out of this one alive.

"Sorry, Sis. I didn't mean to have it sound that way," I

explained.

"Right. Right," she said. "You are your father's son." And she shook her head sadly, a faraway look in her eyes. She took the final sip of wine from her glass. "Fill this for me, will you?"

"Sure," I said and took our glasses to the 'fridge and refilled them. "How am I like our father?"

"He loved his toys, too, as he got older." She took her glass from me, and I sat back down at the kitchen table. It was pitch dark outside, and the fireflies winked like mysterious beacons in the garden.

"Loved his toys, my Aunt Fanny! Ever since he had that '55 T-Bird his taste in cars went to hell in a hand basket. What was he driving when he died, that pale blue WV bug?"

"He still had the bug. It's in the garage. But he had the boat."

"Boat? Here in St. Louis?" I asked. "What kind of boat?" Our father had been in the Navy but, aside from a cruise on a passenger liner down the east coast of South America one summer, had never shown any interest in the water or in boats.

"I assumed you knew all about it," said Sis. "Cheers." And she raised her glass in my direction.

"Cheers," I answered. "I didn't know anything about a boat. He never said anything to me about getting a boat. Where'd he keep it, Lake St. Charles? Alton?"

"I don't know. The title was there among his papers. I assumed you and he had worked on it together, your being in the Navy and all. I thought maybe he'd done it sort of to copy you, in sympathy with you."

"I didn't know anything about it."

Sis looked thoughtful for a moment. "Let's finish this," she said, "and then I'll get the title for you. Give you something to do, playing with the boat." She turned to the stereo. "Sorry about reacting that way to Nash and his Z 281ady, but you guys really are shits, you know."

"Yeah" I guess." She pushed the PLAY button.

Well, I can see the Apple and the top of the peaks of Phu Quoc, so I'd better close.

Do me a favor, Denny.

Don't let the thing with Anne get to you. Best bet might be to do the split city for a while. You said that Uncle wasn't interested in you, so you could do the Mexico trip you and I had been planning. I promise you that Zihuatenejo would be perfect. They even have a shark works. Whether that means they make sharks there or make things out of sharks, I don't know. We never got out to the point where it was located. Just the trip into the dark for the grass. I'll tell you that story sometime.

Oh, yeah. About your question, the one you asked on your last tape. No, there isn't much dope around here. I saw a couple of Vietnamese officers pass a joint back and forth at the O Club in Cam Rahn, but on the boats, we stay real clean. A little beer on the beach at the O club or the EM Clubs, but nothing stronger. I guess it's because we're always on call. They can scramble us at any time, and we go out once a day in any case.

I know I sure as hell wouldn't want some stoned pony next to me if we got in a firefight.

So... We don't smoke any dope here that I've heard about, and I'm kind of glad. It's a lot like being in a fighter squadron in the World War Two movies. We kind of see ourselves as straight shooters, good guys, white scarves, all that sort of thing. I like it. It seems to help us keep straight, and I think it makes some of this shit make sense, somehow.

Take care, Dennis, and send a tape back soon. This is Abbey November 93, out.

"You sound really sad there at the end," Sis commented after a while, and she turned off the hiss of the stereo.

"I do, don't I." I stood up and stretched. "These tapes really take me back there, you know. Kind of spooky the way it happens. I can really sense it, almost feel the same exact way I felt when I was there. It's kind of like reliving it."

"Is that bad or good?" asked Sis, perching on the arm of my chair.

"Neither, really." I relaxed back in the chair and let my legs stretch out straight ahead of me. "There were some good things about being over there. About having command of your own boat. About having all that power."

"In some of the tapes you sent me, you really created a sense of being there for me, a sense of exhilaration about the war." Sis looked down at me and pursed her lips. "You know how I hate it, but you really made me feel it, feel the excitement of it. It was almost sexual, some of your descriptions. In fact, you ever realize how... phallic you made everything sound over there? Almost sounded like you fought the war with your penises instead of shells and bullets. I think that might be the connection to the stupidity of it."

She got up off the chair. "I'll get the boat title, although I don't think it's called that." She walked out of the sunroom through the living room and up the stairs

He comments about phalluses reminded me of Hannah and her friend. Ben Tré and its river. I could see the curve just before the bridge as you entered the town. Indian Territory. All those rivers were Indian Territory.

I shut my eyes and saw a map crisscrossed with rivers, but two rivers, the Cua Lon and the Dam Doi, stood out in my mind's eye. The map was under a sheet of plexiglass on the chart table of the 93 boat. I could see the blue of the river, the yellow of its shores, and the variegated green of the land surrounding the rivers. A photo overlay map, half cartographer's survey, half satellite photograph. Precise. Unambiguous. Fixed. Accurate. Endlessly fascinating.

I would spend hours on watch looking at the map for places along the river, especially the Cua Lon, to explore. Canals. Streams. Whatever. Anywhere a Swift could get in, even if we had to back out. It was an adventure in the early days of being there. Tempting, almost seductive in a physical way. Like imagining sex when you were still a virgin, Nash had told me that once when we had been drinking at the O Club in Vung Tau. I had agreed.

At least it was that way in the beginning. At the end, I didn't want to get off the main rivers anymore.

Things change. We grow up. We are no longer virgins. We use deadly instruments for our pleasure.

"Maybe you should write down some of what went on over there," Sis suggested from the doorway. I hadn't heard her come down the stairs. She had a folded white piece of paper in her hand" Too big for a title, I thought.

"I have," I said. "I'll show it to you. I wrote it last week. Couldn't sleep one night and hauled out the old Smith Corona. But I can't seem to be able to write anything else. It just won't come. A whole year over there, and all I can write is one story!"

"What's it about?"

"An ambush in a canal and a kid on the boat getting hit."

"True story?" asked Sis and tossed the paper into my lap and say down on the couch.

"Mostly."

"I'd like to read it."

I unfolded and looked at the piece of paper Sis had brought. The documentation described, in maritime legalese, an eight-ton self-propelled oil screw vessel registered as *Coast Pilot* with the vessel number No. 46213 carved in a prominent place on the main or other comparable deck beam to the depth of one-half of one inch. Said vessel was the property of one Cyrus Taylor, his place of residence being St. Louis, Missouri, recently transferred from its former owner. *Coast Pilot's* breadth was listed as 9.5 and its depth as 2.5, said vessel being a length of 28.5. This vessel, the document proclaimed, was built in Waren, Rhode Island, and the signature of the principal shipwright seemed to be that of one Henrique Silvera.

"What the hell was he up to?" I said, astonished. "This is a good-sized boat, not a dingy like I thought you meant."

Sis shrugged her shoulders.

"Where does he... did he keep it?"

"I have no idea. I was going to ask you 'cause I was sure you and he were doing the boat together."

"Our dad was a remarkable man," I said, and Sis smiled.

After another glass of wine and a promise to let her read the story I had written, we kissed goodnight, and I went up to my room with the idea of trying to write again. Sis' comments on the phallicy of war had suggested a story about Hannah and her friend.

CHAPTER SIX

Old Bonhomme Road, morning

The next morning at breakfast, I told Sis that I was in trouble.

"Trouble? What kind of trouble? You just got home."

"All the stories I wanted to write about Vietnam are gone. Nothing I'd done over there seems to matter. Whenever I try to write about something important, it doesn't come out on paper. Just like it was all dead inside. Just like me inside. The writing's all worn out, like after making love. You know what I mean?" I stopped. "This sounds crazy, Sis. I'm sorry. I should never have mentioned it."

"Bullshit, Nedgar. Who else are you going to tell? What did you mean about the writing being worn out. After you make love, don't you feel good?"

"Sometimes, yes. Not always."

"Why not?" Sis asked.

"How do women feel after making love?"

"You mean you've never asked one, little brother, little male chauvinist brother?"

"No, I never asked. I thought it would be rude, older sister," I retorted.

"Well, I can only speak from personal experience and hearsay, but I think most women feel warm and filled and

41

loved. If it's been with someone they care about."

"And if it's been with someone they didn't care about?" I asked.

"And why do you think I would know the answer to that?"

"Well, I guess men are different. It's usually a letdown to me. Sometimes I want to just disappear, to not be there with who... whomever I'm with."

"Nice save on that one, Mr. Writer, Sir. Yes. I guess it must be different with us." She waited until she was sure I wasn't going to say anything. "Your writing. What are you trying to write at this point that isn't happening?"

"It's about a girl I met over there."

"Where are you in the story?" asked Sis, sounding like an editor.

"I'm not anywhere. I'm trying to write about this thing I felt when I was in this beautiful French colonial town, Ben Tré. A kind of fear. That sort of thing."

"And...?"

"And nothing. Zip. Zero. It's like it never happened. I can't find anything to say about it. It all seems too talky or philosophy. I don't know."

Sis paused before replying. "What was it like? The fear part? Was it like anything else over there? Was it like anything else that happened to you over there? Think back."

"I'm trying to, but nothing's there," I said after a long pause.

"What else goes on in the story?"

"There's the Donut Dolly."

"Donut Dolly? One of your cute names again, like Puff the Magic Dragon and Jolly Green Giant? What was a Donut Dolly, some kind of tank with breasts?" Sis asked, in her big sister voice. I had heard this voice many times when I was younger. Especially after Mom had died.

"Sorry, Sis. No, a donut dolly is a female Red Cross worker who helps with relief in an area in-country. We'd see them in the bigger towns, where they'd have O Club privileges. As a group, they were pretty easy to get to know."

"In a biblical sense, little brother?"

"Yeah," I answered. "Anyway, the dollies would serve donuts and coffee at the EM Clubs and run libraries and just visit with the troops. They were a good bunch of ladies, but they had reputations for, you know... being pretty easy lays for the officers."

"Tell me about your donut dolly," said Sis's voice. "As repulsive a name as that is, how does she fit into your story? She did have a name, I take it, or did she just call herself Dolly?"

"Her name was Hannah... We had kind of a thing and saw each other a couple of times, but it wasn't what you'd call a great love affair or anything like that," I said.

"You sleep with her?" asked Sis, her voice neutral.

"Sort of."

"How do you sort of sleep with someone?"

I could hear the smile in her voice. "Well, we had sex once," I started and then stopped.

"But?"

"But it was never... consummated. At least not as far as I was concerned."

"Yes?" asked Sis.

"So it wasn't really having sex," I tried to explain.

"You want to tell me?" Her voice was hard, and then she laughed. "Sorry if sometimes I sound a bit offended. Most women since Eve haven't had sex more than once or twice, if you measure it that way." She paused. "Tell me the story."

"I was pretty drunk, OK? Nash and I had just got back from the river. We'd been given some bad coordinates, and we'd almost dropped a couple rounds in on a South Vietnamese outpost."

"This isn't very sexy, Ned," said Sis. "Get to the donut dolly part."

"I am. I'm explaining why I was drunk. I was pretty upset about the outpost. Nash and I had been pretty pissed off about Jimmy, an advisor who'd been killed by the Vietnamese earlier. We'd gotten really 'faced at the O Club. Anyway, I ran into this donut dolly, Hannah, at the Club. She had joked about looking for some sailors to take home, so we decided to take a walk

43

down to the river. Kind of to sober up. She told me she'd had a bad week and all."

I paused, and Sis spoke kindly, pushing me. "Ned, just describe what the two of you did, you and Dolly."

"Hannah. Her name was Hannah."

"OK, Hannah. What did she look like? Describe her. I want to feel as though I know her, so she isn't just a cardboard cutout, a paper doll."

"OK. Hannah was tall, thin but a good build. She had dark hair cut in bangs and hanging down on the side. I had seen her a couple of times at the O Club, and I had talked to her once. We even made out down by the river a couple of times. Just kissing and messing around. Mainly, we talked."

"About what?" asked Sis."

"The boats. What we did on the rivers. The usual small talk. Anyway, this night we had met at the O Club and, all of a sudden, we were walking from down by the river in front of the Club back to her hotel. She was living at the one hotel in town with the other Red Cross types, and she had a room on the third floor. In the front, looking over the river. We never even turned on the lights. We took our clothes off and stood there, just inside the window, French doors out onto a tiny balcony, really, and were kind of hugging." I stopped talking.

"Kind of?" asked Sis.

"We hugged. Our arms around each other, you know? We just held onto each other, like for warmth, but it was already warm in the room and all. We hugged and pulled and pushed against each other together for maybe a couple of minutes. And we were kissing, too. I could tell something was wrong, but I couldn't tell what."

"And then?" Sis asked.

"She told me to go sit on the bed. She asked me if I'd do something for her, something a little strange. I said, 'Sure.' I sat on the edge of the bed, waiting. She opened the bottom drawer and fooled around with something before bringing it over to me on the bed. At first, I thought it was a vibrator, but it was bigger. She lay down on the bed and held it out to me. I had never actually held one, but I could tell what it was. 'Go ahead,' she said."

"A dildo?" asked Sis.

"Not quite. A twenty-millimeter canon shell... a live round. It could go off if you messed around with it."

Sis laughed.

"Oh, come on!" I said. "It gets kind of weird, here."

"It's OK. I want to hear it. Don't worry about me. You won't shock me, really," she promised me.

"I was kind of spacey by this time, and she had to show me what she wanted. She had me make love to her with it. She lay there on her back and with me kneeling there, guided my putting the shell in her and pushing it in and pulling it out until I had it the way she liked. Then she held on to the shell with one hand and reached up and grabbed me and started on me with her other hand. I remember she asked, 'This is OK for you, isn't it, doing this?' "

"I was there jamming her with the live round, and she was kind of singing and crying. I couldn't tell, but she was so rough with that shell I was sure she was going to hurt herself or worse. I guess I was also afraid that she was going to set that sucker off and blow us both up. So, I held on like crazy and she rode me and that thing into the next county. She asked me again if it was OK."

"'Oh, yeah,' I said to her, and, in a way, it was good, but, as soon as I had said it, I knew that it was all fucked up, having sex like this, using a live round on her and her playing with me that way. It wasn't normal, and I was doing it because I wasn't normal anymore, and she wasn't normal anymore either, and none of that fucking place was normal anymore. I wanted out of her hands and that shell out of her body and me out of her room and out of that hotel and out of Ben Tré and out of the rivers and out of the war and out of Vietnam and out of the Navy. I wanted out. No matter how goddamned good it felt!" I stopped, and Sis heard my single sob catch me by surprise.

"Finish it, Ned. How did it end."

I was catching my breath as I said, "I tried to stop with the shell and go into her myself, but she didn't want me to. She wanted me to keep using the shell. So, I did. And she finally

came, holding that shell with one hand and me with the other,"
I finished, my voice so low that I'm surprised Sis could hear
me. "Then... I got up and got dressed, went out and went back
to the boat. I never even kissed her goodbye." My voice had
become stronger.

"Did she say goodbye to you, Ned?"

"No. I think she was asleep by the time I left."

"Weren't you still horny," asked Sis.

"No. I had gone beyond that stage; I was all used up. Felt
hollow. Empty. Used up and used, I guess. Funny," I said,
finally smiling, "I thought only girls, women were supposed to
feel that way."

We were both silent.

Finally, Sis said, "You figured out what the fear was there
at the end. It explains the fear you wrote me about at the end."

"That's what I don't get. I don't see the connection. The
feelings were the same, but I don't understand why," I said.

"I think it's the feeling of being part of something that's
not normal, not clean, not moral. It's a little like fearing for
your soul rather than for your body. The body fears we can
handle; it's the soul fears that get us, make us stop in our
tracks. As old fashioned as it sounds, you felt fear that you
were going to lose your soul there, because you knew what you
were going to have to do, both in the rivers and in that hotel
room with that girl with the live shell," Sis explained. "Why
don't you write that as a story?"

"You mean the Hannah story? I'm not sure which part of
it to write."

"Just type it out," said Sis. "It's already been written. You
wrote it just now, telling it to me. It's been distilling inside of
you, writing itself ever since it happened. You just have to put
it on paper."

I wrote the story that day. As Sis had suggested, I just typed
it out.

CHAPTER SEVEN

Old Bonhomme Road

It took two days of 'phone calls to every marina within a hundred miles of St. Louis to discover that the *Coast Pilot* was nowhere to be found.

Good, I thought. I need something to keep me busy. I didn't need a job, as I had over two thousand dollars of backpay in the form of an as yet uncashed Treasury paycheck, and the bank which was handling our father's estate was footing Sis's and my bills for the time being through a line of credit. I was working on a second story about Vietnam, which was consuming five hours a day; for the rest of the time, having been used to the fully regulated days in the Navy, I was starting to get bored. The mystery of our father's boat was a welcome diversion.

I asked Sis for any bills she had turned up among our father's things at *Dragonwyck*. She joined me for breakfast on Saturday morning in the kitchen with bagels, coffee, and an orange crate full of bank statements, cancelled checks, and numerous bills and receipts.

We separated the box of bills into two huge piles, and Sis took one over to the counter and I kept the other on the table.

"Anything at all that could give us a clue on the … *Coast Pilot* …," I said. "Fuel bill, slip rental receipt, checks written to nautical sounding places. You know."

"How about a check for fifteen dollars written to Fredericks of Hollywood?" Sis asked, looking up from her pile with a shocked look on her face.

"What?" I said, astounded, starting to get up from the table.

"Just kidding, Nedgar," Sis said. "Lighten up, brother. This is just a lark, you know. It's not that serious. Think of it as just another way to get to know Dad."

" It's just that I feel a little like we're prying," I said. "I really don't want to turn up anything I wouldn't want to know about him. I want to remember just the good things."

"It's OK, Ned. I think most of us can survive this kind of poking around. Don't forget, I was the one who had to go through his room, through his bureau drawers and medicine cabinet just after he died. He was clean enough," Sis said. "Anyway, we can use this as an excuse to throw away a lot of junk paperwork; it'll save us some accounting fees for the estate. Think of that as an excuse. One that even Dad would agree to."

"You went through his bureau and medicine chest?" I asked.

"Sure. Why not? I had to get clothes to bury him in, and I didn't want anybody else to find anything... funny, you know, later."

"Oh, I see," I said, considering the matter. "Find anything unusual?"

"Just some men things, that's all."

"Men things?"

"Men things, like a box of playing cards with what I think were described on the box as Art Studies. Basically, big bosoms and lace underwear."

"And?"

"And a little bottle of some exotic root powder, with a name I don't remember."

"What in the world would that be for?" I asked.

"For when you can't get or keep it up, or so I've been led to believe by one of my more experienced girlfriends," Sis said. "Don't worry, I didn't tell her the real reason I wanted to know. The Taylor male secret is safe with me."

"For this relief, much thanks," I said with mock seriousness. "Anything else?"

Sis hesitated before answering. "No. Not really."

"Come on. What else? There's something else."

"A picture, that's all." Sis looked down at the pile of papers in front of her and poked at them with her finger.

"Of?"

"Of Dad and someone else. At a costume party or something. It was a little weird," Sis said. "He was wearing a huge sombrero. A Mexican sombrero," and for a moment I thought she was going to cry.

"What's wrong?" I asked.

Sis just looked at me for a long moment, as if deciding if she should go on. "Oh, it's just that he looked so damned happy in the picture," she finally said. "He had a grin on his face like I hadn't seen in years. It was the first kind of happy picture I'd seen of him since Mom left. He never looked like that lately. And the picture was less than six months old."

"How do you know?"

"The mustache. He didn't have his mustache in the picture, and he had shaved if off about six months ago."

"I didn't know," I said. "Why'd he shave it off?"

"Who knows? Just after Christmas, when he was just back from one of his trips, I had dinner with him at the house and it was gone. Made him look years younger without it. When I asked, he said that he wanted a change."

"Trips?" I asked. "Trips where?"

"Don't know. He never said, and I didn't want to pry. He'd just be gone for a week or so every month. He was really good about not asking about my Bohemian life on Delmar, and I thought I could return the complement. Anyway, he shaved it off for a change, according to him."

"A change? Doesn't sound like our father, old Mr. Conservative, does it? Where's the picture? You still have it?"

"I threw it out," Sis said, looking straight at me. And then, defiantly, "OK?"

"How come?" I asked softly, realizing I'd hit some kind of

nerve.

"You wouldn't understand," she said, "and you'll laugh."

"No, I won't. It was just a picture, Sis."

"The other person in the photograph scared me. Made me feel creepy, somehow. And Dad, too. He looked, OK, happy, but he also looked kind of funny in the picture."

"Funny ha-ha or funny queer?"

"Funny queer. Kind of bizarre, and I just didn't want a picture like that around, Ned. It was too soon after he died, and I'm sure my reaction would be a lot different now." She paused. "I guess I'm just embarrassed that I threw something out like that, without waiting for you and all. It was the last picture taken of him."

"It's OK," I assured her. "I couldn't have even gone through his things, I'm sure. I'm hopeless when it comes to things like that." I crossed to where Sis sat at the counter, and she looked up at me as I bent to kiss her on the forehead. Our lips touched. I felt a shiver of what could have been her guilt at throwing away our father's photograph. "You did just fine," I said.

"Thanks. I'm glad you understand."

We went through every bill or receipt in those two piles and could find no hint of the *Coast Pilot*. Sis was putting her pile into the orange crate when I had an idea.

"Any car rentals?"

"One, I think. Why?"

"Where was it for?"

Sis looked through her pile of papers and extracted a credit card bill. "It just says *Carriage Trade Rentals*. $205.97."

"Bingo," I exclaimed. I looked in the yellow pages and discovered no *Carriage Trade Rentals* in the St. Louis area, so it had to be out of town and far enough away for him not to have driven his own car.

I called the credit card company, and they gave me the telephone number for *Carriage Trade Rentals*. It was a small company in Pennsylvania, nowhere near the water. Sis didn't remember our father having travelled to Pennsylvania in the past year, so I called the company and asked a voice in the billing department to trace a charge for a rental for a Mr. Taylor in the amount of $249.97.

"I'm sorry, Mr. Taylor, but there is no way we can tell you about a rental with just a name and a dollar amount to work with," said a bored male voice from somewhere deep within the bowels of rent-a-car purgatory. "If you would put your request in writing, perhaps someone could help you."

"What about your computers," I asked. "Can't you ask them to search the records for the name and the amount?"

"That would be a very complicated process, I'm afraid, Sir. We are a small company and don't have computers available for this sort of thing." The voice reflected a degree of hopelessness usually reserved for terminal illness. I decided to try a different tack.

"How about the accident report, then? Do you have a copy of that?"

"Accident?" The voice sounded a bit more alert. "What accident would that be, sir?"

"I probably shouldn't be even talking about it. But... I am a bit concerned."

"May I have someone who can help you return your call, sir?" the voice asked hopefully.

"Yes," I said and gave the voice my number. The telephone rang in ten and one-half minutes. I timed it.

"Mr. Cyrus Taylor?" a brighter, more hopeful, even cheerful voice asked. "This is Miss Johnson in customer relations."

"Yes?" I had not used our father's first name on the first call. So they *had* found his record. Good!

"You reported nothing about an accident when you turned in your car last time," Miss Johnson said. I wondered if she'd trained for her present position as a schoolteacher. She had that voice.

"Accident? There was no accident. I just wanted to ask a question about the bill," I explained, hoping she would hear the smile in my voice.

"No accident? But the operator in Billing said that you wanted to know about an accident report."

"Oh, my mistake, I guess. Sorry." I forced myself to stop speaking, hoping Miss Johnson would fill the silence. As a rule, teachers and customer relation types don't appreciate silences.

"Well, I'm glad there wasn't another accident. Not that we considered the broken tail lamp an accident, but you know how proud we are of our cars, Mr. Taylor," Miss Johnson reminded me.

"Oh, yes. Indeed, I do." I paused, trying to figure out how to find out where it took place without sounding like a complete fool, a customer who couldn't remember the location where he'd rented a car. I wanted to ask about the other accident, the taillight one, but figured I'd stick to just one lead at a time. "Now, about my last rental, Miss Johnson. My... accountant needs a breakdown on the charges. How much of the charge was for mileage, can you tell me?"

"Yes, Sir. I have it in front of me."

Yes! Almost there.

"The daily charge was ten dollars, for seven days, making seventy. Livery was thirty-five. The insurance was three dollars a day, for twenty-one; the mileage was 440 at twenty-five cents a mile for another one-hundred-ten. The remaining thirteen-ninety-seven was Florida State tax."

Florida, aha!

"No local tax?" I asked, hoping against hope.

"Miami-Dade has no local tax, Mr. Taylor."

"Oh, fine. Thank you, Miss Johnson. You've been a big help to me, my favorite rental car company, as a matter of fact." Sis was making signs of being sick to her stomach as she listened to me, a demonic expression on her face.

"Why, thank you, Mr. Taylor. You're a favorite customer of ours, too. We'll meet you with your car on the thirtieth. A convertible, correct?"

Pretty sporty, I thought, for our father. And mysterious. "Yes. The convertible's perfect, thank you. What time is the reservation for?"

"We will meet Eastern's flight 42, at 2:40 PM."

"Oh, good. Thank you." I wondered if I could stretch my luck a bit and asked, "Could you possibly send me a copy of my most recent bills? I've misplaced my copies, and I know I'll need them."

"Of course, Mr. Taylor. The past six months or the past year?"

"If you could send me copies of the past year..."

"Surely. To your regular address?"

"Yes, please."

"I'll put them in today's mail."

"Thank you so much. Goodbye."

"Goodbye."

I hung up and turned to Sis. "Miami. Since when did our father hang out in Miami?"

"Since never, as far as I know," she said. "He wasn't the Florida type, he used to say and made fun of the white patent leather set. I can't imagine him in a convertible, either."

"... a remarkable man," we both said in unison.

By Wednesday of the next week, I had combed the Miami-Dade County area by telephone for any sign of the *Coast Pilot,* but I had come up empty. There seemed to have been no connection between the boat and the car rentals after all. I was working on my stories each morning from six until nine and spending the afternoons on the mysterious *Coast Pilot.* My friends all had jobs, so I only saw them in the evenings, usually at *Sir John's Den.* Sis seemed less interested in the boat than I, but she would check with me each evening to check on my progress. She also wanted to keep tabs on me, she admitted, afraid that I might slip into the same funk that had claimed friend Dave.

"I just don't want you to end up like him," she said on Wednesday evening when I was on my way to *Sir John's Den* to meet the Crew.

The next evening after a long day of writing and trying to write, I asked her, "Do you remember finding any bills for motels or hotels? I'm beginning to wonder if Miami is where Dad had the boat. There's not a sign of it."

"I made two piles, Ned. In one I put all the obviously St.

Louis bills. I have all the mystery bills in the second pile," Sis explained. "The mystery bills aren't many. Three of them, to be exact. A check made out to one Tim's Small Engine Repair for thirty-five dollars, dated last February, the same month as the Carriage Trade rental car. There's no such place in the 'phone book here in St. Louis. The second check is made out to a roofing company called something like Stan and Sons, Roofers; again, not a St. Louis company and dated in April. The final one's the real mystery."

"Made out to...?"

"Bee. Wye. Bee. El. Oh. Ess. Byblos, I guess. And it was for two thousand dollars. But the funny part is that there's no check, only the check-book stub in Dad's handwriting. I called the bank, and it hasn't ever cleared. I put a stop payment on it. It was made out on the twenty-first of December, last year."

"Good work," I said. "The mystery continues! I'm going to meet the Crew," I said, changing the subject. "I don't want to make it too late a night 'cause I'm getting up early to write."

CHAPTER EIGHT

Bonhomme Road, the next morning

"I found the boat, Sis!" I yelled upstairs at eleven in the morning. I had waited for the morning mail, looking for the information from *Carriage Trade*. It arrived in a large envelope.

"Great! How'd you do it," she asked, coming into the kitchen.

"He'd rented a car eight times in the past year, and the mileage was almost always the same. It ranged from 430 to 460. The car was always ready for him at the airport, and he caught his return flight to St. Louis from there always about a week later. The gas always needed to be topped off, which he paid for in cash, charging the remainder. The rental in May of this year, he turned in the car with a cracked taillight lens, no charge."

"So, the boat is where?" asked Sis.

"Watch this amazing demonstration, Sis. I will recreate the great discovery. Follow me."

"Oh, you clever boy, you. What place is that far from Miami?"

"That was the funny part. Divide the mileage in half, and you'd think you could figure out where he'd driven to and back, and that would give you the location of the boat, right?"

"Right."

"Unfortunately, the average mileage he always put on the car was 440 or so miles, divided in half made 220 miles. What's 220 miles from Miami? To the north there is Winter Haven. To the west is Sarasota. But they all have airports."

"Why would he fly to Miami and rent a car to drive two and a half hours to a place he could fly to anyway?"

"Exactly. So let's play that scene out," I said, relishing my role as a sleuth. "Figuring that he didn't like to drive more than an hour at one time, that limits us to Boca Raton to the north, the upper keys to the south, and absolutely nothing but Everglades to the west. Ergo?"

"Ergo what?"

"Ergo, he drove somewhere within an hour's drive of the airport."

"But what about the extra mileage?" Sis asked.

"Perhaps it wasn't his mileage," I said and waited.

"Not his? But whose?"

"The rental agency's."

"Explain, but make it quick, Nedgar," said Sis. "You're enjoying this much more than I, you know."

"Point taken. Ok, big finish," I said and paused for dramatic effect. "He arrives by plane at Florida, but not in Miami. He is met by the car rental people. He is met by them, almost as though they aren't there all the time. So I think, Maybe they don't have an office at the airport, and I call Miss Johnson, have an inane conversation with her which allows me to discover that their office is in Miami. They have a kid take the car up to the airport, not in Miami but the one in Ft. Lauderdale, to meet him, he drives the kid back to Miami and then starts his drive to wherever the boat is. He repeats the same thing, but in reverse, at the end of each trip. That was what the "livery" charge was for, the thirty-five bucks. I finally figured out that he flew into Ft. Lauderdale instead of Miami because there are non-stop flights there."

"So how far was the boat from Miami?"

"Ta-da! In a slip in Stock Island just north of Key West at the Cow Key Marina, thank you very much. Thirty miles between Miami and Lauderdale, up and back and up and back again, done twice making 120 miles. That leaves 320 round trip or 160 miles one way. With a road map I drew a rough circle, and the circle touched Key West to the south and the Sebastian Inlet to the north. Since the Gold Coast is pretty much all alike as you go north from Miami, I tried to the south first."

"How do you happen to know so much about the Florida coast?" Sis interrupted.

"Don't forget my two years in Key West in the Navy," I reminded her. "Anyhow, I hit paydirt on my third call. 'Yes, a Mr. Cyrus Taylor keeps his Dyer 29 here, and would I happen to be named Terry?' I explained that I was Mr. Taylor's son, and that Mr. Taylor had passed away and asked who Terry was. The kid on the other end said that he was sorry to hear about Dad and that Mr. Taylor had left instructions that someone named Terry was in charge of the boat."

"This place Cow Key, where Dad kept the boat, what's it called, *Coast Pilot*? What's a *Coast Pilot*?"

"It's a government publication in about eight volumes that describes different sections of the coast of the United States in words rather than with charts or maps. We used them in the Navy."

"Sounds interesting, translating pictures to words."

"I wonder how Dad found out about the Coast Pilot volumes. They're kind of obscure except to sailors,"

"Maybe the boat already had that name when he bought it," suggested Sis.

"I have the document here. Let me look..." I found the paper on the kitchen counter and scanned it. "Yup," I said. "You're right. The boat was built two years before he bought it. He bought the boat and kept its name. It's evidently a big deal to change the name of a documented boat."

I paused, and Sis then added, "I wonder who this Terry person is."

"Curiouser and curiouser..."

"Said Alice," I finished the phrase.

We decided that a trip south to at least see the boat might be in order, and, since there was already an airlines reservation and a rental car reservation made, we'd go on a Sunday, the thirtieth, on Eastern's flight 42, arriving at 2:40 PM in Ft. Lauderdale. Sis made another reservation for herself. There was already a single return booked for a week later.

CHAPTER NINE

Old Bonhomme Road, next day

They next day as we were planning our Florida trip, Sis asked if I was prepared to learn about the mysterious Terry.

"Why? Do you think it is something kinky?" I asked.

"Who knows," Sis said. "There's probably a lot we don't know about Dad. Same as there's a lot we don't know about each other. I'm sure we've both got things we don't really want to share with others."

"Things? What things?"

"Oh, you know, fantasies and all. We all have them," Sis pointed out. "Once I turned nine or ten, I began to wonder what boys would look like with no clothes on."

She smiled as she continued, "I do have to admit I wanted to see specifically what you looked like without any clothes on, too, since I hadn't seen you in the altogether since we were babies. I didn't really have much of an idea about what boys were like down there. I got all fouled up when the biology teacher had us dissect a pig and told us it was like a human body in lots of ways. I couldn't figure out how the penis worked. Mom was gone, so I couldn't ask her. I didn't even consider asking Dad." She sat back and stretched her arms over her head, her fingers reaching higher and higher.

"You're lucky you didn't. Dad on that subject messed me

up but good. I was just about to go away to school, and I thought I needed a good talk about sex. Took me on a fishing trip to Lake Wappapello."

"Dad hated fishing," Sis said simply. She sat forward, placing her arms on the table on either side of her empty coffee cup, her listening position.

"Exactly. He drank warm gin out of a pint bottle while we floated around in an aluminum row boat with an engine that didn't work right. That, and it rained the whole time. Toward the end of the afternoon, he brought up sex and asked me what I wanted to know. I didn't know what I didn't know, so I said I was OK and knew enough to keep me going."

"He must have loved that," Sis said.

"It let him off the hook, anyway. So, then he switched over to his real reason for the trip. I was about to go away to boarding school, so he felt he had to warn me about guys in the shower wanting to touch me. Queers. He told a bunch of dirty jokes about not picking up the soap in the shower and all." I stopped, remembering.

"We were in a part of the lake above the dam where the trees hadn't been all cut down. So, their branches were sticking up out of the water, like hands, grabbing at us and catching our lures every time we cast. Or I cast. I don't remember him fishing. I don't even think he had a pole. Just the bottle of gin. Pretty spooky, and Dad scaring me to death about queers trying to grab me in the shower at school. Shit, I was a wreck by the time we got home from that trip." I looked up at my sister and smiled weakly. "You're damned lucky you didn't go to him to ask about anything like that."

"I guess I am. I'm sorry that happened to you." Sis reached forward and touched my right hand with one finger and then clasped her two hands together. "If I'd known, maybe I could have helped, but I never knew he had that hang-up. He ever talk to you about it again?"

"Once, when I asked to work summer stock on Cape Cod one summer. Remember my talking about Pete Candler at school? The director of the drama club? He used to be the manager of the Melody Tent in Hyannis during the summer, and he asked if I wanted to be an intern there. Dad said, 'No way.' Then he told me, I think he was kind of sauced one night, and he told me about being chased around the hors d'oeuvres table at a party by some older man in New York City when he was with the Triangle, his college drama club. Dad was in charge of publicity for the show."

"That was the guys dressing up in falsies and dresses and doing hairy legged kick lines? I didn't know Dad was into that," Sis said. "Wow, imagine that. Our father consorting with college queens."

"He never did say what finally happened at the party," I continued.

"My bet is the guy caught him," Sis offered. "If he was as uptight about it as it sounds, I bet Dad got caught and woke up in bed with the guy."

"Meaning," I asked, "that Dad was queer? I'm not so sure. He was the same man, don't forget, who tried to bed every woman that came into reach, including Aunt Alice."

"Precisely," said Sis simply.

"Go on," I said. "I don't get it. He collected women like notches in his pistol."

"A truly male metaphor, dear brother. Dad might have been afraid of being queer, or gay, as we say now," explained Sis. "He might have been always trying to prove that he wasn't."

The day before we were to leave for Florida, at breakfast, I was again trying to figure out why I couldn't write my stories.

"I can't say what I want to say when I write. I can't feel." I sat at the table, holding my two hands out in front of me in fists. Sis looked on, unspeaking, waiting. "I went to *Sir John's Den* last night. The gang was there. Dave said I might be able to find a story there to write. Johnny Holmes was holding court, as usual, at the big table in the back. Tim Sullivan was there. He was a warrant in the Army and flew gunships. I joined in for a while, adding my war stories to the collection, but I didn't want to talk anymore, and his were pretty good and I liked to listen, so I just sat along the edge and listened. I could tell how much things had changed. This was a pretty, you know, conservative group and all. Most of them thought it was neat that I had been in Vietnam and liked to hear the stories, but it was almost as though having been there gave me some special status. Made me a special member of the group. But it also made Tim and me special in a bizarre kind of way. It was as though we had this special fascination about us. We had been there. We had done this thing.

" 'Meet Ned. He's just back from 'Nam.' or 'He was in the rivers in 'Nam.' And I'd talk to whomever it was I'd been introduced to and maybe tell a war story, and then the person'd move away and back to the group, and I'd feel, somehow, as though I was still on the outside and could never really be part of that group, the one around the table.

"Because, while having been to Vietnam gave me a ticket into the group, it was only as a special member, a special category. Like being a clown at the party or the token black in a club. I was their token warrior, their prize fighter. I had grown up with them, but I had been changed and was no longer really one of them. I was presentable enough to be a part of their group, and I think they enjoyed some of the stories. Most of them didn't know many people who'd been to Vietnam. But I had been changed, somehow, by the experience, and they could tell. It was as if I wore some kind of patch or sign that identified me.

"The sign let me into the group but only as a special person, like a gladiator. It was as though they wanted me for that but not for what I was inside. No, they definitely didn't want what was inside."

Sis listened as I spoke, her eyes following me as I moved around the kitchen, touching things on the shelves, straightening things.

"You know, Sis, I can't buy a drink at *Sir John's Den*. My money isn't any good. I go up to buy a drink or a round, and the bartender tells me that it has already been taken care of by so- and-so. At first, I thought it was great. But, after a while, I didn't like it so much. In a funny sort of way, you aren't part of a group if you can't join in their games as an equal. And I'm not an equal, that's obvious. I can't buy a drink."

"And... I didn't catch on to this right away... I haven't been invited back to any of the married ones' houses yet. To the single ones, yes. The ones without wives or husbands or kids. But not the settled ones, the ones who have been married for a few years and have young kids. They don't want to have me get too close to their homes. Think I might kill something, there, in front of them at the dinner table. Or shout RANGER out loud during the cocktail party and jump out a window. Or forget to wipe the blood off my boots before entering the house. Or offer someone an ear to nibble on," I said in a hoarse whisper and sat down at the table, exhausted.

Sis took both of my hands in hers and held on.

"I'm sorry," I said.

"I'm not," she answered. "You needed to say those things."

"But I shouldn't have to do it... to you like that."

"It's what we do, Nedgar. We listen and wait and try not to judge very much."

"It's... Well, it's shitty that I have to unload all that on you, but thanks for listening and especially not judging," I said and squeezed Sis's hands in mine. "Thanks."

Sis smiled and I felt better.

"Your story was pretty good, by the way. You going to send it out to anyone?" Sis asked after a while, referring to Killian's getting hit in the canal.

"Thanks. I might send it out eventually, but I don't think it'll stand on its own. I need some other stories to go with it. I'm working on one about a girl I met at a kind of dance over there."

"Love story?"

"Not quite," I answered and then thought maybe it could be, after all.

"Could I see it when it's done? I like your writing," Sis said and indicated the stack of pages in the middle of the table. "Here, you can have these back. I didn't make any notes. I didn't know if you wanted me to."

"Oh, yeah. Make notes. I'd love to find out what you think, how you react to it. I'll give you a copy of the dance story when

I'm done. By the way, what did you want to tell me about the bank?"

"The bank called. Dad owned more than a boat in Florida, evidently. They found a small amount of income from an offshore something-or-other in the Bahamas," Sis explained. "When they checked it out, they found out it was a whole set-up that managed Florida property and things like that."

"What did he own?"

"They can't tell me. It's like this: The offshore... trust, it's called. The offshore trust owns these Florida properties, and owners of the trust, it's like owning a share of stock, get to use the property just like it's theirs. Only they don't have to declare it or anything. It's used to hide real estate from anyone who might want to get at it, like in a divorce. That's the way the bank explained, anyway. As far as anyone can tell, Dad owned shares in the trust, and he could keep those shares out of the country, away from a creditor, unlike a deed to property, which would have to be registered to him in the 'States and could be captured by someone through the courts."

"Why couldn't someone capture the shares?" I asked, amazed at the complexity of it all and equally impressed that Sis seemed to understand it so well. I had evidently underestimated that side of her.

"As the bank explained," Sis said, "the shares are in bearer form. Meaning whoever holds the actual piece of paper, the share certificate itself, is the owner of the shares. Like bonds, really, rather than shares of stock."

"And the location of the property?"

"The trust doesn't have to tell. Their books aren't public."

"I don't get it," I said. "What if someone dies, like Dad, and the property just sits there? Does the trust do anything? Who pays the property taxes? Can anyone sell it? All those questions."

"I'll give you the bank's best guess of what's going on," Sis answered. "It took them about a half hour on the 'phone to work it out with me." Sis made a steeple with her hands and breathed in through her nose. "The property is like a grave site, a cemetery plot. It's bought through the trust, and the purchase price is invested in the real estate and other securities. The income from the other securities pays for the taxes on the property. If someone dies, as Dad has, then the property just sits there, abandoned, with the taxes being paid, until it falls down. The trust is only obligated to keep the books so that taxes can be paid."

"Forever?" I asked.

"Ninety-nine years, under Bahamian law. Then the real estate reverts to the owners of the shares. If you have in your possession share number 675, for instance, you will be given the deed to property number 675, the owner's name part of the deed left blank, for you to fill in. Until then, there are only two people who know who has which piece of property. You know... because you purchased the property in the first place and signed it over to the trust when you joined... and the trust itself. There is a book or a list or something that ties the particular certificates to the particular pieces of property."

"That means that the list of owners could change at any time, then. That if you gave your certificate to someone then that someone would be the new owner of the piece of property the certificate represented. Right?"

"As I understand it, right. Only the list doesn't automatically get updated. The names stay the same on the list unless someone contacts the trust and authorizes them to change the holder's name of certificate 675, for instance, to Mr. Jones. The names on the list don't have any legal force anyway. It's the physical possessor of the certificate who own the property. As the bank said, the property could change owners during a poker game, legally, and no one, not even the trust, would know."

"So, we own a piece of property somewhere," I offered.

"Maybe."

"Why maybe?"

"Can't find the certificate. Bank doesn't have it. It doesn't seem to be here in the house, Bank and I've been through the safe deposit box, and it wasn't there," Sis said. "The only way the bank found out about it was a small amount of income that was distributed last year. Kind of a year-end bonus of a couple of hundred bucks."

"Answer me this," I said. "When the ninety-nine years is up, how does the trust know where to send the deed?"

"They don't. The holder of the certificate has to contact them to get the deed to the property. If no contact is made, the deed just sits there, the taxes go unpaid, and the town or city or country where the property is located has to foreclose or whatever to get its taxes. The trust just lets the deed go."

"How about if the trust ceases to function?"

"I don't know. The bank didn't know either. It's a relatively new thing. They were only first created about ten years ago. None of them have gone out of business yet," Sis answered.

"Another mystery. Like the boat."

"And Terry. Don't forget Terry," Sis reminded me, her green eyes sparkling. "I'm dying to find out about Terry, the boat boy or whatever. Wonder if he has cute buns..."

CHAPTER TEN

Vung Tau, June 14, 2015 hours

Dancing at the Saigon Hotel in Vung Tau happened in a long room on the garden side of the old three-story colonial building. The arrangement of the room and the music made Ned think of the Fortnightly dance classes at the Park Plaza in St. Louis when he was growing up.

The inside wall was lined with straight back chairs arranged facing the tall French doors leading outside to the narrow verandah. The wide steps down to the garden from the verandah were blocked by mesh to protect against grenades thrown from the garden. The tops of the walls around the garden had broken glass stuck in new cement. The garden gate leading to the back street behind the hotel was barricaded with sandbags.

The girls stood in small groups of three or four or sat in pairs and chattered busily with each other, their voices singsongy in a pleasant and comforting way. At the far door sitting on a tall stool an old angry looking woman spoke to three or four very young girls, their faces and bodies identical. Only the colors and embroidered designs on their dresses were different. They did not look like whores to Ned.

The other drivers had taken one of the cyclos back to the base after only one drink in the noisy bar. Dave Sylvester, the ex-Swift driver now XO of the division, stood solidly in the doorway at Ned's left inspecting the crowd of girls. Each girl lowered her eyes as Dave stared at her in turn. A placard on an easel invited in French all patriotic residents of Vung Tau each evening from seven until ten to a tea dance to promote the interchange of Vietnamese and American cultures.

"I'm going to hit the head. Then I'll be in the bar. Nothing new here," he added and was gone, leaving Ned alone in the doorway, a few of the girls looking in his direction. He avoided their eyes by looking at the rest of the room.

A trio, crowded into the far corner in front of one of the pairs of French doors, consisted of a white baby grand piano, a snare drum, and a baritone saxophone. The piano, out of tune and badly played by an elegantly dressed and savagely grinning man, drove the beat of *One of Those Things* while the taller, funereal drummer made the wire brushes on the snare drum hiss. The saxophonist had bleached his hair and was trying to follow the melody, only coinciding with the piano every fifth or sixth note, struggling with transposing the music from tenor to baritone. Ned smiled as he listened. The sounds they made evoked another time in his life when the boys in the room were not in a war and the girls were not paid to dance.

Three couples danced in the center of the room. A short red headed boy with freckles awkwardly held a girl in a white ao di with a blue dragon on each sleeve. A serious faced black soldier barely moved, his huge arms surrounding a tiny girl dressed in a long yellow dress with red flowers down the left side. He was all in white, and Ned thought they made a dazzling couple. The third man was Vietnamese. He dressed like a businessman from the American Midwest, complete with a Rotary pin in the lapel of his shiny brown suit. His partner, wearing a white dress with a long slit up the side, was young enough to be his daughter. Her arms hung at her sides while his hands rested on her shoulders. Ned could see her hands occasionally brush across his crotch. The man's chin barely touched the top of her head, and he did not smile. His eyes were tightly shut.

The music stopped and Ned stepped across the floor to a

table with a large, chromed punch bowl in the center. He would have some punch and pick a girl to ask to dance but there were no glasses or cups near the punch bowl. He saw them carefully piled on a table next to the angry old woman. Ned looked around the room. No one was drinking punch. A pretty girl with sad mouth and eyes in a peach-colored cotton dress walked up and stood next to him. She said nothing and only looked in the direction of the trio. She was tall for a Vietnamese. The trio began to play again but he could not recognize the tune. Ned turned to her, and only her mouth smiled. Her sad eyes did not quite meet his.

"You are an officer?" she asked. Her voice was very soft and surprisingly deep.

"Yes. In the Navy." He wore no rank badge.

Her smile brightened but her eyes didn't change. They weren't quite the eyes of a Vietnamese. Maybe she was part European. "You please buy drink?"

"Can we dance?" Ned answered. He felt nervous.

"You must first buy drink."

"Even if I am not thirsty?"

"I cannot dance unless you first buy drink. You do not have to drink. I would like some champagne."

"Can we go somewhere else? I don't really want to dance."

"You want to date me?" She looked up at him and her eyes finally smiled too and then she looked down again. "You must buy me." Her hand almost touched his sleeve. "Then we leave."

Some tea dance, thought Ned. "How much?" He only had twenty dollars in Military Payment Certificates and another ten in piasters.

"I will ask," she said. She walked away from him to the old woman guarding the door. He could not see her figure very well under the peach-colored cotton dress. Her black hair was long in back, almost down to her waist. She spoke something to the old woman who looked up and across the room at Ned. The girl nodded her head as the old woman spoke in answer. The girl shook her head once in the middle of the old woman's answer.

"One hundred p," the girl said, her eyes looking down, when she returned to Ned at the punch table. She had small breasts and was almost as tall as Ned. Her hair in front was cut in bangs just above her round eyes.

"One hundred?" He didn't have enough money to buy her and now felt foolish that he had asked. "You must be a very good dancer to be so expensive," Ned said, trying to hide his embarrassment. "I cannot dance that well. One hundred is beaucoup piasters."

"Not so much. It only cost you one hundred." She stopped and almost touched his sleeve again but still avoided his eyes. "I would like to have date with you. We go my apartment and have a date. It will cost only one hundred to go with me. You not even have to tip me if you do not like our date." She looked up then and her eyes smiled at him.

"Where do you live?" Ned asked, embarrassed by her insistence. Maybe he could borrow the money.

"It is very near here."

Ned went into the bar to look for Dave.

The girl's apartment was three blocks from the hotel on Tran Hung Dao Street and she insisted on taking a cyclo. The two of them sat facing each other with their knees touching and did not speak. Ned had to pay the cyclo driver double the usual fare because of the shortness of the trip.

The front door of the girl's apartment building stood between a bicycle repair shop and a grocery, both closed for the night. Two old women squatted in the vestibule and stopped talking as Ned and the girl walked past them and up the dim lit stairs to the third-floor landing where the girl motioned him to wait. She knocked once at a door in the shadows and immediately opened it and went in, silently closing the door behind her. Ned only saw for a moment a dull yellow glow from inside where the girl went. He thought about Vung Tau being for R and R for both sides of the war and how there wasn't any danger in being where he was, but he could still feel the beginnings of the excitement he felt in the rivers. Maybe it was being with this girl whose hand would almost touch him and whose eyes had finally smiled at him.

The door opened and a slight figure stood there for an instant. It was an old woman in black pajamas, and she scurried past, her eyes not meeting his, and went down the stairs behind him. He wanted to leave then when the girl looked out into the hallway and motioned him in. He felt hollow and tight, and his excitement was growing as he went into the room.

There was now a dim red glow in the room coming from a single lamp on a table in the far corner. A chair sat to the right of the table. A pile of boxes the size of wine crates ran along the right wall. Opposite the door was a window with yellow curtains drawn. Under the window was a long, low open box. Along the left wall was a simple camp style bed with a pile of large pillows arranged to make it serve as a couch. At the foot of the bed stood a three-drawer bureau against the wall. A single framed photograph of a young child with an unlit candle in front sat on the top of the bureau.

The girl stood in the middle of the room.

"Come in, please. "

Ned shut the door, the excitement of being with a girl again making him nervous.

"You would like a beer?" the girl asked. "I have Ba Mi Ba beer if you would like."

"Yes, please," Ned answered, nervous at being in this girl's room. "A very nice room." He paused. "Who was that?"

"My aunt. She stay here while I am at the hotel. They steal my things if no one here."

"Is that your little girl?" asked Ned pointing to the child in the picture on the bureau.

"Oh, no," she said quickly. "Is my sister's baby." She paused and then added, "I am still virgin." She turned to one of the boxes on the floor along the right wall and withdrew a single bottle. "Here is your beer." She opened the bottle with an opener that lay on a tray on the table, carefully poured half of the foamy beer into a wine glass and handed Ned the glass.

"Thank you," he said looking at the warm beer. He didn't want to drink the beer.

"Do you want to have a date now?" she said and started to unbutton the front of her dress.

"Yes," Ned said. "Let me watch you undress."

"If you like to."

"You are very pretty."

"Not so much," she said raising her arms and slipping the dress over her head. The red glow of the light made her skin the same color as the rest of the room. Her black hair and eyes stood out in the dimness while the rest of her body was indistinct. Ned looked around the room and when he looked back her bra and panties were off and she was in front of him, her arms at her sides. He tried not to stare at the black hair between her legs and looked instead at her breasts. He put the wine glass with the warm beer down on the table. He wanted her and wanted her to touch him.

"Will you take my clothes off?"

"If you like." He stood facing the middle of the room as she began by kneeling and untying his shoes.

"I am a virgin too," he said smiling down at her.

"You are very old to be virgin," she said seriously. As she carefully rolled each sock down, he lifted his foot, keeping his balance by placing his hands on her shoulders. Her skin was soft and cool. She placed his socks carefully in his shoes and slid them under the chair.

Next, she stood up and began unbuttoning his shirt. She stepped behind him and pulled the sleeves off one by one, one of her breasts brushing against his bare back. He wanted to be inside of her very much as she unbuttoned his pants and lowered the zipper. Her fingers touched gently as she pulled his pants to the floor, and he stepped out of them. She giggled as she tried to slip his shorts off, and he stood there with his arms away from his sides and let her touch him.

"We have our date now," she suggested and giggled.

"Just us two virgins, huh?" Ned was enjoying the feeling of wanting her.

The two of them moved to the bed, and he sat on the edge, and she began to move into his lap and he tried to stop the memory that was coming back of how he had held Killian on the bow of the boat in the canal. He could hear the girl whispering to him and he could see Killian's face as he held him. The girl's face looked up and the voice from the canal whispered to him.

"You do not want me?" Her voice was quiet in the quiet room. She did not move in his arms, and he still held her. But she had it right, and he did not want her anymore. His face was hot, and he was ashamed. It had happened once before, and he could still remember how it had scared him.

"It's not you," he tried to explain. "No, don't move. Stay there," he said as she started to get up. Her body relaxed and she lay there in his arms.

"Don't, please. That won't do any good," he said after a while. "Just lie here."

Then he started to tell in a low voice of the canal and the mine and about how he had hated Killian before he was wounded and about how he had almost died in his arms the way he had died with her in his arms. He told about all that and in the telling of it tried to feel again the hatred he had felt toward Killian. He thought somehow that the hatred might help him with her. She lay there in his arms and her head rested against his shoulder. It made no difference that she did not understand much of what he said. When he came to the end of the story, he still could not feel the hatred he had felt, only the shame of hating Killian and then seeing him wounded like that and the other shame that he felt now.

"You are afraid when there is this fight?" she asked him.

"Yes. "

"You are afraid now?"

"I don't think so. I don't know. Maybe." He wasn't sure.

"You want me now?" she asked him quietly.

"No, I don't think so," he said, remembering Killian.

The shame had ebbed now and only bitterness was left. He was beginning to hate Killian again. That shit, he thought. That shit gets me even here after he's dead. He could feel the hatred rise now.

Good, he thought. The hot hating feeling began to swell inside of him and then the girl was touching him again and he realized that it wasn't he who was dead.

CHAPTER ELEVEN

Vung Tau, 4 December, 2010 hours

At the Officer's Club on the Navy base in Vung Tau, Republic of South Vietnam, with three days left, Ned lowered his hand and drained his beer in two swallows. Dog was writing something in his small notebook. When he was finished, he put the stub of the pencil inside the notebook, folded it shut, and slipped it inside its small waterproof pouch. He put the pouch inside his breast pocket.

"Keeping track of the bets, Dog?" Ned asked, and Dog's smile told him that he had guessed right. Dog was one careful driver. A good man to have on your wing or when the bets were down.

Ned was just about to pour the last of his second beer into his glass when the door opened, letting in a warm gust of salty air scented with diesel fuel and tidal mud flats. Lieutenant Commander Frederick, the Division Commander, stood in the doorway. He smiled at the six drivers seated around the table and collected a beer bottle and glass in one hand from the beaming bartender, crossing to the round table, his other hand holding a folded yellow sheet of foolscap between thumb and forefinger. The door slowly shut behind him with a tiny sigh from the hydraulic closer.

"May I join you, gentlemen?" he asked.

Dog and Marco had both half risen to their feet, their chairs scraping across the floor, as Frederick motioned them down with both hands.

"Somebody grab a chair for the boss," said O'Connor, who only looked up for a moment and then continued to stare at his beer bottle which he had waddled to the center of the table. Marco pulled a chair from the table behind and made room for it between his and Ned's chair. The Division Commander hooked the chair into position with his foot and dropped into it. He clanked the bottle and glass down onto the plywood table in front of him.

"What brings you to the trenches, Sir?" asked Sleek-hood. "You've got news on my parts, maybe?"

"No, Diego. We're still waiting, but don't worry. You'll be ready for turnover on time. Guaranteed. " Frederick paused and looked at the six young men facing him. "I've got some back news, guys. Don Cherry bought it. Back at *Sea Float.*"

"No," Ned said.

"What happened?" asked Dog, leaning forward, his head cocked to one side.

"When?" asked Marco. His black eyes stared dully.

"On a SEAL op," answered Frederick. "Yesterday. Cherry and a SEAL got hit by a claymore on the Duong Keo."

"Stupid bastard," muttered O'Connor in a small voice.

"He always gave us real good skinny, guys," said Davis. "Always out there nosing around, going on ops with us and the SEALs."

"What kind of op?" wondered Dog aloud.

"They went in to see if they couldn't get that .51 that's been down there for the last year or so. Thought there might be some kind of sapper or rocket team getting set up to bust *Solid Anchor*, now that we've pulled out."

"Solid anchor. Who are they?" asked Sleek-hood.

"*Sea Float*, Diego," answered Frederick. "They've started to move the barges out of the river and are just using the land base now. Calling it *Solid Anchor.*"

"Five acres of muddy sand, eh, Sir?" O'Connor smiled at his beer bottle. "We made it what it is today, boys."

"You guys helped build it, all right," Frederick spoke quietly, and the other six were silent, waiting for O'Connor to continue.

O'Connor looked up at Frederick. "Was he married?"

"Don? No. Engaged, I think, but even that had kind of fallen by the wayside when he upped for another six months," Frederick said, looking down at his hands. He hadn't touched his beer. The beads of sweat had started to puddle at the base of the bottle, making a ring on the table. "At least, that's what he told me before we left the Float."

O'Connor raised his glass to eye level. "Gentlemen," he stated.

Each of the others at the table except Frederick raised his glass. The Division Commander hastily picked up his beer bottle in his right hand and wiped the top with his left. All eyes turned toward O'Connor, his red hair making his face seem unnaturally pale in the fluorescent light of the small room.

"To Don Cherry," O'Connor spoke slowly and took a sip of beer. "To his mostly intelligent intelligence."

"A hell of a guy," said Marco. Dog looked at the American flag to the left of the door to the small room.

Ned spoke the intelligence officer's name quietly, under his breath and finished his glass of beer in a slow swallow.

Davis, Sleek-hood, and Frederick each took a sip of beer, echoing, "Don."

"He was supposed to come out of the river with us," said Ned. "What happened?"

Frederick pushed his chair back an inch farther from the table. He held his beer bottle by the mouth with three fingers. He raised it an inch above the table and let it drop with a clunk to the plywood. It wobbled from side to side, almost tipping over, but finally settled onto its bottom. "Missed his flight out on the next to last Sea Wolf to go on the SEAL op. They were going to bring him up with the STAB boats. A last run up the canals. My Tho, Ben Thuy, Saigon, and home."

"Hell of run that would be," said Ned, thinking of the thirty foot barge shaped STABs, only two feet of their hull showing above the water at rest. Their flat black painted hulls could hold an entire SEAL team, enough mini-gun ammo for a two-minute fire fight, and two Chrysler Hemis. The bastards would do forty-five knots in calm water and were so muffled that you never heard them coming, only going away. They used to drop them in by helo at the top of canals and the STABs would run the whole canal at full bore, hosing down both sides with their mini-guns, just to show Charlie that he didn't control the water. What a trip that would be, Ned thought and smiled. Slam, bam, thank you, ma'am. "Bet they were going to call it an intel mission," Ned said.

"What else!" agreed Dog smiling at the thought of travelling cross country on the canals and rivers that way. "You know that canal between the Bassac and Cui Tu, just below My Tho?" he said to Ned, his voice low and his eyes shining.

Ned nodded and the two of them talked in low voices. Marco, Davis, and Frederick talked about fuel filters while O'Connor and Sleek-hood each stared ahead of him at his own beer bottle and glass. Sleek-hood's face in the cold light seemed peaceful, but O'Connor's eyes looked hollow and empty. Neither of them spoke.

Davis was the first to stand and start for the bar, but Frederick stopped him with a hand on his arm.

"Hold it, guys," he said. "I've got something for you, and before the next round I want to lay it out. " He tapped the yellow paper that lay on the table in front of him. "I want you all to hear me real good on this one, OK?"

They all looked at him. O'Connor's eyes were half closed, but his attention was riveted on the Division Commander's moving lips. Marco and Davis exchanged glances. Ned leaned forward, his forearms on the plywood table. Dog sat up straight in his chair. Sleek-hood smiled, reminding Ned of a garishly colored print of the Buddha he saw hanging in a shop window in Vung Tau during the past week.

"You don't have to do this, any of you," said the flat voice of the Division Commander. "This group has officially stood down from combat." He looked around the table from Marco at his right to Ned on his left. "This is purely a volunteer operation, OK?" He paused and no one spoke. "And you can't volunteer if you've been drinking here. Got it?" Again, no one spoke. Ned looked at the clock. He had been in the small room just about an hour and was working on his second beer.

"An old Victory class freighter is expected in early tomorrow morning. It's supposed to hit the Sea Buoy off Nui Vung Tau between 0200 and 0400. It'll take the pilot aboard just inside of the three-mile limit and will head up the river to Saigon to unload jeep parts and sewing machines."

"Jeep parts," echoed Davis and his eyes blinked.

"It's a Chinese ship from Taiwan," continued the Division Commander. "MACV has been asked, unofficially, by the Taiwanese, to help out their intelligence types."

"Where do we come in?" asked Dog.

"MACV has asked us to take the Taiwanese intel people, their whatevers, out to this freighter and put them aboard instead of the pilot they'll be expecting."

"Why do they need us?" Marcos at back in his chair as he spoke the words."

"Why can't they just use the pilot boat to put these whatevers aboard?" Davis's voice sounded tired. He wasn't on the blade, thought Ned.

"They think there might be some... problems."

"With what? What kind of problems, Sir?" asked Marco, sitting forward again.

"They think there might be another boat going out to meet this ship. A boat with some ARVNs aboard." Frederick paused. "A South Vietnamese Swift."

Slick-hood whistled and Ned suddenly felt embarrassed for him. He always reacted the wrong way.

"They think the Swift will be out there to pick up some contraband. Perfume. Or whiskey. Black market stuff for Cholon. "

"Why don't the Viets send one of their boats out to do the drop off?" This was Dog.

"They don't know which ones are involved," came the answer from Frederick. "It seems they have a group of their Swifts who are trying to go private on them. Setting up in business for themselves. A group out of Saigon. None of their coastal swifts from here will go up against them." Frederick stopped talking.

He's said too much already, thought Ned.

"Rules of engagement?" asked Dog.

"Fire only if fired upon," came the instant answer, "and only with permission from Saigon." He's thought this one out, Ned knew. There's going to be some trouble with this one.

O'Connor made a bridge of his two hands over his beer bottle. "How many boats do they expect to attend this party?"

"One Viet Swift. They would like two of ours. One to carry the whatevers and the other to ride shotgun. "

Ned thought for a moment and said, "This Viet Swift. Where is it supposed to be now?"

"We're not sure," Frederick said slowly. "We can't just go ask them. They would want to know why we wanted to know. MACV says we can't tell them. " He touched the mouth of his beer bottle with a finger. "Not until after the drop."

"Whose bad dream is this supposed to be?"

Ned and Marco looked down at the bare plywood in front of them as O'Connor spoke aloud their inner thoughts, his voice too loud for the small group at the table. "What a load of crap."

Ned could hear the red head's voice begin to fill with anger, but Ned would not look up at him. "How can they ask us to do this? We're shut down. finished. Out of the war. Retired from the service. All that good stuff." His voice began to shake. "Bastards don't give us a chance, do they? Finally give it to us just to yank it away at the last minute," the words beginning to tumble together, his tongue alternately licking first one side then the other of his mouth.

Ned looked up into his dancing, angry eyes. Across the room, behind the bar, the Vietnamese bartender stared, his mouth slightly open, no longer smiling. "Fuckers don't care, do they!" O'Connor shouted, finally. "Don't care a rat's ass."

"Hold on, Pat," said Frederick softly. "This is our choice. It would be our op."

"Damned right I'll hold on," snapped O'Connor, his voice now almost a whine, its power beginning to wane. "I'll hold on to what I've got left, all right. What I've got left of me, I'll sure as hell hold on to. And my crew. And the crew. I'll hold on for them, too."

O'Connor took a breath and continued. "What a stupid goddamned idea! Go out against some Viet Swift who can blow us out of the water with our own goddamned ordinance." He squeezed his eyes shut and dropped his voice to a hoarse rattle. "Fire only if fired upon. My sweet ass." Another breath. "Jesus H. Christ." Ned counted to five before O'Connor spoke again. "How can they tell us to do something so damned dumb? So goddamned dumb."

"Pat, Pat," coaxed Frederick, "It's only if someone wants to do it. Only if a couple of you and two crews want to go out. Nobody's saying anyone has to."

"What about the crews?" asked Ned. "Do they have a choice, too?"

"Hell, yes," said Frederick, still looking at O'Connor who was now holding his empty beer bottle tightly in both hands. "The Chief is over at the EM Club right now, checking with them, with any of the sober ones, that is." Frederick smiled and Marco and Davis laughed, some of the tension disappearing. Even O'Connor smiled. "Can't go out if you've got a buzz on, can you?"

There were nods of comprehension all around the table. O'Connor's grip on the bottle slackened. "Credi'll be faced by now, I'll bet," the red head said, his voice almost normal again.

"You're probably right, Pat," said Frederick, his face calm and kind. "That old gunny can sure as hell put them away." Ned looked into Frederick's eyes and saw the Division Commander take the kindest way out. "He's your best man, isn't he, Pat?"

"Yes, Sir. I guess." O'Connor was thinking more clearly now. Both hands lay restlessly on the table, the pale fingers encircling the beer bottle. "All the others worth a damn went home on the flight last week. Credi's a boozer but he knows his stuff. Master and Lippert are still pretty green, and Robinson's useless." Pat sat up straight and looked around the table. Ned spoke first.

"Don't you do it, Pat."

"Not without Credi," added Dog.

There was silence as O'Connor shifted in his chair.

"Oh, hell," he said at last and stood up. "Think I'll pass on this one, sir, if it's OK with you. Get myself another one of these beauties," he added and walked toward the bar. "Get anyone else one while I'm up?"

"If no one minds, I will have just one," said Sleek-hood's voice and Ned smiled. That's two down.

"No, thanks," Nash Davis said, and Ned heard the thickness in his voice. "Too bright in here already." He pulled the aviator glasses down with his middle finger and pushed them against the bridge of his nose, his smile fading to a frown as he tilted his empty bottle over his glass. "I've had it." Three down, three to go.

"No, thanks, Pat," said Dog. Ned couldn't read anything behind the words he was hearing. Was Dog saying yes to the op? "I might just listen to some more of this Chinese story and wait to see if I have a crew that's sober."

Ned heard his own voice speaking softly, carefully. "I'll wait this round out, Pat. Thanks, though." What the hell, he thought. What am I doing? He could feel the smooth, damp plywood table under his palms and the rough fabric of his fatigues across his thighs. He touched his finger inside his shirt collar where it touched his neck. His dog tags felt cool against his chest. He wished he had put on a T-shirt.

Pat leaned against the bar. The bartender's head nodded up and down, up and down, his smile flashing. Pat looked at Marco. "Wop? A beer?"

"Screw you very much. But make sure it's cold, you witless Mick," said Marco holding up his middle finger. "And a clean glass, please."

"You got it," said the red head with a grin. He held up two fingers to the bartender who plunged his arms into the ice filled sink behind the bar and quickly held up two bottles of beer, high above his head, like a referee holding the hands of two boxers. One bottle was green and the other brown. He lowered them to the bar and placed a single, clean glass beside them.

"The green meanie for me," said Marco. Neither bottle had a label, but the odds were good on the green bottle containing a German or Dutch beer.

"You can have it," answered O'Connor as he slapped a damp pile of the small, pink and blue Military Payment Certificates on the bar's sticky surface and picked up the two bottles and the glass with the fingers of his right hand. "I need the Ba Mi Ba's formaldehyde to keep me from rotting in this paradise." He turned his back on the bar. "Keep the change, my man," he said over his shoulder with a wave of his left hand. "Save your MPCs... The South shall get it up again!" He sat heavily in his chair and pushed the glass and the green bottle toward Marco. Their eyes met and they both smiled. Marco filled his glass.

"Cheers, Mick."

"The same, Wop."

They both drank deep, Pat straight from the brown bottle. What the hell, thought Ned. Why not?

"The ninety three'll go. If my crew's sober," Ned said.

Dog smiled and held out his hand to Ned. "Knew I couldn't leave her that easy, the bitch." Ned and Dog shook. "Count me in, too."

Division Commander Frederick smiled.

Vung Tau, 4 December, 2030 hours

Ned sat below in the cabin of the 93 boat and waited for his crew to return from the EM Club. He had stopped by the nurses' barracks; Lee, the nurse Ned had met in Can Tho, wouldn't be back from Saigon until later that night, he was told by Willie, her roommate. Dog was still talking to Frederick up at Division and the others, all except O'Connor, had gone back to their boats or into town. O'Connor would keep slamming back the beers until he got sick or passed out. He had been performing the same ritual each night for the past week. Ned touched the teletyped after-action report that he had been asked to edit or approve by Division.

The report read, in part, *"On 5 August his craft received an urgent request to extract a team of United States Navy SEALs at the culmination of an intelligence gathering mission. He entered a narrow river and came under heavy enemy automatic weapons and rocket attack..."* Whoever wrote this one up made a screwed-up mission sound a whole lot better than it really was, Ned thought as he closed his eyes and remembered the operation.

CHAPTER TWELVE

Dam Doi River, 5 August, 1915 hours

They had put Arapaho on the beach just before twilight. The main river in the silver light looked solid, hard as a steel ribbon unwinding into the dark green interior, up toward the village of Dam Doi and away from the safety offered by *Sea Float*.

"How long you think it'll take?"

"Two hours. Three at the most," said Cooper, leader of the eight-man SEAL team. Cooper's skin was painted black and green and brown, and he wore loose black pajamas. At his waist he wore a K-Bar knife in a black sheath. On his feet were yellow plastic flip-flops which had been spray painted flat black. His face paint made his eyes seem rimmed with red and his mouth glistened hungrily as Ned and he looked at the map spread on top of the clear plastic chart table cover. "The Dam Doi's a bitch. Only got about two, three feet at max up as far as the village. Then it goes real thin."

"Do you know which side you want to use yet?"

"If there's going to be any shit, it'll come from the village side on the north. We'll wait for you on the south bank. Maybe about two hundred yards this side of the village."

"Call sign?"

"We're Arapaho tonight. You guys still Abbey

November?" They had worked together three other times, always to the west of *Sea Float*. This was their first time working the more uncertain eastern end of the river. Ned wrote the call sign and the extraction time, 2200-2300, on the plastic chart table cover.

"Yeah. We're Abbey November nine three and the other boat's one two seven. You know Pat O'Connor?"

"You mean 'Seamus' from Boston? Sure. His old man works at Merrill Lynch. Sent me a shit load of stuff on the market."

"Pat's got the 127 boat He'll stay about fifty yards down the Dam Doi from us. He doesn't have reverse in his port engine, so he's got to be careful not to get too far in so he can't turn around," Ned added. "Don't worry. Pat's got a good boat. He'll be there to give you some fire support with the eighty-one if you want. Besides, only one of us could extract at a time."

Cooper touched Ned's shoulder with his closed fist and grinned hideously in the gloom. The yellow kerosene lights in the hootches in the resettlement village winked on one by one. The two boats drifted quietly, their engines shut down, in the main river, the Cua Lon, a tidal river at the southern tip of the country that ran both ways. The tide was running to the east and would be low just after midnight. The mission had been called for 2000, so they had left *Sea Float* at 1900.

"You going to walk in?" Ned asked.

"No. Sampans. Three of them on the south bank just where the Dam Doi meets the Cua Lon. "

"How'd they get there?"

"Team Two left them there last night after their recon. They're the ones told us about the old man we're going to snatch."

"Old man?"

"Village chief. We want to bring him in to talk to him. Seems he's been keeping bad company."

"What if he won't come in?" Ned asked. He felt naive whenever he worked with SEALs.

"Oh. They always come," said Cooper and his smile flashed

white again.

I'll bet they do, thought Ned.

At 2008 Ned wrote the time in the log and the bow of the 93 briefly touched the east bank of the Cua Lon after it turns south where it meets the Dam Doi. The night was warm and quiet. No moon shone, but the stars in the sky gave light enough to define the river and give some substance to the shore. The 127 had continued south toward the sea, opening one of its engine hatches to make extra noise. The 93 had cut its engines and drifted to the bank. The eight SEALs had jumped from the bow to the bank below. They had pushed the Swift away from the bank, and Ned could barely see them. Disembodied eyes and teeth gleamed in the soft darkness.

"Abbey November nine-three, this is Arapaho. Radio check, over," came a whisper from the speaker in the pilot house. Arapaho's voice spoke with the slow self-assurance of a California surfer.

"Arapaho, nine-three. Loud and clear. How me, over?" Ned heard Tom, the driver, answer.

"Read you the same. Out."

It was almost an hour later when the first call came in.

"This is Arapaho, over."

The crew sat below in the half-darkness created by the red night lighting. Tom and Ned sat in the pilot house. Downstream, a hundred yards closer to the mouth of the river sat the low silhouette of the 127, no lights showing. Ned had the radio turned down as he always did when he worked with SEALs. Arapaho's voice was low and sinister in the darkness.

"This is nine-three. Go ahead, Arapaho," Ned answered.

"'We are ready for pick-up, over." The voice was neutral. Its earlier Southern California cadence was missing.

"On our way. Break. One-two-seven, this is nine-three. Did you copy?"

"Affirmative. We'll be at the end of the street if you need us," answered Pat O'Connor. They would wait at the junction of the Cua Lon and the Dam Doi. There wasn't enough room for both Swifts to maneuver in the narrow river. The 127 would only be two or three hundred yards away at the most.

"Call mother for me on the other push, OK? Let her know how we are." Ned asked. Pat could give the scheduled progress report to *Sea Float*.

"You've got it. Out."

At a nod from Ned, Tom started the two huge engines. As they began to reach idle and smooth out, the rest of the crew of the 93 came up from below and took their positions. Harris climbed up into the gun tub through the pilot house opening at the bottom. Tom closed his flak jacket and settled his helmet on the back of his head. Ned looked aft and saw Shawgo, who was just riding the boat until his permanent assignment came back from refit in Cam Rahn, at the 81 mm mortar with the .50 piggybacked on top. CB, who had been sitting alone on the stern, moved past him heading for his position in the peak tank on the bow. By now the engines ran smoothly, and Ned walked to the stern to see cooling water pouring evenly from both exhausts.

"The other boat'll wait for us at the mouth," he said to Tracy, the black-haired farm boy from west Texas. Tracy's eyes grew wider, and he smiled in answer. "Piece of cake," assured Ned and returned to the pilot house. "Let's do it to it," he spoke quietly to Tom.

Tom eased back on the engines and the boat pulled free of the mud bank, turned its bow to the north and started up the fifty yards to the Dam Doi.

"Abbey November nine-three, this is Arapaho. Radio check, over," spoke the radio. The voice was once again Southern California.

"Arapaho, this is nine-three. Loud and clear, over." He's being pretty chatty, Ned thought. Nerves?

"Roger. Out."

The boat traveled slowly up the center of the river, leaving little wake and making the minimum of noise. Harris squatted down in the gun tub and spoke down into the pilot house.

"What kind of light are we looking for?"

"Don't know. When we see it, we'll let them know the color

and they'll confirm."

"OK," said Haris and stood up again.

They had been moving up the Dam Doi for about five minutes when Ned saw a red light gleam on the left hand bank about one hundred yards ahead of them.

"Arapaho, this is nine-three. I have a red light, over."

The radio remained silent.

"Hold it here, Tom." The boat, its engines muttering at idle, sat in the middle of the river and waited. The red light remained steady, eighty yards ahead of them. Ned took the starlight scope down from its rack and thumbed it on. The high pitch whine of its light amplifier was loud in the silence of the pilot house. Ned aimed the scope at the red light on the north bank of the river and could see only the white brightness of the light itself in the monochrome viewfinder. There was no sign of the SEAL team. He wondered why Cooper had changed his mind about the side of the river they would wait on.

"Arapaho, this is Abbey November nine-three. I have a red light, over." He knew not to give away the team by saying the location of the light over the radio.

Silence. Ned turned the radio louder and adjusted the squelch. The radio hissed for a moment and was silent.

"See anything, Harris?" Ned whispered into the bottom of the gun tub."

"Quiet as the grave," came the answer from above.

The red light continued to glow in the darkness. Ned picked out the indistinct smear of a cooking fire in the darkness of a group of huts in the village ahead. The boat sat in the river, its engines still muttering. When the radio's voice spoke, it made Ned and Tom jump.

"Abbey November, get the fuck out of here! We don't…"

A bright blue flash illuminated the interior of the pilot house and Tom's hand was frozen in the act of scratching his left ear. The crack of an exploding charge followed an instant later, and leaves and twigs rained down on the deck. Ned could hear the rattle of small arms fire from somewhere ahead. A rocket hissed across the river in front of them, arcing from left to right. Ned heard a low thump an instant later.

"Hold your fire," spoke Ned out the door of the pilot house. "Everybody OK?"

"OK back here," came Tracy's west Texas drawl in answer.

"Let's hold it right here for a bit," Ned told Tom.

The small arms fire ahead increased. Ned could hear the rapid fire of a SEAL Stoner, its 1,000 rounds a minute cutting high and clear like tearing canvas.

"Yeah. Boss. Fine here," came Harris' voice from up in the gun tub. "That rocket..."

Two yellow explosions to starboard were followed by a splash astern of them. Water cascaded down on the stern of the boat. Ned heard Tracy swear in amazement.

"Abbey November, come get us. This is Arapaho. We'll give you a light from the south bank." There's that California voice, Ned thought and nodded. Tom put the engines into gear, and the boat started to move forward. At just under ten knots they would leave little wake and the engines would be fairly quiet.

"Roger, Arapaho. Coming up on you now."

Ned could see the red light clearly now. It was attached to a stick in a garden. Farther ahead on the opposite bank, he could see a green light flash once, twice, three times and then go out. Something rushed across the bow from the south to the north bank two feet off the water and trailing sparks, maybe another rocket. The Stoner fired again in the dark ahead.

"I have a green light, flashing three times, over," Ned spoke into the radio.

"That's us. That you coming up the middle of the river?" asked the California voice.

"Affirmative. We're almost there." Ned hung out of the pilot house door and spoke up to the gun tub. "Harris, keep an eye out for a green light on the south bank on the right just ahead and see if you can see the team. Here's the starlight," and Ned handed the scope up into the darkness and felt it being taken firmly by Harris.

"Got it."

There were no tracer rounds to show where the shooting was, only sounds echoing across the flat water. The boat eased over to port to clear a fish trap that extended out from the south bank.

"Remember that one, Tom, for our way out." They could now see muzzle flashes on both banks of the river ahead. I hope that stuff is over by the time we get there, Ned thought. Not being able to shoot back gives me the willies. Too much time to think about being killed.

Harris' voice came clearly down from the gun tub. "I see the team. I count six."

A yellow flash from the north bank on Ned's side made him jump, and he felt a solid thump on the hull under him. Ned could see the shape of a launch-bomb, half of it buried in the aluminum hull just below his feet.

Then there was no sound or time or anything except his being on the river and waiting, hearing his thoughts as they told him like a small, dry voice telling an old story to a child, calmly. I am going to die tonight on this river, torn apart the way a piece of chicken is torn apart as it is eaten. In this death of yours there will not be very much blood except maybe from the mouth or ears because everything that does the damage happens inside. I will probably fall overboard where I will lie in the water face down floating, arms out to each side like a crucifixion seen from behind, my boots gone and my helmet too. Sometimes the clothes are gone too, blown off, and there is just the body, broken inside and looking soft and lumpy outside at first and then swollen and tight to bursting as it lies there waiting to be carried back to base.

He had seen bodies that had been killed like this, and he always wondered about the pain. Where there was blood, he could imagine how much the pain had been but where there was just the blast and joints pulled apart, each bone from its socket so the body would be limp as a rag doll, he couldn't imagine the pain or how bad it could be.

He was still thinking about the pain when the launch-bomb, of its own weight and the vibration of the hull, fell out of the hole and into the river, splashing in the water and disappearing until they were well past it and the moment of his dying was over.

But the image of him lying face down in the water, limp as a rag doll, was still there now in his head, created out of what the launch-bomb had done and the dead bodies he'd seen while he had been in the rivers. At the repair shop up at An Thoi he had looked carefully at the damage done to boats by rockets. He had also seen dead bodies. These two images had been separate until tonight when they had come together as one image like the twin eye pieces of a pair of binoculars bringing a distant scene into sharp focus. His own death looked very clear to him now.

"...the green light, Boss?" Tom's voice brought him back to the river. Rifle shots. Two, three. He thought he heard a baby crying. A dog barked and he could smell fish. They were opposite the village. He felt a chill and realized with shame that he had peed in his pants.

"What?" Ned asked. He could not hear the Stoner, but an AK-47 fired two short bursts ahead to his left on the north bank.

"Want to land at the green light?" Tom's hands were pale in the lights from the instrument panel. His left hand gripped the wheel, and the right one made a fist enclosing the knobs on top of both throttle levers.

"Yeah. Land at the green light, Tom." They were thirty yards downstream from the green light on the south bank. "But let's hold here until they wave us in. I'll be up forward. Watch for my hand signals."

He went out onto the short foredeck and knelt. The engines backed for a moment and the boat was still. He could sense rather than see CB next to him with his M-79 grenade launcher. CB could drop a grenade into a trash can at fifty yards. Ned had won ten bucks when he had bet on him back at *Sea Float* at the July 4th picnic. "You OK, CB?"

"Yeah, Boss. Shitty, huh, not being able to shoot back?"

"You bet... Harris?" he called up to the gun tub, not turning his head. A single shot echoed in the darkness ahead.

"Boss?"

The dog barked again. The baby still cried. Poor kid, Ned thought. Tom's voice from the pilot house was saying something. Probably on the radio with 127. "Still see the team?" Ned spoke up to Harris.

"All eight. Plus a package. Wish they'd smile."

"Smile?" Ned repeated.

"Yeah. So I could see them better in the scope," the black gunner's mate said. Ned could hear him smiling.

"Hey, Boss," CB said. "'Were we hit back there? That last thump?"

"Yeah. A launch-bomb. Probably a 105 round."

"Lucky it was a dud," CB said.

"Yeah. Lucky," Ned agreed and realized that the image of him lying dead in the water was no longer as clear as it had been. He hoped the wet on his trousers wouldn't show.

"They're waving us in," said Harris.

"Ready to cover them," Ned said.

Ned motioned Tom forward with his hand.

"Ready," answered Harris. The 93 edged toward the green light and came to a stop about a foot from shore. Steep sides, Ned thought. He stood up and looked down over the bow into the darkness and eyes looking up at him. The river and the village and the men on the bank were all silent.

"Get us the hell out of here," Cooper's voice spoke. "We're screwed up real good."

Seven SEAL team members scrambled up the landing net and crouched on the bow. Two of them leaned over the edge and accepted a bundle the size of a grain sack from below and laid it carefully on the deck up against the pilot house. The eighth member of the team came over the bow.

"Let's move it," said Cooper's voice and Ned signaled Tom to back off the bank. A shot to their left broke the silence and the engines roared as the boat backed in a rush to the center of the river, its stern swinging to port as its bow pointed downstream. There was a moment of hesitation as the engines idled, the transmissions shifting through neutral to forward, and the engines roared again. The bow rose just as a rocket arced ahead of them and exploded on the opposite bank with a white flash. Shrapnel and debris splattered the boat.

Ned could see the red light ahead of them on the north bank still shining in the garden. Their wake was beginning to pull water away from the banks into a wave behind them. There was no more firing from the village.

Cooper looked at Ned. "OK to return fire? The other boat clear?"

"The 127 is out near the main river. Go ahead," Ned answered.

"Prep fire both banks," Cooper told his men. "Make sure you toss a few charges up into the village as we go out." The night erupted into pounding and hammering as the 93 boat roared out along the length of the Dam Doi.

"Call the one-twenty-seven and tell them we're on our way out. Wait for us just below where we'll come out," Ned told Tom. Cooper stood next to Ned in the doorway of the pilot house. Harris was firing the twin .50s to starboard; they could just hear each other.

"My radioman says he heard our call sign," Ned said and waited. "Someone called us in for an extraction."

"Wasn't us. We weren't done yet."

"You set up a red light on the north bank, in a garden near the village?" Ned asked.

"Nope. We only used green tonight. Was it an American voice that called you in?" Cooper's voice was flat even though he had to shout to be heard over the slamming of the .50s.

"Sounded American, but I didn't think it sounded like your kid from California."

"Radioman's from Norfolk."

"He talks like a surfer," Ned tried to explain.

"What the fuck's the difference what he talks like? It wasn't him and you busted up our snatch. Came in too early." Cooper's flat voice shouting in his ear hurt, but Ned couldn't move away. Cooper was shouting to be heard over the guns, but he didn't sound angry.

"What would you have done, Cooper?" Ned finally asked, shouting.

"Same asshole thing you did, what do you think?"

"But you got the old man." Ned tried to sound positive. Harris had stopped firing the .50s. There was sporadic M-16 fire from the SEALs on the stem.

"Huh?" Cooper looked blank.

"In the sack. There," said Ned, pointing down at the bundle on the deck.

"Oh, him," said Cooper with a shrug. "That's his kid. We missed the old man, so we grabbed his kid. Little bastard tried to roll a grenade at us. Can you imagine that? A grenade?"

They were almost out of the Dam Doi, and the firing had completely stopped. The comfortable roar of the diesels filled the river, echoing from the black walls that rushed past in the darkness.

Cooper walked back toward the stern.

"By the way," Cooper said and he stopped and turned back toward Ned who was staring down at the bundle on the deck. "That was good the way you held your fire back there. Took some guts. We could have gotten chewed up real bad if you'd started firing."

CHAPTER THIRTEEN

Sea Float, 6 August, 0100 hours

The kid had been shot in the foot. Not even the SEALs knew this until all their gear was off the 93 boat tied up to Sea Float and the bundle still was rolled up on the deck next to the pilot house. Ned was working on his report of the operation when CB pointed out the bundle still on the bow.

"Your kid's still on board!" Ned yelled to Cooper who was walking down the barge toward the SEAL hootch at the far end.

"Oh, yeah," said Cooper but he didn't stop. "We can't keep him. Already have one Viet family living in the guest hootch. See if Cherry in Intel wants him." Cooper turned the corner of the galley hootch and was gone.

Ned looked down at the bundle. In the glare of the arc lights high above the eight barges lashed together that was Sea Float, Ned could see that the bundle consisted of a dirty poncho liner and some black cotton cloth. A small dirty naked human foot with dried blood on it stuck out from the end closest to him. Ned didn't want to look very closely at the wound.

"Keep an eye on this... prisoner, CB," Ned said pointing at the bundle. "It's only a kid but he rolled a grenade at the SEALs." Ned went to find Don Cherry, the Navy intelligence officer at Sea Float. Kid has guts, he thought.

An hour later Ned carried a very pale ten-year-old Viet Cong in his arms to the medical hootch next to the helo pad at the west end of Sea Float. The boy was either asleep or had passed out. When Ned and CB had carefully unwrapped him, the child had looked up at them and had then closed his eyes. His pale face was pinched, and his straight, black hair hung dry and lifeless. His legs and arms were pitifully thin, and Ned could feel his ribs through his shirt as he carried him. So this is a VC, thought Ned. The kid doesn't seem very dangerous. Ned thought of a picture on his father's bureau at home of Ned when he was eight or nine dangling a crab fiercely holding on to a bit of meat at the end of a piece of string. The kid's about that age now, Ned guessed.

Can Tho, 20 August, 1000 hours

Two weeks later Ned and the 93 boat were in the Bassac River as part of Operation Blue Shark. They pulled into Can Tho, the Navy's largest inland base in the Delta, late afternoon on a muggy and overcast Thursday. The 93 boat didn't have an operation scheduled with the local ARVN until Sunday. Most of the Navy's fixed wing aircraft flew out of Can Tho and there was a hospital there, the one where Killian, Ned's old bow gunner, had died.

Ned remembered this as he went to look for the kid the SEALs had brought aboard during the Dam Doi mission. The kid had also been dusted off to the hospital here at Can Tho, but Ned had heard, through Don Cherry, that they had saved the kid's foot.

After checking with several offices at the hospital, Ned found himself standing in front of a quonset hut with a blue and gold sign over the door which read RELOCATION. The hut was separated by about a hundred yards from the other hospital buildings. It stood next to an asphalt landing pad with a helo circle on it near one of the taxiways of the airfield. To the right of the entrance of the hut someone had planted a small flower garden. Two rose bushes and some bright yellow flowers that could have been bougainvillea shared space with pansies and green and white ferns. Around the outside of the garden nested egg-shaped stones, each one painted white. A small square of plywood nailed to a stake in the ground was also painted white. The tiny sign had the words FLOWERS: DON'T KILL painted on it in red.

Ned walked through the door of the quonset hut and entered a small office. There were two gray file cabinets, an Army green steel desk with a gray IBM typewriter on it and a typing chair behind it. A framed color photograph of the Chief of Naval Operations stared across the room at another of the President of the United States on the opposite wall. The only touch of humanity in the office was a green plant Ned didn't recognize in a cut down 5-inch brass shell casing on top of the right file cabinet. The green plant bore a single blood-red bud. A blond corpsman in fatigues had his back to Ned and was looking through the top drawer of the other file cabinet. Ned waited for a moment and then cleared his throat. "I'm looking for a ten-year-old Vietnamese boy who was brought up from *Sea Float* a little over a week ago. He'd been wounded in the foot."

"The boy's gone. You with intelligence?" The corpsman's voice asked, still busy in the drawer of the file cabinet. The voice was unusually soft, and it had a pleasing sound.

"No. Just normal Navy. Swift boats. We brought the boy in with the SEALs who captured him," Ned answered.

"Who shot him, you mean. " The sentence was a statement, not a question.

"He tried to roll a grenade at them."

"He was only ten years old, for Christ's sake," said the corpsman and turned around to face Ned.

"Yeah, but..." said Ned and stopped. It was like looking at himself in a mirror. The same dark blond hair. The same eyes, brown and set apart, taking attention away from a nose that was almost too short. The ears were delicate, set close to the head. High cheekbones and a strong chin. The clear complexion radiated aggressive healthiness. The face looking back at him was almost his own.

But the mirror image wasn't perfect. The corpsman who stared back at him was a girl, a young woman. A Navy nurse. The short hair had been what had fooled him. That and her body looking like a boy's in the green fatigues. A girl with his own eyes and a wide mouth that wore no lipstick and was not smiling. He looked at all of her. Small breasts and slim hips. Boyish. Ned felt something, a shiver, go through him. How weird, he thought. He wondered if he was blushing.

"You tough guys shot him in the foot," the nurse was saying. Her eyes were angry. She pointed a pencil at him. In her other hand she held the folder she had pulled from the still open file drawer.

"I didn't shoot him," Ned said. "He was caught in a firefight during a SEAL operation. Those things happen."

"You guys should be better than that," she said and sat down behind the desk. The plastic name plate said ENS. MORGAN. "A ten-year-old kid, for God's sake." She opened the file in front of her. Her short hair was parted on the left. As she read the file, she used her fingertips to push some stray hair back behind her right ear. She did this three times while he watched her. "What do you want with the kid?" She didn't look up or smile when she said it. Her anger was close to the surface, just barely under control.

"Hey, come on. We did our best. It was a sour mission. No one's proud of it. We just try to do a good job," Ned said, and she looked up sharply at him. He'd read that somewhere and it had stuck with him. I don't have to be proud of it. I only have to do it well. He thought he believed in the truth of that.

He looked at her and waited, not knowing what to say back to her anger anymore. He felt embarrassed, staring at her like this, like getting caught admiring someone. But he couldn't help it.

"Do you want anything else?" she asked.

"Just checking on the kid. I carried him off the boat and he seemed so helpless. I just wanted to see how he was doing. That's all."

"He'll live. Also, he's a child, not a goat. He's been sent to the resettlement base back down in Ca Mau." Her eyes were less angry. They met his but only for a moment. She went back to looking at the file in front of her.

"Good," Ned said. "Lousy thing for a kid... a child to get hurt like that. I'm glad he'll be OK."

"Oh, he'll be grand." Her anger flashed again. "He just won't ever use that leg for walking. I hope the mission was worth it."

He could think of nothing to say. The mission had been a failure. But at least none of the Americans had been killed. He stood there and looked down at the floor. It had once been painted gray, but the bare plywood showed through. "I'm sorry," he said at last.

"Yeah," she said and looked up at him.

"What's the name of the village? Where they sent him?"

"New Nam Can."

New Nam Can, my ass, he thought. He knew the place. A slum on the north bank of the river at *Sea Float*. Nam Can used to be a village of charcoal makers on the south bank of the Cua Lon just west of Sea Float until the area was defoliated and the charcoal ovens all blown up. Once the trees and the ovens were ruined, the people were resettled in New Nam Can. "Shit," he said and then apologized. "Sorry."

"Don't worry about it. I've said it a few times myself lately," she said and for just an instant she smiled. "Thanks for the thought, though." She pushed her hair back over her ear and looked down. After a moment she looked up at him again. "Anything else?"

"Thanks. "

"For what? I didn't do anything for you. Same as I couldn't do anything for the boy." She wouldn't look up at him, but he could feel her anger again across the desk.

"Well, thanks for answering my question. For telling me about the child. Know his name?" Ned asked.

"What?" She hadn't been listening. She had been thinking.

"His name. Do you have his name?"

She twisted a clipboard off a hook on the side of her desk

and raised the metal cover. Her eyes followed her finger down the page.

"He didn't have a name," she said. "The dust-off crew called him Chuck, so that's what we called him." She shut the clip board and returned it to its hook.

"Thanks. See you," Ned said and turned and walked to the screen door and stopped, looking out through the screen into the silver and green of the delta evening. Her anger radiated even this far. She's as uncomfortable being here with me and talking about this kid or this child as I am, he thought. But at least she has her anger. I don't even feel that. I've been in the rivers too long. "Nice view from here," Ned said because he had to say something.

"Yeah. Take care," she said.

"Thanks. I will. You too," he said and meant it.

"Yeah."

He could feel her looking at him as he went out through the screen door of the quonset hut. He imagined her looking at him, but he didn't look back. It had been like looking in the mirror.

"There's a nurse named Morgan over at the hospital," Ned explained to Tom Flynn, Officer-in-Charge of small craft maintenance at the base. "You know her?"

"Lee Morgan? Yeah," said Tom. "She's out of Vung Tau, sent up here a month or so ago on temporary duty to set up the relocation program for civilian casualties." Ned and Tom were sitting on the screened porch of the Can Tho Officer's Club. They hadn't seen each other since they were both on the *Calcaterra*, a destroyer escort out of Key West. "She doesn't like guys, if you know what I mean," Tom continued and sipped his beer. "Tried to date her, but she wasn't having any of it. Told me she didn't date."

Tom was a tall, soft spoken Irishman from Boston and had been Ned's roommate in the small apartment on Catherine Street in Key West. Sitting across the table from Tom reminded Ned of the two good months of sailing out of the marina on Cow Key in the 5.5 meter sloop they had named *New Providence*. They had bought the boat, originally named *Atalante*, for $500, dried out and black paint peeling from sitting in the sun for months, from a Chief who lived in Sigsbee Park, a Navy housing complex at the wrong end of the island. The two of them had learned to sail her in and out of the slip. A rusty single cylinder gas engine lay in her bilges, but no one could get it started. Their friendship had grown strong from sharing this boat without an engine. Ned hadn't seen Tom for at least six months.

"She doesn't like guys?" Ned repeated Tom's words.

"She told me up front when I asked her for a date. She's nice enough, though," Tom offered. "Why? You interested in her? Good luck, Nedgar." No one else in the Navy called him Nedgar, but Ned liked the sound of it and the friendliness behind it.

"Funny how that works," Ned said. "When I first walked in, I thought she was a guy. She had her back to me, and I thought she was a corpsman."

"Might as well be a guy," Tom joked. "I really thought she was cute though. Shame she's off limits."

"Yeah. Maybe I can convert her," said Ned, making a joke of it. He was sorry that she was that way.

"Right," Tom laughed. "But you better get to it. She's going back to Vung Tau in another week or so."

"So, what happened to the *New Providence*? " Ned asked, glad to change the subject.

"I had her hauled out at that old marina in Garrison Bight. The one where we painted her and fixed that plank," Tom said. "The old guy there said he'd keep her for me until I got back. I just have to pay storage when I claim her."

"I'd like to sail her again," said Ned as he remembered the narrow racing boat with the tiny cabin. He used to stand on her stern, holding the backstay as she steered herself to weather. "Remember that weekend we took her out to the Marquesas? She averaged five knots out and back. Jesus, I haven't been that drunk since. Johnny Walker Black and illegal lobster tails. That was peace on earth."

"Yeah, those were good times. A lot's changed since then." Tom paused and looked at Ned. "You seen much action where you are?"

"Enough. But I've got a good boat, so it isn't too bad," Ned said and thought of his crew. They seemed hours and miles away. When he had left them, they were shooting pool, playing pinball, and chain drinking beers in the EM Club next door. He was lucky to have them.

"Let's have another," Tom decided, "and then we'll go get relaxed."

"You're on."

The Chicago-a-Go-Go sat at the end of a short alley off Can Tho's single paved road, a block outside of the main gate. The words SAUNA and MASSAGE were painted in red along the front of the building in foot high letters. The sign for the place was a piece of edge lit plexiglas from a Navy combat status board display. Some patron had donated it, Tom offered, probably having appropriated it from the air traffic control office at the base. The sign, a bad imitation of a Toulouse-Lautrec Can-Can poster with some obvious and physically improbable embellishments below the dancers' waists, was the classiest thing about the place, Ned decided, but the lobby looked clean. A miniature potted palm tree with the remains of silver and blue tinsel in its fronds stood in the corner of the square space. Plastic chairs lined three of the walls. A pile of magazines, *Playboy* and *Life* among them, sat on a Navy issue metal desk. The new Crosby, Stills, Nash, and Young single, *Our House*, squeaked from a loud speaker hanging above the door to the interior.

The tall, skinny manager dressed in white pyjamas directed first Tom and then Ned through the interior door to separate plywood cubicles at the near end of a long and red lit hall. The manager reminded Ned of an older Lauren Bacall, but in the dim light Ned couldn't tell if she was a man or a woman. He could hear Tom's voice out in the long hall demanding a particular girl.

The cubicle was small with room enough only for a wooden, straight-backed chair with a towel on the seat and a tall table covered with a thin plastic pad. Over the table, on the partition wall, hung a brightly colored picture of Jesus bearing his chest to point to His Sacred Heart. Ned took off his clothes, hung them over the chair, wrapped a towel around his waist, and, with his wallet and some coins in his hand, went out through the bright blue cloth curtain. He walked down the hall toward the door marked SAUNA. There were a dozen cubicles, each with a different colored cloth curtain. The sounds of flesh slapping on flesh echoed in the dim hall.

In a cubicle on the right with its red curtain open, Ned saw Tom with his hands on the naked hips of a girl half his height.

"Be right with you, Nedgar," Tom said over his shoulder. "Lee and I are concluding a little business deal for later. See you in the sauna."

"Sure. Sorry," Ned said, embarrassed, and continued down the narrow hall. Through a break in a green curtain on the left Ned saw a tiny Vietnamese girl in white culottes and a middy blouse intently massaging the shoulder muscles of a huge black man. His towel lay discreetly draped over his rump. He appeared to be asleep.

The curtains of the next cubicle were tightly drawn. Ned could hear a mixture of giggles and pleasurable moans. Ned moved on.

"For me, Kim. Do it for me," whispered a woman's voice from a cubicle with a purple curtain. Ned paused and listened. He could hear the soft twang of the Florida panhandle in her voice.

"But you are not sailor," a soft Vietnamese voice answered. Fascinated by the two voices, Ned stepped into the cubicle next to the one with the purple curtain. He had to strain to hear the voices through the partition.

"It is all right, Kim. I won't tell. Do it, please," the Florida voice pleaded.

"You pay me?"

"Sure, I'll pay you, same as a man pays. I paid you for massage, didn't I?" The Florida voice seemed on the verge of tears. Ned felt a sadness surround him.

"You pay me now for this," the Vietnamese voice demanded softly.

"And you will do it?" the Florida voice questioned.

"Yes, but you must not tell mama san. She say it wrong. Only do massage for women, she say. Not do the other"

"I won't tell. Please, Kim. Here. Here's the money." There was hope now in the Florida voice.

"OK. You lie down," the Vietnamese voice said. "But I no kiss you, OK?"

There was no further sound from the cubicle. What the hell, Ned thought. It takes all kinds and it's sad, but the picture of what was happening in the next cubicle excited him. He liked thinking about it.

"Oh, yes. That's it," the Florida voice whispered in triumph. "Yes, now... God!"

Ned left the cubicle, walked down the hall to the door marked SAUNA, and entered the steam filled room.

CHAPTER FOURTEEN

Lambert Field, St. Louis

By the end of the month, the stories were beginning to write a bit easier, and I, not wanting to lose the momentum, bought a portable typewriter to take down to Florida with us. We even thought we might take a quick trip down to the islands after Florida, so Sis arranged with a friend to take care of *Dragonwyck*. We drove out to the airport in her car, and, as we were walking from the long- term parking lot, I off-handedly mentioned to Sis the recording I'd found at the end of the tape. At the terminal we sat in a pair of chairs shaped like an old-fashioned love seat, the two chairs connected at their waists, facing in opposite directions. Sis faced the gate while I sat looking up the long ramp to the main terminal. I sipped a lukewarm coffee, the portable typewriter between my feet. Sis had a copy of my latest story, the one about the Vietnamese girl in Vung Tau, *Tea Dance*.

"This is good story, Ned. I really can put myself in the girl's place."

"I think that's because you and she are both girls, women. From a woman's point of view, what about the character Ned? Can you feel what he's feeling or sense what he's going through?"

Sis thought for a moment. "He seems to see himself

playing out that scene with the dead boy on the boat, right?"

"Killian, yes."

"OK. The only part I don't really understand is how the anger he feels about the boy dying like that lets him make love to the girl at the end," said Sis. Somewhere overhead, a disembodied voice announced an Eastern flight to Chicago.

"Not anger. Hatred. He remembers how much he hated Killian."

"How does hatred work in with sex?"

Ned let his shoulders slump, and he slid his legs out in front of him, releasing the typewriter. He flopped his hands into his lap. "I don't know," he said at last. "I just wrote the story, kind of the way I imagined it and kind of the way it happened in Vietnam."

"Which parts are true?" Sis leaned back so she could watch my face.

"Only the parts where Ned is really a neat guy, Sis," I said as sincerely sounding as I could, but in the end I smiled. "The ambush in the canal. I did go home with a girl in Vung Tau. Only in real life I had to sell my Timex to the Vietnamese bartender to be able to afford her. And I really did feel guilty about this guy Killian."

"About the hate and sex?"

"That's something I think I feel now more than I felt then," I answered after a long pause. "I don't think I felt much of anything over there for a long time. That's why the sex was so important, why it seems to be almost as important as the fighting. When you don't feel things anymore, you tend to do rougher and rougher things, just so you'll feel something, anything." I took another swallow of the coffee.

Sis put her hands out in front of her on her legs. "So, you used hatred to get you turned on?"

"The fictional Ned, Sis, not me." We both smiled. "I think that Ned discovered that he could use the memory of his hatred to get himself turned on."

"I guess that's the part that, maybe as a woman, I don't get. What's the connection between hatred and sex? Is this just in your story, or is it out there, in real life?" Sis was now looking straight at me, and she had lowered her voice.

"I don't know... I guess it's got to be out there somewhere," I said, feeling very uncomfortable thinking about the story in this light. I had been just trying to get what happened down on paper in a believable way, to make it true in that sense. I hadn't even tried to figure out what was making the characters do what they did.

For a second, I wanted to ask Sis why the Vietnamese girl did what she did. Sis might even know, where I didn't, even though I wrote the story, created the characters.

"Hatred," I said, "is an emotion, the one that's opposite to love, I guess. And it seems to drive a lot of what we do. Maybe half of what we do. I guess that when there isn't love there, as there isn't between Ned and the girl, he kind of digs around for something to get his love engine going," and Sis gave me a dirty look.

"He is really mixed up there. He's almost hallucinating between the three of them, Killian, the girl, and himself. He finally can make love when he realizes that it's Killian who's dead and not him. Up until then, when he can't have sex with her, he feels dead."

"Go on," Sis said.

"See, it's like a kid, a little kid. When a little kid sees something dead, maybe even kills something. Seeing it dead like that proves to the kid, somehow, that he's alive. Kind of like, 'I think, therefore I am.'"

"Do you know how screwed up that is, Ned?"

"But it's true, isn't it?"

"But screwed up," insisted Sis. "OK. I see the connection between calling on his memory of Killian and being able to have sex, but I need to have you make the connection for me between sex and all the other negative things. Is sex negative? I always kind of thought of it as positive, one of the good things."

"Then you must have had a very different growing up," I said.

"Maybe. But what is the connection between war and sex? Why is your war story a story about sex too?"

"Do you read Hemingway, Sis?"

"He's a pig, Ned. All his women are either bitches or virgins." I could tell that I had touched a nerve. "Reading his stories are like...," she paused, "sleeping with a relative or something."

"What in the world does that mean?" I asked, never having heard Sis sound so prejudiced or biased about a writer before. She had always been a thoughtful and caring reader, even of some of the most unabashedly masculine literature. She even liked Zane Gray and the Travis Magee novels.

"Forget I said that. I just mean I don't get anything out of his stories. Maybe they're just for male readers, I don't know."

"Well, anyway, I'll give you the one about working with the SEALs, the Navy commandos, when I get it finished in Florida," I promised. "I've got about a day's work to do on it, but first I have to write down this dream I keep having. Before I forget it."

"A bad one, a nightmare?" asked Sis, alert as always to any sign that I was unhappy or upset. She had become very protective of me once she had understood that the nonchalant kid who went off to war had come back grown-up and up tight. They were taking our tickets and motioning us toward the door to the boarding ramp.

"I haven't had it lately," I explained. "But it scares me that it'll come back. Sometimes waiting for it is almost worse than the dream itself. Like I used to have a bad dream in Vietnam, when I was in the rivers, that they were sending me back to survival school. In the dream, survival school was worse than the real thing."

"I used to be afraid of swimming in muddy water," Sis said, apropos of nothing as we reached the plane, a 727. Her voice was kind of dreamy. The rush and hum of the boarding process flowed all around us.

"Huh?"

"Tell you as soon as we get settled," Sis said as we entered the cabin.

At cruising altitude, when the seat belt sign had been turned off, Sis swiveled around in her seat and, with her legs tucked under her in a pose I had come to associate as her most comfortable, faced me.

"Tell me," she ordered. "The dream."

I told her about the nightmare, tempering the description only slightly due to the full light of day and the fact that my listener was, while a woman, my sister and not my lover,

"Sexy," was her immediate comment, followed by, "and, except for the castration bit at the end, not as adolescently male as I would have thought. I can even relate to some of the things you experienced."

"Such as?"

Sis didn't hesitate for an instant. "Your being afraid of being hurt by your lover. I can vouch for that fear."

"The virginity thing?"

"Sure," Sis said. "No matter how much we might have fantasized being swept away and conquered by our male partner, there is that very real fear of what that thing sticking out there is going to do to us. It's very, very threatening. A lot like being stabbed or stuck with a spear." She paused. "I imagine it's why there are a lot of women who never lose their virginity and stay old maids. It takes quite a bit to get a girl to the point where she'll allow a guy inside of her like that."

"Lesbians?"

"What about them?"

"Is that why women become lesbians?" I asked.

"Maybe. I guess some of them can find the love they want from another female, and the main thing the female offers is not something he's going to ram into her," Sis analyzed. "Do you know what most women want?"

"Absolutely not," I answered without a pause. "I haven't the foggiest."

"Didn't you ever try to figure it out?"

"When I had just gotten in the Navy, and we were sitting around chewing the fat in boot camp, we'd tell stories about what we were going to do on leave or on liberty. The most usual comment that you'd hear about what women wanted was very physical and on a par with a summer sausage. and I think a lot of guys really had been convinced of that."

"Remember what Dad would say when he came home from work? The phrase he used when he'd make himself a highball?"

"What I need is a good, stiff drink?" He used that same phrase every night. "That's it. A good, stiff drink. Where do you think that tidy phrase comes from? What I need, or what you need, looking at the young lady in question, is a good, stiff... Finish it yourself."

"Isn't that a bit Freudian?"

"Not really. Men do an awful lot of reasoning with their penises."

"What about women? Don't they manipulate with their bodies, too?" I said a bit loudly and defensively.

A voice at my elbow answered, "Not always. Would you like a drink?" The stewardess looked at us with a perfectly innocent and professional smile.

"Uh...," was all I could manage.

"White wine, if you have it," Sis laughed. "And a Roy Rodgers for my baby brother, perhaps."

"A white wine would be fine," I said. The stewardess gave us each a tiny bottle of room temperature California wine and asked the couple across the aisle for their drink order.

"What does the dream mean?" I said when the stewardess had moved on two more rows.

"Let me think about this one, Nedgar. There's a lot happening in it."

After a starchy lunch, we began our decent into "the Ft. Lauderdale area." Sis had a pencil out and was going through my *Tea Dance* story, trying, she said. to figure out which parts were fact and which were fiction. She was underlining the facts.

I thought of the girls in my stories. The real Vietnamese girl had had a name, Tuong, and she had been less shy than the fictional girl in the story. Just as Lee Morgan had been less shy in real life than I had made her in the story that I was thinking about writing about her. I usually thought about the characters and what happened in one story while I was actually writing another story. It sometimes got confusing, but I found that the story I was thinking about needed that extra time to ferment.

Lee and what had happened to the two of us haunted me, though, and I was having a hard time even letting it simmer while I worked on the SEAL story. Maybe Florida would unlock it for me, just as I hoped that Florida would unlock what had become the mystery of my father.

Ft. Lauderdale, Florida

"You look like your father," said the tall, poised black man named Tom as he helped us put our bags in the trunk of the light blue Buick skylark. He had been holding a sign that read TAYLOR in front of him as we got off the plane. He wore pale yellow slacks and a rose-colored polo shirt. His hair was silver, and Sis whispered that he was the most elegant man she'd seen since Hector was a pup, her brother excluded, of course. I had explained to Tom that our father had passed, but that we had decided to come down in his place.

"I don't think he knew me, but we all knew him," said Tom as we worked our way along Griffin Road toward 95 South, Sis in the front seat and me in the back, the top down, enjoying the exhilaration of the ride. "Hs was one of those customers it is hard to forget. The first time he came down, if I may be excused for saying it, he was very rude and obviously a very unhappy man."

Sis and I looked at each other. Sounded like the father I remembered. His rudeness had been legend among my teenaged friends in St. Louis, although they had liked him well enough, probably because he had genuinely liked them and had treated them like adults. But he had been an irascible bastard at times.

"We had even decided not to take any further reservations from him. And then, when he returned the car at the end of the week, we changed our minds. He was a new man," Tom said and slapped the steering wheel. "A new man! He was polite and happy and told us some of the funniest jokes there in the office. All very risqué, but, somehow, in good taste, even for the ladies who work there. A charmer is what your father had become. A real charmer. One of the ladies, and I hope I'm not speaking out of turn, even wondered if he was married." Tom smiled at the memory. "He will be missed. You children should know that. He will be missed."

Sis and I were stunned. Was this the same man we had grown up with?

"How long had he been here when you noticed this change, Tom?" asked Sis.

"Exactly a week, Miss."

"Where had he been, did he say?"

"No, Miss. He never said. But I think he was in the Keys. I found a Monroe County map in the glove compartment when I was cleaning the car once when he returned it."

"Aren't the Keys in Monroe County?" asked Sis.

"All of the Keys. That's Monroe County. From Key Largo to Key West."

"But he never said where he went down there?" I pursued.

"No, sir, and we didn't ask." Tom paused. "He did mention a reunion, I remember, and I thought, perhaps, at first, he had a lady friend down there, and that's why we saw such a wonderful change, but he came back down from St. Louis still in a good mood, so perhaps the change was more permanent and not just because of a good vacation in the Keys. I hope you don't think me impertinent, going on this way about your father."

"Not at all, Tom," assured Sis. "We are trying to get to know him, and anything you can tell us is a big help. As a matter of fact, there's another thing we're trying to find out about. Did Dad ever mention any property he might have had down here?"

"Let me think," said Tom, as he negotiated his way up the

ramp onto 95 South. "He did sound a bit worried on one trip, last summer it was, when there was a tropical storm or depression in the offing. He asked if anyone in the office knew where he could get a storm tracking chart. One of the women in the back room knew and told him. He said he felt as though there was now a reason to keep in touch with the weather down here."

"Because?" prompted Sis.

"He didn't say, but I had the feeling it was more because of an emotional attachment than a physical thing, like a house or car."

"He had a boat in Key West," I said. "That's where we're going."

"Perhaps that was it," said Tom. After a while he added, "But, as I said, it almost seemed as though he was anxious about something more than a boat."

"Well, you know how some people are about boats," suggested Sis. "They even name some of them after women and all."

"Yes, Miss. Perhaps it was his boat he was worried about." But Tom didn't sound convinced.

I-95 Southbound, Florida

"You said you used to be afraid of muddy water," I said as we drove south on 95 after dropping Tom off at the Miami office of the rental company. The greens of the shallower water and the deep paint blue of the Gulf Stream sparkled to our left.

Sis didn't answer for a while, and I didn't press her. She seemed to be lost in thought, and, when she finally answered, I heard a new quality in her voice. "Ned, I'm a pretty rational person, even if I'm a sculptress. But I used to be really afraid of swimming anywhere where the water was not absolutely clear, like in a swimming pool. I knew what, symbolically at least, this meant. I'd read all the Freudian dream books in school. I was afraid of getting into my unconscious or sub-

115

conscious and finding stuff there, like I'd find I had an Electra complex or whatever. I knew that, but the fear of swimming in murky water still was there. It ruined all the float trips we'd go on, when Jim and I'd go down to the Ozarks or on the Quivver or the Coat- Away."

"When was this," I asked.

"When you were in the Navy. It started about the time you went in. Jim and I were really seeing a lot of each other, and we really loved to go camping with our friends. Fielding and Christie would bring his collection of good rock tapes and their damned candelabra and china and silver service. Bird and Marion would bring some good wine, and Jim and I would bring the food.

It was great, all except when we'd get out to go swimming. unless we were at a gravel pool that was perfectly clear, I'd have to sit in the canoe or up on the bank. At first it was just an inconvenience, but later it really became a thing with me. I freaked out. I'd get all shaky and sit there with my knees drawn up and hugging myself to keep from rattling apart from the shakes. It finally got so bad on the float we took on the 4th of July that I didn't go the next time. I couldn't do it. Jim took it OK, but he was a little worried because I wouldn't even be able to talk about it much, just to say that the water scared me, and I didn't want to go on a float trip just then. So he went alone, without me, and I knew then that this thing was really screwing me up."

"I did a really bizarre thing, Ned. I went to see Awree. You remember her?"

"Awree! Marie Reeves? The little old colored lady used to be our nurse when Mom... when we were really young. I remember her. Where'd you find her? I somehow though that she'd died."

A flood of memories, of living all together, our father and mother and Sis and me, swirled around me, and I had to concentrate on keeping the Skylark in the right lane. "'Wow, yeah. I remember her."

"I went to see her. She lives over on the other side of Delmar in the colored section of town. She looked older than hell, but she had a grip in those little old hands of hers that could have bent iron. She hugged and hugged me, and I hugged her back and even found myself crying and sobbing all over her just standing in the doorway to her little house.

She pulled me inside and made me sit down in the front room and gave me a Kleenex, just like she used to do when I was a kid. Just like then, too, I didn't tell her there was anything wrong. She knew it, of course, and didn't ask me and knew I'd tell it to her when I was ready. She hadn't changed at all. I hadn't either, I guess.

So, I told her I was afraid, and she got a funny look on her face and asked me why I came to her. I told her that I had remembered when we were really little she had told us that she was a witch."

"You should have seen me, Nedgar. Sitting there in the front room of this little old brick house in the colored part of town telling our old nurse that I thought she was a witch."

"What did she say?" I asked.

"She just looked at me and said, 'What do you need a witch for, honey?' I told her what I was afraid of. She gave me another Kleenex and got up and told me she'd be right back."

"She went somewhere into the back of the house and came back with something in her hand, and she sat down again across from me and held out her hand. It looked like a tea bag, but it was made of cloth. 'Here, take this and put it somewhere in your clothes, so it's next to your body.' I asked her what it was supposed to do, and she just said, 'Make you dream, honey. It just make you dream.' I asked her to explain, but she would only tell me the same thing. Finally, she said, 'You always come to Awree when you hurt as a little girl and I make things better?' I said that that was true" "Then you just do as I say, honey, and you see if it don't work. Now you just put that little thing down inside your clothes and let it do what it have to.'"

"We both stood up and I put the packet down the front of my shirt, down next to my skin in the front of my bra. She took both of my hands in hers and walked, kind of pulled me, to the door and out onto a little front porch with a glider and

117

some scruffy looking plants in red clay pots. Not flowers. Herbs, mostly. I wanted to give her something, but I didn't know how to do it."

"'Can I give you something, Awree?' I said, and she said, 'You see that building down there?' and she pointed at what used to be a Rexall drug store but had its windows all painted white on the inside. The big, pressed tin Rexall sign was still there, but it had been painted white too. 'That's my church, honey. You go there and put ten dollars in the poor box just inside the door" That be perfect for me.' So, I kissed her goodbye and went down the street and put the money inside the box, and when I came out of the church, she had gone back inside the house and shut the door."

"I started to dream about water about three nights later."

"You're kidding," I said. Sis was one of the least suggestive people I'd ever known.

"No. for real" At first it was just dreams about swimming in a pool, like the one at the Country Club" And then I was in the ocean or a big lake. And, finally, the third night I dreamed I was in a river. A muddy river." It was gross, really. I was standing in water about up to my knees, and the water was a kind of chocolatey brown. I could feel the mud squidging through my toes, and I was sure there were all sorts of great things down there underwater just waiting to get at me. I didn't know why I was there until suddenly there is this woman standing there in front of me with her hands on her hips in a real threatening way. And she's all in leather, like a biker's outfit. And over her shoulder I can see there's a boat coming towards us. A steamboat. A Mississippi stern-wheeler."

"Who is the woman?" I interrupted.

"I don't know. I had never seen her before. Just a woman. And I start to move out of the way, over toward the bank of the river, and she moves too and blocks me. like she's trying to keep me where I am. and the river boat just keeps on coming, and she won't let me get out of the way, so I start to fight her, to push past her, and she and I start to wrestle."

"She's much stronger than I am, and it's not long before she has me down on my back. I'm in the water, and she's now standing over me, trying to push me under, to drown me, and the damned steamboat's coming closer, bearing right down on us. I'm in a real panic. If I let her win, she'll drown me. But, if I keep fighting, we're both going to get smashed up by the steamboat, especially by the stern wheel. I can even hear it now, going whap-whap-whap in the water..."

"So, I decide. I just give in and hold my breath and let her push me under the water. I let her push me under the water and even into the mud there on the bottom. And I can feel the rumble of the steamboat and the crash of the paddles in the water as it goes right over us, me in the mud on the bottom, being held there by this woman in the leather suit."

Sis paused, dramatically. I had a hard time keeping my eyes on the road. She just sat there, the story unfinished.

"Yes?" I said.

"I woke up."

"And that's it? You woke up?"

"That's all. I woke up and knew that I wasn't afraid of the water anymore," Sis said, pride in her voice. "And it was true. Jim and I and the gang went on a float trip that next weekend, and I tubed down the rapids there below the Highway 5 bridge and all. I went swimming all the time, everywhere. I was cured. The dream cured me. By letting the woman push me down, by giving in and letting it happen, I was saved. Awree's little pouch, her little teabag, made me dream, and I worked it out in the dream."

"The woman in the dream. What happened to her?"

Sis waited before answering. "She must have been killed, but you know how dreams work. Who knows? Here," Sis said, and she tossed something into my lap.

I jumped. "What the hell is that?" I asked and reached down to pick it up.

It was the little tea bag, Awree's little pouch.

"Maybe you can use it sometime," Sis said with a grin, but I knew she was serious, so I slipped it into my trouser pocket.

Key Largo, evening

We crossed Jewfish Creek at about six in the evening and were checked into a small, clean cabin at the Islander Motel in Key Largo by six-thirty. The cabin and everything in it looked bleached, cleaned to a dead whiteness by the sun, relieved only by the green leaves and bright red blossoms of bougainvillea which seemed to be sprouting any place there was the least amount of black dirt. Even this late in the day, the heat was oppressive. Huge thunderheads wallowed in the sky overhead.

We had an early dinner of excellent broiled snapper and huge steak fries at the almost deserted *Queen Conch*. We split a pitcher of a dark and delicious draft beer and finished the meal with rich Cuban coffee and Key Lime pie. We questioned the bartender/cook/owner about how long such a simple restaurant could continue to serve such great food and not be swamped by tourists. He told us, between swipes of his towel across an already spotless bar, that the summer was no time for tourists and that the locals would start to drift in about eight, when the light was gone and the heat had died down.

We got back to the cabin at eight and started to get ready for bed without turning on the ceiling light. The cabin had a shower stall and toilet in a small closet sized room through a louvered door in the back wall. The wash basin was in the main room, along with a bureau, two single beds, a large jalousie window, and a slow-moving ceiling fan that supported the single light bulb.

There was no room to undress in the bathroom unless you chose to stand in the shower. We both hesitated, and then both started to undress at the same time. I normally slept in just boxer shorts, and I guess Sis usually slept in a camisole, sort of a French undershirt, and her bikini briefs. When she turned away from me to unhook her bra, I, as a joke, whistled. She, also as a joke I think, turned back toward me, her bra dangling from her right hand.

I guess the look on my face must have been foolish, for Sis smiled and just stood there and let me look. "Do you want to see it all?" she said at last. "I'll show you mine if you'll show me yours," she teased.

"I...," was all I could get out at first. "I'm sorry. That was rude of me to whistle.""

"I'm proud of my body, Ned," Sis said simply. "You should be proud of yours too."

"This scar," I said, pointing down at the reddish line that started just above my shorts.

"Honorably earned, I would say. Nothing to be ashamed of," said Sis. "Show me."

"Now? Here?"

"As good a time as any, since we're both undressing for bed."

I stood there and wondered why I felt the way I did. I thought my sister's body was I beautiful. She had a full and well-muscled but womanly figure. She was neither fleshy nor slender. I had a picture of her taken at a picnic we'd both gone to when I was a junior in college, where her back is to the camera. She is leaning on the roof of her car, a yellow Capri. She is wearing a grey-green sweater, pushed up to her elbows, a pair of tight cut off white Levis, and plaid knee socks. One hand is absently tugging at one leg of the cut-offs down so it is sure to cover the full cheek of her right butt. She is talking to someone in front of her who you can't see in the photograph.

I kept this photograph in my room during my senior year in college, and it travelled with me in the Navy. I never told anyone it was my sister; that would have been too weird. But that picture modelled, for me, the ideal body shape for a girl her age.

And now, I was being shown this perfect body. And it was and was not like I was looking at my sister. I felt the same feelings I would feel looking at any beautiful body, a stirring of both wonder and yearning.

"Has anyone seen the scar, outside of the hospital?" asked Sis, breaking into my thoughts.

"The nurse I knew over in Vietnam. She saw it, but she was being a nurse then, not a... friend."

"How much of what's happening with you has been

because of the way you feel about the scar?" Sis asked.

"I don't know... I hadn't thought about the scar that way."

"Show me the scar," Sis said as though it were the simplest thing in the world, and she dropped her bra and slipped down her briefs and stepped out of them. The light had faded, and deep shadows filled the room, but I could see her so clearly, standing like a beautiful statue.

I responded by pulling off my shorts and facing her. I looked down and saw that I was partially obscured in shadow. I moved back a step, and I could clearly see the scar now.

"It's not bad, Ned, really," Sis said sincerely. "If anything, it's interesting and not at all gross. Really."

"That's because you're my sister."

"You're kind of cute, even," she went on, "and your... parts are all in proportion, too. I should do a torso of you sometime."

"Oh, cut it out. It's embarrassing," I protested and wanted to turn away, but I couldn't stop looking at her. I could see that she, too, was beautifully proportioned, her pomegranate sized breasts, the flat and lightly muscled stomach, the curved surface of her pubic triangle. She was resting her weight on her left leg, and her right hip was slightly raised.

She moved her left hand to her hip and grinned. "So wouldn't we make a pair of statues. Brother and sister in the purest Carrara." She seemed to be looking directly in my eyes, although I couldn't be sure because of the dim light. I was trying to figure out where to look at her and was looking everywhere, frankly ensnared by her beautiful body, when she said, "Tomorrow's the big day. I'm for bed."

She pulled the camisole over her head and put her briefs back on. I put my boxer shorts on and went over to the wash basin, and she went into the bathroom and closed the door. When she came out, I was in the bed closest to the window.

"You know, I'd sleep with you if you asked me to, Ned," Sis said as she got into bed after brushing her teeth. The cabin was completely dark. Tree frogs thrummed in the night outside. The ocean air smelled salty, rich, damp.

"So please don't ever ask, OK?"

"Me, too," I said and was surprised at how easy my desire for her was to admit. "I won't ever ask. I promise. Night-night, Sis."

"Night."

CHAPTER FIFTEEN

Can Tho, 24 August, 2115 hours

Operation Blue Shark was ready to begin four days later. The first stage was to be a Swift boat supported sweep of three islands near the mouth of the Bassac south of Can Tho. Ned's 93 boat had been undergoing routine maintenance and had not left the dock for four days. His men slept in the air-conditioned barracks on the base, so he had the berthing area of the boat to himself. It had been months since he had slept without the presence of other humans breathing and snoring around him. Part of him enjoyed the privacy while another part missed the company.

He ate dinner at the O Club each evening. He had seen Lee Morgan there several times. They had talked about being in the Navy and about home but not about the boy, Chuck, or what Lee did for the civilians or Ned did in the rivers. Lee was from Cape Cod and loved to sail. She was brought up by her grandmother, went to college in upstate New York where she was an English Lit major, read Dylan Thomas and wrote long poems about her childhood and growing up near the water.

She had become a nurse in Newport, Rhode Island about six months after Ned had gone through Officer Candidate School. Her favorite music was jazz, Miles Davis in particular, and she thought that *Love Story* was crap but had read it straight through in one sitting. She had read The *Alexandria Quartet* by Durrell on her own in college in Elmira and thought that Clea was a better first name than Lee.

"It conjures images," she told Ned. "Lee doesn't do anything for me. I'd like a name that makes me want to meet me. Know what I mean?"

Ned agreed and they laughed over how unexciting the name Edgar was.

He asked her to join him for dinner twice and the second time he had been surprised when she said, "Yes."

As they talked over dinner the first night, Ned marveled at their physical similarity, at how much she looked like his sister

"We do look like at least cousins," was all she said when he mentioned how they looked alike. "But you're cuter than I am," she added with a smile. "It must be the nose looks better on a guy." He didn't mention their resemblance again.

It did make him jumpy inside, like all his dates in Junior High, to sit next to and talk with a girl who could be his sister or his cousin and want to touch her. The more he thought about how much she was like him, the more he wanted her and the more he thought about what Tom had told him about her not liking men. She seemed to enjoy being with him, Ned thought, but maybe just like a sister enjoys the company of a brother.

Ned felt strange wanting her and wondered if other men ever wanted their sisters or cousins. When his thoughts took him that far, he stopped thinking about brothers and sisters and just thought about the girl across the table from him. Her mouth didn't move very much when she spoke, and her eyes never stopped roving around the room, looking and smiling at everything.

Even Tom noticed how they looked together the first time Ned and Lee had dinner. Tom turned to Ned when they were both at the bar getting drinks. "Two of you make a handsome couple. Too bad she's one of the guys," he teased Ned. Tom whistled as he gathered four rum and Cokes and departed for a group of giggling nurses as a table in the center of the room. Ned watched the nurses divide up the drinks and saw Tom hunch forward the way he always did when he was telling a dirty story.

Ned found he didn't mind Tom's teasing. He remembered the electric thrill he had felt when Lee's hand would touch his hand for emphasis. She told him about how happy she had been to get flower seeds for the little garden from the States, even though some of them hadn't sprouted yet.

He thought the time he was spending with her was wonderful. The only women he'd been with lately had been the massage girls or whores, and he didn't speak their language. The women in Vietnam whom Ned had met spoke only enough English to clean hootches, do laundry, or agree to silent and clumsy sex. The desire to share their common pasts and present experiences drove both Ned and Lee to tell each other everything they had done since coming in-country in a great rush. They also told each other college stories, comparing their memories of the East Coast. So many of the men he'd met in Vietnam were from California, and all Ned had in common with them were their Navy experiences. At times Ned almost believed he was back in the States on a date, not sitting in a Navy building with a commissioned officer who could have been his sister.

The bar closed at nine.

"I'd invite you up for a nightcap, but I have a roommate," Lee said.

I shouldn't give up so easily, thought Ned.

He took her to the front door to her barracks, a one-story white stucco building with barred windows and sandbagged sentry posts at the doors and the corners. Ned shook hands goodnight, although he wasn't sure if the shy look she had given him as they parted had been some kind of invitation.

The second night they had dinner they sat across from each other at a corner table for four and turned their chairs so they could look out through the screens toward the river. An occasional brightly lighted tug and barge churned up the main channel. Ned felt relaxed and happy. They were still drinking coffee and talking when a voice behind them made Ned jump.

"Hey, there, Nanny Goat. Is this your Swifty?"

Ned turned around at the sound of the familiar Florida panhandle voice, the voice in the cubicle in the massage parlor. He looked at a tall, statuesque redhead with a half full beer bottle and glass in her left hand and a wide smile on her angular face. She wore a bottle green cotton blouse and khaki trousers" She was strikingly handsome. She looked like a figurehead from a clipper ship, thought Ned. He couldn't associate the woman standing in front of him with the sad and hungry voice from behind the purple curtain at the Chicago-a-Go-Go.

She tossed her curly red hair and stuck out her free hand at Ned. "I'm Willie, Nanny Goat's roommate. She told me she met a guy off the river boats. I told her to keep her pants on 'cause you guys only got one thing on your mind. How you doin'?"

She certainly was direct, Ned thought. "Hi. Fine, I guess. I'm Ned. Join us?"

Lee smiled but didn't say anything. Willie pulled out the chair between Ned and Lee, sat down in a single easy motion that belied her height, and poured the rest of her beer into her glass. She propped her elbows on the table, holding her beer glass with both hands.

"I've heard a rumor you Swifties travel with a net bag full of dirty laundry, a Rolex watch, and a hard-on. That true?" Willie asked Ned sternly. Is she angry at me or just kidding, Ned wondered.

"Oh, come on, Willie," said Lee with a giggle. "He's not like that."

"Let him answer, then," continued Willie. She looked directly into Ned's eyes.

"My watch's a Timex and I do my own laundry," Ned said, hoping his smile was convincing.

"You oughta do the hard-on at the same time." The red head of hair shook with her laugh, and Willie broke eye contact with Ned. "At least you've got a sense of humor," Willie said with a smile and turned to Lee. "You're right. He's OK, but watch yourself, Nanny Goat."

She downed her beer and stood up. "I've got a couple of

doctors to shape up. See you around," she said to Ned and, putting her right hand gently on Lee's shoulder, warned her, "Don't be too late." Ned couldn't tell if there was anger there or if it was directed at him. One thing sure, Willie was telling Lee not to play games with him.

"Night, Willie. Don't worry about me," Lee said. "We'll be OK." She smiled at Ned.

Ned smiled back, unsure of what he had just agreed to. Willie covered the distance between their table and the doors to the screened porch in long, athletic strides. The doors slammed behind her. Her beer bottle and empty glass sat between them on the table. Ned moved them next to the sugar bowl and salt and pepper shakers at the center. He could hear Willie's panhandle voice from out on the porch and the answering sound of male laughter.

"That's quite a roommate you've got," Ned said.

"She comes on strong, I know, but she's really wonderful. Willie's taught me a lot since I've been over here."

I wonder if she's keeping you for herself, Ned thought.

On board the 93 boat, ten minutes later, they sat across from each other at the main cabin table arranged like a booth in a diner and drank coffee. They had crossed the brightly lit compound down to the river's edge and walked slowly through the warm night to the moored barge used as a floating dock for the Swift boats. The 93 boat was rafted outside of the 70 boat at the upstream end of the barge. The boat crew was billeted in the air conditioned barracks; Ned and Lee were alone on board.

They had stood on deck at first and listened to the river rush by and the squeak of the tires the boats used as fenders. Across the Bassac winked the lights of single occasional cars on the highway to Vihn Long. The ferry had stopped running at dusk and only the occasional lights of a sampan moved slowly up or quickly down the far shore of the river. Most river traffic avoided the base side of the river at night with its bright orange lights and its nervous sentries.

They had gone below and opened the sliding ports on the

river side and sat in the shadows on either side of the table. Dim light reflected off of the river from the bright security lights outside and danced throughout the cabin.

"Can you spend the night on the boat?" he asked during a pause in the conversation.

"I'm not sure that would be such a good idea," she said matter-of-factly.

"Why not?" He took a sip of his coffee. He could not see the expression on her face in the dimness of the shadow she sat in.

"Things happen sometimes that shouldn't." Her hands lay quietly, palms down on the table between them.

"Why shouldn't they happen?" The thought of sleeping with her excited him. He tried to keep the eagerness out of his voice.

"Oh, because people get hurt by them," she said sadly.

"Nobody has to get hurt. We're grown-ups," he assured her.

"I don't feel very grown up right now."

"I can't tell what you feel."

"About what?"

"About me, for instance," he said.

"A friend. The first man friend I've had for a long time. I feel comfortable with you. I don't with most of the men here." He thought he could see a smile soften her face.

"What about Willie?"

"Willie's different," she said. He could see her head tilt down.

"I'll say. Doesn't that bother you?" he asked.

"You mean that she doesn't trust men?" She was now looking straight at him.

"It's more than that." And Ned told her what he had heard at the Chicago-d-Go-Go.

There was a pause before Lee spoke. "I thought she might have found someplace in town," she said quietly. "There are a few real dykes here on the base, but I never see Willie with them. She's loud and not very lady-like, but she doesn't push it with any of the girls here. Not that way."

130

Neither of them spoke. Out on the river a horn blew a single, lonely note.

"What were you doing at that place, anyway?" Lee asked Ned.

"What do you think?" Ned couldn't keep a smile out of his voice. He felt embarrassed to be talking about this. He was glad his face was hidden in the shadow.

"Oh, I have a pretty good idea, but I'd like to hear how you'd describe it."

"You're teasing," he said, trying to sound serious. "I was getting a massage."

"I'll bet. That all?" she insisted. He could hear her smiling.

"Not exactly. You want me to describe it to you?" he challenged.

"Sure. I'd love to hear how a man would describe it."

"You're liable to get carried away with the passion of it all." He tried to sound mock- serious, but he was intrigued by her suggestion that he describe his "massage."

"I'll be able to handle the heat," she joked.

"That's not exactly a compliment, you know. Aren't you supposed to be swept away by my masculine presence?"

"Only in the movies. It's a little like being clubbed. I'd rather just be comfortable with you. What makes men have to sweep women away?" she asked, a new seriousness in her voice. She leaned forward.

"It's what most women seem to expect. It's normal."

"Bullshit. I know a lot of women who don't like it," she snapped, and he could feel the anger that he felt when he first met her at the hospital.

"But Willie's not normal," he said to get even.

"No... but maybe I'm not either." Her voice was flat, unemotional. She sat up straight.

"Is that why you're her roommate."

Lee paused before answering.

"You think I'm like her." There were tears or a smile in her voice. Ned couldn't tell which.

"No?" he pressed.

"How long have you thought that?" she asked after a pause.

He could see her face, pale, floating in the dimness across from him.

"Ever since Tom Flynn told me you wouldn't go out with him. Finding out that you roomed with Willie also helps."

They looked at each other across the table.

"Good Jesus!" she said in a small voice at last. "Just because I don't fuck every other guy on this base means I'm a lesbian, huh?" Her words shocked him.

"No, that's not what I said."

"It's what you meant, though, isn't it?"

"I don't know. I'm confused," Ned said unhappily. He had gone quickly out of his depth, into somewhere he had never thought about before.

"You sure as hell are," Lee answered. "I really like you, Ned. A lot. Because you didn't push it with me. You didn't try to come on to me the first night."

"I guess what Tom said slowed me down," he admitted.

"It was nice. Not having to constantly push you out of my lap. I liked it," she said as she leaned forward again.

"It can stay the same."

"Can it? I don't see how. Now that you don't know what I am, you'll either try to take me to bed to prove it one way or you'll get horny and go off to get laid somewhere else," she said sadly. "Either way, I lose you as a friend."

"I guess I seem to have a one-track mind. Why do you think I like being with you?" Ned wondered if she heard the hurt in his voice. "It's not to get sex from you. I didn't think you wanted sex... not with me anyway. I just liked being with you. Only when we started to get along so well, I started thinking again about wanting to go to bed with you. Anyhow..."

"Anyhow what?"

"It was kind of a relief. Thinking you weren't interested in guys that way." Ned blushed when he said it. "I didn't feel like I had to... impress you or make the, you know, earth move."

Lee laughed and leaned across the table toward him. "Come here," she said. He leaned forward, out of the shadows, and she kissed him lightly on the cheek. "You are a jackass,

Ned Taylor, you know that?" She sat back and he grinned.

For a full minute, they sat back in the shadows and neither of them spoke. A shot echoed flatly from across the river. There was no answering shot. Ned looked out the open sliding port at the lights on the river and he knew that Lee was watching him. Where does this go from here? he wondered.

"Will you play a game with me?" she said at last, her voice serious.

"What kind of a game?"

"You have to promise that whatever happens you won't try to fuck me."

The word's tough, violent sound was like a slap, and Ned was shocked by her using the word. "OK," he said.

"Say it," she insisted. "Say you won't try to fuck me."

"Jesus. Sure. I promise I won't." He couldn't say the word.

"Come on," she said. "Just promise you won't fuck me. Say the word. It's OK. It's war time."

He was blushing again. "I'm not used to talking this way to girls." Ned took a breath "All right. I promise not to try to fuck you. Whatever happens. There," he said with relief, "I've said it. This is sure as hell a strange game."

I wonder where this is going, he thought. The two of us sit here in the dark using dirty words with each other. And we've got this strange promise between us.

"Thank you," Lee said, and he could hear the smile in her voice again. She had made him say it, made him use the ugly word out loud. Why was he being thanked?

"I got married my last term in nursing school," she said after a long silence.

Damn, he thought. From trying to date a girl who doesn't like men to making a pass at a married woman. I ought to have stayed in the rivers.

"His name was Jeremy. A nice boy I met in college. Very bright, very sweet. He was tall and blond and had a beautiful body. I was a virgin, kind of a rarity in those days. We used to love to touch each other, but we both decided to save the big moment for after the wedding."

What an old-fashioned idea, Ned thought. "I didn't think couples did that anymore."

"We did and we made it a game" We would see how much we could turn each other on. See how close to going all the way we could get. Without doing it."

"Did you make it to the honeymoon?" Ned asked. I

"Just barely. We got married in the fall, on a Friday afternoon in Boston, and were at a friend's cabin out in Provincetown on the Cape by eight that evening. We drank a couple of glasses of wine and lay down on a rug in front of the fireplace. We both knew that the time had come."

Ned could imagine her lying in the firelight in that friend's cabin. He felt the same ache for her now sitting with her on his boat in Vietnam as that boy must have felt.

"That's when I knew I didn't want him to," she said and then paused.

"You knew... what was involved?" Ned asked uneasily, unable to find any other word than the one she had used, the word she had made him say.

"Oh, come on, Ned. I'd read all the pillow books and some of the crotch novels. I was in nursing school and worked in the hospital every day. I knew what was supposed to happen. I had touched him all over before. I'd even teased him, you know, when we were playing the game, but all of a sudden it was different. There he was, ready to put that thing in me. And I didn't want him to," she said with a sigh. "It wasn't that I was scared of being hurt." She gave a sad little laugh. "He wasn't actually all that big. I just didn't want him inside me. Having him inside of me seemed so violent, so much like being stabbed. Dirty, somehow. "

"What did you do?"

"I told him I loved him and would find a way to satisfy him and wanted to just keep playing the game," she said, "but he got on top of me and said he was going to do it because we were supposed to. It was what men and women did when they got married."

"And?" asked Ned.

"He fucked me," she said, and the word slapped him again. "And I cried.,."

"He forced you?" Ned interrupted.

"...but not because it hurt." Lee stopped for a moment. Ned heard her take a deep breath. "No," she answered. "He didn't force me. I let him do it, but I kept telling him I didn't want to. He didn't seem to care. Like what he was doing had nothing to do with me." She stopped speaking just as the tears started.

Ned reached across the table and touched her hand.

Her voice was strong again in the darkness. "The marriage was annulled a few weeks later. We said it hadn't been consummated."

Ned could hear both anger and sadness across from him and could hear the echoes of that night in Provincetown with the sweet, bright boy with the beautiful body who wouldn't keep playing the game. "I graduated, started working as a nurse, and joined the Navy," Lee said.

"So, here we are," was all Ned could find to say.

"That's why I tell Tom and the others I don't date. I just don't want to have that happen to me again," she said. "It's why Willie and I make good roommates."

"I'm sorry," he said. He was apologizing for himself, for the time he had done the same thing, and he was apologizing for Jeremy. For all the horny boys and aggressive men. He felt the stinging heat of tears come to his eyes. What's happening to me? He rubbed his eyes and sat looking into the darkness across from him.

Through the open port came the whup-whup-whup of a Medivac helicopter landing at the hospital and, a minute later, the muted, staccato pulse of a motorized junk from across the river.

Lee was the first to speak. "I'm heading back to Vung Tau soon."

"Tom said you would." Ned cleared his throat. "Can I... Is it all right if we have dinner or drinks again?"

"I'd like that. Here," she said in the darkness, "hold my hand. I like it when you touch me. Just don't try to..."

"I know. I know," Ned interrupted and took her hand. "I got the message." Even with the sadness and hurt, there was something delicious and forbidden in the touch of her fingers across the palm of his hand. "Don't tease," he said.

"I can't help it," she admitted to him. "You're so nice that I almost want to hurt you."

"Try it," he said. "I've been in the rivers so long, I probably won't even feel it." Still holding his hand, she came around to his side of the dinette and knelt, facing him" "Feel this, John Wayne," she said and started to tickle him.

Later that night as they lay together on the narrow berth, their shoulders and hips touching, she asked him again if he thought he could continue to play the game, to play with and touch and tease each other but not fuck.

"Why do you have to use that word?" Ned asked.

"Because it's a horrible word and it's so perfect for it. Can you keep playing the game, Ned, or does it have to be *normal?* Tell me now, so we don't get all tangled up later."

"Yes," Ned said into the darkness as the water lapped at the hull. The single, lonely horn sounded on the river outside.

The hard boots of his crew on the metal decks of the barge woke him from a dream of lying in the grass on a blanket by a lake. It was 0500 by his watch. This morning would see the start of the operation called *Lemming Drive*. He knew that Lee was not there anymore even before he looked around the gray cabin of the 93 boat. A note on the dinette table said simply

Thanks for the game.
You really are nice,
Nanny Goat

CHAPTER SIXTEEN

Florida Keys, morning

At eight o'clock the next morning Sis and I drove from Key Largo to Stock Island, the key just east of Key West. I had dreamed during the night, but I couldn't remember what about. I was sure that it wasn't the nightmare again. I wasn't wearing Awree's packet next to my skin, I joked to myself, but I said nothing to Sis.

After checking into a small but clean motel at the corner of White and Truman Streets in Key West at noon, we presented ourselves at the office of the Cow Key Marina on the ocean side of Stock Island.

The marina was a ramshackle series of hurricane shelters, low roofed sheds over deep slips cut into the bone-white marl that made up the structure of the keys. The water was black from the constant steeping of the mangrove islands, but the boats seemed well cared for, their lines neatly coiled or tied properly around cleats and pilings. I knew why as soon as we entered the dim room of the collection of boards, cement block, and tin that served as bait shop, gas dock, and office. Behind the counter, a glass candy store case filled with fishing gear with the word Necco frosted in the cut glass on the front, stood the Chief. He was short, perhaps five feet four inches, and he had a deeply tanned face with a neatly trimmed jet-black beard. He was dressed like a Chief Bos'n Mate, even down to the khaki webbed belt and black shoes, but he wore no insignias on his uniform. His uniform cap, drum tight, sat square on the glass case within arm's reach, and it, too, was missing the fouled anchor insignia.

"Morning, Chief," I said. I had seen the cast bronze name plate hanging behind him from a shelf of whipping twine, oakum, and cards with needles on them. Senior Chief Boatswains Mate William Nunnery, USN.

"Morning, Captain... M'am," he answered cheerily. "Help you?"

"I'm Ned Taylor, Cyrus Taylor's son and this is his daughter, Sis," I introduced us. "We've come down to see about his boat, the *Coast Pilot*."

"Nice boat, *Coast Pilot*. How's Mr. Taylor doing? He's due back pretty soon, isn't he?"

"He passed away, Chief, about a month ago," Sis said.

The Chief's face lost its cheerful openness. "Damn. Well, I am sorry to hear that. I really liked him. I'm sorry." He moved slightly to the left and then back to the right, like a boxer's feint.

"Thank you, Chief," I said, and I handed him a copy of the letter the bank had given us to present to anyone who might wonder what authority we had to be concerned with the affairs of Cyrus Taylor, deceased. One moment the letter was in my hand, and the next it was open in his hand. This man moves fast, I thought. I hadn't even felt him taking it from me.

"Uhm, yes," he said after looking over the letter carefully through a pair of reading glasses he had magically produced from inside of his cap. "I kind of thought he might have had a family. Didn't seem the kind of man to be on his own all his life. Said he was in the war. Destroyers. We used to talk." The Chief paused. "Finally figured out how to drive that boat. Took him a while, but he really worked at it and could finally make a pretty decent landing, even with a tide. Good on him, I say. Good on him!"

"Could we see the boat?" I asked after the letter was back in my hand. I guessed that the Chief had handed the letter back. His glasses were gone, back in his cap I imagined

"Follow me," said the Chief his hand appearing in front of a rack of unlabeled keys on the wall behind him and snicking a plastic bobber or float in the shape of a red, cone shaped navigation buoy with some keys hanging from it. "She's out here," and he disappeared out the back door. We followed him, and I wondered if he always moved that quickly.

"Am I just slow this morning, or is that man some kind of slight-of-hand artist?" Sis whispered as we walked along down the white marl path that ran between patches of well clipped green lawn that appeared to be all crab grass. Low banana trees and coconut palms lined the path. White painted rocks defined the roadway snaking along to our left. "I've never seen anything like it""

"He's something else, all right. Not actually Navy issue," I commented, watching the Chief disappear into the farthest hurricane shelter. "There he goes."

We entered the relative dimness of the shelter and could see a long row of assorted powerboats. The first three were local fishing boats, old wooden boats in various states of repair with their official numbers painted high on their hulls amidships under their steering stations. The next half dozen boats were almost identical yachts, their spotless hulls lined up at attention, each of them between forty and fifty feet in length, all of them white in color. From the bow of each flew a triangular burgee with a red O on a blue background. Inside the O was the letter R.

"Ocean Reef Club," answered the Chief s voice out of the dimness ahead, although I had not spoken my question aloud or even really looked that carefully at the little flags.

"'Weird," said Sis.

"Here she be," the Chief's voice spoke, and I could see that, a dozen boats ahead, the bow of a dark hulled smaller boat rocked slightly. As we walked closer, I could make out a smaller boat with a dark blue hull and a white boot stripe at the water. It was packed in among larger, more formidable yachts, all at least two decks above the waterline, but its lines were of a finer nature.

From a teak bowsprit off of which hung a plow shaped anchor, back toward a tidy raised forward cabin, a rakish two paned windshield, and a khaki-colored canvas soft top over the cockpit, the *Coast Pilot* seemed a breed apart from these others. We turned left to go down the narrow finger pier between *Coast Pilot* and the boat to her left. From the top of her windshield to the end of her long but narrow cockpit, ran a single, flowing line that carried the eye aft in a sweep.

She was beautiful! Her hull was not just blue, but a deep ocean blue, a color I had only seen when I had been days offshore during an ocean transit. The decks were a light cream color. The interior of the cockpit was painted a slightly lighter beige. The cushions of the helm seat and the navigator's seat were of the same dark blue as her hull.

"How comfortable looking," said Sis. "I had no idea."

The Chief had the engine box open and was wiping the end of the tidy red six-cylinder Perkin's dip stick with a red rag. I could hear the purr of a bilge pump from under the deck \ somewhere. Then it stopped.

"I disconnected shore power," said the Chief. "The cable's all stowed." And he was suddenly down in the small cabin, flipping switches on the circuit breaker panel. "Running lights, Sir?"

I walked around the bow to the port side and back along to the stern. "All running lights are bright lights, Chief." "She's topped up with fuel, 100 gallons. Take you about 250 miles if you're not too greedy. She has 25 gallons of fresh water in a tank under the v-berths. There's no head on board, just a cedar bucket with a nice oak seat in here."

The Chief tapped on a paneled door to starboard. "The last owner kept it real simple. Kerosene, two-burner stove with a couple flowerpots for heat, ice box with room for about a twenty-pound block. That's what I've got in there now. And a six pack of 7- Up and one of Dr. Pepper."

Sis was standing to starboard, listening to the Chief s inventory. I climbed aboard from the port side, aft and was amazed at the low freeboard. She looked sleek and maneuverable.

"Come on aboard, Sis," I said. "Maybe the Chief could give us a quick lesson?"

"It's simple, Sir. Being a Swift driver and all, you should have no sweat. Same twin Morse controls, clutch to port." The Chief was off the boat to port and around the bow in a moment where he busied himself with adjusting the fit of the plow anchor and checking the keeper pin. "Twelve feet of chain, 'cause of the coral. 150 feet of half inch nylon rode. The storm's in the lazarette with three-quarter inch warp, another 150 feet of nylon. OK as a tow line, too."

"Chief..." I started to ask, but his answer cut me off.

"Your father and I. We talked lots about you and you, too, Ma'm," he said, switching his eyes to Sis, who seemed as stunned as I was by the Chief.

"How did you know we'd be here today to put ice on board?" Sis asked.

"Your father kept a pretty regular schedule, Ma'm," answered the Chief as he checked the starboard bow line.

"And the right flavor sodas? Out father didn't drink soda, did he?" she asked, the expression on her face reflecting fascination rather than suspicion.

"No, but he said you two might come down, so I kept some aboard." He was tugging at the forward starboard spring line.

"But the controls," I said. "You said the Morse controls were the same as on the Swifts. How did you know that? Dad couldn't have told you. He wouldn't have known a Morse control from Adam's house cat."

"Oh, he picked up a lot, did your Dad. From your tapes. From around here. A bit from me, now and again," said the Chief, who was all the way aft, inspecting the stern mooring line.

"She's a Dyer. Built up in New England" Rhode Island, I think. Your Dad bought her after being out on her only once. As far as I know, she's the only one around. She backs to starboard, though. Reverse gear on the Perkin's a bit unusual," and the Chief pointed to the windscreen. There, just under the wiper motor, was a small brass arrow tacked to the wooden windshield frame, its point to the right. "That's why the arrow." The Chief was up at the bow. Sis and I stood in the cockpit. We looked at each other. "Come up to the office when you're ready, and I'11 give you his logbook," said the Chief and he was gone.

"Curiouser..." Sis said.

"...and curiouser," I answered.

By the time we had thoroughly inspected *Coast Pilot*, it was noon and the summer heat was baking the hurricane shelter. It seemed a good time to take the boat out for a run. We went up to the office to find that the Chief was off on some errand. The same boy who had answered the 'phone when I had originally found *Coast Pilot* gave us our father's logbook. He asked if we needed help getting underway

"No, I don't think so," I said. "Anything I should know about the turning basin or about the channel out of here?"

"Nothing special," said the boy. "You're at half tide, coming in. She only draws two and a half feet, so you should be OK."

"Thanks," I said.

The boy pointed up to a sign on the wall I hadn't noticed before. "Chief said always remember this one." The sign said simply DON'T GO WHERE YOU SEE BIRDS WALKING.

Good advice, I thought.

Back on board, we looked at the logbook. It was a simple child's school composition book with heavy cardboard covers in a speckled black and white pattern. On the cover it said *Coast Pilot* in black ink in a strong hand. Below that was the word Byblos in a shaky hand.

I went aft to look over the stern of the boat. Above a teak swim platform in gold leaf letters was *Coast Pilot*, and, just below in a size smaller lettering was her hailing port, *Byblos*, both name and port outlined in red.

We sat together on the engine box on top of which had been fastened a cushion. A small, hinged panel at the end of the engine box, with the addition of another cushion, would make an adequate spare berth.

On the first page of the log, in his shaky but readable script, was a list of what seemed to be supplies for the boat. The second and third page contained instructions on how to perform various tasks around the boat, like changing the oil and checking the batteries for water. The fourth and following dozen page contained a series of what appeared to be longer numbers and shorter numbers with plus signs after some of them in bunches or paragraphs. There were no descriptions of the objects the longer numbers might be bearings to, if in fact the three-digit numbers were bearings. The first entry, alone on page four, made no sense at all to me.

110 225 77+ RL
045 77+ 2

I got out a chart of the area from under the port v-berth and set the parallel rules I'd found in a small teak rack to starboard of the helm to the first three-digit number, 110. I started at our location, the Cow Key Marina. A course of 110 degrees would have taken the *Coast Pilot* up on the beach and into the restrooms of the Hogfish Bar and Grill. I then walked the rules around the chart looking for courses of 110 degrees. The only one I could find near the marina was on the ocean side, from the mouth of Cow Key Cut out to the number "2" daymark flashing a red light every 4 seconds, about a mile and a half south of Stock Island. None of the other numbers made any sense, especially the numbers 2 or 3+ on either side of the 110 degrees. They couldn't be miles.

Most bearings are paired with distances for navigation, as in "Steer 090 degrees (due east) for 6 miles." This might be noted as 090° 6 or 6 090°, but nothing on the local chart supported our father's strange notes. Maybe they weren't bearings. The next page contained another series of long and short numbers, some with the pluses.

110 285 20+ 8
105 20+ 2

I tried using the individual numbers as corrections to magnetic compass courses, but they were too small to make much difference. I did notice that both number paragraphs started with 110 but couldn't figure out what that signified, if anything. I was stumped.

To Sis, who wasn't particularly interested in navigation problems, the boat was fascinating for different reasons. She searched through every nook and cranny of *Coast Pilot* for evidence of our father's secret life in the Keys. In the cupboard over the galley counter, she found an open package of Twinning's Lapsang Souchong tea bags. Our father only drank coffee. There was a small basket containing pink packages of artificial sweetener, but sugar was our father's usual choice. Two pressed paper beer coasters advertised The Tide's Inn on Flagler Boulevard, but every Florida city on the East Coast had a Flagler Street or Boulevard. She also uncovered two spent .22 caliber shells and a Popular Mechanics featuring articles on solar panels, water purification systems, and LORAN, any one of which could have been of interest to a boater, but not to our father under normal circumstances.

In the locker under the port bunk were two adult sized sets of swim fins, snorkels, and masks. This man, Sis pointed out when she found a copy of *Petersen's Guide to North American Birds* on the small shelf above the port bunk, was quite a different human being than the one we thought we knew in St. Louis. Another startling revelation was the lack of any alcohol whatsoever aboard *Coast Pilot*. For as long as I could remember, our father always had a bottle of gin near at hand.

After spending a half hour looking over the boat, Sis disembarked and went back to the marina office to call the bank in St. Louis. They had been doing some research for us about the Offshore Trust our father had invested in, his mysterious Florida property.

I surveyed the *Coast Pilot* and found her sound, serviceable, and well equipped. Aside from some minor scrapes to her starboard rub rail, she was in perfect shape. I would use the snorkeling gear and dive on her hull later, but I was sure that she would be clean and undamaged.

Offshore, Key West

The horizon held a thin band of deepest blue to the east and a fine line of green to the west. We were headed southwest on a course of 245° at 2,200 RPM about a mile offshore. The fathometer read 155 feet. The breeze was light and right on our nose. Tiny splashes of spray spattered against the windshield as the Dyer cut elegantly through the one-to-two-foot chop. The memory of the humidity of St. Louis had been earlier erased by the solid heat of the Keys. This memory, too, was now supplanted by the delight of a twenty-knot breeze and a sparkling, sunny afternoon. Sis has shucked her jeans and oxford shirt and now wore a deep green two-piece swimsuit, and I wore a striped bathing suit.

"She handles beautifully!" I called to Sis as we came abeam of the Southernmost Point near the Casa Marina. "I don't even really need to steer. She holds a course like she was on auto pilot."

"That's nice, dear," Sis answered, her eyes shut against the sun's glare. She was stretched out on a towel on the cockpit deck, working on her tan.

"How about the bank?"

"Must I interrupt this important activity and speak of business?" Sis moaned.

"Just the good news," I said.

"No record at all of anything called Offshore Trust or anything related to Florida or the Bahamas." And in a smaller voice. "It was as if he was really trying to hide this."

"How could he have had this separate life, and we not know anything about it?"

"Well, there's no way you would have known because you were away in the Navy. I've been trying to figure out why I didn't know, and I think I've got it. Since I lived on Delmar and only saw him maybe once a month for dinner at the Country Club, that had become a ritual for us. I thought back about when we did have dinner, and it was almost always on the first Sunday night of each month. I had no idea it had become such a routine. Dad would call up and suggest dinner next week, how about Sunday evening? and I would say fine. I'd meet him there, we'd have a few cocktails, and then a long, talky dinner."

"I'd table-hop a bit and Dad would scowl at his fellow members. Maybe a few would stop over to pay their respects, but it was always the same. We'd split up around nine or so, and I'd kind of make sure he was OK to drive. This last year, in fact, he was much better and had cut back to only one martini before dinner and no wine. I remember telling him how proud I was. He beamed." Sis stopped.

She wiped her eyes with the back of her hands and then continued. "He could be such a dear old thing when he wanted to. Anyway, he never mentioned Florida, and I never asked specifically what he was doing each month. We mainly talked about me, I guess. And you. We planned out your life for you, I hope you know."

"My life? I thought Uncle Sam was in charge of my life over the past three years."

"I mean when you got home. We had it all set," Sis said with a grin, "Dad in particular, what you should do after the Navy. Back to grad school, a degree in English, perhaps teach at Country Day. A little writing on the side. Marry and have kids. Get a house in Ladue. Join the Racquet and STLCC."

"Think it will ever happen, this domestic little scene?" I asked Sis over my shoulder as I swung the boat in a wide arc and headed for the Sea Bouy at the head of the main channel into the harbor at Key West. I thought that our father had been pretty brave to have ventured out here.

"A life like that seems pretty far away right now, doesn't it?"

"It does. The writing is the only thing that's on schedule, and even that's not going as well as I'd like it to."

"Trouble, again?'

"I'm working on a piece about the last operation we went on, the one that I got hit in. And I can't seem to finish it. It's

146

come to a dead stop, and I'm finding it hard to work on any of the other ones I want to do while that one is stalled."

"Do you want to talk it out?" Sis offered.

"Sure."

"Let me tell you one thing the bank did say, and then we can do the story, OK?"

I really loved it when the two of us were in sync. "Go for it," I said.

"The bank said they found a huge draft, a sight draft they called it, drawn last year in April. It was cleared through a New York bank in early May. The amount, they said, was enough to purchase a small house. With some left over as seed money for a trust to pay local property taxes."

"This might be just what we need." I was really impressed with Sis's sleuthing. She had told the bank what to look for. "Anything else?"

"Once a month, during the last year or so, Dad had cashed a pretty good-sized check," Sis said. "I had given them the dates of the car rentals over the 'phone and the checks cashed matched most of those dates within a week." Sis sat up and blinked. "Pretty neat, huh?"

"What?"

"He had it all worked out. Came down here every month for a week, and nobody at home ever knew." She smiled and nodded her head. "I'm kind of happy he was able to do it."

"Do what?" I asked.

"Pull off something like this. Have a secret life and all. He'd always been so straight that I'm glad he was able to do something a little out of the ordinary for once in his life."

"I don't remember. Maybe you do. Had he been down here just before he died?"

"The week before."

"And you had had dinner with him when?"

"The week he died. He told me that Sunday night he was going in for the tests." Sis asked.

"'Was there any connection between the tests or his dying like that and the Florida trips?"

"Dad's doctor told me that Dad knew he was going to die,

that his liver was pretty well shot. The tests were just to track progress. The last set of tests, by the way?" Sis paused and I gave her a look over my shoulder. "They were surprisingly positive. He was doing much better. Not enough to save him, but enough to let the doctor know that Dad was behaving himself a little better."

"Tell me about the story that won't write," Sis said as we made the swing to starboard to bring us in line with the range markers indicating the main ship channel. We passed Mallory Square to starboard and Christmas Tree Island to port, cruised by the shrimp boats squashed together at the commercial docks southwest of the Navy Annex, where my ship, the *Calcaterra*, had been berthed. We then turned south, past Mallory Square again, and out the channel to the Sea Buoy.

The run back to the marina had been silent, each of us thinking out separate thoughts about our father's last weeks and days. I hoped that Florida had been good for him.

"I've called it Final Op, and it's about the group of us getting ready to come home and getting a last chance to go out and take on a Chinese freighter. Well, not take it on, but put some customs agents aboard it. I've got our hero ready to go, and he has a last talk with his girl, Lee. That's where it gets bogged down. I can't seem to get the two of them talking."

"What do they want to talk about?" Sis asked.

"She doesn't want him to go. He feels that he has to."

"Why? In each case, why?"

"He wants to go because... Wait a sec." I throttled back and let *Coast Pilot* come off her plane. I had almost missed our turn, a deceptively narrow entrance to the channel into the marina. I had to use reverse and bring the helm hard left to slew the bow around to port. We drifted sideways for a bit, our wake pushing us broadside toward a daymark to the right of the channel. At the last moment, as our bow lined up for the new course, I came ahead at about half throttle, and we slipped into the narrow channel, just missing the daymark.

"Nicely done!" Sis said. "I'm impressed. The Navy really did teach you something. I though sure that you'd stuffed it with that one. Dad would be proud of you, Ned."

"Thanks." I did hope that he would have been proud.

"What did you and Lee talk about? Wait," she interrupted herself. "Were you two in love?"

Sis had not seen any of the Lee story yet.

"It's kind of complicated. Ned and Lee are friends but not really lovers. Well, they do fool around, but she doesn't want to... Ned's not sure if she's a lesbian or not because she won't let him sleep with her. They have sex but just don't go all the way. It's kind of strange."

"OK... So why does Ned want to go on this operation. Aren't they all about to go home?"

"That's kind of it. They're about to go home and Ned's still feeling afraid."

"Of what?"

"Of being killed, I think. He first feels it when he's with the SEALs. Remember?" I asked. "When they're up the Dam Doi and they get hit with the launch bomb."

"I haven't read that one yet."

"Oh, sorry. I've got a copy back at the motel. What happens is upsetting. Ned thinks he's about to die, and he gets really scared. He even pees in his pants."

"But isn't it normal?" As Sis spoke, a heron noisily took off from the mangroves to our right."

"What?"

"To be afraid. To feel fear. You sound like there's something wrong with Ned, and that's what makes him go on this operation."

"But it's not OK to be afraid. The whole thing about the training is so you're not afraid, so you do what you have to do without being afraid," I explained.

"I don't get it," Sis said.

"Maybe when you read the story."

"Maybe," she said. "But why can't you finish it and fill in the dialogue later. You told me you don't always write these in the order they happened."

"That's another thing, Sis. I don't really know how it did end."

"That battle at the end?"

"The firefight, yes. They told me at the hospital and all. I've read the action report, but I have a big blank spot. From about when Lee leaves the boat before we go out until I wake up in the hospital."

"You don't remember anything?"

"Oh, bits and pieces, OK. Like I can remember the call signs we used. And some of the bearings to the position where the ship anchored. But I can't remember what I was thinking or feeling much after Lee and I had our last conversation." We were passing the desalinization plant to starboard.

"How did it end?"

"The op?"

"The conversation with Lee."

"Not well. She got pissed off and left... I spilled my coffee. I remember that!"

After tying up *Coast Pilot*, we checked in at the office, but the Chief was still out. We drove back to the motel, and I gave Sis a copy of the SEAL story. I let her look at what I'd finished of the Lee stories as we had dinner at the *4th of July*, my favorite Cuban restaurant.

"Pretty complex lady, Ned, but it sounds like you handled it OK," she said as she gave me back my draft of *Can Tho Girls*, the working title for the story about Lee and Willie. When I pressed for more of a reaction, Sis asked for some time to think about it.

"Where would we look if we wanted to find out about a piece of property being bought or sold down here?" I asked the bartender, a sallow skinned, gaunt old man who sat morosely behind the bar, as if in a trance.

"Town office, I would," he said, his eyes blinking once, twice, three times, like an old sea turtle.

"What about for other towns in the Keys? There a central place we could look?"

"Monroe Country Court House here in Key West, I would." He blinked twice again.

"Thank you," said Sis.

He blinked a final time as we went out into the evening.

The next three days were taken up with short trips in *Coast Pilot*, as I got the feel of her single screw. All of my experience in the Navy had been in ships or boats with two propellers, so I wanted to get some sea time with a single. Sis sunbathed and read as I played games in the twisty creeks winding through the mangroves and in the ocean and in Florida Bay. We spent half a day exploring the deed records of Monroe County, all to no avail. There hadn't been any sales of property during April or May of last year in those towns to an Offshore Trust or anyone or thing like that. The records clerk either knew the owners or showed us a mainland address that couldn't have had any connection to our father. We put a few extra miles on the rental car, checking out a house three keys to the east, ate some wonderful fresh fish and conch chowder, and saw John Wayne in *The Green Berets* at a local drive-in movie on Stock Island. I wondered aloud if the world was ready for my version of Vietnam after hearing the hoots, hollers, and cheers from the customized pick-up trucks, rusted-out jeeps, and ancient station wagons surrounding us.

"Just write your stories, Ned," assured Sis, "and even these folks'll figure it out in time."

It seemed like the first vacation either of us had had in ages as I spent long stretches at the typewriter while Sis lay on the deck of *Coast Pilot*. The Chief had let us tie her up on a dock outside of the hurricane shelter so we could enjoy the weather and sunshine. We followed no schedule and made no rules to follow. We spent long periods of silence punctuated by sporadic conversations, some serious and most wonderfully foolish. We got to know each other on a wordless level.

A new serenity was beginning to fill in some of the cracks in my life, and I could almost imagine what my father had felt when he was down here, but I still needed to know what had so changed him in that last year.

It was mid-morning on the third day, as Sis sunbathed, and I sat in the navigator's seat of *Coast Pilot* anchored out off of the Naval Air Station at Boca Chica that I began to unravel the code in the log of the *Coast Pilot*. I had shown the log entries to the Chief and asked him if he had any ideas. He had confided that our father had seemed unable to read a navigational chart, but he had always jotted down directions as fast as they could be given. The Chief had told our father where the best snorkeling places were, for instance, and where he could go to take a photograph of the sunset or watch the Navy jets take off and land, for instance. Perhaps these numbers were directions, taken in shorthand form.

The Chief did remember telling our father that Coast Pilot's compass should read 110° when she sat tied up, 110° being the heading of her slip. That might explain why the first number of each paragraph was 110. Maybe some of the other numbers were not distances but times. The Chief had told our father another bit of local lore, that in the old days you could cross the Gulf Stream by travelling south, against the current, for five minutes for each fifty-five minutes spent travelling east. Again, time used instead of distance.

I rewrote the first number paragraph in the log, putting the three-digit bearing, if that was what it was, at the beginning of each new line.

110
225 77+ RL
045 77+ 2

And, on the fifth page of the notebook

110
285 20+ 8
105 20+ 2

By writing the number this way I could see the pattern I had been missing. Leaving out the first number, the 110 our father had used to check his compass each time he went out, the other numbers described a round trip of some sort because the first two numbers were the reciprocals, or reverse, of the last two, as were the middle two numbers.

On the 360 degree card of a compass, 225 is the reverse of 045, and 105 is the opposite direction to 285, in each case subtracting 180 degrees from the larger number to get the smaller.

I tried it with a third number paragraph on page six, this time leaving off the first 110, to verify my discovery.

300 2+
037 3+
217 3+
120 2+

It worked! The numbers described a trip to somewhere, out and back. The second number in each line was always the same number used in the corresponding reciprocal or reverse direction line. The only odd parts were the notations at the end of some lines, an RL and a 2 on the first set and an 8 and 2 on the second set. Nautical charts all contain thousands of the number 2 and 8, so that would be no help, but the number RL was unusual. I looked at the local area chart for the number RL that could mean something.

I found an "RL" daymark near Sand Key, to the southwest of Key West, a favorite place to snorkel or skin-dive. I tried using ten knots as a speed. Ten knots for 77 minutes didn't get me anywhere, so I tried 12 knots. That put me halfway to the Gulf Stream. 14 knots did it. That took us to the red lighthouse on Sand Key, the RL in our father's strange notes.

At last!

It was time to check out *Coast Pilot's* running gear. I put on the flippers, mask, and snorkel. I put up the dive flag that I had discovered in the cabin. I climbed over the transom out onto the swim platform and stepped off into the clear water of the Atlantic. A moment later Sis, too, slid in beside me. I motioned for her to hang onto the mooring line I had trailed in the water astern of the Dyer, and we began our inspection.

The four bladed propeller was free of nicks and smoothly polished. The twin nuts holding the prop to the shaft were secure and the cotter pin securing them was neatly spread. The shaft seemed true, and no monofilament line was wrapped anywhere. The cutlass bearing halfway down the shaft appeared clean and snug. The bronze pipe skeg was coated with bottom paint on all but the bottom surface, indicating the boat had kissed the bottom a few times, but I could find no damage whatsoever. Our father became quite a pilot at the end, I thought to myself. Good for him!

Sis and I moved forward and inspected the rest of the hull. The bottom seemed clean of weed, suggesting that the anti-fouling paint was doing its job. We drifted aft to the swim platform and hung there together, enjoying the ocean and the sky and the freedom offered by *Coast Pilot*.

"Dad must have felt some of this," Sis said, tipping her head back so her hair fell in a single wave down her back.

"I hope so," I answered, feeling differently toward him than I had all those years, having now shared this experience with him, even so separated in time as we were. I thought of the last two stanzas of the Frost poem I had memorized in school,

And dreaming, as it were, held brotherly speech
With one whose thought I had not hoped to reach.
"Men work together," I told him from the heart,
"Whether they work together or apart."

We dried off and put on suntan oil. I started the engine and brought her up to cruising speed on a course of 285 degrees. Sis lay forward on the cabin top on the cushions from on top of the engine box. I kept the course with my foot, gently adjusting every minute or so. The Dyer tracked beautifully through the gentle swells, and the morning passed into afternoon with neither of us speaking, each lost in the sweet drone of the diesel and the slow baking of the sun.

When we could just make out the "2" buoy making the seaward end of the channel back into the marina, we anchored again, and Sis made sandwiches for both of us. We ate in silence. She simply smiled at me in answer to my "Thank you."

"I could out here forever," I mused.

"Me, too," answered Sis. "Can I ask you something?"

"Shoot."

"Was Willie's Present true?" Sis had read the first part of my latest piece, this one about an encounter between Ned and a very young Vietnamese whom Lee's friend, Willie, had paid to give Ned a massage. I hadn't finished it, but I had told Sis how it was going to end.

"The part about what happened at the end," I said and raised up on one elbow to watch a pair of fighter land at Boca Chica. "Only it wasn't Willie who gave her to me. I was completely on my own. A couple of other Swifties and I had been out drinking and went to one of the massage places in Can Tho. The old lady running the place asked me if I cared who gave me the massage, and I said I didn't. I ended up with someone pretty much like Willie's present, and I was just drunk enough to not really care what happened. Until it was all over, that is."

"How do you feel about it now?" Sis's voice came from the cabin.

"I'm not sure how I feel or how I felt at the time," I said. "That's kind of why I started writing it, to get it all clear in my mind, to figure it out."

There was silence between us for a while.

"What was there to figure out?" Sis asked.

"I'm not sure." I sat up and hugged my knees. "There was one other part didn't make it into the story."

"Like?"

"Like the part that I was drunk enough so it could have been... either."

"Either what?" asked Sis.

"This kid could have been either sex, and I wouldn't have known. Or cared. I wrote the story with a girl just so it wouldn't seem so... queer."

"That's what I mean," said Sis. "If you feel guilty about having sex with a kid, maybe that's what's keeping you from being able to write some of your stories."

"So what happens, then? How can I prove it one way or another, that I'm either queer or normal."

"I don't think it works like that. It's what you believe that's important, not what you can prove or disprove. It's how you feel. Look at Lee. Was she a lesbian?"

"I don't think so, not like Willie. She just had rough time with that guy she married," I said.

"Let me ask you this. Did she ever have sex with Willie?"

I didn't answer for almost a minute, but Sis waited.

"Yes," I said at last.

"How do you know?"

I didn't answer right away.

"She told me. The two of them had been pinned down in one of the bunkers near the hospital for about a half an hour during a mortar attack. This had been about a month before I had arrived on the scene. The VC had dropped about ten rounds in on the base. Two were close ones, and it took a while after the attack was over to clear out some of the debris that had blocked the bunker door."

"By the time the two of them got out, Lee was a nervous wreck, and Willie wasn't much better. They both went to the O Club and drank a couple glasses of wine, Lee said. By the time they got back to their room, Lee was shaking and thought she would burst into tears any moment. She couldn't stop shaking."

"Willie suggested a hot shower, and Lee took one. She got into bed, and Willie put an extra blanket on top for warmth because Lee was getting chills, a reaction to the wine and the mortar attack." Willie had calmed down quite a bit by this time, Lee said, and, when Lee had not been able to stop shaking, Willie had come over and sat on the edge of her bed and held her, to comfort her. It felt so much better, Lee said, that she just kind of curled up in Willie's arms. Willie pulled the blanket up around them both. After a while the shaking got better, and Lee finally drifted off to sleep.

"She woke up sometime later and could feel Willie silently crying beside her. 'What's wrong?' Lee asked Willie. 'I want you,' was Willie's answer. 'Don't cry,' Lee told her, and Lee then put her arms around Willie. 'What do you want?' Lee asked Willie, and Willie told her.

"Lee said that she thought about it and remembered how she had felt during the mortar attack and afterwards, so she said, 'OK.'"

I stopped telling the story as the sun touched the horizon in the West. I could imagine the hiss of the drowning sun.

"And?" asked Sis.

"And so, I guess they made love together. That's as much as Lee would tell me."

"So, do you think Lee and Willie were regular lovers?"

"No. I'm pretty sure they weren't," I said. "By the time Lee was down at Vung Tau, the night of the last operation, Willie had a new roommate and everything. Lee and I were going out together all the time."

"So, her experience with Willie didn't make her a lesbian?"

"Well, I'm not sure what it did. It just seemed to have happened; I don't think it changed anything inside of her, if that's what you mean," I said.

"And you and Willie's present? Did that make you a dirty old man or a pederast?" pressed Sis.

"No. Guess not. Thinking about it later scared the hell out of me, though," I admitted. "That I could let myself go that way."

We got underway and returned to the marina, put *Coast Pilot* away, and returned to Key West. After dinner, I drifted into sleep that night trying to complete the connection between what was going on with my writing and what had happened with Willie's present.

CHAPTER SEVENTEEN

Can Tho, August, evening

He inhaled four times deeply from the tightly rolled joint in the men's room of the O Club, flushed it down the toilet, and washed away the pungent taste with a beer from the service bar. The smoke had made him cough, and his eyes watered a bit at first. Nash had said it would take just a couple of minutes to kick in. He would offer Lee the other one he had in his pocket up in hers and Willie's room. She didn't have to take any if she didn't want to, but Ned thought she would. She said she wanted to make love but just... couldn't. This might help, Ned thought.

"Be ready for it," Nash had warned. "It's not like being hit by a train or anything. Kind of slow and easy, but you'll know it's there when it starts. I always take one before a massage or before running a canal. Lasts an hour or so, maybe two. Your nurse'll love you for it," Nash said with a lewd wink.

Nash had guessed that Ned was having trouble getting Lee to sleep with him. Ned had not directly denied the suggestion, so Nash had suggested the pot as a solution. "You both take a few hits with a beer at the O Club and the two of you'll be screwing in the parking lot in half an hour!" Nash guaranteed. "One of my buddies, a SEAL, brought a few back from the border last time. Said they smoked them with girls in the

WILLIAM W. STANARD

villages up there. Part pot, part something else. Grows horns on you like a bitch. Gave one to one of the girls at the Chicago and thought she was going to swallow me whole. Almost convinced her to pay me. Bitchin'!"

In Willie's and Lee's room on the second floor of the hospital staff barracks Ned began to feel the insides of his arms tingle like a mild electric shock. He felt nervous and alert and glanced out of the window down at the moving brown river for only a moment before crossing the room to the table and reading the titles of the paperbacks stacked there. His hands felt for and found the tightly rolled second joint in his pocket. He crossed the room in a few quick strides and entered the small bathroom.

Ned looked at the toilet with its blue plastic toilet seat, the beige fiberglass shower stall, the wash basin with a stool and three towels under it, and the bookshelf with magazines scattered haphazardly on two of the three shelves. The middle shelf held an assortment of bottles and jars and a square white box with blue letters on its lid. He stood in front of the toilet and unzipped himself.

He smiled as he watched the stream of urine splash into the clear water of the bowl, turning it more and more yellow. *The Yellow River*, by I. P. Daily, Ned thought and then knew that the pot was beginning to work. He felt giddy, excited, "Ready for it all," he thought and realized he'd spoken aloud. He flushed the toilet, zipped his trousers, and went back into the other room, pausing to look at the table of paperbacks again.

Wonder what's keeping Lee? he thought. He saw the note for the first time, folded like a pup tent, off to the left side of the books.

Nanny Goat had to fill in for another of the girls in post-op, so she has to break your date. I've put together a little present for you who will show up at seven. Relax and let it go where it takes you. Everything's been paid for.
Willie

Cow Key Marina, Stock Island

Try as he might, Ned couldn't continue the story. Maybe when I'm back in St. Louis, he thought, but he knew that this was as far as he could go. Leave it up to the reader's imagination. The unwritten truth that the author does not tell but is always there behind the story.

CHAPTER EIGHTEEN

Key West, afternoon

The next afternoon Sis and I took *Coast Pilot* out again. As we drew due south of "2", a growing roar caught both our attentions, and we looked to our left over the low keys in time to see a pair of F-4s bank to the south and soon disappear over the horizon toward Cuba.

"Hairbrush," I said.

"What does that mean?" asked Sis.

"It's the old radio code for a scramble to come down and help us out when I was on the *Calcaterra* down here. We would steam for days on end about twelve miles off Havana Harbor, and 'Hairbrush' was the code word to get help. If we were being harassed or attacked by Fidel's boys. Wouldn't have done any good, though."

"So why did they bother, having a secret word and all?"

"Made us feel better, I guess." I thought about it for a moment. "We would do these things if we just had half a sense that we'd be backed up if things got tough."

Two more F-4s roared up from Boca Chica and headed for Cuba. *Coast Pilot* skimmed along on a flat sea toward red buoy number "2" off of Boca Chica Channel where we changed course to 260 degrees for red buoy "12" at the end of the first dogleg of the main ship channel going into Key West. We lined up the two ranges on what the locals called Christmas Tree Island, a haven for hippy dropouts and high school kids who wanted to get high. As we came up even with the submarine pens at the Navy Base, I brought *Coast Pilot* into line with the ranges on Fleming Key, compensating for the push of the current by holding the Dyer slightly askew from our course. Between the current and our crabbing motion, the Dyer stayed exactly where I wanted her, just to starboard of mid-channel. We would get fuel at the shrimp docks before heading back to the marina. Once we had passed port side to port side with an untidy wooden hulled shrimper named *Caliope* starting to lower her outriggers for stability, the harbor looked clear of traffic.

A small, single engine plane was buzzing around Middle Ground, a good fishing area to our northwest, like an angry gnat, and Sis and I were keeping an eye on its antics when we heard a shout above the thrum of the diesel. We looked at each other, and her shrug told me that she had no idea where it came from. I throttled back and went into neutral. The current had half-filled the harbor with the rising tide, and *Coat Pilot* was being swept at a good clip up toward the turning basin at the Navy Annex. We waited for the shout again.

"Watch out, man!" The shout came from somewhere ahead of us, so I backed down *Coast Pilot*, swinging the helm to port to counteract her stern's walking sideways to starboard. It took fifteen seconds to get sternway on against the current.

"Keep a look out astern, Sis."

"Got it," Sis answered. "You're OK right now. Nearest boat's, say, a hundred feet or so. They're docking""

As we gained momentum astern, I saw a group of well-tanned faces appear over the deck edge at the bow, and a hand grab the blade of the plow anchor.

"We'll get out of here, man. Sorry," said a quiet male voice from the group at *Coast Pilot's* bow, and a small dingy with maybe six people aboard slipped to starboard from under our bow and proceeded across the channel, two of its occupants paddling steadily with what looked like canoe paddles, and the rest just holding onto the gunwales and rolling their heads drunkenly.

"Look at this, Sis," I said over my shoulder, and she turned from keeping watch astern just in time to see the whole dingy load of humanity upend itself and dump its cargo into the harbor.

"Wow, man," came the quiet voice again, and the bodies separated themselves from each other and began to swim in separate directions. I saw two girls and three men. Two of the men were strong swimmers and had no trouble, one heading for the shrimp docks and the other for an anchored short-masted schooner, the *Western Union*.

"I'm going to stick around and make sure everyone makes it," I told Sis who was standing at the navigator's station to port. I tapped the engine astern to help keep our position just northeast of the Customs House.

The third man dog paddled for a bit and then rolled over onto his back and floated, his hands clasped across his very noticeable belly. He dog paddled again and then rolled over to float. He repeated this strange method of travel until he disappeared around the breakwater of the sub pens. The two girls swam with strong, coordinated strokes, almost like precision dancers, toward the beach at the *Pier House*. I could see now that they weren't wearing bikini tops, but I didn't imagine that anyone at the *Pier House* would mind.

"Weren't there six, Ned?" asked Sis. "I think I saw six when they first started swimming."

I looked around the harbor, and it took enough time for us to have drifted almost even with the *Pier House* beach before I saw first the girl's head and then her mahogany tanned body through the clear water of the harbor. She was hanging onto one of the pilings of the dock at the north end of the Customs House Landing. Her head was tipped back, and her hair spread like a fan behind her. Even from fifty feet away I could see the tension in her arms. I put the engine into reverse, hoping to back *Coast Pilot* close enough to help her aboard by the swim platform.

"Can you grab the boat hook there," I said to Sis, indicating the port side of the cockpit, under the side deck. It was then I heard the clunk and felt the wheel stiffen. The engine then labored for a bit before I could get it into neutral. "Shit. We hit something," I said and thought of another swimmer in the water.

"A piece of driftwood," said Sis from the stern. "I saw it earlier as we went by."

"The steering's gone," I said. "Keep an eye on the girl, and I'll try to free this bastard." I had the lazarette cover up and checked the quadrant. It was clear of obstacles, so I knew it had to be underwater where the steering was jammed between the rudder and the prop or the skeg.

"She's slipping. I'll get her," Sis said and was over the side of *Coast Pilot* before I could react. I shut down the diesel, tied the starboard aft mooring line off to the stern clean, and threw the bitter end into the water. A quick rummage in the aftermost underdeck locker found one of the swim masks. I climbed onto the swim platform and jumped into the water, one hand on the mooring line. The piece of driftwood, as big around as my wrist, was jammed between the rudder and the skeg. The prop had made a couple of good nicks in it, but it still looked solid enough. I came up for a breath of air and saw that Sis had arrived at the Customs House Landing and was next to the girl. No one on the land seemed to be aware of our difficulties. With a deep breath, I went under the boat again. Letting go of the mooring line, bracing both feet on the skeg, and grabbing the driftwood with both hands, I was able to move it about a foot, but part of it caught on the shaft this time.

I surfaced for another breath, noticed that we had drifted to a point opposite the Turtle Kraals, and went down again. One more tug with both hands did it. I put the driftwood on the swim platform and heaved myself up. The driftwood went into the cockpit and the mooring line followed. I didn't want to wrap that half inch nylon around the shaft.

Sis had her left arm around the girl, holding on to the Customs house dock's underpinnings. There was no easy way up onto the land from where they were, so I would need to bring the Dyer over to them so they could get aboard. After starting the diesel, I put the helm over hard to starboard and gave the engine a good goose in forward. The Dyer slipped through the water easily, and I was able to spin it around at the last moment, so her stern faced the Customs House, presenting the two swimmers with what I thought was the easiest was aboard.

"I'm going to need a hand with her, Ned. She's weak," said Sis.

I maneuvered to the south of where they were and, from the cockpit, held the boat hook out toward Sis, who let go of the piling she was holding on to and grabbed the boat hook, keeping her left arm around the girl. I could see pale skin on the girl's scalp through her matted hair, but the rest of her body was deeply tanned.

"Let go now," said Sis to the girl. "I've got you."

The girl let go of the piling. Sis turned her around in the water, and I started to pull them toward the boat. As they reached the swim platform, I leaned over the side and took the girl under her arms and held her while Sis swam around behind her. Between the two of us, we tugged and pushed her up onto the platform into a half lying, half sitting position, her feet trailing in the water. Sis climbed aboard and sat next to her.

"Hold on to her, Sis, and I'll get us into a dock," and I went back to the controls.

There was an open space at the Texaco fuel dock in the middle of the fleet of shrimpers, and I slipped *Coast Pilot* in astern of a steel hull named the *Carol Anne*.

"She'll take about fifty," I said to the old man on duty at the pump who had taken our stern line, "with the low-pressure hose. I'll get the deck plate."

I killed the engine and opened the starboard side deck fill and took the offered nozzle. Once it was in the fill and was pumping fuel, I went aft in the cockpit to check on my sister and our guest. The girl had her head forward, her wet hair tumbled around her face. She wore a dark green, one-piece racing or tank suit that showed off her well-tanned body, a dancer's body. Her arms and back were smoothly muscled, and she looked fit.

"I was fine until I took a mouthful of harbor water down the wrong way!" the girl said, as if in answer to my unspoken question. "I'm really embarrassed."

"Are you OK now?" asked Sis.

"I think I've caught my breath, yes. Thank you, again," the girl said and, with both hands, cleared the hair away from in front of her face. "I'm Annie Gerard"

"I'm Sis Taylor and the staring one there is my brother, Ned."

"I..." was as close as I could get to an apology, for I had been rudely staring. Annie had an amazing face. Her eyes were blue, set wide apart in a broad, almost Indian face with high cheekbones. A thin, straight nose seemed at odds with the flare of her nostrils. They swelled and relaxed as she breathed. Her mouth was wide and her lips full, and, when she looked up at the expression on my face, her eyes almost closed in amusement. Her neck was long, making her torso seem thinner than it actually was. Her fingers seemed very long, but her hands were large but delicate.

"Hello, Ned Taylor," said Annie and she looked directly through my eyes and into me. "You guys make a useful team."

I finished fueling and, as I was paying up in the office, asked the dock master where we could get a place to tie up. As long as we didn't need shore power or water, he could give a place in the back row, outboard of a pair of shrimpers that didn't plan to go out for a while. Engine trouble, he guessed.

As we moved over toward where we could tie up, Annie explained that she was getting a ride to the town landing from the island with the fat man in the dingy when the others got aboard. One of them thought it would be fun to hitch a ride on the passing shrimper, so he grabbed a trailing line. When he let go, they found themselves in the middle of the channel, just under our bow. They were so stoned, Annie said, that they probably won't even remember what happened. She hadn't known any of them, and the one with the belly had just seen her on the beach and offered her a ride from the island to the landing.

We slipped in outboard of the *Belle*, rigged a pair of white vinyl fenders and tied off, adding spring lines fore and aft. Annie watched us as we worked. I found myself staring at her a couple of times, and I think she noticed because she looked back at me each time. She sat on the transom, her legs crossed at the ankles, and it was soon hard to imagine her in trouble in the water or anywhere for that matter.

Sis must have noticed me staring at Annie because she poked me in the ribs when we were both forward adjusting the bow line.

"Go ahead," Sis whispered. "Ask her."

"What?" I asked.

"Whatever it is you want to ask her. She can't take her eyes off of you, either."

"Oh," I said. "What should I ask her?"

"About a better place to stay than the motel we're in now. I'm ready to move up a notch."

We went aft, and I tried to speak to her but found myself becoming tongue tied. "A place to stay. Know of any?"

"You aren't conchs?" Annie said. "I thought I'd seen your boat before. In fact, I'm sure I have, although I never saw who was driving it."

"It's... It was our father's boat. He used to drive it around here," I said. "So, *we* don't know our way around, at least not as far as places to stay. I was here in the Navy, but even from here I can see it's changed in the last year or so." At least I could make the words hang together in sentences"

"It's all pretty expensive, even in summer. How long are you going to stay for?"

"We are doing some research in the County Court House. It should take a couple of days," I said. "'We're not on a very strict schedule."

"Well, I'll be down here for another two days. I have rooms at a guest house on William Street, about three blocks from here. You two could stay with me there, as long as you don't mind sharing quarters with a couple hundred crabs."

"Crabs?" Sis asked.

"I'm tagging crabs. I'm a marine biologist. I collect them

down here on the island once a year and then number them. I let them go and check on them again the next year"'"

"How long have you been doing this? It sounds neat," Sis said.

"I'm into my fifth season," Annie answered. "I work at the University of Miami. This is kind of my summer holiday. A way to get out of the city and relax, get my research done, and get paid for it all at the same time. You guys could have the beds in the crab room. Don't worry, they're all in tanks, most of the time anyway. I owe you two a lot. Come on!"

"If you're sure it's OK," Sis said after looking at me and seeing the grin on my face. "What would the owner think?"

"No problem; here on the island they think they invented the ménage à trois." Annie smiled. "This is great. It would make us almost even."

"Is that what we'd be?" asked Sis with a grin, and Annie blushed. "Even, or a ménage à trois?"

A little girl who made sure we knew that her name was Robin met us at the door to The Chimneys Guest House at 45 William Street, so named because of its two brick chimneys, one of which would have been unusual in a town that never has experienced frost. The record low temperature in Key West was thirty-four degrees, Annie reminded us. While she talked to the owner, Robin's mother, somewhere in the back of the house, Sis and I waited on the front porch. The street was heavy with summer flowers and alive with birds. A huge gumbo limbo tree in the front yard cast a green shadow over the house, making it seem as though we were underwater.

"Nice place," observed Sis. "Hope the crabs aren't going to be a pain. What do you think about Annie?"

"Pretty," I offered. "Does she seem at all strange to you or is it just me?"

"No. As a matter of fact, she seems quite self-possessed to me, very much in charge of herself. You haven't known too many women like that since Mom. Does her attitude bother you?" Sis asked.

"I'm not sure."

"Most men don't know how to treat women like her. These women don't fit the two stereotypes men have created for us. Men cast us as either Madonnas or whores," Sis said seriously, "excepting your mothers and some of your sisters. You're even bothered by my relationship with Jim, aren't you? Why? I'm a big girl."

"I just have a hard time imagining you as, well... having an affair with someone."

"You mean a hard time imagining me having sex, right?" asked Sis.

"Sort of." I was quickly slipping out of my depth.

"What about our fantasies when we were younger? What about the other night? We both could imagine really well the other one in bed, right?" Sis leaned forward and tapped my left knee with her finger. "What was the real difference between the other night and your imagining me in bed with another man, with Jim, or with anybody else?"

"I'm not sure... I don't know."

"Try this: it's all right for you but not all right for another man or another person to make love, to have sex, to sleep with me, right?" At each step in her argument, Sis tapped my knee.

"I know it's not OK for me, either," I admitted. "But I did want to, I guess."

"It's not OK only because I'm your sister, right?"

"Right. Brothers and sisters aren't supposed to."

"Unless they're Hawaiians or Egyptians," Sis reminded me.

"But if we weren't related, think of how you'd feel. You wouldn't want to think of me with any other person, right?"

"Right. It does bother me, thinking of you with another man. And you're right about it being because I'm a man, not your brother."

"You wouldn't even like to think of me with another person..." and Sis took my hands, forcing me to look into her eyes, "...another woman, would you?"

I wondered what was coming.

"Annie?" I asked.

"Just answer me, Ned. Would you be bothered by my being

with another woman?"

I thought for at least a minute.

"Maybe," I said at last.

"Because...?"

"Because... it wasn't me. Just because it was she and not me," I admitted to Sis and to myself.

"Well," Sis said with a sigh and sat back, letting go of my hands. "I don't think you have to worry about that with me. I think I'm pretty well queer for guys. Jim in particular. You, too, if you weren't my brother. But...," and Sis paused.

I felt confused by where Sis had brought me with her questions.

"But I want you to think about how you feel about women. How you think about them. What they really are to you." Sis smiled gently at me, but I think she was also enjoying seeing me struggle. "It may tell you something about where you were with Lee Morgan. Even where you might be with Annie, if it's going that way. And you'll also see where you are with me, although I think where we two are is somehow very different."

"How different?"

"We'll probably have a... affair..."

"No," I interrupted.

"But it won't be on a physical plane. I think it's much more bodiless, more mystical," said Sis slowly.

"It's certainly more unreal," I agreed and reached over toward her, "but I've really needed it." As I raised my hand, palm toward her, so did she, and our palms touched in greeting.

We had brought a single duffle bag of clothes that we kept on the boat for the two of us, and Sis had loaned Annie a pair of sandals, hers having been lost overboard when the dingy upset. I pulled a copy of the piece I was working on out of the duffle bag, one about an Army major I'd had a run-in with on a river operation south of Can Tho. I started to go through it, making penciled notes, when Annie returned to the porch.

"Come on up," she announced. "It's fine. Mrs. Harris'll

bring up another two sets of towels. There're already sheets on the two beds. No charge, she said, when I told her what you two did for me."

We each showered and collected ourselves on the front porch. Sis had changed into a pair of cut off Levis and a bright yellow t-shirt. I had put on a green polo shirt and khakis. Annie wore a sleeveless white cotton sun dress with a subtle white printed pattern. With her dark tan, she looked spectacular. She wore no makeup or nail polish. Now that her hair was dry, I could see how red it was. I'm sure I was staring again, but she seemed to enjoy it. I kept catching her looking at me too, so I guess our enjoyment was mutual.

I asked our landlady to call a cab, I retrieved our clothes and checked out of our motel, leaving Sis and Annie and Robin talking on the porch.

"Let's celebrate our new digs," Sis suggested when I returned.

"Where to?" asked Annie.

"How about starting with a beer at Sloppy Joe's, in honor of Papa," I suggested.

"Let's do it," agreed Sis.

We sat under the slowly turning paddles of the ceiling fans in Sloppy Joe's Saloon at the corner of Greene and Duval Streets and drank a beer to Papa Hemingway's memory. It was almost five as we finished our beers, and Sis excused herself to make a 'phone call from the ancient booth in the back of the barroom. When she returned with a smile on her face, "Tell you later," is all she would say in answer to my quizzical expression.

We then were led by Annie to a tiny French restaurant on the second floor of South Florida's only Romanesque bank building where we all had escargots and Annie and I had sweetbreads while Sis just ate a green salad. Annie bought another pair of sandals at Kino's on Front Street and gave back

Sis's pair. I bought a straw hat with a purple band at Annie's suggestion and couldn't get Sis to explain why she was grinning at me.

"It's not the hat, really, Ned. It's just you," was all Sis would say. I could tell from the look that passed between the two of them that Annie shared in the joke. Sis bought a polished white coral necklace, and, as Annie fastened it around Sis' neck, I suddenly realized how much alike they were. Not in physical appearance so much, for Sis was fairer skinned and Annie finer boned, but alike in attitude or spirit. As we walked through the town, the two of them chatted together, and I seemed to fall easily into step a few paces behind them. I felt proud, somehow, as though I were privileged to be with them. Two striking young women and their trusted escort on the town in old Key West. What could have been better, I wondered. Life had changed course 180 degrees since my return to St. Louis a month ago.

We wandered around in the evening of the town, crossing our path many times, finally arriving at Captain Tony's Saloon where I wanted to show my two ladies the calling card I'd thumb tacked to the cork board, adding to the saloon's collection when I was first stationed in Key West three years ago. It was a tradition for visitors to add their card to the cork board covering almost all of the free surface of the bar itself, the columns supporting the roof, and the walls. The famous ones were on the wall above the bottles behind the bar. My card was on a soffit just above where we were able to get seats at the bar. It had yellowed a bit, although it was whiter than most of them.

Edgar C. Taylor, Ensign, USNR it read, and, underneath, someone had written something in light pencil.

"Return to thy house, O beautiful boy," read Annie. "Looks like you have an admirer."

"Oh, great," I said. "I really need this."

"Ned, come on. It's not that. It's a quote from somewhere, I think" said Sis" "I remember it from college. It's Old Testament or something."

"Weird," said Annie and touched my arm for just a

moment, "but nice."

"Curiouser...," said Sis.

"...and curiouser""

"...said Alice," finished Annie, and Sis and I looked at each other. Sis was smiling an extravagant smile.

We were sitting at the counter at Shorty's on Duval Street, eating scrambled eggs and grits at midnight and drinking Cuban coffee from small cups. We had been prowling the streets for hours, visiting all of the bars and clubs I'd remembered from when I had been stationed on the island. Annie introduced us to a few others that she knew about. The drinks were plentiful, the natives friendly, and we were finally running out of steam and were just about ready to head back to The Chimneys.

As I finished the last of my eggs I began to notice the night people around us. There were two sailors, obvious because of their close haircuts and polyester Navy Exchange clothes, trying to pick up two local Cuban girls who giggled and talked only to each other in rapid Spanish. An old woman arguing quietly with herself stood in the corner near the open front doors. A couple of indeterminate gender sat hunched in a booth at the back, sipping Cokes through straws, just like the old magazine and billboard ads, straws crossed, glasses touching, and heads bowed. A uniformed medic, his ambulance parked on the street outside, sipped at a tiny cup of Cuban coffee opposite a pair of Shore Patrol, their identical helmet liners hanging on the coat rack behind them. They were devouring hamburgers and fries in tandem with military precision. And there we were. To anyone passing by, who was our trio and what was their relationship to each other?

As we walked down Duval Street toward the waterfront, we passed Cuban couples walking hand in hand, demurely making their paseo. A solitary drunk hung on for dear life to what must have been to him a wildly lurching telephone pole.

A strange couple, a young girl, not yet a teenager, with a blond Dutch Boy haircut, stood waiting at the corner of Eaton

Street with a thin gray-haired oldster with a long cane or staff. The girl wore neatly cut-off jean shorts and a brightly tie-dyed t-shirt while the older of the two wore a leather vest, denim shirt, and baggy chino pants. Both wore sandals. I noticed them because they so strangely contrasted with the other night people on Duval Street, the drunks, the military, the refugees.

Out of the red front door of a bar across the street wove a conga line of half a dozen late night revelers, their leader a man in his sixties wearing a white linen suit and a Panama hat and chanting drunkenly, "… my children, and you shall hear of the midnight slide of my career."

He waved a wine glass aloft in his right hand, like a beacon, and a sheaf of papers in his left hand. From the strong young man holding, perhaps guiding, his hips from behind him through the middles ones, all young and quite drunk or stoned, to the last of the human chain, a frowsy woman with henna hair and sea green pants, they seemed to me a joyless sight, their gaiety forced by drink or drugs, and I suddenly wondered if this was the life that our father had found here in Key West. It was as if someone had stepped on my grave.

I felt cold and alone, and, almost automatically, reached to the right and left, taking both Annie and Sis by their hands. The energy that flowed through us as we walked on that street together nearly dispelled the melancholy I had suddenly felt there. The rest of our walk back to The Chimneys passed in silence.

"Jim's home," Sis said, as the three of us were sitting on the small, second floor porch off of Annie's room having a late night glass of wine. "I think I'll see about heading back to St. Louis tomorrow," continued Sis. "If it's OK for Ned to stay on, that is," she said to Annie.

I never would have been able to be as direct as that, I thought. Sis really seems to feel comfortable with Annie, even though they've only known each other for a few hours.

"No problem," answered Annie from inside her room. "The crabs'll enjoy the company. And I can use the help,"

Annie said as she came out onto the porch, turning off the light in her room behind her" She had removed the cotton sun dress she had worn to dinner and had on just an extra-large large white t-shirt that came down to mid-thigh. Her hair was loose and spread out across her shoulders. She was lovely in the soft light from the street. When she smiled, her teeth flashed white across her tanned face.

"Thank you, Annie," said Sis. "Jim's going to make a reservation for me from Miami to St. Louis through his company. I'll call first thing tomorrow to confirm it."

"You're not going to help find the house?" I asked Sis.

"Annie will help," Sis said. "We've already talked about it. She has a friend at the Courthouse."

I felt a little out of control of what was happening, and I said with a smile, "You two are ganging up on me."

"You'll be fine, Ned," said Sis. "Annie's just taking over for me is all. You can help her with her crabs, and she can help you with looking for Dad's house. The two of you will make a great team." Sis paused and looked into her wine glass. "Anyhow, it's been a long time since I've seen Jim, and I really miss him." I had felt secure with Sis along on this trip, and now she was going back to her life in St. Louis.

I felt scared, but, as I looked up at Annie's looking at me, I imagined that she might offer another safety.

"Anybody need another wine?" Sis asked and disappeared without waiting for an answer into Annie's room where the wine sat in small refrigerator,

"She's special, isn't she?" observed Annie after a pause. "The two of you have a really intimate relationship. I've always wanted to have a man as a brother."

"You can have mine for a while," Sis's voice said out of the darkness, and a deal seemed to have been made between the two of them.

Annie and Sis and I found a cab over on Duval Street at six the next morning, and the three of us drove to the airport. We had coffee in the small cafe and waited for the seven o'clock plane to Marathon and Miami. Sis had called Jim and found that she had a non-stop Miami-St. Louis flight that left Miami at eleven, so we had to get her to the early morning Miami plane.

Sis was excited to be going home to see her Jim. Annie seemed exhilarated to be part of the dynamics of our family. I wasn't sure how I felt, but I enjoyed the company of the two beautiful women, bathing in the envious looks from the airport ground crew, four young men and one black Cuban girl of about twenty with startlingly curly short hair of the deepest jet color. She wore a gold ring the diameter of a dime through her left nostril, and her eyes constantly appraised the other crew members and the three of us.

Sis and I said little to each other until her flight was called. Annie walked out onto the ramp ahead of us.

"I'll miss you, Sis. You made all this seem easy. I'm not sure I would have kept going if it hadn't been for you being there. That and you figuring all this stuff out about the trust and the property."

"You'll do fine with Annie, Ned. She's a good one; believe your sister on this one. I can tell."

"Well, I'm not sure I need a second sister. I do have you."

"Don't worry about what she'll be, Ned. Just count her as a friend, OK. Don't try to make her anything. She's just a girl, a woman. Pretend she's a sister and you'll be a lot better off than if you invent some other kind of role for her. Just let her be there."

"She says she wants a brother, huh?"

"That's what she said, so let her have one, Ned. Think of it as something you can do for her. And she'll help you find Dad's house."

"I'll miss you, Sis," I said as we hugged quickly, and, as Annie came up next to me, Sis trotted across the blacktop toward the sputtering yellow DC-3 that squatted far out on the apron. She was the last one aboard, and the black Cuban girl said something to her as Sis turned in the doorway of the plane. Sis said something in answer to the girl, and, as she shut the oval door behind Sis, I could see the girl grin and look over toward Annie and me. As Annie and I turned to go up to the observation deck to watch Sis take off, the curly haired girl waved. Annie waved back, but I was only able to give a smile.

Annie and I spent the rest of the morning at the Monroe County Courthouse. Avrila, a small, middle-aged woman with large honest eyes, the friend of Annie's, showed us the card file index to property records for the county, introduced us to the old conch clerk who had to shuffle off into the dank tombs below to retrieve the heavy ledgers with the handwritten and photocopied facsimiles of the deeds.

"Where did you meet Annie?" asked Avrila when Annie had gone across the street for coffee. Nothing in business in Key West seemed to happen without constant attention to coffee.

"At the harbor," I answered, keeping it simple.

"She's been a good friend. I have relations in Cuba who cannot visit the United States, and Annie has had some of her Miami friends get in touch with them for me. I keep in touch with my family through her."

It was not long before I realized that Annie's Avrila was going to be extremely helpful. Finding out about property transfers at the Courthouse had been much more difficult without Avrila's help, and seeing the actual records had been nearly impossible. The posted times for property review was late afternoon on Thursday, almost a week away. I judged that even a small "gift" to the clerk would not have helped as much as the OK from Avrila.

"What do you do here at the Courthouse," I asked.

"I'm in charge of the dead," Avrila said and picked up her telephone as it started to ring.

"Yes. Yes. I'll come see. Excuse me, Annie, Mr. Taylor. I'll be right back," she said as she left the room.

"What in the world does in charge of the dead mean?" I asked Annie.

"She translates for all the Cubans who have to deal with burial permits and relatives' estates here in the Courthouse,"

Annie explained, stirring her coffee. "Two sugars, right?"

"Two would be great."

"It's a big job, and she's very important to the community. As she explained it to me, she is paid by subscription in the community," said Annie as she passed me my coffee. "All the Cubans here in Key West pay her salary, since she makes their life easier, kind of like Cerberus."

"Nice picture, that. The bureaucratic guard dog of the underworld." I reached for a wooden coffee stirrer from the pile on Avrila's desk, and my hand brushed Annie's. She quickly pulled her hand away and turned to look through the card file catalogue of deed transfers.

"What dates am I looking for?" she asked.

"Late April, early May, last year," I answered, wondering why she jumped so at my touch.

We were looking for a property transfer to the Offshore Trust dated around the end of April or the beginning of May. We knew the approximate dollar amount of the April-May sight draft, but really had only the anonymous character of the new owner to go by. By noon we had discovered a dozen properties, five in Key West and seven in the lower keys which could fit our profile. We bought a city map upstairs and drew Xs on it at the locations of the properties.

Two of the sales happened to occur at the same address and only minutes apart. Avrila explained that this could have been either a condominium project with multiple units or that we could be looking at a strawman sale which she explained as the transfer of property, through a lawyer or other intermediary, the strawman, out of a family or marriage because of divorce or death. We decided these two properties wouldn't fit.

The third property was on Simonton Street, four blocks from the courthouse, the fourth on Flagler Boulevard out near the Navy Hospital, and the fifth on Von Phister Street, about ten blocks away from downtown. We wrote down the locations of the lower key's properties, thanked the old conch porter with a five dollar tip, and returned to Avrila's office.

"You have been a big help," Annie said. "Can you have

dinner with us tonight? We'd like to thank you properly, Avrila."

"I'd love to, but I must be home with my brother," Avrila said, her honest eyes sparkling. "He is not able to take care of himself, and I must be there for him. But thank you. Having helped a friend of yours, Annie, means I need no other thanks. You have done so much for me."

Annie and Avrila hugged, I took Avrila's hand and gave her a short bow, something I hadn't done since I had been a little boy, making my manners. It evidently was just the right thing, for Avrila smiled at Annie and gave me a pat on the arm,

"She likes you because you are polite," said Annie as we walked down the front steps of the Courthouse, "and so do I."

I wondered what that meant for our relationship.

"Sis said you were writing. Can I read one of your stories?" Annie asked as we sat at the counter for lunch at the *4th of July*, evidently a favorite of Annie's too, plates of its ground Cuban beef, black beans, and rice before us.

In my sheaf of papers about the properties we were looking at this afternoon, I still had the working copy of the piece about the Army Major.

"It isn't really finished yet, but I could always use a first reader," I said and handed her the stapled sheaf of paper. As an introduction, I told her briefly about my Vietnam tour, leaving out my being wounded in the last operation just days before coming home.

"Thanks," she said and pulled a pair of glasses out from her canvas shoulder bag. "Go ahead and start. I'm going to read for a bit, OK?" She hunched over the table, the glasses catching the light of the bright noontime sun reflecting off the counter. Her lips moved minutely as she read, but her eyes hopped from line to line incredibly quickly. "You use a lot of sounds in your writing, huh?" she said without looking up.

I don't think she even heard my answer.

CHAPTER NINETEEN

Can Tho, 25 August, 0530 hours

Ned crossed over the barge and walked across the compound to the officers' barracks. The morning was cool but the high clouds piling up to the south promised rain by afternoon. He would take a quick shower while the crew topped off the fuel of the 93 boat. The dusty compound was still asleep, the only noises coming from the Swift boat crews down on the barge at the river's edge. Everything Ned could see was coated with a reddish-brown dust.

The nearest living green he could see was an island close to the western shore just upstream from the Navy base. A white sign on the southern tip of the island was lettered in red, ISLAND OFF LIMITS. UNEXPLODED ORDINANCE. The sign also said something in Vietnamese which Ned couldn't read. The river was a dull reddish brown and sluggish in the early morning light. Across the river a single sampan powered by a noisy long-shaft engine worked its way up-river against the current. Ned was glad he wasn't permanently stationed at Can Tho.

As he entered the changing room with its two open shower stalls at one end, he saw Blue Shark's operational commander, an Army Major named Britton, toweling himself dry looking out through one of the two barred windows toward the river.

He was heavy set and well-muscled, but his dark farmer's tan, leaving all but his face and lower arms a pasty white, reminded Ned of a hairy harlequin. He heard Ned enter and turned, smiling, his thin lips stretched tight over perfect teeth. The head clown, Ned thought bitterly. He didn't like working for the Army.

"Gonna keep you nifty-Navy types busy all day today and out on the river tonight with the Ruff-Puffs. Give them some moral support, if you know what I mean," the Major said as he dried his crotch.

"Yes, sir," answered Ned. "We're taking on fuel now."

"Good. Don't leave any gear here, 'cause I might not want to bring you back right away. " The Major covered his head and face with the towel and started to dry his hair. Ned stripped off his shorts and t-shirt, kicked his flip-flops off, and pulled his underpants down. As always, he felt embarrassed undressing in front of someone else. He put his clothes on a wooden bench that lay along the wall opposite the window"

"None of these bastards been in combat yet," said the Major's muffled voice from under the towel, "so they're pretty scared. You guys going to be the only on-scene, permanent fire support they've got, so we want to put on a big show."

"They usually like the .50s," offered Ned. "A lot of noise. Scatters a lot of twigs and leaves. Pretty impressive splashes in the water, too."

"Yeah. Shouldn't be too difficult to impress them," said the Major and he tossed his towel into the canvas hamper. "Two points, eh?" He stood looking at Ned, his hands on his hips., "Bring you all back here in a couple days or so or maybe send you to Ben Tre. We'll see."

The two naked men faced each other, the Major aggressive and Ned just waiting.

"You Navy types aren't afraid of spending the night out, are you? It'll be just like kiddie camp."

"Looking forward to it," said Ned, forcing a smile, and he wrapped his towel around his hips and started for the showers. "See you on board about 0630, Sir. Underway at 0700, as planned?"

"Yeah," said the Major who then smiled and farted. "Aha! First of the day. Sign of a healthy gut." He started to pick through a pile of starched olive drab laundry he had unwrapped from a brown paper parcel. "0530. Right on schedule."

Ned hung the towel on a hook just outside of the shower stall, stepped in, and turned on the single tap. The water was lukewarm. As he stood under the water, Ned watched the Major dress, selecting a pair of olive drab bikini briefs and slipping them on. He arranged himself to his satisfaction, smoothing the pouch with both hands as he looked at himself in the full length mirror.

Male plumbing, thought Ned. Some men are certainly proud of their equipment. He looked down at his and thought that maybe Lee was right, that some of our parts were highly overrated.

Bassac River, 25 August, 0800 hours

There were two Swifts involved in Operation Blue Shark, the 93 and 70 boats, both from *Sea Float*. They each had twenty Regional and Popular Forces troops aboard and Major Britton ran the operation from the pilot house of Ned's boat.

They left Can Tho in convoy with 93 leading and 70 bringing up the rear. Ned and Dog, the skipper of the 70 boat, had decided to use a second radio frequency separate from the primary to keep in touch with each other. Like wingmen in the World War Two fighter pilot tradition, the Swifts always worked with partners. The Ruff-Puffs, a name that Ned thought described their combat attitude well, sat on the engine hatches and mortar box back aft and ate what looked like breakfast out of brown paper bags or cloth pouches. With their mismatched tan and olive drab uniforms and red scarves they looked more like a poorly organized Boy Scout picnic than a fighting force ready to go into enemy territory. The two boats turned south and headed for a cluster of three islands near the mouth of the Bassac river, about thirty miles south of

Can Tho.

By 0800 the Sunday sun had warmed the river, and the familiar smell of diesel fumes and hot metal was replaced by the odor of rotting and growing vegetation and the faint fishiness that always seemed to breathe from the rivers and canals of the delta. The tactical radio, its squelch adjusted poorly by Major Britton, hissed and popped constantly. Messages in the clear between Can Tho and the Major announced to anyone with a radio what was going on.

"Roger that," said the Major into the radio microphone that hung down over the helmsman's seat. Tom, the 93 boat's driver, had moved to the aft steering station to escape the Major's body hanging over him and constantly banging into him. "We'll be on the beach by ten hundred. I'll give you a sit rep by eleven hundred. Have the other half of the force on the friendly bank by noon and we'll sweep to you, over."

"Roger. Over and out," came the reply from Can Tho.

"Should we be telling everybody what we are up to?" Ned asked as they approached the northern end of Dung Island, the largest and middle island of the three.

"Calling the operation Lemming Drive should confuse them," said Britton. "The slopes can't find their own asses in the dark, so I'm not worried about them finding us."

"They don't have to find us. They just have to know we're coming," Ned said, but the Major shook his head. Ned noticed that the Major's left hand was cupped over his crotch. Protection or just playing with himself, wondered Ned.

"We've got Charlie trapped on the island. Even if they know we're coming, the ARVN on the south bank of the Bassac'll pick 'em off as they try to cross. Neat. Clean. Army style. Don't get your balls in an uproar, Taylor." Both of the Major's hands were now gripping the back of the helmsman's seat.

"Sir," answered Ned, and again he knew why he hated working with the Army. He remembered what his boss at *Sea Float* had said. That they're different from us, even though we all wear the same color uniforms over here. Maybe it's because there are so many of them that they think it doesn't show if they do a sloppy job. Lieutenant Commander Frederick had been advisor of a RAG group, a river assault group, headquartered on a Vietnamese LST when an Army unit working with the Vietnamese had called in artillery on the ship as it lay at anchor in the middle of the Cua Lon River. Three US sailors wounded seriously and one killed. Only fools could think that a hundred-and-fifty-foot LST could be an enemy outpost, Frederick had written in his casualty report.

"Don't worry so much about radio security. The Charlies around here don't even speak English," Britton added and farted. "First of the day! Sign of good health."

This man isn't even house broken, Ned thought. And I hope he knows the enemy a lot better than he can count.

As the two Swift boats passed to the north of a group of three small islands on the south bank of the river, they swung close to a pair of small sampans tied to some poles in the shallow water near the bank. Fish trap, thought Ned. Tom brought their boat speed down to just under ten knots and Ned called the 70 boat on the radio. "Slowing for local traffic."

"Don't slow for these bastards, Lieutenant; we're on a mission," ordered the Major.

"'We always slow if we can, Major. We do share the river with them. Be nice if they were on our side," Ned replied. Standing in the closest sampan was a naked boy about ten years old pulling bits of trash from the net. Ned thought of the lame VC boy he had carried ashore. I wonder if he ever worked the fish traps on the Dam Doi like this. Or will ever do it again.

"You gook lovers are all the same," the Major said, shaking his head in disgust. "It's why we're losing this war.""

"What is?"

"These bastards understand only one thing. You know what that is?"

"Respect," Ned answered. In the far sampan Ned could see an old man, maybe the boy's grandfather, mending a rip in the monofilament net. The old man smiled a gap-toothed smile and nodded.

WILLIAM W. STANARD

"Respect, shit. It's power. They understand power. Whoever's got it is going to win this war and they know it." The Major put his fingertips on the chart table, keeping his arms stiff. He's going to make a speech, Ned thought as the Major stared out through the pilot house windscreen. "You can't show weakness with them. They don't respect weakness. They respect power and we've got the power right now." He paused. "If you slow down out here in the river, you're telling them that you don't have the power."

Bullshit, Ned thought. "How are you ever going to win their hearts and minds?" he asked the Major, referring to the recent directives from Saigon proposing that the Viet Cong's influence might be lessened by more good works and fewer bullets on our part.

"Yeah. Hearts and minds." The Major laughed. It made an ugly sound. "The truth is, Lieutenant, you grab 'em by the balls and their hearts and minds'll follow. That's the way it really works." The old man and young boy working at their fish trap were now astern of the two Swift boats.

At a nod from Ned, Tom pushed the throttles forward and the 93 boat began to pick up speed.

"Seven zero. Nine three. Tally-ho."

"Yoiks," came the answer.

Ned wrote in his log that the 93 boat passed the northern tip of Dung island at 0945.

"Seven zero this is nine three, over," Ned said into the radio mic when he had lifted his head from the black rubber hood of the radar scope. He glanced at the spinning orange of the depth finder.

"Seven zero. Go."

"Feeter-meter says three to five. Ten thousand to go. Keep to the middle 'til we get there. Let's keep a c-note between us."

Tim Barnes on the 70 boat keyed his mic twice without saying anything, acknowledging the information. A c-note meant one hundred yards.

"Come on back up here," Ned said out the door to Tom.

"I've got the helm."

Tom pulled the disconnect on the after steering, shut the cover over the throttles, and came forward to the pilot house. Ned rested his right hand on the wheel.

"Excuse me, sir," Tom said as he squeezed into the helmsman's seat past the Major who stood, hands on hips, trying to balance without holding on. The Swift was rolling gently at twenty knots, barely planing.

"Yeah, sorry," said the Major, who did not move.

"I've got it, Boss," said Tom once he was settled in the seat. Ned took his hand off the wheel. Tom changed course a few degrees to starboard, keeping the Swift exactly in the middle of the river. Ned checked the radar and was pleased to see the other boat precisely one hundred yards astern. Right on the money, Dog, he thought proudly. We'll show the Major how the Navy does it.

"Seven zero, nine three. Coming up to two grand, over," Ned said and heard the two clicks in answer. The bow of the 93 boat raised slightly as the boat picked up speed to 2,000 RPM for its plunge between the islands. Ten minutes to go.

"Prep fire both banks?" Ned asked the Major.

"Yeah. We'd like some heavy .50 fire for about a half mile before we put them on the beach." The Major poked at the map on the chart table to the left of the helm. Ned noticed his fingernails were bitten. "We'll insert about a mile in. Put 'em on the south island. That's Dung, the big one. The three islands have been off limits for a week now. We won't have to worry about the locals on this operation."

"Anyone live on the island?" asked Ned.

"Probably not. It's used mainly as a staging camp for Charlie for supplies heading down toward Ca Mau, south of the Delta."

There were tiny circles, each one the symbol for a village, dotted across the three islands, but there were no names to identify the circles. Either the villages no longer existed, or their names had simply been erased.

Ned wondered about the no-name villages as they approached the north end of Con Coc Island which was to form the left bank of the slot. Five minutes to go.

"No civilians?" he again asked the Major.

"Shouldn't be. They've been told to keep out," the Major assured him.

The 93 boat started to fire as soon as it entered the slot between Con Coc and Dung Island. Ned stood just outside the port door of the pilot house and looked over his boat. Harris, an unlit cigar clamped between his teeth up in the twin- .50 caliber gun tub above the pilot house, concentrated his fire twenty to thirty yards ahead of the boat on the right hand, southern bank, while Tracy, his Australian bush hat pushed well back on his head, fired at right angles directly into the left or northern bank with the aft .50 caliber.

The Ruff-Puffs, filling all of the deck space on the stern, knelt nervously or sat on their haunches, holding their weapons by the barrels, the rifle butts on the deck. Some of them appeared to be praying, looking down and moving their lips. Even in the bright morning light, Ned could see the red tracers arc purposefully into the all-absorbing green walls of the narrow space between the islands. A moment later the 70 boat entered the slot and began to fire at both banks. Ned noted, once again, that the heavy firing had no visible effect on either bank.

Just like us being in this river or this war, he thought. This heavy fire's supposed to keep the enemy's head down so the troops can be landed easily with no firefight and start their sweep. Prep firing before inserting troops was more for the troops' morale than for any real tactical advantage, Ned knew. Anyone interested in ambushing this raggedy-assed bunch of clerks and farmers just has to wait until they're on the ground and away from the covering fire of the boats before springing the trap.

If Charlie wants to wallop a boat, he only had to set up a remote-controlled ambush. He'll use rockets or launch-bombs fired from a point upstream from where he'll be sitting, only his head peeking out from a hole in the ground. When he gets us lined up with his two aiming stakes, he'll touch two wires together and pow! The rockets come out of the bushes, slamming into the side of the boat. An attack like that is damned near impossible to spot in advance and, in a small canal, almost a guaranteed hit. Even prep firing like we're doing now won't help much because Charlie can let us have it a hundred yards before we ever get to where he's sitting in his hole, waiting for us.

Harris was firing well ahead of the rushing Swift as a precaution against just such an ambush. The gap between the islands had narrowed to a stream barely a hundred feet wide. The stream turned to the right five hundred yards ahead and disappeared into the thick green mat of nipa palms and creepers.

"Just around the next bend," shouted the Major into Ned's ear. "Put 'em in on the right bank." The Major described what he wanted with his hands.

"Yes, sir," Ned acknowledged and looked at Tom who nodded his head.

Ned moved behind Tom and went out the starboard door of the pilot house. He waved his hand to catch Harris' attention. The cigar was still clamped tightly in Harris' mouth, but half of it had been eaten. How does he do it? Ned wondered. By the end of this run the whole cigar'll be gone and Harris will still be smiling. The black gunner stopped firing and leaned forward to listen to Ned. Tracy's piggybacked .50 stopped too.

"We'll stop and wait mid-stream for about ten seconds so seven-zero can catch up. Lay it in pretty heavy and then let up as soon as we're on the beach."

"Got it, Boss," said Harris around the cigar stump as he swiveled the twin-.50s forward and began firing again. He never lights them, either, thought Ned. It's his pacifier. Tracy's .50 began to fire again. It's a real team, Ned thought as he went around the front of the pilot house to the port side, smiling down at CB whose head and shoulders bobbed up out of the chain locker, the forward gunner's position.

CB held an M-60 machine gun at the ready, the copper,

brass, and lead rounds looping over a C-ration can clipped to the side of the weapon to insure a fair lead for the belted ammunition. He had briefed the crew before leaving Can Tho on what to expect and they were ready. Ned stepped into the pilot house and put a grease pencil dot on the chart to indicate their current position.

"Why'd you stop firing?" the Major demanded.

"Telling Harris something," Ned said.

The Major grunted.

Get off my case, Ned thought. You run your Ruff-Puffs, and I'll run my boat.

The twin-.5Os stopped firing just as a flash of white ahead and to the right made Ned look up from his map on the chart table in front of him.

A small sampan was slowly making its way out from the side of the river about one hundred yards ahead of the 93 boat. A man in white shirt and black trousers stood in the stern, sculling with an oar. Amidship sat a woman in a white ao-di.

"Hold it here, Tom," said Ned as he grabbed for the mic. "Seven zero, nine three. Cease fire. We're going to hold here, over." Tracy's stern.50 had stopped firing.

"What the fuck's that?" bellowed the Major, leaning forward to glare through the pilot house windscreen. He was unsnapping the cover on the holster of his .45. As the 93 boat cut her speed, the bow dropped until it was parallel to the water. "'We're not there yet. That boat shouldn't be here. It's a restricted zone. Keep firing," the Major shouted at Ned.

The Ruff-Puffs, thinking that they had reached the insertion point, all stood up and started to move up the side decks toward the bow of the Swift. They stopped just aft of the pilot house. And waited.

Ten yards beyond the first sampan appeared another, then another, until there were at least a dozen in mid-stream heading toward the two now silent and motionless Swifts, each sampan having emerged from the heavy foliage at the sides of the river, each sampan with a single or a couple of Vietnamese dressed in white and black. In one sampan in the middle of the strange flotilla, a sitting woman held a white parasol, the lace trimmed fringe torn and ragged. The man standing, sculling behind her wore what looked to Ned like what remained of a straw planter's hat.

The sampans moved slowly toward the two Swifts in the center of the river. Where the hell'd they come from? wondered Ned. They must have heard us coming and hid in the undergrowth. Lucky they showed themselves when they did. "What's today?" he asked the Major, whose .45 was drawn. The lead sampan was less than fifty yards from the 93 boat.

"Let's go. Keep up the prep fire," the Major said. He pushed past Ned out of the pilot house and stood on the bow next to CB. The lead sampan and two of the others carried tiny yellow and red South Vietnamese flags on short sticks at their bows"

"Kneel down, so Tom can see, OK?" Ned asked from the pilot house door. "What day of the week is today, Major?"

"They shouldn't be here. Start firing again, Taylor. Come on," said the Major, motioning forward with his .45. He didn't kneel.

"Sunday," came the answer, but from Tom who was now standing to be able to see the river.

"That's what's going on. They're heading for church. Or market," Ned said. "We'll have to wait 'til they're clear. There might be others up ahead still hiding from us." The sampans were twenty yards away from the Swifts. Ned was still holding the mic. He keyed it and said, "Seven zero, nine three. We've got some fans on the field. We'll wait until they're clear and then we'll get on with it, over."

"Bullshit. They know they're not supposed to be here. Keep going," the Major said, turning to face Ned. "Start firing!"

"Roger, nine three. Standing by," came the reply from the 70 boat.

"We'll have to wait here, sir," Ned said. He could feel the Major's anger grow as he saw his face become flushed. Here it comes, Ned thought.

"You candy asses start firing, and that's an order!" shouted the Major, his red face inches from Ned's. Ned stepped back from the Major and keyed the mic.

"Blue Shark, this is Abbey November nine three, over." His voice sounded calm. I wonder what I'm going to say to Blue Shark, he thought.

"Give me that fucking mic," the Major said, "and start firing. They know they're not supposed to be here." His left hand reached toward the mic. His right hand held the .45. Ned noticed that the huge, black handgun was aimed at the deck at Ned's feet.

"Sorry, sir, but we've got to tell Can Tho about these civilians," Ned said. He returned the mic to his lips and waited. Come on, Blue Shark, answer me. This guy's going to blow.

"The mic, Lieutenant. I want it, now." The Major's left hand closed around the mic cord. The .45's barrel raised slightly. It pointed somewhere above Ned's legs. "You goddamned gook loving water taxis don't run this war."

Ned didn't move. He's actually going to shoot me, Ned thought. The Swift boats were now surrounded by the sampans. The nervous occupants smiled and nodded first to the 93 and then to the 70 boat. They spoke to the troops crowding the side decks of the 93 boat.

"This is my op," said the Major. "Start shooting. That's an order."

A voice from above them spoke clearly and quietly in the silence.

"Any trouble, gentlemen?" asked Harris, resting on his arms over the edge of the gun tub like a preacher leaning down from a pulpit. His huge right fist held a tiny pistol carelessly pointing at the Major's upturned face. "You were about to make a call, Boss?" Harris' cigar was gone, Ned noticed.

The air was heavy with the promise of rain. Huge thunderheads towered in the sky over the Delta and the islands and the two gray Swift boats surrounded by sampans. As the sampans sculled slowly past, none of the Americans moved aboard the 93 boat.

Ned saw his reflection in the side window of the pilot house, his regulation t-shirt under his fatigue shirt, his dog tags flashing once in the sunlight as the boat rocked slightly, his last

194

name stitched in black thread above his left breast pocket, backwards and to his right in the reflection, his Division pin, Snoopy firing a .50, sitting on a miniature Swift boat, winking from the center of his other breast pocket flap. The face reflected in the window seemed pale, washed out, overexposed in the full noon sun, like a photograph taken with a cheap camera. Ned saw himself holding the mic to his lips. Thunder cracked and rumbled somewhere overhead.

Major Britton held the black spiral of the mic cord in his left fist at a point six inches away from the cigarette pack sized black plastic microphone in Ned's hand. From on board the 70 boat, Dog told Ned later, it looked like the Major was shaking his fist under Ned's nose. Tiny dark blood vessels crisscrossed the fleshy parts of the Major's nose. He had not clipped the hairs that bristled from his nostrils. They flared and relaxed as his red rimmed eyes stared hard at Ned. A mosquito landed on the Major's right cheek and plunged her needle into the tanned skin. The Major had huge pores.

Harris' blue-black face hovered in the air above the Major and reminded Ned of the face of a god in a ceiling fresco. His white eyes, tinged with yellow, stared down at them from his gun tub. His thin lips were tightly shut. The knuckles of his hand enclosing the small pistol were scarred, the clean fingernails of the trigger finger and thumb left long. Harris' naked arms glistened, and his huge hands almost touched as if in prayer. The pistol, a snub nosed .38 police special, the bluing worn along the short barrel missing its front sight, never wavered from the Major's face.

No air moved across the flat brown water of the river. The tall trees and creepers around the two gray boats and the dozen sampans hung heavy and green in the intense and oppressive heat. Thunder cracked once, twice to the north of them.

Ned could see Tom standing at the helm in the cool shadows of the pilot house, staring out at the two officers. His left hand gripped the gray rim of the wheel and his right hand rested atop the twin Morse engine controls. His damp reddish blond hair stuck to his forehead below the blue bandana headband. His helmet was still too large. A scattering of freckles, accented because of his pallor, further emphasized his prominent cheeks. He can't see Harris, Ned thought, and is worse scared than I am.

A single, huge drop of rain fell on the grey top of the pilothouse and almost immediately evaporated. Another raindrop hit Ned's helmet. A third drop splashed on the red-brown hairs of the Majors left forearm.

Ned didn't turn his head, but he could hear the guttural twittering as the Ruff-Puffs gossiped nervously with the occupants of the sampans. The echo of a crash of nearby thunder was drowned out by the hiss and then roar of rain hitting the water and the leaves of the trees as the storm swept over them. Ned watched the Major's left hand open and release the mic cord. The cord thrummed through the air between them, and Ned almost let go of the mic. The Major, staring hard at a point over Ned's shoulder through the downpour, slowly lowered his pistol.

"We're fine, Harris. Just discussing tactics," Ned said as he released his held breath.

The Major said nothing but turned away, holstering his .45, and walked back along the side deck of the 93 boat into the now sodden collection of Ruff-Puffs standing dejectedly on the stern. One of them, a small soldier with almost European eyes, looked past the Major at Ned and smiled. He then raised his head toward the pouring sky and caught the drops of rainwater with his tongue as they poured over his upturned, happy face. There would be no sweep of the island this afternoon. The helos they might have to call on for air support couldn't fly in a downpour like this.

"Thanks, Harris," Ned said, but the gunner was back sitting between his twin-.50s again, staring straight ahead into the downpour.

"Abbey November niner-three, this is Blue Shark, over," the radio said. Ned keyed the mic.

"Blue Shark, niner three. We have civilians in sampans in the mission area during prep fire, over.""

"Niner three, Blue Shark. Any casualties? Over."

"Negative casualties, over," Ned said.

But it was damned close.

CHAPTER TWENTY

Key West

The first floor of the Simonton Street property, owned now by Anonymous Ink, hid behind a blank façade painted black. To the world outside it presented an arched door painted bright green with a Judas hole in the middle. A beautifully detailed sign involving a dragon performing obscene acts with several blond maidens suggested that the building had once been a tattoo parlor offering other recreation on the side as an afterthought.

We knocked, expecting no answer, and we were surprised to hear abuzz and click of an electric latch. I pushed open the door, and the two of us entered a dim anteroom smelling of disinfectant and medicinal alcohol. Around the perimeter of the room were plastic covered armchairs and sofas, all empty. From a door on the opposite side of the room came an electric hum. We crossed to the door and looked into the next room.

A huge naked body, neither of us could tell, even later, whether the mound was female or male, sat hunched over, its back toward us, while a dwarfish, hairy creature with a long, unkempt beard, obviously male, climbed on an oak chair busying itself with a buzzing electric needle. A large tattoo of an upside-down seahorse was emerging across his client's back, its tail wrapped under one armpit, and its nose or muzzle sniffing between the client's buttocks.

"Be with you in a second. I'm almost done this color," said the hairy artist. "Or do you both want Gah, here?"

It was obvious that we had the wrong property, so I tried to take our leave as quickly as possible.

"How much for a small spider under my breast?" Annie asked as she paused at the door of the room as we were leaving.

"In trade or cash?" asked the dwarf, just the top of his head visible from the other side of Gah.

"What's to trade?"

"An hour's work entertaining the clients gets you fifteen minutes under the needle."

"I'll be in touch," promised Annie. "Thanks."

"See you," said the small man. Gah had said nothing.

Our next stop was a tiny cinderblock house on Flagler that sat squarely in the center of a bare, barren lot. The pounded red earth looked like Georgia clay. It may have been someone's idea of paradise, but not my father's, I told Annie as we arrived.

I had collected the rental from the marina and kept it parked in various spots around the neighborhood near The Chimneys, so we were able to travel easily around Key West.

The deed gave the owner's name as Island Paradise. We were so sure that this was not my father's mysterious property that we kept the engine running while I went up to the painted plywood door decorated with gaudy tropical birds and lizards. A young couple had bought the house, we were told by the old woman who answered the door, and she was the cleaning lady. We were asked if we wanted to wait, but we said that we couldn't.

"Tell them we came about the electric fencing. We'll call them later this week," said Annie to the cleaning lady. "We just wanted to make them feel at home in the neighborhood."

As we got back into the cab, Annie pointed out the tree in the back yard hung with green tinsel. It sparkled in the sunlight

as a tiny breeze blew hot air across the red clay
    "Nice place," I said as we drove off.

    65 Von Phister Street was a two-story conch house painted
a dove gray and set deep on its overgrown but tidy lot. Across
the front of the property, next to the road, for there were no
sidewalks on Von Phister Street, stood a tall, thick hedge
covered with tiny red flowers and long thorns. The house was
old, perhaps built soon after the Civil War, and its most
dominant feature was its double porch, one atop the other,
across the narrow front of each floor and down the right side
from front to back. These heavily ginger breaded porches were
completely screened in, giving the house a gauzy, slightly out
of focus look. The dark green front door on the first floor
promised an even deeper quiet within, even though Von
Phister was a residential street far removed from the bustle of
downtown Key West. The number, 65, was carved in a huge
slab of dark polished wood that seemed to be half swallowed
by the kapok tree to the left of the path through the hedge
leading up to the front entrance. A globe shaped clay bell hung
from the old tree and the leather thong invited it to be rung.
    "A friendly shore to be washed up on" I said.
    "Looks well taken care of," Annie said and walked around
the back of the house.
    "Annie," I called out, for she was nowhere to be seen. I
looked again at the huge tree and its carved number 65. The
plank must have been very old, for the kapok tree had almost
completely enveloped it in its corky folds. The clay bell was
decorated with strange glyphs, hawks and dog headed humans,
all very Egyptian, I thought. Out of the corner of my eye, a bit
of yellow fluff moved, and I looked into the flat face of a tough
looking but tiny tawny cat at eye level in the kapok tree. As I
looked at it, it disappeared through a crotch between branches
away from me down the back side of the tree. I was about to
ring the bell when Annie came around the back of the left side
of the house.
    "Don't bother," she said in a low voice. "There's no one

home. The gardner's in back, and he said there's been no one here for a little over a month."

"Does he know who..."

"No. He's hired by a grounds-keeping company here in town. Never gets to see his customers usually. Just keeps this place picked up and the grass trimmed."

"Let's go look around," I said and started up the brick path. Above the dark green front door, the screened transom light was slightly open. The door to the screened porch on the first floor was ajar, not quite latched. I knocked on the front door and then tried the handle. Locked.

I was looking up at the transom light, about to suggest to Annie that we walk around the porch and look through a window, when I noticed the small brass plaque just above the front door. In old fashioned hand engraving, it read simply *Byblos*.

And I didn't quite know what to feel. A sadness and loss of direction had replaced the excitement of the hunt. A father with just a somewhat obscure side to his life had given way to reveal a completely dimensioned and unknown person. I had spent years using as one of the definitions of myself, that I was the son of Cyrus Taylor. Now that Cyrus Taylor was someone else, not the person that I thought he was, my own definition had slipped, leaving me as precarious as ever in the Who am I? department.

Which was maybe why I gave a start when Annie touched my shoulder, and, then, seeing the *Byblos* plaque too, she said, "Oh, Ned. This is spooky, isn't it. That's the name Sis said you were looking for."

"I didn't think about it this way, as a house with a personality, with a life of its own. It's not like the boat, which is just transportation like a car. This is a whole life he had down here," I tried to explain. "This means there was this whole person I didn't know." I wiped my eyes.

"That will be the gardener leaving," Annie said as I reacted to a car door slamming from the alley behind the house. She pushed at the screened door to the porch. "Come on." Around the corner of the porch peeked the tawny cat. "Oh, look, a kitty," Annie said, and the cat disappeared.

We moved across the front of the house, past two tall windows whose sills almost reached the floor. The windows were closed and we could see that the latches were locked. Curtains were drawn, and we couldn't see in. Down the side of the porch there were three windows, and we could see as soon as we turned the comer that the middle one was slightly open at the top. The curtains were pulled aside, and we looked in on a small bedroom. The cat had disappeared.

We both looked through the window for a long time before Annie said, "Come one," again and started to lift the window.

We ducked and entered the room, Annie first. Across from where we stood was a simple iron single bed, with brass fittings on a low headboard. A bright East Indian print covered the single pillow and what appeared to be apricot-colored sheets. A tall but utilitarian oak bureau with six drawers stood to the right of the bed, and a bed side table was on the left with a lamp made out of a huge blue-green bottle filled with beach glass, a brass alarm clock, and a pile of three hardcover books. There were no pictures on the white painted walls, and a simple reed mat covered the center of the pale green painted floor. One door led toward the back of the house, and another led toward the front of the house.

I went through the door toward the back of the house and found myself in a small bathroom containing a claw footed tub, a pedestal basin with ceramic handles, a narrow closet, open and empty, a jalousie window high up on the wall, and a rag rug on the floor. Over the basin was a mirrored medicine cabinet. I hesitated but finally opened the cabinet, knowing that I would find another picture of my father in its contents.

Half a bottle of aspirin. An underarm deodorant stick. Q-tips. A razor and a pack of three blades. A can of Barbasol shaving cream. An almost brand-new green toothbrush and a slightly squeezed tube of Colgate toothpaste. A black plastic comb. A brown glass bottle of Coppertone suntan oil, half full. A pack of Stim-U-Dents. A tiny metal capped glass bottle containing a roll of dental floss. A yellow metal shaker can of powder for athlete's foot. A styptic pencil, half gone. A minute squat bottle of Tiger Balm salve. And a pair of nail clippers in a leatherette case.

Cyrus Taylor. A portrait in objects of little consequence. A life entire.

I shut the cabinet and returned to the bedroom. Annie had gone through the door into the rest of the house, but I hesitated at the table next to the bed. The two top books were recent mystery novels, but the bottom book had no identification on its red cloth cover, simply a gold squiggle of a symbol along the spine. I slipped the red book out from under the other two and opened it. Its title page read simply *Book of the Dead*. A handwritten signature that I could not decipher stood out below the title in blue-black ink. The rest of the book contained excepts from the *Tibetan Book of the Dead* made popular in the late 1960s by Leary and Alpert, the two Harvard professors at the focus of the LSD movement.

Had my father tuned in, turned on, and dropped out? I somehow didn't think so.

At the bottom of the back page of the book was printed simply

EDITED, HAND SET, & HAND PRINTED
KEY WEST IN THE FLORIDAS
1970

"What's that?" asked Annie from the doorway.

"My father was into some unusual reading. This is an LSD tripper's guide, I think, but it's privately printed, so he might have it just because of the edition. Strange." I returned the book to the bedside table. "What did you find?"

"Come see."

Annie had opened the white linen curtains. The front room of the house was almost as starkly furnished as the bedroom, but the walls were hung with black and white photographs sandwiched between panes of glass held together with springs and clips. A long, low couch faced the two front windows, and in front of it squatted what appeared to be a coffee table made of a narrow, six foot long, open mahogany box topped by a thick pane of glass. Inside the box lay an assortment of strange objects. I couldn't make them all out, but I could identify some of them.

"Look at these," I said to Annie who was peering at one of the photographs.

"I know. I've seen them. Do they mean anything to you? They look personal."

I could see a roll of parchment, tired with a dark ribbon. A diploma? A small silver stemmed cup. A crucifix, wooden with a brass or bronze Christ. A large diaper pin mounted with an amber stone. An airmail envelope with no stamp, but an address and a return address, neither of which I could read because of the dimness of the light in the box. A letter opener in the shape of a small dagger. A Toledo steel Zippo lighter case. A cylindrical glass pepper mill, just like...

Then it struck me. These were all objects that I associated with my father, things that he had surrounded himself with throughout his life. The crucifix he had brought back from Mexico and used to hang in his office at home. The pepper mill was a Peugeot from a trip to France in the early sixties and used to have pride of place in the center of the kitchen table in St. Louis. The silver cup was a golf trophy from the Country Club.

Why these objects would be appropriate to decorate the inside of a coffee table, I had no idea. They weren't really special enough or valuable enough to be *objects d'art* in themselves. I could imagine how Sis or I might make a shrine of them in our father's memory (if we were different people than we were, I thought), but I couldn't figure out why our father would see them as so special. I looked up in time to catch the cat staring in at me through the right front window. It quickly dipped out of sight.

"Look at this," said Annie from the corner of the room nearest the door to the center of the house. She was looking at one of the photographs on the wall. I crossed the room and looked over her shoulder. The wall held perhaps twenty photographs, but I could see where another dozen had been taken down, the white shadows of their having been there still visible. In the center of the photograph Annie was pointing at stood my father, wearing a Mexican sombrero. The scene was a nighttime street party illuminated by the photographer's flash. Most of the people were in their twenties or thirties, although a few younger boys and girls could be picked out among the crowd of gaily dressed party goers. All of the people in the photograph seemed to be looking at my father, some with their hands caught in the flash together and some apart as if clapping for him, some with their arms out as if welcoming him, all of them smiling.

My father looked self-conscious but happy. From the trees and buildings in the background I could tell that the scene of the party was Key West. The house might have been in the same neighborhood as the one we were in. My father looked older and frailer than I remembered him. His mustache was gone, too, making this a fairly recent photograph. Next to him, mugging for the camera was a young man, still really a boy, wearing camouflage fatigues, all the rage in the last few years. I thought for a moment I had seen that kid before.

"Was wearing funny hats one of his things?" asked Annie, but her voice was amused rather than cruel. "Is it a family trait I should know about?"

"Not as far as I know" What the hell was he up to? Look at all these young people," I said and then suddenly felt as though I were going to faint. My eyes unfocused, and I felt dizzy. The room tilted, and I needed air. Annie must have noticed because she turned and caught me around the middle and helped me into a low canvas chair a few feet away.

"Are you OK? You look awful!"

I couldn't speak. My pulse was racing, and I felt as if I wanted to throw up, but I couldn't move. I waved my hand that I was OK

"Just sit there. I'll get some water from the kitchen," Annie said and disappeared.

I slumped in the chair and watched as dust motes swam in a single beam of sunlight that came in through the front window on the right. The light through kapok tree outside bathed the rest of the room in a green mist. It was as though I was not myself at all but was standing over me, looking down at my body in the chair. I could see my lips push apart with each breath I exhaled, see my nostrils flare and relax with each inhalation. My hands were on my knees. My eyes were open and blinked rhythmically. I could move my fingers, one at a time, first on my right hand and then on my left. I could tap my toes, left foot first, then right.

And in my head flashed pictures and sounds of the coast of Vietnam, off Vung Tau.

I saw two Swifts heading for the mouth of a small river. One of them was in the channel and the other was weaving its way through a maze of fish stakes. I saw Lee standing in the dim light of the cabin of the 93 boat. I heard Dog's voice over the radio saying the word Fellini over and over. And I heard Annie saying that I had to take it. I had to take it.

"Take it. Here, take it," and a glass of water was being pressed into my hand.

I drank some of the water.

"Thanks. Sorry. I just kind of... I think I must have almost fainted. I don't know why." I was back inside of me again. "I'm OK now."

"You scared me, Ned. I thought you'd lost it. I've never seen a face go so blank as yours just did, like you were gone." Annie hunched down on the floor in front of me as I straightened myself in the chair.

"Well, as a matter of fact, I was gone for a time. Like I was on the outside looking in," I explained, but even that didn't quite say what I wanted it to.

"Where were you?"

"Here, looking down at myself. And in Vietnam. It was the night of that last op, the one I got wounded on. I actually remembered some things I hadn't been able to before." And I described to Annie what I could remember of the Vietnam part.

"What triggered it?" Annie asked.

"That's what's weird," I explained. "I was looking at the picture when I started getting dizzy. I don't get a connection."

Annie stood up and looked at the photograph again. "Nothing here about Vietnam that I can see. Just your dad and a lot of other folks at a party, only he looks kind of silly with that hat on. Most of the people in the picture look normal, around his age. Some younger. Oh," Annie exclaimed, "here's one I've seen," and she pointed to the photograph.

"Describe it. I just want to sit for a bit."

"It's the little girl we saw last night. The one with the Dutch Boy hair, remember?"

"Yeah. She was with the old man."

"I thought it was an old woman," said Annie. "But I don't see her, or him, anywhere."

"Whichever. But the girl's in the photograph, huh?" I said.

"In the background, like in the last row. She's waving. And saying something."

Annie came and sat down again on the floor. She handed me a faded 4 by 5 photo. "I found this one on the floor, sort of half under the rug, like it fell down there."

I put the photograph down without looking at it.

"How are you doing?" she asked me.

"OK, now. I'll be fine," and I leaned forward and rested my arms on my legs. "It's just some of the Vietnam stuff coming back. They told me it might happen after the trauma of being hit. They said it might come back in pieces like that. Just let it come back, the docs said. Don't judge it or feel like you have to make excuses for it. Just accept it."

"Accept what?"

"Oh. Some of the memories might not be of the best sort of things, they said. We might remember doing things that weren't so... so rational or moral or whatever" Sometimes that's why we forget them. To protect us from them."

"Do you think something happened when you were wounded that you don't want to remember?"

"I don't know. They read me what happened over the telephone from Saigon when I got back to the States. It all seemed pretty normal, except that it was a great cock-up. Nothing particularly startling. We took some fire, and a stray round got me. The other boat didn't get hit, but a Vietnamese Swift in the area got blown up by a water mine just inside a nearby river. It was a typical screw up. South Vietnamese thought we were the bad guys and we though they were. Friendly fire, it's called. We spent most of our time over there trying to avoid it."

"Were you able to, most of the time?" Annie asked.

"Most of the time."

The cat was back, staring at me through the same window. This time it didn't disappear.

I felt better and got up again to look at the other photographs on the walls. All of the photographs were of Key West scenes. The Southernmost Point. The lighthouse. Hemingway's house. The Audubon House. An abandoned cigar factory on a back street. One of the Martello towers. A DC-3 parked on the ramp in front of the International Airport. And all of these photographs were of the same sharp focus and same balanced exposure. The paper wasn't a glossy finish, but the images were clear and sharp, the kind I associated with a 4 by 5 press camera and not a 35mm. While the compositions showed no real originality in subject matter, the photographs were all of a professional technical quality. I wondered if my father had taken them. The one Annie had found on the floor wasn't recent, however, and wasn't of the same quality as the others.

It looked like an enlargement of a snapshot. My father in his Navy uniform and mother in a 'forties style dress stood on either side of a handsome young man in tennis whites. In the background was the Casa Marina. It had to have been taken during World War Two.

We explored the rest of the house. Upstairs was the kitchen, not too unusual an arrangement in a conch house, Annie explained. The cooking wouldn't heat up the rest of the house this way. When I had been stationed on the island, I had spent most of my time either at the Stock Island Marina aboard the *New Providence* with Tom Flynn or in a room at the BOQ overlooking Garrison Bight, so I had been in very few conch houses.

Down the hall behind the kitchen there was another

bathroom and another large bedroom, the same size as the one downstairs. All the walls were of white painted plaster, and the wood moldings were stained dark and varnished. The board floors were painted a pale green throughout the house. No pictures or other decorations were to be found in any of the rooms. The kitchen had all of the staples in neat rows on shelves in a spacious larder. The refrigerator, its door propped open, was turned off and empty except for a box of baking soda.

Everything was spotlessly clean and tidy. The beds were made. The floors swept. The windows washed. The wastebaskets empty with oval pieces of white paper in the bottom.

It was as if, except for those two photographs in the living room and the assortment of objects in the glass topped coffee table, my father, or no other person for that matter, had never lived here.

"So this house, this *Byblos*, belongs now to you and Sis," said Annie as we looked out onto the second floor screened porch from the back bedroom. "It's a neat place, isn't it? It even seems to come with its own cat. I can see it out on the front lawn, stalking geckos."

"That's another strange thing. My father didn't like pets. If you had known him, you'd say it was a little spooky. Nothing here's at all like him. He was a normally messy person, not too bad, but not this neat, certainly. It is as if this has all been sterilized. And he never would have had a cat."

"Maybe the kitty isn't his, and maybe he has a cleaning service. They can be pretty impersonal. I have one in Miami, and the lady they send over scours and scrubs everything in my place until there's nothing of me left. But you're right, it looks a bit like a motel room. There's no clutter."

"That's what it is, Annie. You're right. There's no clutter at all. none of the little things that people abandon when they leave a room or a house." I stopped and looked at her back. she was looking out onto the street through the porch screen. "I have something to ask you, but I don't want you to take it the wrong way," I said after a long silence.

"Go ahead. Try me. I don't bite... usually, and then only when asked to."

"Well, you said tonight is your last night at The Chimneys, and now that I have this place, do you want to stay here?" The words came tumbling out in a rush. "There... I've said it!" I was blushing like a high schooler asking for a first date. I noticed her shoulders drop just a bit and thought the question might have disappointed her.

"Depends on your intentions," Annie said in a serious voice, not turning from looking out onto the street. "I'm just getting used to having a brother."

"You could stay a few days before going back to Miami."

"Let me think about it, but I suppose it might be OK, don't you?" Annie looked around at me; I knew she was waiting for my answer.

"Yes."

We walked four blocks down to a Cuban bodega on White Street where we bought milk, two loaves of Cuban bread, assorted cold cuts and cheese, a jar of mayonnaise, a large bottle of white Chilean wine, and a carton of eggs. We talked about what Annie did during the rest of the year, when she wasn't tagging crabs. As we returned up the quiet of White Street, the municipal fishing pier in the distance jutting out into the green shallows of the Atlantic, a large, white garbage truck rattled and banged across White headed north on the street just beyond Von Phister. We turned onto Von Phister toward the house, and, from the more human perspective of walking, I was able to really look at the neighborhood for the first time in some detail.

All of the houses were very different. Some were just better than shacks and some were quite formal, but they all seemed clean and well cared for, each one painted a distinct pair of colors, for none of them were merely white. Their traditional gardens or tropical foliage, depending on their owner's tastes, were all well-tended and lushly watered.

#65, my father's house, my house, *Byblos*, seemed to be

about average for this street, and it didn't stand out at all except for the carved board in the kapok tree. From the next street over I heard a dog bark and the rattle of the garbage truck.

Annie and I walked side by side on the north side of the street until we were in front of the house. The tawny cat watched us, this time from inside the screen up on the second-floor porch. As we watched, it batted at a flying bug with its right paw, pinning it against the screen. It curled its claws around the bug and popped it into its mouth, the bug buzzing loudly and then stopping. The cat then withdrew from the edge of the porch and disappeared.

"It's like a wood spirit or something," observed Annie. "I bet your dad didn't have him as a pet but the other way around."

"The neighbors must have known my father," I said, looking around. "Even if he were only here occasionally. This is such a tidy little neighborhood, I'm sure everybody kept track of everybody else's business."

"Actually, I grew up in a neighborhood like this in Lake Forest," said Annie. "There were the grand houses, out on Bayberry and Deerpath and so on, but most of the town was little neighborhoods like this. Big and little houses all mixed in. Takes a long time to make a neighborhood like this."

"I'm going to ask," I said, put my grocery bag down in front of the path to #65, and headed across the street toward a two-story shotgun house painted light blue with ocher trim

"No. You can't," said Annie. She dumped her bag down quickly and ran after me, catching me as I approached mid-street. "I watched him from upstairs. He's too..."

A middle-aged man with salt-and-pepper hair looked up from his garden work, and I knew why Annie did not want me to speak to him. He stood on the lawn side of a low hedge made of woven cactus leaves. He was continuing the weave higher, braiding the long yellow and green leaves into an impenetrable mesh. He had a thin, well clipped mustache, huge ears, and bright blue eyes. His arms and legs were skinny, but he had a wonderful pot belly that he balanced carefully in front of his straight back between a faded canvas belt on his navy shorts and an immaculate white t-shirt that was two sizes too small. As we approached him, his navel peeked out, and he tugged his t-short down over it.

"Interesting hedge," I said as he looked up at us nearsightedly. In the brief silence that followed, the garbage truck rattled and banged on the next street. I could feel Annie stiffen next to me. It was the first time I had known her to be out of control. Her mirth seemed to bubble up out of her.

"Keeps in what needs to be kept in and vice versa," he said in a mild Southern accent. Virginia, I thought.

"We're staying over across the street," I said and held out my hand. "I'm Ned and this is Annie."

"I saw you arrive." His navel peeked out again. He tugged down on the t-shirt. "Guests?"

"Going to stay for a few days. Just thought we'd introduce ourselves."

"I'm Clayton Person," he offered. "Friends of his?"

"Friends?" I said, hoping Clayton Person would elaborate. I wanted to know how his neighbors might have regarded my father.

"Friends of Cyrus Taylor." His navel winked at us before he could tug the t-shirt over it. Annie gave a little coughing sound and turned away toward #65. I could hear the garbage truck change gears. "He'll be here soon, I should think. He's about due. I take care of Pug for him when he's gone. Keep the dish filled and all."

"Pug?"

"His cat. Actually, it's not his. It just came with the house, but the little devil keeps the palm rats under control. He's looking at us now."

I looked across the street to where Clayton Person was pointing and could see the tawny cat stalking stiff legged through the vegetation under the front of the porch, staring at us sideways. "We sort of met," I said.

"Pug can't wait 'till he gets back. Always brings him something, like a catnip mouse. Wonder what it'll be this time," and Clayton Person held the bottom of his t-shirt to keep his navel from peeking out.

"I'm Cyrus' son, Mr. Person. Actually, my father passed away last month. In St. Louis."

"I'm sorry... really sorry," said Clayton Person, his mouth remaining open. A single tear fell from his left eye onto his sun-tanned cheek and stayed there. "I...," and he turned abruptly and went in a shuffling run up the walk toward his house, disappearing through the screen door, letting it slam shut behind him.

Annie had turned back toward Clayton Person's house, her amusement squelched by his obvious sorrow and shock. "Come on," she said. "He'll be OK. Maybe they were good friends."

"I think I told him too quickly. I should have kind of eased into it." I turned toward #65 in time to see the yellow cat disappear under the porch. "Damn. I forget how other people take these things. It's almost like I don't feel things anymore, you know?"

"I think so, but you didn't say anything wrong, really," counseled Annie. "It just caught him by surprise. Let's go put these things away."

The rattle and bang of the garbage truck had come around the comer onto our block of Von Phister. We stood across from #65 and watched it pull up to a pile of brown paper sacks and palm fronds two houses north. The younger of the two men hanging on the back jumped down and tossed the bags into the maw at the back. The other man pulled the hydraulic lever, starting the crushing process. The high-pitched whine quickly dipped to a low moan, and the truck lurched ahead and started to gain speed, heading for the next pile, about five houses beyond us up the street.

Just then a dark brown shape streaked from where the pile of trash had been to a spot in the street in front of the white truck's front tires and froze, turned a complete circle, and started again across the street.

"Fuggin' rat," the man on the near side of the truck cursed. "Git it, Fammy. Pop the sucka!"

The truck's engine whined louder and the palm rat just

slipped from in front of its tires and made it to the center of the street. Annie's hand came up in front of her mouth.

"The kitten... Stop!" she shouted, and we both watched as the tawny yellow cat, in full pursuit of the terrified palm rat, shot out toward the truck, seemed to bump once against the side of the right front tire and fell back to the edge of the street in a confused tumble. Annie started across the street with me right behind her as the garbage truck rattled past.

The truck continued up the street in low gear, shifted to the next higher, and braked to a stop at the next pile of trash. The two men on the back went about their work, not giving a look back in our direction. I tried to stare them into some response, but they didn't seem to notice me standing in the middle of the street, my hands at my sides, fists clenched.

Annie had disappeared and the cat, too, was gone. Annie's grocery bag still sat next to mine on the edge of the street. I picked both up and headed toward the front porch. I deposited the two bags there are went around to the back of the house. Annie was kneeling, bent over something on the ground next to the house where, under a tiny lean-to, sat a bowl of water and some dried cat food in a tin dish.

"The kitten... Pug," she said, and I could hear the tears in her voice. "He made it here OK, but... I don't think he's going to..."

I looked down at the tiny lump on the ground. There was no blood, just a ragged yellow bundle of fur, its mouth opening and closing, like a fish out of water. As we watched, its tiny eyes blinked twice, stayed open, and its mouth stopped moving. It never made a sound.

"I can't," Annie said and got up from in front of the dead kitten.

"I'll do it."

"See you upstairs," she said and turned toward the front of the house. "Thank you, Ned."

I poked around in a small shed at the back of #65 and found a garden trowel. I walked once around the house and settled on a spot under a bush with a shower of tiny yellow and red flowers. I dug carefully, making sure that the hole was deep enough, trying not to cut the roots of the bush.

I had a hard time keeping digging. I would stop for a time and just rest my fists on the ground on either side of the hole, staring into the rich black dirt. then, when I would dig again, it was as if a great sadness settled over me, weighting me down so that I would have to stop again.

The third time I had to stop digging, I realized that I was out of breath. Tears were now flowing down my face and splashing into the dirt and onto my hands and the trowel. By the time I had picked up the dead Pug, I couldn't hold back the sobs any longer. As I knelt and placed the tiny yellow cat in the hole, I could feel the dam burst inside and was just able to cover him over and put two bricks on top when I had to sit back on the ground, against the house, and weep.

Annie must have heard me because, the next thing I knew, she was sitting next to me, her arm around my shoulder, saying nothing, holding me.

There I was in Key West, a thousand miles from home, burying a dead, wild creature that hadn't belonged to my father any more than he had belonged to me, and I was suddenly, finally able to cry for the death of my father. Somehow the cat's meaningless death had released in me the sorrow I had been unable to feel for my father's death. I couldn't see the connection yet but felt grateful for it.

I sat against the house with a girl I hardly knew and let hot tears wash down my face and sobs shudder from deep inside of me. I was grieving at last and couldn't stop even if I had wanted to. For the first time since the boy on the bow had lain there bleeding to death across my lap up that canal in Vietnam, I was in the grip of a response I could not control.

I was crying for my dead father, for this dead cat, for the dead boy on the boat, and somehow for part of me too.

It was midafternoon when we drove back to *The Chimneys*, and Annie let me talk or be silent according to my whim. We returned to #65, to *Byblos*, Annie's collapsed specimen boxes, nets, and record books filling the back seat of the car, a box of live, skittering crabs balanced on each of our laps, her canvas suitcase on the front seat, and a suit bag of dresses over the front seat. My canvas boat bag lay on the floor at my feet.

An hour later, as the rain fell in single huge drops at first and then more quickly, turning the blacktop of the street at first oily and then jet black, Annie and I sat on the screened porch on the first floor with the windows wide opened behind us and drank cups of rich Cuban coffee. Thunder heads had started to build out over the Gulf Stream around two, and, by four, the heat was pressing down like an anvil, crushing the energy out of us. The rain at five came as a relief. The coffee, although hot, gave us the caffeine energy to keep going. I had taken my bag up to the upstairs bedroom while Annie had hung up her suit bag in what had been Dad's room on the first floor.

Annie wore a pair of old jeans and a bikini top. I wore khaki shorts and a blue chambray shirt. I wrote holding the typewriter on my lap, page after page, the story flowing easily, almost telling itself. I had just gotten to the place where the Army is giving us instructions to drop mortar rounds in on what might be a friendly outpost.

Annie sat cross legged on the porch floor, pouring through two photograph albums. One of them I had found high up and in back on the shelf in the front hall closet. It had both my father's and my mother's initials on its dark leather cover in gold. The other album was mine; I had carried it all through Vietnam and had brought it down from St. Louis because it had some river photos in it I wanted for my writing. Annie was looking through my album, and occasionally she would hold up a picture. I would try to identify the subject.

"The Lincolns, friends from St. Louis, at the christening of their younger daughter's baby, I think. Susie was about three years, no, just a year younger than I. Before I left my ship here in the States, Dad told me she had a baby. He was kind of surprised I hadn't gotten an invitation to her wedding. He sent me the picture to me over in Vietnam."

"Go out with her?"

"A bit. We were kind of pushed into it by our folks. Why?"

I asked.

"That would explain why you didn't get an invitation," Annie offered. "Did you two, you know... go steady?"

"No, we didn't," I said, looking up from my typewriter. "We would have, I think, but we went just far enough for Susie to tell her mom and her mom to tell my dad."

"Sorry if I'm being nosey, but every piece I asked you about has been an unfinished painting, a broken piece of something really nice that you collected and put away. Like you were going to mend them some day. All your photos are kind of incomplete."

I rested my hands on the keys and listened.

"You have all these unfinished things around you. You're like one of my crabs who digs a hole in the sand or dirt and keeps a little heap of goodies just outside, kind of a refuse pile that he can pull in on him for protection. Every once and a while you see one of these little guys skittering around and going through this pile of stuff, moving it around, sorting through it, like it was looking for something it had misplaced, you know?"

"And I'm like that?" I asked, smiling.

"Kind of, only a bit neater."

"How so?"

"Instead of a pile of things and stuff and memories and people, you have all that in jour photos and in your stories. Like the one about the Major who wanted you to fire at the people in the sampans," explained Annie, her hands resting palm up on her knees, Buddha style. My photograph album lay open on her lap.

"I'm not with you," I said. "In what way is that story unfinished? I'm still proofing it, but the story itself is done. I got to the end of what happened, and I stopped writing."

"That's what I mean. You left a lot out."

"What?"

"You left the photographer... you left you out. It's like these photographs. There's always someone missing, someone who needs to be in there to make the picture complete. The person who recorded the event in the first place. If you take them yourself, if you're the photographer, it's OK 'cause you look at them later and fill in your part because you were there." Annie pointed in through the open living room window into the darkness inside. "Remember the picture of your father in the giant sombrero? Who took it?"

"I have no idea."

"Wouldn't it make experiencing the photograph more complete if you knew who took it and why?"

"Yes, I guess, but how does this connect to my writing?" I asked. I put the typewriter down on the floor. "I'm going to get some more coffee. Want some?" I ducked in through the window.

"No, thanks."

"Keep talking. I can hear you." I climbed the stairs to the kitchen, tip toeing so I could hear her voice. It was soft, easy to listen to, and it was telling me things I had not thought about or heard before.

"I really like your writing, Ned, and you tell a good story. All the Navy stuff is interesting and all, even to someone who's never been in a war. But when you get to the good part, the part where your character, Ned, can react to something happening or somebody, you disappear. Or, rather, Ned's reactions disappear. Like this." She paused, I poured the last of the pot of coffee into the small white double sized demitasse cup, and Annie started to read.

"He stood looking at Ned, his hands on his hips. 'Bring you all back here in a couple days or so or maybe send you to Ben Tre. We'll see.'

The two naked men faced each other, the Major aggressive with his hips forward and Ned just waiting.

'You Navy types aren't afraid of spending the night out, are you? It'll be just like kiddie camp.'

'Looking forward to it,' said Ned, forcing a smile, and he wrapped his towel around his hips and started for the showers. 'See you onboard about 0630, sir. Underway at 0700, as planned?'

'Yeah,' said the Major who then smiled and farted."

I stood in the window, looking down at her reading. Her silver dollar sized granny glasses sat on the end of her nose, the pages of the story scattered over her lap. I remembered standing in another window looking down, unobserved, at another girl, sunbathing.

"What was Ned thinking?" Annie asked, and she looked up in time to see me standing there, watching her.

I walked through the window, careful not to spill my coffee.

"He's just waiting, is all. The ball's in the Major's court. Ned just wants to see, no, he has to wait and see what's next," I answered as I sat in my chair again, putting the coffee on the floor in front of me"

"What I want to know, as a reader, Ned," and Annie's glasses flashed as she looked up at me as she shuffled the story back together again, "is what Ned thinks when he's looking at this other naked man."

"In the story?"

"Yes. This Major guy has his... his hips thrust out ahead of him like some half-goat, half-human. Surely Ned must think something when he's presented with it that way. It's so direct a threat to him. Almost a come-on, let's fight. Know what I mean?"

"Ned's kind of shy about his body, right?" I answered. "So, he would be very put off by this aggressiveness. He would just see what way the scene was going. Then he would react."

"I know, but what actual thoughts go through his mind as... as he looks at this other man's… thing poked out there in front like that?"

"I guess he thinks about whether the Major's is bigger than his, for one thing."

"Is it?" Annie's face darkened, even under her tan, but she was smiling, looking down at the papers in her lap.

"It never comes up in the story… ooops!"

"Ned!" Nancy laughed despite herself.

"Sorry. That was bad."

"I'm serious about this."

"So am I. If the size of their plumbing isn't part of the scene, then he might think about it as any man might, being in a scene like that, a stand-off, but the reality of whose is bigger just doesn't matter. Does it. To the reader, I mean?"

"What matters to me, is what actual thoughts and feelings and emotions go through Ned during the scene. That's why I read about people, to experience what they have experienced. Even if it's private and strange, I want to know all of his thoughts."

"How do you mean, all?" I asked. No one had ever talked about writing like this with me before.

"I want to know what Ned thinks about the Major's body, as he looks at him standing there. I've been in a shower room alongside another woman and wondered about her body. Compared it to mine. And I want to know if a man does the same thing," Annie spoke slowly, earnestly.

"In the story?"

"Or in real life! Did this happen? Did you ever meet the Major in the shower room for real in Vietnam?"

"The Major's real. The shower room's real. But Ned and the Major were never there at the same time," I said after a pause. I had to think back to Vietnam, and it took a moment to focus on the historical place and on the fictional one.

"So, when the two of them meet in this scene, how do you know what to tell about. How do you know what happens or doesn't?"

"I put Ned into a scene, and... This'll sound kind of strange, Annie."

"Go on; I'm listening. You put him in a scene, and then what?"

"He just does what he would do. If I've created him well enough, he'll have a life of his own in the scene and will act the way Ned would act."

"What makes you decide to tell as much or as little as you do about what Ned is thinking?"

"I actually try to stay as much as possible outside of Ned consciousness, and I do that for a reason. The reader should be like another character in the story. Think of yourself as an invisible, non-participating bystander. I let you know as much about Ned as that bystander would know from being there."

"Is that enough?"

"It gives a lot of realism to the story, I think."

Annie looked at me and took her glasses off. "And the Major? How do you animate him if you have put him in scenes he's never been in. Or the real-life Major was never in."

"Same thing. If he's written right, I can give him his lead and he'll follow it, saying all the right things, doing what the Major would do if the scene were... history."

"You mean real?"

"No, not precisely. History," I answered.

"The scene is real, in a way, even if it never actually happened in history. In some cases, it's more vivid than what happened over there. More involving, in any case. More real. The scene spends more time in my head rehearsing and replaying itself than anything else in my life. There are events in the story more real to me than, say, my father's death, Sis and my coming down here, or the two of us right now."

Annie arched her eyebrows. "So, your Major can be more real than I am?"

"No, you are a most tangible presence in my life right now," I answered with a smile, and immediately wished that I hadn't made such a declaration. Annie's body stiffened, and she dropped her eyes from mine. Was she embarrassed? I couldn't tell. I picked up my coffee and took a long swallow. "Anyway," I began again, "I've spent a lot of my life in the past month or so inside the stories. Most of the time it's been more real in the stories than in real life, although there are exceptions."

"I meant to ask you about them at some point. Do you have an exception at home in St. Louis?" Annie was looking down at the papers in her lap when she asked the question. "Sis didn't mention anyone when I asked her if you were... dating anyone in particular."

Annie waited for me to answer. "I'm not having sex with anyone, if that's what you're asking."

"Why do so many relationships seem to build on sex?" she persisted. Annie and I sat across from each other and waited for an answer. "Can a normal couple have a relationship that doesn't rely on sex?" she asked.

That one I could try to answer, so I said, "We seem to,

don't we?"

"Do we?" Annie asked as she got to her feet, went to the porch edge, and looked out across the street. "I've been so afraid it would come to this. Just asking the question seems to make it part of what there is between us. Sis told us that we were going to be like brother and sister, but there's that tension always there." She leaned forward on the porch rail, her arms straight, staring into the gloom. "It's like some animal in the attic... really, I think it's probably in the cellar... just sitting there, breathing in the dark, waiting."

It seemed preferable for me to just sit there and wait, too. I even tried holding my breath.

I carried my typewriter into the upstairs bedroom. "I'm going to take a shower. What do you want to eat for dinner?" I called down the stairs.

"You choose," Annie's voice answered. "I'm too beat to think, and you know this town as well as I do."

"We've tried French" How about seafood?"

"I'd love it. Give me half an hour," and I heard her door shut.

We sat across from each other at a porch table at Anthony's Fish Market after spending the walk from #65 sightseeing. We had stopped at the chain link fence surrounding the abandoned Casa Marina Hotel, and I had told Annie how my mother, pregnant with me, had played cards and had tea there waiting for my father's ship to come back to port during World War Two. We had watched the sun set from the Southernmost Point at the end of Whitehead Street and had crossed to the south side of the street to avoid passing too close to the oldest bar in town, El Papagayo, a depression era undertaker's parlor that had been reborn as a biker's bar.

The waiter at Anthony's came to the table and took our drink order. In his left ear he wore a gold earring.

"Does the earing in that ear mean he's spoken for or is

available?" Annie wondered aloud. "Is it like the hibiscus behind a Tahitian girl's ear?"

"I can't keep track. Probably why I don't wear one. Even when I was stationed here, I had to watch out which bars I went to. I ended up hanging out at a little place called the Tide's Inn over near Garrison Bight. It was a real beer bar, complete with pickled eggs and twenty-five cent drafts, run by a guy named Bernie from Brooklyn," I said. "I watched the moon landing from there. And felt fairly safe."

The waiter brought our carafe of wine and left us a pair of menus; I poured for the two of us.

"I've only got a week before..." Annie began.

"Wait," I stopped her. "Don't say it. I know you have to go back for classes, but I don't want to deal with it just yet. I'm between lives right now, and I like having you here. Very selfish, but humor me, OK?"

"I'm not sure I understand."

"I'm not sure I do either, but what you said about the unfinished photographs or stories this afternoon has been bugging me. I think I'm beginning to get my head around the idea. See, I'm kind of suspended in the air, between where I was, Vietnam, and where I am supposed to be, St. Louis, Missouri. I haven't landed. I'm circling, waiting for clearance. It's like I can't raise anybody on the radio. 'Hello, hello... Anybody there? This is Ned Taylor, requesting permission to land. Hello? Hello?'"

"You don't need anybody else's permission..."

"Probably not," I interrupted, "but right now it's very important that I get it anyway."

"How do I give you permission to... land? Unless, of course, you are taking this metaphor to new depths and are suggesting that you are going to land on me..." Annie said, and I listened for the same anger I'd heard earlier in the afternoon.

"No. Not at all. Never even crossed my mind," I back-pedaled furiously. "By getting permission to land I mean being accepted for who I am right now. Not as a returned Vietnam Vet, wearing his American Legion or VFW cap to all the picnics and parades. And not the half-hippy, half-preppy someone I was before Vietnam, but just what everybody sees in front of them."

"Everybody sees someone different. I'm sure you see a different me than the one who's inside."

"Here's where I need help." I leaned forward across the table and touched the fingers of my right hand to the back of Annie's hand holding the stem of her glass of wine. "What do you see, for instance?"

Annie thought for a full minute before answering. I sensed that she wanted to pull her hand away, but she was polite enough to keep it there.

"I see a man who needs other people or another person near him. People or someone to act as a mirror, so he can see his own reflection..."

"Go on," I prompted.

"I see a writer who has escaped into his writing enough so that it has become almost more real than his life..."

"Yes."

"I see someone I would take as a lover in a second, if I was in the market for a lover at the moment..."

"OK." and I was surprised my voice worked at all at that point.

"And I see someone who has defined himself by others for his entire life and is finding out that that doesn't work very well. You have stepped out of the system. Or the system has thrown you out. In either case, all of the others by whom you've defined yourself for so long no longer apply. Your dad's dead. Your sister brought you as far as she could and has returned to her life with Jim. All of the women in your life have either moved on or no longer need you. And you are feeling very much adrift. Unable to land. The metaphor is equally valid for flying a plane or sailing a boat." Annie paused. "How am I doing?"

"Keep going." I had released her hand by now, and I was settled forward on my elbows, my hands under my chin, listening as I came to life in her words. She was no longer looking directly at me. I wondered for how long she had been thinking of me like this, for her perceptions hadn't come to her on the spur of the moment, only in response to my question of who she saw sitting here across from her.

The waiter returned and hovered long enough to gather an order for two plates of shrimp, a large green salad, and a side order of red beans. As he disappeared through the swinging door into the kitchen, Annie looked over my shoulder, and the expression on her face changed.

"What is it?" I asked "You look as though you've seen the proverbial..."

"It's the little girl again. She's coming this way."

I turned in my seat and looked along the aisle between the tables. The little girl with the Dutch Boy haircut was walking in the direction of our table, but she wasn't looking at either of us. She was perhaps eleven or twelve years old, dressed in the same bib overalls and T-shirt we had seen her in the night before on Duval Street. This time her t-shirt had Mickey Mouse with a burst of light behind him. Only his ears and the top of his oval eyes peeped over the bib. She wore red, high-top basketball sneakers and her hair was held in place on each side with a red plastic barrette in the shape of a bow.

"Hi," she said as she passed our table.

"Hi," answered Annie, and the little girl sat down with a young couple and a baby in a basket on the floor two tables away. The couple had the identical roasted skin tones of sunburned tourists. He wore a brightly flowered shirt, and her straw planter's hat sat firmly centered on her head. They both looked exhausted but happy. The little girl fussed for a moment with the sleeping baby in the basket and then sipped her orange drink through a straw, holding the large glass with both hands.

"She's in the picture of your dad in the sombrero."

"I'd love to know if she knows what was going on. It must have been last New Year's because she looks about the same age," I said. "Think I could ask her?"

"I will if you like," offered Annie.

"Please."

Annie got up and walked over to the couple's table. I watched as she pointed back toward our table and gestured with her hands, smiling as she spoke. Her body moved easily, and she seemed comfortable in conversation with the couple. The little girl, I noticed, said very little, looking up at Annie with big eyes, cocking her head to one side and then the other, considering carefully what Annie was saying. Finally, the couple and Annie were all three focused on the little girl and seemed to be waiting for a response. I could not hear what she said, but Annie waved goodbye to the little girl as she returned to our table.

"They don't really look like conchs," I said as Annie sat. "As I watched you over there, I wondered if they were even here last New Year's Eve."

"The couple are tourists, but she's not. Her name's Cassie, and she's their babysitter. They hired her through the *Pier House* front desk to watch their baby while they went out for dinner, but she was so pleasant they brought her and the baby along."

"So does Cassie remember Dad?"

"We'll find out. I asked her if I could talk to her again tomorrow. Her mom works at the *Pier House* desk during the day, and Cassie'll be on the beach by nine."

I tried to pay for both of our dinners, but Annie would have none of it. She split the check down the middle, told me the amount I owed, paid with a credit card, and she left the tip in cash.

"For giving me a place to stay, it's the least I can do," she explained. We made it an early evening, walking back to #65 down the main streets of town, window shopping and talking about Annie's experiences as a marine biologist. It was ten o'clock by the time we reached Von Phister Street. As we approached the spot where the little cat had been hit, we slowed, and I reached out and took Annie's hand.

"Thank you for what you did this afternoon," I said. Whether my taking her hand or my thanking her had made her uncomfortable, I could not tell, but Annie suddenly seemed tongue-tied and tense.

"Sure." She quickened her pace and turned up the path to the house. "You were upset."

I let go of her hand and fell in line a few paces behind. She was silhouetted for a moment in the light from the single globe on the porch. Her hair was down over her shoulders. I watched her long legs through the thin cotton of her skirt as she opened the screen door and walked into the front hall. She stopped in front of the tall mirror on the left, raised both of her bare arms above her head, and stretched like a cat. Her breasts moved easily under the thin cotton. "I'm thinking I'm going to call it a day, Ned," she said as I walked in from the porch. "Dinner was great." She yawned luxuriously and then caught herself. I might take it as an invitation, she must have thought. "Sorry, that was rude."

"Nightcap," I suggested.

"No, thanks. I had a great time, but I'm out of steam."

Annie's message to me seemed clear. She did not want me as a complication in her life at this moment, so I had to be content to play the role of friend or brother.

Our eyes met in the mirror" Annie grinned, so I smiled back.

"Curiouser..," I said.

"...and curiouser..," she continued.

"...said Annie," I teased and went up the stairs.

I could hear her getting ready for bed downstairs as I sat on the second-floor porch with a glass of wine. A moon had started to peer through the black clouds out above the Atlantic. A single set of lights, two white and a green, indicated a ship tucked in close to the Keys, headed south against the Stream. A crow in the top of a royal palm at the corner of street cawed once and was answered by a single caw from further down the block. From below I heard Annie step out onto the porch through the window from Dad's old room. I followed the slight sounds of her movements as she eased into the canvas chair I had sat in this afternoon. I sat in the dark and listened as she settled herself. A clink of china on wood told me she was finishing what was left of my afternoon coffee.

Out at the edge of the Stream, the moon illuminated the ship for a moment, and I could see that it was a lightly loaded tanker, only half in ballast, heading back to the Gulf Coast. I had steamed those waters when I was on the *Calcaterra*, so for the next five minutes I was on her bridge, taking the danger bearings of Sand Key Light, marking the minutes until we could make the turn for our run to the northwest and the Gulf, when Loggerhead Light in the Dry Tortugas would bear just aft of amidships. I could imagine the heavy thrum of the diesels, more felt than heard. I could see our wake from the wing of the bridge playing hide-and-seek with the moon's bright trail.

I took a drink of the wine and remembered the feeling of awe I had felt as Officer-of-the-Deck on those night passages. As one hundred and fifty men slept below, with the help of five other men, I had guided our ship along the invisible ocean paths. And I had known exactly my duties and who I was.

CHAPTER TWENTY-ONE

Ben Tré, September 5, late afternoon

Indian Territory was what they called those parts of the river where they might get ambushed, and Indian Territory went right up to the eastern edge of Ben Tré where the river dog- legged first right past the RF-PF outpost and then left where the Route 5 bridge to Saigon once crossed. The local watermen had put fish traps sticking out where the stone bridge supports used to be. About a month earlier one of the patrol boats ran up on the sharp end of a steel girder underwater and it gouged a two-foot hole in the aluminum hull. The boats had to watch themselves near that bridge.

The story went that Ben Tré was where the war really started in the South. There was a woman, a professor, who tried to get the French kicked out. The French locked the woman up, and, when she died, her friends used her death as an excuse to activate the Viet Minh. They were the political ones and the Viet Cong were the soldiers. It was strange to Ned to be in the town where the war had started almost twenty years ago.

It was a small French colonial town, all the red roof tiles, low stucco buildings, green lawns, and children playing along the river and up and down the canals. Almost like there wasn't a war. Kids would stop, all smiling, and wave at the boats, usually two at a time going along just fast enough not to throw a wake, engine exhausts steaming in the bright morning air. The boats had 12-cylinder diesels, and even with the engine hatches closed we could hear them up the river for miles, growling or purring or roaring like restless animals in a zoo. We could tell when something was up by the change in the sound they made.

At the end of a mission the boats would come into town one behind the other, going full bore until the last possible minute, cutting their speed suddenly, the big waves they carried behind them catching up and giving them a last push, wallowing through the right hand turn at the outpost and then the left-hand bend at the fish traps near the old bridge site. They had to go too slow once they got that close to the town but at least they were out of Indian Territory and almost home.

They always wanted at least ten knots on when they were underway, so if they came under fire there wouldn't be that bad couple of moments when the boat squatted down in the water, their throttles all the way open, and the boat going nowhere. The noise of an ambush would already have started, engines and machine guns and the shouting. Usually, the gunner up in the twin-.5Os, a turret mounted above the pilot house, would hear or see it first and open up. His barrels stuck out just over the pilot house door so the first they'd know of it would be the physical slap of their own guns, not the sound of Charlie's. Usually there would be some splashes in the water around the boat; occasionally there would be the smoke trail of a B-40 or one of their homemade rockets, kind of a flat arc from one side of the river across to the other, just high enough so it would hit the boat just below the pilot house. If the boat driver saw the rocket smoke then he knew he was OK.

He would try to grab the radio and get his voice down low enough, so he didn't sound like the new skippers, their voices high and worried and scaring the others a little because they knew what the virgins were going through, and the virgin would tell whoever was controlling his radio network where he was and how bad it was.

When a radio transmission would come in from a boat

caught in an ambush all the other drivers would listen carefully to what was going on behind the voice. One time there was a real slow pounding of a .51 caliber, one of those Chinese machine guns on wheels with a slow rate of fire like they have on display at the base in Vung Tau, just pounding away behind the skipper's voice, chewing away at them. The other drivers could hear it behind his voice, and it frightened them because they didn't think that there was a machine gun that big in the lower Delta. The .51 scared everyone and they always listened for them when they picked up an ambush on the radio. Some of the boat drivers hated going south of the Cua Lon River because they had been the ones who had heard and remembered the sound of that .51 down there that one time.

It was near the middle of the rainy season and Ned had the 93 boat, carrying an American advisor and twelve child-sized Montagnard mercenaries, and Nash had the 127 boat and another squad of 'Yards, both returning from an afternoon security sweep of an island downstream. One of his crew took a photograph that day showing Nash and Ned standing back on the stern of his boat next to the mortar. Ned's hair is cut shorter than Nash's, and Ned has the beginnings of a mustache. They are wearing camouflaged fatigues, flak jackets, and jungle boots. Nash is holding a .45 and Ned has a .38 in a holster on his belt. The 'Yards in the background of the photograph look like kids dressed up in Army costumes. Nash and Ned are posing and smiling and don't look like there's a war going on at all.

The two boats cut speed together and rumbled slowly in single file through the right-hand bend of the dog-leg on the edge of Ben Tré. The 'Yards were Meo hill people and hated all Vietnamese but especially the Viet Cong who would come into their villages and take their food and any medical supplies that they had. The 'Yards were great fighters, hating the Vietnamese the way they did. Ned thought they were the ones who started that business of collecting ears because the American advisers would pay them for a dead VC only when they turned in a right ear.

Jimmy Bascom, their American advisor, a young kid with a

Midwest accent and a real baby face, had just given the order for the soldiers to clear the live rounds from their weapons. Nash and Ned had worked with Jimmy before and they knew that he was good but had pretty much gone native, eating and living with the 'Yards and all, and sure enough there they were gathered around him like campers around a counselor at story time and he was explaining something to them in Meo, that funny kind of language they spoke. Ned was talking to his gunner up in the twin-.5Os and reminding him to clear his guns when Ned felt and then heard the crack of a single bullet.

Jimmy went down in a heap, his teeth bared and his eyes shining white in the almost dark, his canvas hat with its bright red band rolling across the deck and down and away into the brown water. He didn't speak or cry out and his eyes stayed open. The 'Yard squad leader ripped Jimmy's shirt open from the top on down to the bottom button which was some kind of an animal's tooth, and another 'Yard put his hand over the neat, black hole of the chest wound. No one spoke. Ned didn't know any more to do than the 'Yards so he stayed put in the pilot house looking out through the windshield onto the bow.

Ned could see the squad of 'Yards chambering rounds in their M-16s, getting ready to shoot back if they could find something or someone to aim at. "Everyone, hold your fire," Ned said slowly using the mic for the loudspeaker mounted on the boat's utility mast. They don't speak English, Ned thought. "Don't shoot!" Ned said again even more slowly. He tried to keep his voice from cracking.

The two boats were well inside the town limits. "Nash, we've taken fire from the Ruff-Puff outpost," Ned said over the loudspeaker to the other boat and Ned heard his engines start to wind up. Ruff-Puffs, the Regional and Popular Forces, were charged with the duty of guarding the town. They were famous for disappearing when things got hot. None of the drivers trusted them and the 'Yards looked down on them as little better than Cub Scouts. An RF-PF outpost near Saigon once called in American artillery on a Montagnard basecamp, just to get even for a brawl in a bar the night before. The 'Yards and the Ruff-Puffs were always fighting over whose territory the bars and their girls were in.

Ned hung out of the pilot house door to get a better look at Jimmy up on the bow. He didn't look good.

"Di di mau," the squad leader said, pointing toward the center of town, but the two boats were already almost on plane, pulling huge wakes behind them as they roared up the river into the center of Ben Tré. Ned took the radio mic from its clip and took a deep breath.

"Blue Shark, Blue Shark. This is Abbey November nine three. We are taking friendly fire from..." Ned paused, "...from the west side of the river, near the RF-PF outpost. Over."

Both boats were at full speed. "Nine three. You OK over there?" Nash asked over his loudspeaker, not wanting to say anything over the radio.

Ned keyed his loudspeaker. "Jimmy's down."

"Nine three, this is Blue Shark. Say again, over," said the voice of the American base in Ben Tré.

"Blue Shark," Ned said over the radio. "This is nine three. We have taken one round from the RF-PF outpost. Request you stand by with a dust-off at the dock. Over." A dust-off was a helicopter used to carry wounded.

Ned heard the voice of one of the 'Yards on Nash's boat over his loudspeaker. All the men on the bow of the 93 boat turned toward 127 . Then the brown face of the squad leader was looking up at Ned, his hand gesturing for the loudspeaker mic. The high sing-song of the Meo language echoed above the roar of the diesels as the two boats talked to each other as they ran side by side the mile left to the town dock and the dust-off, but Jimmy Bascom was dead before they got there.

Ned heard the next day that one of the Ruff-Puffs who had been on duty that night at the outpost was found dead, shot in the heart. His right ear had been cut off, but they found it lying next to the body.

About a week later Nash and Ned were on loan again to the Army to support some sort of big sweep with ARVN troops cleaning up islands along the west bank of the Bassac

River, one of the branches of the Mekong in the Delta. They had been given H & I duty, harassing and interdiction fire, just anchoring in the middle of the river and firing twenty mortar rounds at odd intervals during the night at a specific target, just to keep the VC from moving too easily through the area on the canals and rivers.

They tied up together and swung off Nash's anchor in about twenty feet of water just east of the main ship channel. The Army sent coordinates in the late afternoon, and they were supposed to start firing around midnight. One high explosive round, one white parachute flare round, alternating like that, all through the night.

"You plotted the coordinates yet?" Nash asked, leaning out his pilot house door. The rainy season had just ended, and it was still hot and humid on the river, so he wore camouflaged fatigue trousers, a white t-shirt, and black low cut Navy boots. Mirrored aviator glasses with wire frames were pushed up on his forehead. He looked beyond Ned as he spoke. For the past three weeks his eyes were always scanning the horizon as though he was expecting something to appear there.

"Yeah. It's where two canals intersect," Ned answered, looking up at Nash's bright eyes, following them to watch a tug and barge churning up the east channel of the river.

"Anything there on your map?" Ned looked at his map and didn't see anything except two blue lines at right angles, the way the French always dug their canals, straight and precise. "Two canals is all," Ned answered. "Why?"

Nash studied his map again and carried it over to the 93 boat and spread it out over Ned's map. "There's a building on my map," he said. "Right here," he pointed. Just above his finger, its nail chewed short, was a small triangle. Outpost or Fort, the legend of the map said.

"Check the coordinates?" Ned asked, reaching for the yellow Snoopy notebook he used as a radio message log.

"They're good numbers," Nash said, comparing his finger's position on the map with some figures in pencil written in the margin. "I broke them myself. Twice." He paused, his fingers fishing a pair of dividers from the olive drab c-ration can in the bin behind the chart table. He walked the dividers along the map's right margin, brought them into the center again. Next he moved from the bottom margin to the straight blue canals and twisting streams that cut across the light greens of the map to the left of the Bassac River, two inches wide, running north to south along the right edge of the map. "35,707 and 65, 890. Right on the money."

Ned looked up the code for the week and did the numbers again. "35...707 and 65...890. I agree." One of Ned's crew came up from down below carrying a bucket. He trudged to the stern and poured the day's garbage over the transom, a lettuce leaf and some coffee grounds spilling on the deck. He tied a line to the bucket, plopped it into the river, hauled it up full, and sluiced down the deck.

Both drivers both stared at Nash's map. The wake of the tug and barge slapped against the bows of the two boats. Nash's map was dated three years earlier than Ned's.

"I don't like the idea of firing at an outpost," Nash said quietly, looking steadily at where the river blended evenly into the sky at the horizon, "even if it's not on the new maps." The tug first and then the barge began to be swallowed up by the long island that separated the east channel from the main ship channel. Soon all the two could see was the top of the tug's pilot house above the trees of the island. They both watched the tug disappear and thought about the outpost.

"Maybe it's gone. Destroyed," Ned suggested at last.

Nash's blond hair hung long in front, almost hiding his blue eyes. He took his aviator glasses in his right hand, shook his head, and went up onto the foredeck. Ned followed. "Even so," he said as he tapped the taut bow line with his right boot, "somebody's going to be still using what's left of the building. Ruff-Puffs, maybe." Nash walked back into the pilot house and Ned still followed. His mentioning Ruff-Puffs like that seemed funny to Ned, but Ned remembered how Nash had taken Jimmy's death pretty hard. He wouldn't talk about it or anything. "It would serve the bastards right if we did drop a few in on them," Nash said at last.

For a minute neither one of them said anything. Ned

thought back to Jimmy's wide open surprised eyes as he lay there on the deck.

"Do you want to call in or should I?" Nash asked.

"I'd rather not go up against Britton," Ned said. "He's still pissed after our little dance with the Sunday shoppers." Ned had told Nash about the confrontation in the narrow river during Lemming Drive.

"I'll check on it," Nash said and held the black single sideband radio mic to his lips. Communications were tricky this far from base, so they used a longer ranged but less reliable and more complicated radio. Nash used Ned's call sign because he was using the radio on Ned's boat. "Blue Shark... Blue Shark... Blue Shark... This is Abbey November nine three, over."

The tug's pilot house disappeared for a while behind some taller trees on the island. It was a minute before Ben Tré answered. Ned thought about Jimmy's chest wound and the tiny kissing sound it must have made as they had tried to get him back to Ben Tré.

"Nine three, this is Blue Shark. Roger, over." The voice was high pitched, nasal, and hollow. Like the voice of a robot.

"Roger, Blue Shark." Nash tapped twice with the dividers on the intersection of the two canals on the map. "Reference your hotel india for tonight...Request you confirm and send the numbers again." Nash looked over his shoulder at Ned and Ned nodded. "We have some problems with the target... Over," he finished.

"Roger. Stand by," spoke the robot voice.

The tug and barge had cleared the upper end of the island by the time a different voice broke the silence. "Abbey November nine three, this is Blue Shark," and Ned could picture the sour expression on the face of Major Britton. "Do you have some problem? Over." Ned wondered if the Major was holding his crotch with his left hand.

"'We read an outpost at the location for tonight's business," Nash said. He used the week's code word for an outpost or fort. There was silence from the radio speaker, broken only by the clicking and popping of the atmosphere. "Do you copy?"

Nash asked after a while.

"'We have negative information on any structure," the Major's voice whined through the speaker. "Proceed with your mission. Out."

The wake from the tug and barge would reach the two boats in another thirty seconds. "Request you stand by. Over," said Nash and turned to Ned. Ned was thinking of Jimmy Bascom and the Ruff-Puffs. "I don't know," Nash said. "That lazy bastard probably didn't even check."

"I bet he's right, though," Ned said even though he didn't believe it. "Let's not worry about it. "

"Right," Nash said slowly and took a breath. "Blue Shark, this is Abbey November nine three."

"Go, nine three."

"Will proceed with mission. Over. "

"Roger. Good hunting. Out."

The wake of the tug and barge rocked the two boats together, banging their gunwales against each other. Nash held the edge of the chart table and looked at the river meeting the sky while Ned steadied himself against the radar scope and noticed that he was conscious of his body, of where it touched the rough fabric of his uniform. He could feel the cool metal of his dog tags. He tried to recall having been as aware of his body, of being as sensitive to his clothes before. He couldn't remember.

Oh, yes I do, he thought a few minutes later as he stood on the stern of the 93 boat, looking downstream to where, miles away, the smooth brown river was forever pouring into the choppy blue South China Sea. In eighth or ninth grade. But back then I usually had had an erection to go along with it, and Ned smiled.

I am not dead, he thought, remembering how he had felt with the girl from the dance once he had begun to hate Killian again.

Later that night, ten minutes before they were supposed to start firing, the radio stopped hissing and popping and began to speak.

"Abbey November nine three, this is Blue Shark, over."

Nash's boat was keeping the radio watch. Ned was trying to work his way through a USO Library copy of *The Caine Mutiny* in his pilot house and Nash was doing a crossword on 127. Ned had always worked for good captains, so the novel seemed made up until he remembered the Major from Can Tho.

Both boats had their red cabin lights on to protect their night vision even though there was a half-moon above some high thin clouds. The two crews had had steak and eggs for dinner but neither skipper could sleep. Ned had tried to record a tape to send home to his father, but he still couldn't get the words right. Ned's grandmother had died the month before, and Ned hadn't been able to tell his father how he felt except in that one telegram they let him send home when someone dies. Ned wanted to tell about being dead and being alive, but he knew the words would sound all wrong to his father.

"This is one two seven. Roger, over," Nash spoke into the mic. He and Ned had told their crews they could turn in. The two skippers had decided that it was OK to fire the mission with just the two of them on duty.

"One two seven, this is Blue Shark. Local RF-PF units request you confirm the coordinates for tonight. I say again, confirm the coordinates for tonight's mission, over." Ned couldn't tell if it was the Major's voice or not. He couldn't picture the face, but that could have been just because of the hollow, eerie sound the single sideband radio was making.

Across the water in the main ship channel a single tug was moving quickly downstream, its bright orange deck lights dancing on the river. Nash put the mic down on the chart table and turned the volume down and stared at the tug. Ned looked down at his book. The radio squealed as someone adjusted the frequency at Ben Tré.

"Abbey November nine three, Abbey November one two seven, this is Blue Shark. Did you copy my last, over?"

The automobile tires hung out as fenders squealed in protest, the two boats grinding together as the wake of the tug reached them.

Ned thought of Jimmy on the bow of the 93 with the 'Yards all around him and how he couldn't do anything to help the advisor. Ned looked over at the red light making dark shadows in Nash's pilot house. The two skippers looked at each other as the boats rocked in the wake, and Ned watched as Nash put the mic back in its clip on the radio, checked his compass heading, gathered his notebook, and went aft to his mortar. Ned crossed over to the stern of Nash's boat. Nash and Ned worked together without speaking, training the mortar to the bearing, setting the elevation of the barrel.

"One two seven, this is Blue Shark, over," the radio whispered.

Back at the mortar the two men listened to the voice all the way from Ben Tré. Ned slid a white phosphorus mortar round from its plastic container and stripped four bags of powder from its tail, leaving eight. White phosphorus burned when it exploded, and nothing would put it out. It made a terrific anti-personnel round. Especially when white phosphorous was alternated with high explosives. Willy-Pete and HE…

"Confirming range… two thousand. Eight bags. Willy-Pete. One round," Ned said. He was aware that he had an erection.

"Range… two thousand, check," answered Nash.

"Abbey November units nine three or one two seven, this is Blue Shark. Local RF-PF units request you confirm the coordinates for tonight. There may be a problem with the numbers you have. Over," the radio hissed urgently from the pilot house, and the two boats rocked gently in the river.

"Tube set on drop fire?"

"Drop fire," Nash answered.

Ned slid the mortar round into the tube, held it around its waist for a moment until the rocking of the boat stilled, said, "Fire in the hole," ducked his head, and let go.

The voice of Blue Shark continued for five minutes more before it was replaced by the empty noises of the atmosphere.

CHAPTER TWENTY-TWO

Key West, morning

At nine o'clock on Thursday morning, the beach of the Pier House was almost deserted. Down by the water's edge the little girl named Cassie with the Dutch Boy haircut was digging a moat around a half-buried glass fishing float. She wore ragged jean cut-offs and a white t-shirt with Snow White's Dopey on the front. Sitting on top of the float was the bleached shell of a crab, the number 348 in red paint on its back. Annie sat on her heels in the sand and watched as Cassie walked her fingers up the side of the moat and climbed to the top of the pale blue glass float. I sat in a beach chair partly shaded by a stunted coconut palm.

"And when the princess gets to the top of the castle, she puts on the armor," Cassie was saying. She picked up the crab shell and placed it on top of her walking fingers. "Then she's ready to battle with the monsters."

"Will she win?" asked Annie.

"If she's loyal and true and knows the magic words."

"What are the magic words? Can you tell me?"

"I can tell you two of them," the little girl said proudly. "Pin-pig-twiggle is one and shaz- zam is the other. But the third one I'm not supposed to tell, ever."

"Those are neat words, Cassie. Thank you."

"You said you wanted to ask me about the man with the giant hat."

"Yes, I do," said Annie, and she started to make a little path through the sand from the moat around the glass float down to the water's edge. I leaned forward so I could listen better.

"He was nice," Cassie said, walking the shell down the side of the float. "We had ice cream and little soft brown cookies wrapped in paper."

"Amoretto di Sarono. One of Dad's addictions," I said to Annie, who just nodded.

"Was it a party?" Annie asked.

"It was New Year's Eve, but it wasn't midnight. I couldn't stay up all the way 'til then, but next year I will and we're going to go down to the parade in the harbor and get to ride on a raft over to the island and help with the fireworks."

"How did you get to meet the man in the hat?"

"At his house, the one with the funny name and the board stuck in the tree outside," Cassie said and walked the crab shell over to Annie's little trench. Annie took the shell and put it on her walking fingers. "We can share the armor, too, if you want to."

"Thank you, Cassie. I'm old number 348, Old Fred, I think," Annie said in a deep voice, and then in her regular voice, "Tell about the first time you went to the house with the funny name."

"We were walking."

"Do you walk a lot?"

"Every day. Sometimes we walk in the morning. Sometimes we can't walk until night. I saw you two the other night when we were walking. Remember?"

"Yes. I remember," I said, and Cassie looked at me. "We were on Duval Street. We had been at Shorty's for a midnight snack."

"Did you have ice cream? We have ice cream at Shorty's," Cassie said to Annie.

"No. No ice cream," answered Annie as she walked in her armor up to the top of the float. "We had scrambled eggs and grits."

"Yuk," said Cassie.

"I think you're right," agreed Annie. "Ice cream would have been better."

"Where's the third lady? His sister," Cassie said, pointing at me.

Annie and I waited, stunned. How did this little girl know that Sis and I were brother and sister?

Annie finally smiled and said, "She went back home, back to St. Louis. How did you know that she was Ned's sister?"

"It's part of what we do when we walk. We talk about everybody we see. Who they are and where they live and what they've done and everything. That, and I've seen them together in the pictures at the house. When they'd talk, I got to look through the books of pictures, and I've seen pictures of him and the other lady. I liked the one where they were in the little truck together, the one with the ladders on the side."

Annie looked at me.

"I know the photo Cassie means. I thought it was back in St. Louis. It's of a birthday party when we were almost in our teens. Mom's sister had sent us a double birthday present from New York City. This great cardboard fire engine that you could get in. It was much too small for us. I think she thought we were both younger than we were, but we got in it anyway and someone took our picture. I remember it because it really made us look like twins."

"I wish I had a truck like that," said Cassie.

"It's probably still in the attic in St. Louis. If it is, I'll send it to you," I promised.

"Thank you."

"You're welcome."

"Who was talking at the house when you were looking at the pictures?" Annie asked.

"Terri and the man who lives there."

"Terri?"

"I take Terri for walks. I told you."

"And the two of you talk?"

"Mainly we just walk. Terri tells me which streets to go down, and I go down them and answer Terri's questions about everything."

"Tell me one of Terri's questions," I asked.

Cassie looked at Annie.

"It's OK. He's with me," Annie explained and grinned at me.

"What color bird is that singing in that tree? Who is on the street just ahead of us? What store is it that we're passing right now? Things like that."

"Is Terri blind?" Annie asked.

"Almost," Cassie answered.

"And you help him out and lead him?"

"I just walk where we're going, and Terri keeps one hand on my shoulder. Mainly I answer Terri's questions." Cassie thought for a moment as she dug a small trench to connect where she was with Annie's trench. Old Fred, crab number 348, sat on top of the blue glass float. "Mom says I can answer all his questions, no matter how silly they sound. But Terri is the only person I can talk to that way. I can't ever ever talk to strangers, Mom said. It's OK to talk to you, though."

"How do you know that?" I asked.

"Terri told Mom I could. Terri said you would ask me about the man at the house and that it was OK to answer. Only he didn't know it would be you," Cassie said, indicating Annie. "He said it would be the other lady. His sister," pointing at me. "But you're nice, too," she continued, looking Annie square in the eye. "You like her, don't you?"

This last remark was aimed at me.

"Uh... Yes, very...," I said, caught off guard.

"That's what Terri said."

We left Cassie down by the water's edge under the watchful eye of the lifeguard who came on duty at nine-thirty. A yellow red-label Rolls Royce pulled up to the street entrance of the hotel just as we walked in. The Roll's driver disappeared into an office behind the desk just as a tall, sun-tanned young woman with blond hair worn in a long, Indian braid down her back came out from behind the counter.

"Let's go out on the porch," she said to us, and we followed her toward the street. She wore a Mexican peasant dress with bright birds and flowers in crewel work over white homespun. In her face I could see where Cassie would be in ten or fifteen years, and I felt sorry for the young men's hearts which would be broken. I'm Mrs. Prime, Cassandra's mom."

We introduced ourselves and shook hands.

"Terri said you'd be by but not when. I saw you talking to Cassandra down on the beach."

"I hope you don't mind," said Annie. "I told her last night to let you know we would be coming by and to check with you if it was all right."

"No, it's perfectly all right. She told me you had seen her at the restaurant. Was she able to help? Something about your father?"

The three of us stopped at the end of the porch and looked out over the harbor. Tourists were beginning to appear in twos and threes on the streets, and shops were beginning to open for the day.

"Who is Terri, Mrs. Prime?" I asked.

"I guess you'd have to say Terri is one of our local characters," Cassie's mom said. "During World War Two, he was in charge of supplies for a destroyer squadron home ported here. In the early 'fifties he retired here on his service pension and never left. He has a small apartment in one of David's old houses in Conch Town."

"How did Cassie and he meet?" Annie asked.

Cassie's mom gave Annie a funny look, but explained readily enough, "Cassie has been babysitting for guests at the hotel for a couple of years now, and David, the owner, asked me if it would be OK if Cassie kind of acted as a babysitter for an old friend of his, Terri." She paused and crossed her arms on the porch railing. "I know you'll think I'm probably not a very good mother, but, after I met Terri, I didn't see any reason why not, and Terri, through David, pays Cassie what she'd earn babysitting. It all goes into a savings account. Plus, and this is what really made me say that it was all right, Terri is teaching Cassie so much. She knows all the trees and animals on the island and all the local history and wonderful stories about the people and so much more that she wouldn't ever get from the public schools."

"She seems very bright," I offered

"Oh, she is. Her father was a... very intellectual sort of person," she said, her expression darkening for a moment. "It's a tough life for a little girl growing up like this. I earn enough to make ends meet, but I'm always looking for ways to make things better for Cassie. Spending time with Terri this way will give her a real edge in life."

"It sounds to me like Cassie is lucky to have you as her mom," said Annie. "Where is Terri from?"

"As far as I know, Terri has always been from here."

"Can we meet Terri? Can you introduce us to him, Mrs. Prime?" I asked.

"I'll have Cassie tell Terri you'd like a visit," said Cassie's mom, and I wondered at the strange look she gave me, just like the look she had given Annie.

We walked across town in the relative cool of the mid-morning to the *4th of July* for breakfast. Behind the counter sat their famous Cuban coffee machine, a shiny brass and chrome monster four feet high that wheezed, hissed, and thumped as it produced cup after cup for the steady stream of customers who poured through the restaurant's old fashioned swinging saloon doors. As I attacked the mound of scrambled eggs and ham, twice as much piled on the plate as a normal person would ever consider eating, Annie chewed on a piece of toasted Cuban bread, sipped at a mug of thick black coffee, and read the first draft of *Friendly Fire*.

She made a funny noise, and I looked over at her. "You got an... You got excited when you were fighting?" Annie asked, looking up over her glasses.

"Not always. Sometimes," I said through a mouthful of egg and realized that I must have amplified Annie's image of the complete Neanderthal.

"Some of you guys must have some real confusions now

that you're back home. Does it work the same way in reverse?"

"How do you mean?"

"Do you fight when you... have sex?"

I couldn't tell if Annie's question was serious or not, so I just smiled. I realized that I didn't even know the answer to that question. It had been so long since I had been normal with a woman.

Annie wanted to go out to Christmas Tree Island in the harbor to check on some crabs she had let go the day Sis had pulled her out of the harbor. After breakfast, which Annie again insisted was to be Dutch treat, I brought *Coast Pilot* in on the back side of the island where the currents had scoured a channel close in with a depth of five feet. I eased the nose of the Dyer up to the beach, and Annie ran the bow line over to a low but sturdy looking evergreen and tied it off. While she went around the island with her notebooks, jotting down shell numbers and locations, I got out a small holy stone and began to scrub the teak toe rail around the edge of the deck.

Annie was on the far side of the island, and I was on my hands and knees on the bow trying to get a piece of tar off the teak rail. A shadow fell across the deck, and I looked up into an old, weatherbeaten face. "You look like him," said a voice as thin and dry as paper.

"Terri?" I asked.

"He was never able to keep this boat in as good condition as he knew it should be."

The hand holding the tall, polished staff was emaciated and delicately boned. The arm was thin and well-tanned. Terri wore the same clothes as that first night on Duval Street, a leather vest, denim shirt, and baggy chino pants. Grey hair, pulled tight in a long pony tail, was circled by a red bandana, American Indian style. A gaunt nose and high cheek bones supported a pair of soft grey eyes that stared sightlessly straight ahead.

"You will keep it the way he wished it should be done," Terri continued.

"You knew my father well, it sounds like."

"Once he began to know himself, he was easy to get to

know. I liked your father a great deal. He and I talked about many things together. The hours passed quickly at his house."

"Where did the name come from, *Byblos*?" I asked, and as I spoke a thought struck me. I looked hard into Terri's face.

"You must have many questions," Terri said and looked down, away from my stare. "I will come visit, if I may, tomorrow. Is there any time that is better?"

"Any time is fine. We will be there this afternoon."

"The little girl, Cassie, likes the almond cookies which come wrapped in paper... To be truthful, so do I, even if they are too sweet for me, and..." the thin voice trailed off into silence.

"Where can I..." I started to say.

"...there should be a tin under the berth on the port side. That is where your father used to keep them," resumed Terri, "for us."

I got to my feet and went back along the side deck to the cockpit. I ducked down into the cabin and lifted the port bunk cushion and the locker lid. There was the red and orange tin of almond cookies, Amaretto di Sarono. I took a handful out into the cockpit and went forward along the port side.

Terri was gone.

The beach was deserted. I didn't see anyone in the water. I felt foolish, but I jumped down and looked on the sand beneath the overhanging bow. Yes, there were footprints, all right. I could even see where Terri's staff had poked into the sand. The island was small, about the size of a football field; as I scanned the trees, looking for where Terri had disappeared, Annie walked up to the bow of the Dyer.

"You didn't see Terri?" I asked.

"No. Was he here?"

"Yes, big as life. And another thing, Annie," I said as I handed her an almond cookie, "I'm not sure Terri's a guy."

After an early dinner at the *Black and Blue*, a steak house with an excellent jazz trio playing in the background, I had a feeling that Annie wanted to head back to #65. She had been quiet for the last half hour of the meal. We had spent a lot of time in the sun, and I thought maybe the island climate had finally caught up with her. I was feeling a bit scorched myself.

"Do want me to get a taxi, or do you want to walk back to Von Phister?" I asked as we walked out into the relative cool of the evening. It felt like rain.

"Oh, I wasn't really ready to head home yet," Annie said with a bright smile. "Are you tired?"

"No, not really. I just thought that you seemed a little quiet. Like the sun had gotten to you, maybe."

"No. I was just into the music is all. When they played *Blue Rondo*, I remembered some of the good times in college. I'm raring to go," she said, and started to walk fast down Greene Street toward Duval.

When I caught up with her at the corner, she took my wrist in her hand and looked into my eyes. "I didn't pay much attention to you back there. I'm sorry. I'll make it up, promise. It was just so nice to sit there and listen and not feel as though I had to make small talk."

"Thank you."

"For what?"

"For... nothing. Just thank you," and she gave me a very sisterly kiss on the end of my nose.

We sat at Sloppy Joe's and watched the tourists in their dull colored plumage wash up and down the street like so much flotsam and jetsam. Occasionally they would be caught in an eddy in front of store or outside of a noisy bar. The brightly colored natives seemed to constantly buck the flow, noisily talking and gesturing. When natives met tourists, the natives would part to allow the more irresistible forces to flow past.

"It's like watching the halls between classes in a high school. That terrible press of humanity as it goes about its work selecting, sorting, sniffing, judging, touching, challenging, collecting, discarding, urging, pushing, shoving, feeling, and all trying to find a place just to land and rest and be yourself," said Annie. "God, how I hated that. I always felt like I was part of a cattle drive or a livestock auction." She shuddered. "Ned, occasionally remind.me that I'm an OK person, huh?"

I put my arm around her waist and gave her a squeeze. "You're a good woman, Annie Gerard," I told her. After a pause I continued. "I used to hate that part of school, too. Even a guy gets to feel just like so much meat."

"In the end, it's all we are, but I do want to reach up out of the slime a bit along the way toward joining the food chain again. I guess it's why I do research and teach and haven't joined my sorority sisters at the altar who have lined up on their backs to make babies just yet."

"You make it sound pretty grim."

"It is pretty grim, isn't it? You've been there, Ned. You know exactly how grim it can be. It's the female equivalent of combat. Making babies and cleaning house and not doing anything with your life." Annie stopped and looked at me. Her eyes swam out of focus for a moment. "I'm getting the sads, Ned. don't let me get the sads 'cause I become an awful creep."

"Let's go back to Von Phister," I suggested.

We sat on the porch upstairs after the slow walk home. Annie hadn't said much along the way, and I had held her around the waist and told her stories about training in San Fransisco and R & R in Hong Kong. By the time we reached the house, Annie said she felt better and even suggested a nightcap.

"What do you see when you look at me?" she asked as I settled into the canvas chair. She sat on a cushion, had propped herself against the wall, and was looking out over the trees toward the ocean.

"I see an intelligent young woman."

"Am I sexy, too?"

"Yes."

Annie's voice dropped to a whisper, and I had to strain to make out what she was asking me. "Have you wanted to seduce me?"

"Yes."

"Why haven't you tried?"

I didn't know the answer to that one, not the answer I was going to give to Annie in any case, so I didn't say anything.

"Did you think I didn't want you to?" she asked.

"Among other things," I answered.

"What other things?"

Again, I didn't answer.

"Do you want to seduce me now?" she asked.

"You've had quite a bit of wine and so have I."

"What if we both have some more wine? Will you try to seduce me then?"

"I don't know," I said. "Maybe you will try to seduce me."

"What makes you think I'm that kind of girl?"

"What makes you think I'm that kind of boy?"

"I would like another glass of wine, Ned, please."

I took her glass from her outstretched hand and went to the kitchen. I poured us each a full glass and put them on the counter while I went down the hall to the bathroom. When I returned to the porch with the wine glasses, Annie was leaning back against the wall. Her steady, deep breathing told me that she was asleep.

"I think I should tell you, Annie, that I very much want to seduce you. But I've screwed up with so many other women that I'm afraid to try. So, if you want to get laid by me, you are going to have to help out, I guess," I said to her. "You've said that you like this brother- sister thing we're doing. Well, so do I, but I don't know how to move on to anything else."

I stopped speaking to the sleeping Annie and slowly drank my wine as I watched the moon's reflections play tag across the ocean.

"I'm afraid to try with you, Annie. The same way I've been afraid with all the others."

I stretched my legs out in front of me, settling back in the canvas chair, and spoke up toward the darkness, the night breeze slowly turning the blades of the ceiling fan. "I think I want to spend more time with you, Annie Gerard, but I'm so afraid to ask that I'll probably let you slip away. That's how bad it is. So, if it seems I don't want you, it's only because I'm afraid of what will happen if I tell you how much I really do."

I shut my eyes and could feel Annie there next to me. I ached to wake her up and invite her to my bed. "I want you Annie, but right now it just won't go. That's how bad it is."

I could feel the wine tugging me down toward sleep. I could hear a rain shower hissing through the trees off toward the north. The moon was still bright over the water, but the rain was washing down the island from north to south. "For you, it's that animal you hear breathing in the cellar, and for me it's that terror I keep locked up in the same place."

And I sat there with her breathing next to me in the night and tried to put a face to that fear. A gust of cool air driven before the advancing rain made me shiver, and I wanted someone to hug me.

CHAPTER TWENTY-THREE

Key West, after midnight

I woke up in the chair and looked at my watch. Well past midnight and the effects of the wine seemed to have worn off; I looked over next to me and could see that Annie had gone to bed. So much for my scintillating observations on life.

The street was silent except for the splat of water drops from high in the trees hitting the elephant ear plants next to the house. I stretched some of the stiffness out of my body and went in through the window of the bedroom. On the chair at the foot of the bed was the canvas boat bag, and in the bag was the tape recorder. I wanted to hear a particular tape I had sent home to Sis. I carried the recorder, the tape I wanted, and a blank tape out to the porch and sat down, the recorder in my lap.

The neighborhood was dark, but I could see the pulsating glow of the red lights on the Navy communications antenna at the end of White Street. A few bright stars peered through the broken clouds. Stretching my legs out in front of me, I shut my eyes. I put the tape in the machine and pressed the PLAY button. The silence turned to a gentle hiss, and I heard my voice speaking from miles and months away.

It has rained so hard and for so long that the war stopped this morning just after dawn.

At first the drops are large and heavy and come crashing down through the leaves of the trees and palms along the rivers and canals around Can Tho. We hear the hiss and then roar of the rain coming for about thirty seconds before it hits us. Once it arrives, we know that it has come to stay. We are all experts on rain by this time.

Each of us knows that sometimes the rain catches you out in the open and comes at you in single drops that splat around you like angry yellow jackets. Other times, once monsoon season has started, the drops are so many and coming down at you so thickly that it is like being hit with a bucket of water thrown at you. The rain comes at you in different ways depending on the kind of storm, but always the rain stays with you the same way, persistently, for hours and sometimes days.

The rain gets in everywhere on the boats. You notice it in your clothes first. We wash our clothes in the river, so the fatigues and socks and underwear are never really clean. The rain makes your clothes feel and smell like you've worn them for a couple of days even if they are clean and starched looking and you have just put them on. You might think that you can get used to the smell of our clothes when it rains, but some of us can't.

The rain finds its way into the electronics on the boats. Radars go on the fritz and the scopes have no pictures. Radios drift off frequency and cut out in the middle of transmissions, and the batteries run out at critical times. The starting circuits you use to get the big diesels going pop and spark whenever it has rained for longer than a few hours. Tom, the helmsman, always swears he can feel an electrical current running through the wheel in the pilot house on the second day of a rain. The depth sounder, the kind with the little spinning orange light on it, gives funny readings during rainstorms, so none of us trust what it indicates.

Usually when it rains in the Delta there is no wind at all, and the rain falls vertically from the sky in what looks like long strings of beads or strands of fine thread. This means that whatever you are trying to keep dry and out of the rain just needs to be under cover. This works for the first hour of the rain. Then, when everything around is thoroughly soaked, the rain starts to seep. While we know that raindrops can only travel down, we are never convinced that individual drops and sometimes rivulets of rainwater can't travel uphill. We find puddles of rainwater everywhere on board. In between plates stacked in lockers. Inside of the cellophane of unopened packs of cigarettes. In small pools in the middle of the dinette table. In coffee mugs hanging on hooks under shelves. Everywhere.

Sometimes, to test our endurance, the rain arrives with huge gusts of wind. The boats, if tied up at a dock or bow into some riverbank during an ambush, slide sideways and heel gently to the onslaught of wind and rain. The wind driven rain at first pelts and then rattles and finally clatters against the aluminum sides of the cabin and pilot house. This constant drumming sometimes goes on for hours, so, after the first thirty minutes, all of us are so enveloped by the sound that none of us notices it. Until the wind stops. Then the rain takes on what is almost a velvet sound, a warm, comforting purr it has lacked before. The awful rain, without the roughhouse wind, becomes almost friendly. Like a not quite tamed pet or a difficult child, the rain and the wind alternate between outrageous behavior and sweet companionship.

The colors of our rivers, canals, and jungle change dramatically in the rain. The sullen rain mutes the loud yellow greens of nipa palms and creepers to the same dull olive as the dusty leaved mangroves. The light tan of the main rivers under the peppering of the rain becomes indistinguishable from the darker browns of small canals and rachs. The sharp relief and vivid textures of everything around us seen in the usual harsh white light of tropical sun mellows to slightly fuzzy outlines and indistinct surfaces as the rain washes over us, rendering our world in the dull colors of an old newspaper's rotogravure travel section.

Our personalities change in the rain, too. We pull back into ourselves, choosing to be apart from our shipmates. Each of us tries to find a corner of the pilot house or main cabin or berthing area into which he can withdraw.

The usually outgoing Tom props himself up on the ledge in front of the starboard rear window in the pilot house and rereads letters from his friends and relatives in Akron. Tom gets at least two letters at every mail call although I don't remember seeing him ever writing a letter to anyone.

Harris, our gunner, takes apart and cleans all the small arms and rifles on board, spreading the tiny parts and pieces all over the dinette table.

The Kid scrunches down across from Harris in the dinette so just his shoulders and head show over the edge of the table. There he sits, reading his slowly swelling collection of war comics.

CB disappears into his engine room after carefully hanging a DO NOT DISTURB sign he has somehow acquired from the Continental

Hotel in Saigon over the start buttons for the main engines in the pilot house.

Tracy always sleeps in his bunk below when it rains.

I sit in the helmsman's seat in the pilot house.

This Thursday morning when the war stops because of the rain I start reading the book my aunt has just sent me. I wrote to her in answer to one of her letters after I had been in-country for about two months to get it for me, and it has taken about a month for her to find it and then send it over. She lives on the Gold Coast in Florida, and I guess there aren't many bookstores that carry books like Heart of Darkness. *I read it in high school. I want to reread it, wondering if my memory of the journey Marlow took up the unnamed, African river is as accurate a portrayal of my present journey through the rivers of Vietnam as I think it might be. I feel a shiver of déja vu as I join the group of men listening to Marlow tell his tale as they sit on the yawl* Nellie *and wait for the tide to turn. I am sitting on a boat in a river waiting for the rain to stop.*

The scene in which the French ship lobs shell after useless shell into the African coast reminds me of what we do in this river. We escort gigantic rusty steel barges filled with sand towed by huge red and yellow ocean-going tugs, one Swift behind and the other ahead. Charlie's rocket teams take pot shots at the sandbagged bridges of the tugs, earning the crews their monthly $1,000 combat bonus. The Swifts respond to these almost daily ambushes by skittering around like water bugs, spraying the banks of the river with ineffective machine gun fire.

The rocket team has already gone. They only want to show us that they still control the rivers. We ferry poorly trained and ill- equipped troops from place to place where they refuse to fight. They occasionally do draw fire from the guerillas. Once the troops stumble into an ambush, we bring them back aboard and take them home. As we leave the area with our now joyous warriors, the artillery barrage starts, followed by the air strikes of Phantoms and C-47 gunships.

The Vietnamese artillery is inaccurate, and we all cringe in expectation until we are well clear of the area. The joint American- Vietnamese Phantoms then make their ear shattering rums, raining napalm accurately but uselessly down on the all-absorbing jungle. As night falls, we listen for a single C- 47 with its 6,000 round per minute minigun, its call sign Puff, the Magic Dragon. *Instead of a flying serpent breathing fire, I imagine a giant ogre pissing blood as the red tracers arc in a steep and brilliant cure from the gunship to the empty jungle or uninhabited rice fields 500 feet below. Charlie is long gone. He left after making contact with the Ruff Puffs hours ago.*

Marlow describes the station on the river where the Europeans blast cliffs, dig holes, and generally use the natives as slave labor to build a railroad that goes nowhere.

I think of Solid Anchor, *the destination for hundreds of barges of sand brought in by* RMK, *an American construction company. The mud in the Delta's so unstable that conventional buildings can't be built. Someone thought that by adding sand to the soup we could put a base there.*

All we have for our pains is millions of yards of sandy mud and a bunch of barracks that have sunk two feet in the past month. The Vietnamese love the project. Building a base, even if it's going to sink out of sight in two years, is a better duty than going out on patrol. The whole project is inappropriate, an American answer to a Vietnamese situation. In our part of the Delta the war takes until Friday around noon to get going again, so we have a stand down for over twenty-four hours. None of us knows what to do. Send me a tape, Sis. When I start talking like this, you know it's getting to me. I'll start going native or acting like some crazy commando, going off my rocker and fighting my own war.

Keep the baby, Faith!

The tape ran out to the end before I turned it off. Somewhere down the street a dog gave a single bark and was quiet again. I thought that I could hear the roar of the surf in the distance, but there was no wind so there was no surf. I was hearing the roar of the silence around me. Part of me, I knew, hadn't come back from the rivers. I had gone on that last operation and been wounded, but what was missing was an exact memory of what had happened after I had been hit out by the freighter. I thought that if I could just piece together those final minutes before I passed out and woke up at the hospital in Vung Tau, I could put that scene behind me. I needed to write it as a story, make Ned more alive on the pages than the real Ned was, sitting on that porch in his dead father's house in the midnight silence.

I would have to try again, I thought, picking up the story where it left off, on the boat at the dock, waiting to get underway for the mission. I put the blank tape in the recorder and pushed RECORD and PLAY. It still wasn't easy to dictate into the recorder, but the dialogue sounded better if I spoke it aloud before putting it down on the page. I considered having another glass of wine, but I thought it might be better to be clear headed, to remember a few more of the pieces of that final op.

Setting, Vung Tau; date, early December, let's put down 4 December; time, about 9:15, so we'll put 2115 hours. Ned's on board the 93 boat at the dock. they've already been given the mission, and he's just waiting around for things to get rolling. He is looking at a medal he'd gotten for the SEAL op. At this point Dog arrives at the boat.

*"Saw Morgan up at the O Club. She just got back from Saigon,"
announced Dog as he stepped through the pilot house door of the 93 boat. The 70 boat was rafted alongside.*

"Did you tell her?" asked Ned.

"Didn't have to," said Dog as he began to rummage through Ned's charts. "O'Connor spilled the beans. Telling the whole goddamned base."

"She pissed?" asked Ned.

"Not too damned happy about it, as far as I could tell, but she doesn't like much of anything we do, I guess," Dog said with a laugh.

I pushed the STOP button. I had tried to call Tim the first week I had been back in the States, but his family said that he had left for a vacation trip to England. Tim had loved what he regarded as the *art* of navigation and had promised himself that, if he ever made it out of the rivers in one or, at most, two pieces, he would treat himself to a trip to the museum at Greenwich and, finally, set his watch correctly. I had left a message with his parents to have him call me in St. Louis, but I hadn't heard from him yet. Maybe I should try him again. Since there was no telephone at #65, I would need to use a pay phone. OK, I thought, rewound the tape, and pushed PLAY.

...asked Ned.

"Not too damned happy about it, as far as I could tell, but she doesn't like much of

anything we do, I guess," Dog said with a laugh.

I pushed STOP and then PLAY and RECORD.

Lee and Dog reserved their most outrageous arguments for each other, providing entertainment for all who gathered at the O Club. Dog teased her at every turn, even stitching an olive drab and black peace sign on the right breast pocket of his uniform. To pay him back, Lee had put Dog's name on three mailing lists promising new worlds of peace and sharing.

"I like the hippy beads they wear in the brochures they send," Dog had told Lee one night in the O Club, waving a handful of glossy fact sheets, "but I had at least hoped to see a little bare tit, Morgan...

I pushed STOP, REWIND, STOP, and PLAY. Tim Barnes wouldn't have used that word.

...hoped to see

I pushed STOP and then PLAY and RECORD.

a little bare mammary, Morgan.

Better, I thought.

...Come on, get me on a good list. Like nudist peaceniks maybe. Volleyball games and sleep-ins." Ned enjoyed the competition between them.

"She'll be down here to the dock as soon as she checks in at the hospital," Dog said as he pulled out a South China Sea chart and spread it smooth. "Let's set up some freqs for this game. Any favorites, Ned?"

Ned didn't answer right away. He wondered for a moment why he had volunteered. The rest of the base was dark and silent. Only the thrum and hiss of the two generators broke the silence of the Navy base. A full moon hid behind a low overcast, making the low huts and rickety wooden docks glow peacefully in the dark. One last good op, he thought. Something a little more like the real Navy. Something with ships and the sea and no brown water and jungle rivers.

Ned looked around the pilot house, all its red lights dimmed. "My built-in's got a bum circuit," he said slowly, "so I'm using a portable. I'd like the low end for our private chat, and we can let Division monitor channel 77."

Dog consulted his small notebook and looked up. "How about 70? Usually only SEALs use that one, and I don't think there are any teams in the area."

I pushed PAUSE. Was all this radio stuff too much technical stuff? I wondered. It was important in the story later,

I decided, so I released the PAUSE button.

"Good. I'll send the Kid up and he can tell Frederick." Ned turned from the chart table and spoke into the dim cabin, lit only by a single red night light. "Kid? You down there?"

"Yeah, Boss," came the young voice. "What you need?" In a moment the Kid's shaggy head popped up into the pilothouse. He was grinning. The Kid was always grinning.

"Run up to division and tell them we'll be on 77 for this op, OK?"

"You got it," said the Kid and started to duck back into the cabin below. "Back in a flash."

Ned touched him on the shoulder. "Hey, Kid. Wait a sec. Get what call signs they want us to use. OK? Ask them for ones that don't use our numbers."

The Kid's head was swallowed by the dim redness below. "I'm gone!" said the voice.

"He's like a kid at a carnival, isn't he?" observed Dog as they heard him clang out through the aft cabin door and take the steps up to the dock in one noisy leap. "Full of piss and vinegar and willing to do anything to please."

Dog looked out into the night across the silent base. The moon tried to shine out through a thinness in the low clouds, but its light was again dimmed to an eerie glow. Dog slowly put his notebook away in its package and the package in his breast pocket. "Must be nice, huh? To be that turned on by everything."

"Yeah," admitted Ned. Wish I could get the same jolt out of it I used to. When we first got here, it was like being on a constant high. You know, a real rush all the time we were in the rivers. But now it's like it takes a fire fight or some hellatious storm to even get me interested."

"What about being scared?" Dog spoke in a quiet voice Ned hadn't heard before. "Davis was scared, you know, back at the Club. So were the others."

I pressed PAUSE again. I *was* scared that night. I almost didn't go on the op. Tim talked me into it, though. I decided not to put that into the story, but I knew the fear would be there behind everything I did, behind all the decisions I made. I wondered if Lee knew how scared I had been behind the bravado. I wondered if my fear had screwed things up once the op got going.

I would have to write it down to find out, I decided. I thought that if I could just remember the last part, the part after I was hit but before I came to in the OR in Vung Tau, that I might be able to shake the feeling I'd been having ever since I started writing the stories, a feeling that I was lying to myself, lying in the stories.

I knew that fear sat right in the center of it, like a dead thing in the road. Maybe, I thought, my finger on the PAUSE button, I should write about the fear, where it came from, what it made me feel and do. I tried to remember specifically when I realized that I was living with the fear.

It was like the day I admitted to myself that my father was an alcoholic. Sis had known it for a couple of years already, and, when I told her what I had discovered, she took my two hands in hers and looked me in the eye.

"Just because you know now that he's a drunk doesn't make him a different person, Ned," she had said. "He's still the same man. Just you have changed because of what you figured out."

I pressed the STOP button. This story of the final op would have to wait until I was able to write the other, the one about my fear. By my watch it was two in the morning. I listened for a minute to the night sounds of the house and then went in through the window to the bedroom, lay down on the bed, and was quickly asleep.

The next morning, Annie was full of life and stories as we walked to the *4th of July* for another huge breakfast. I had set my alarm for five and had written non-stop until nine-fifteen, sketching in the facts of an ambush along the Cua Lon, the main river of the Ca Mau where we were based at *Sea Float*. It was along that river, and especially at the mouth of the river, where I first knew the constant fear.

"But isn't everyone scared when they go into the rivers?" Annie asked when I told her about writing down the story to get at the fear. I hadn't told her why fear had become important to me again. She didn't seem to remember much of what she or I had said on the porch last night. I was glad to start the day with a clean slate.

"Ninety per cent of the time in the rivers we were bored to tears," I answered. "Nine per cent of the time we were in the thick of it, going up a canal or supporting some op or other along the main river. One per cent of the time were fire fights, ambushes, and taking fire. In the beginning, once we knew that life didn't come to an end as soon as the shooting started, we almost enjoyed the fire fights. I think the adrenalin did that. It was a rush, a thrill, kind of a neat sensation, like being high. I've never felt anything like it, before or since. It's probably why one of the skippers planned to become a narc when he got home. Imagine that, wanting to be a narc! But I know why. He knew that he needed the rush or the high, and there aren't many places to get it except in a war.

"So, you weren't scared in the beginning?"

"No. Not really. This'll sound a bit weird, but I wrote it in some of the other stories. It was almost like sex. Like being on a year-long date. We went up and down the rivers, and what would someday be fear was just anticipation, like being horny."

"The metaphor of foreplay comes to mind," said Annie, but I couldn't tell if she meant it as a humorous observation or as a criticism. "Some of this explains why war seems to be a particularly male enterprise." She began to rearrange the salt and pepper cellars and the sugar shaker in the center of the table.

"Don't worry, Annie," I tried to soothe her. "It changed after a while. And once the anticipation turned to fear, I rode around waiting to be blown away. I think the final two months were like that. And the one per cent of high or rush wasn't enough to offset the nine per cent of being scared in the canals. It became an almost physical feeling, the fear. Like being nauseated."

"How could you operate like that, feeling that way all the time?"

"You have no choice. You just go out on patrol and spend a lot of time feeling a little sick inside, hoping that it will go away, sometimes doing things to make it go away."

"Like what?" asked Annie. "What would you do to make it go away?"

"I didn't do it so much, but some of the other drivers would put themselves in really dangerous situations, would go out looking for trouble, would try to tempt Charlie into a fire fight. Like volunteering for all the SEAL operations. Some of our guys became real maniacs about it."

"What did you do, once you began to be scared?"

"I'll let you read the story," I promised and dug into my pile of eggs and ham.

Terri arrived at #65 at noon. They made a strange sight, the tall, skinny figure with the staff preceded by the bright blond little girl wearing a black swimsuit with a yellow, tie-dyed T-shirt over it. This time they both wore flip-flops. Annie took Cassie to one side of the porch to show her the crabs, while I arranged the two chairs so that Terri and I could talk together quietly. Annie and I had wondered how to find out how Terri and Dad fit together, and she had suggested some questions to ask.

"You know that my father died?"

"I knew that when he left the island the last time that I would not see him again, yes."

"How well did you know him?" I asked, watching the fine lines around Terri's eyes and mouth, looking for some sign of truth or a lie. As I looked at the old face, I wondered why I had assumed that Terri had been a woman.

Back hunched, arm holding the staff, legs together, Terri stared straight ahead.

"As he knew himself better each time he visited during the past year and then stayed longer and finally bought this house, we grew to know each other."

"How did you meet?"

"He was staying down by the harbor, and we met on the beach. I was able to steer him away from what could have been an unfortunate mistake."

"What happened?"

"You didn't love your father..."

"No!" I interrupted. "That's not true."

Terri continued through my interruption. "...just for his more perfect qualities: his legal mind, his love of Dickens' characters, his sense of personal honor."

"I'm sorry," I said.

"You loved him for the total man he had become. This was the man I met on the beach late one afternoon as he was trying to convince a sweet young creature named Billie Rose to join him in his bed."

"My father was a bit of a ladies' man," I said and knew as soon as I said it that it sounded too much like an apology.

"That appetite would have been strangely served," Terri continued, the thin voice filling with amusement, and I watched, surprised, as the dead grey eyes smiled, "for young Miss Rose, the object of your father's attention, is every inch a male of the species, the featured dancer at one of the more interesting clubs off of Duval Street."

"My father was propositioning a man?"

"He didn't know, of course. For all his sophistication, your father was beautifully naive about much of this world. I steered him away from Queen Billy; he never knew of his error. I was going to tell him someday, but I knew how sensitive he was to that particular subject."

"Yes, he was."

"To get back to how we got to know each other, I still had partial sight at that point, so I didn't need Cassie's help getting around. I was on my own. We were both part of the same Navy reunion, so we had dinner together that night. He talked of you and your sister. Of St. Louis. Of how he no longer enjoyed the Law. You had left Key West but were not yet in Vietnam, I think. You were out in California?"

"Vallejo. Mare Island, near San Francisco. I trained there for a few months before going to Vietnam."

"The more we talked that evening, the more your father realized that we had in fact met before, during the war, here in Key West. I had changed quite a bit from the young man he knew in 1944."

"I don't want to pry, but…" I began.

Terri's right hand rose, palm forward, in silent protest. "Your questions at this point do not invade his life. He wanted you to know these things. I think he knew that you would find out about the house and boat, would seek the facts of his life down here. You or your sister."

"We found out by accident."

"I have never been sure whether believing in accidents is presumptuous or vice versa," Terri said with a smile, and I laughed. "You have your father's appreciation of indirection, a craft the two of us enjoyed exercising."

"You don't answer my questions," I complained. Annie had told me to be straight with Terri; I hoped that I wouldn't scare him away. "How did the two of you meet during the war?"

"I will get to that. He was, as you know, stationed on a destroyer home-ported here during the war. He told me that he was so proud that you requested his old duty station, even though the ships had changed, and the missions were different. He felt somehow that the continuum remained unbroken, a concept we had discussed many times, sitting here on this very porch, he where you sit and I here, the light behind me, the little girl around the corner as she is now, reading quietly, playing make believe with the stuffed animals your father brought from St. Louis. A monkey with a short red jacket, missing an ear, was her favorite."

"Mine, from when I was little," I said, feeling one of the invisible connections vibrate slightly.

"And the alligator with the button eyes?"

"Sis's favorite."

"Your father said he did not love or understand children, but he could touch them quite skillfully. He believed he needed to find some of these connections between whom he had been and who he was at that point in his life. Your going to the war in Vietnam and his uncertainty about his health released certain… energies… in him. He started looking for himself, and the path seemed to start for him down here, back in the war years, while he and your mother lived here." Terri stopped speaking, his thin voice trailing off into dry silence.

"Would you two like some tea?" Annie asked, appearing at my side from around the corner of the porch.

"Tea would be most refreshing, thank you. Ned..."

"Yes. Wonderful. Tea.," I said, thinking of the dark Cuban coffee I had grown so fond of in the past days.

"...might prefer some coffee, as did his father. I am old, and the tea is more soothing. The coffee is too strong now, but I still allow myself a small cup now and again. Thank you, Miss Annie."

"My mother used to call me that, Terri. She used to call me Miss Annie."

"Everyone as a child should experience the dignity of being called by the right name," Terri responded, and Annie went into the house and up the stairs to the kitchen. "She has come a long way to find this island, and I think that it agrees with her. She has blossomed in the past years."

"You have seen... I'm sorry. You have known her before this time?" I asked.

"Miss Annie makes her fifth trip to the island. The first two times were with other students from the University who did not share, I can call them her attentions, to the life of our shores. They preferred to roam the streets finding more meaty sport. Miss Annie came down here the third and fourth times alone, pursued her studies on her own, and earned the respect of her colleagues. She is soon to be an Associate Professor of Marine Science for her work. A high position, I think, for a beautiful young girl." Terri's right hand reached out and touched my knee lightly. "She is much more unsure socially than in her profession where she looks forward to a title as confirmation of her worth. You must supply direction to those movements of spirit which the two of you share. We carry much that is of old use with us on our everyday rounds."

"What directions?" I asked. As far as I could tell, there was no relationship beyond the friendship the two of us had spoken of. Part of me also wondered why I was considering advice from this old man, but there was something compelling in the ideas, in the voice.

"If a woman is to seem more to a man than his sister or his mother, a man must move through the stages of becoming. You are first a woman's son. Next you are the brother of a woman. Then, when you have the knowledge of what is dangerous in human relationships and what is also beautiful, then you are at the third stage of being a man with a woman."

"The Garden of Eden."

"The word *Genesis* means *becoming*," said Terri and a smile flickered across his old face. "A fitting name, I have always thought, for instruction books and history texts. Ah, our refreshment."

Annie paused at the screen door, framed for a moment in the gingerbread of the old-fashioned house. It may have been a trick of the afternoon light, but her presence on the porch emerged into sharper focus. The scene before me was caught for a moment, frozen. The long-armed girl bearing a tray, an ancient, blind man telling stories. I was astounded at myself for taking it all in so passively, without question, but I felt part of a larger mechanism, part of an ancient ritual.

Annie placed the tray between us, taking two glasses of lemonade and a small pile of Almond cookies for Cassie and herself. Terri sipped his tea while I finished half my coffee in a gulp.

"What did my father find when he returned here? Was he looking for anything in particular?" I asked, once Terri had settled back, having unerringly returned the mug of tea to the tray Annie had placed between us.

"Your older sister accompanied your mother and father down here in 1943. While your father's ship was out to sea, your mother would play bridge or she and the baby girl would sit together and play in the sand at the hotel beach where your mother could see the ships as they came in past the Sea Bouy, down the main ship channel, and into the harbor. By the time the ship was tied to the shore, your mother would be there, waiting, waving. Your mother was not yet pregnant. When the ship would return, your father would hire a Cuban woman to take care of your sister at the hotel. Your mother and father would then spend all their short time together discovering the town, swimming, going fishing, and making love. Then your father would again go off to sea, your sister and your mother would once again play on the beach, or your mother would play bridge. These trips would last a month, usually, and there were six of them, with a week or ten day's stay in port between each one."

"It doesn't sound like much of a life for my mother," I commented.

"Your father knew this, but he did not know how else he could have her company. He was, as you remarked, a sensual man, especially when he was young. The war patrols, too, served to whet these appetites." Teri spoke without blaming.

"After the fifth period ashore with your father, your mother learned that she was pregnant. Your father wanted his wife, daughter, and new baby out of harm's way, so plans were made for your mother to go back to St. Louis. This next month would be the last time the little girl and the young woman would play on the beach, waiting for the sailor to come home from the sea, for, even though it was not an exciting life for your mother, it was a time of peace with her little girl, a time when she could enjoy the simple pleasures of motherhood without the ceremonial duties of a warrior's wife."

"I guess I'm surprised that my father realized this."

"Most men do not know the roles the women in their life play. Men, especially those in war, define all those around them in warrior terms. Your father, like all of the men in the service with him, placed himself at the center of things and did not consider the roles their wives and lovers played."

"Did you and he talk about this when he returned here last year?" I could not imagine my father having these perceptions, much less revealing them to as unconventional a creature as Terri. But the man I left on going over to Vietnam was certainly not the same as the one who lived in this house at the end of his life. Maybe he had taken to sharing a part of himself with this old man, I thought, but, as soon as I formed the words, I knew that I meant them cruelly. I was jealous that my father had evidently told Terri much of his life and yet had not been able to answer my tapes from Vietnam.

"We talked of many things in both our lives. Men, women, wars; these things all come up. What I am telling you now are parts of his past your father looked for. He may not have discovered every one of them in as ordered a way as I now tell you, but he developed what I might call an appreciation for a woman's role as a sailor's companion. Your father and your mother had their last liberty together at Easter time, just before your mother left for the North."

"Once your mother was home in St. Louis with her parents, a situation she did not care for, I believe, from what your father told me of her letters to him, the tempo of the war patrols increased, and your father returned to the island for shorter periods of time between patrols. He would now come ashore and stay at the Hotel on his own, going fishing or swimming and sitting by the beach, reading. His second homecoming without a woman's attention found him looking for companionship in the town. And he found it. He renewed this intimacy on subsequent calls in port until an Easter leave in St. Louis with your mother and her as-yet unborn baby reminded him of his familial commitment."

"And I was born in November," I said.

"Your father returned to the island and to his patrols. Your mother had her baby, a boy, who became you. Your mother returned to the rhythm of Key West in January of 1945, this time with two children in tow, but it took the entire period of his stay ashore that time for the two of them to find the intimacy lost after your birth."

"What was wrong?"

"Your father told me that after you were born, after he had strayed from his marriage while your mother was in St. Louis, that he and she had a hard time being intimate," Terri explained.

"So, how did he end up at the reunion in Key West all those years later?" I asked, trying to steer the conversation away from my parents' sex life.

"I made sure that he was on the list of invitees to the Pork Chops Reunion."

"You? I don't understand."

Terri, taking a small bite of a cookie, explained. "As a local who still lived here, I was in charge of putting together the reunion of the Pork-Chops, what they used to call the supply officers during the war. My job was to call each of them who were either stationed here or on ships that were home-ported here, or write them a letter, inviting them to a reunion held at the Truman Annex last winter. When I saw your father's name on the roster, I realized that I wanted to see him again. I didn't explain to your father that the fellow calling him had known him during the war, and I don't think he remembered me."

"You two knew each other?"

"We had spent some time together when he was ashore and not on patrol. Going out drinking, playing bridge, that kind of thing." Terry paused. "He didn't seem to remember me, and I didn't remind him. In the end, he said that he wouldn't be able to make the reunion, so I sweetened the pot for him by offering a free stay at the Pier House during the reunion, an arrangement I had worked out with David, the owner. I even managed to get him to bring up that his son, you, had been stationed here for two years, hoping that this would make him curious. Evidently, over the two years you had been stationed here you had spoken to him about your time here, and so he became interested, I think, to see if it matched his memories of Key West. In the end, he attended the reunion," Terri finished.

"Did you get a chance to reminisce?"

"Not at first. I wasn't sure he would want to renew our acquaintance. I stayed in the background and only got together with him directly when I ran into him on the beach with Billy Rose. It was then that he realized who I was. I had, of course, changed a great deal since he had seen me last. It had been a quarter of a century since we had seen each other."

"We talked of old times and of what we had each done in the interim, everything but our time in the Navy together. He seemed to have a hard time remembering all the barhopping and bridge games, and I finally realized why. We had briefly become more than just Navy buddies; we had become, if only for a few inebriated evenings, intimate. He didn't, almost couldn't, remember those times."

"You and my father?" I asked, astonished.

"We were briefly lovers, yes," Terri answered simply.

"Oh," was all I could manage.

After a pause in our conversation that lasted for many minutes, I asked Terri, "Is that why he came back down here those times and bought the house and the boat?"

"Yes. We smoked some marijuana the last evening at the Pork Chop reunion, and, in its glow, he finally was able to reminisce about our "affair."

"The next day, we spoke of it quite openly, even making fun of two old queers here in Key West. He then left for St. Louis and promised to return. He already knew that his health was questionable, and that he did not have a lot of time left, and he said that he wanted to spend it in a place that had good memories."

It helped explain some of the changes my father had undergone in the last year of his life.

"In any case," Terri continued, "your father and I had a series of visits and, by the time he returned to St. Louis for the last time, he was a much happier man than he had been when we met on that beach with Billy Rose."

"And, no, in case you were wondering, we did not become lovers again. The renewed friendship was enough fuel for those old fires. But he did some things that changed my life for the better."

For the first time since sitting on the porch, Teni's eyes blinked, and I thought I saw tears glisten on their grayness. "I used to own *Coast Pilot*, but I could no longer take her out because of my failing eyesight. So, he bought her from me, and I taught him to drive her. We spent many hours on her whenever he would come down here, one week every month. He also rented and then bought this house and let me live here because, as he put it, he and I should have a comfortable place to spend our days and nights."

Cassie had sensed or heard Terri rise from the chair and presented herself as guide. Terri laid a thin, bony hand lightly on her shoulder.

"Thank you for the cookies," the little girl said to Annie. "They were great! And I loved the picture book and the crabs. You're fun."

Annie beamed at this ultimate compliment.

"Your father told me to send this to you and your sister if you didn't come for it within a year," Terri said, producing a blue bound folded sheaf of papers and a small, white envelope from inside of her leather vest. "Thank you for the tea, and I hope I was able to answer some questions for you. Your father was, at the end, a much more peaceful person than the one you left when you went to Vietnam."

I took the offered papers and envelope and placed them on the chair. "Thank you. I can't think that this is the end of the story. We need to meet again. Where are you staying?"

"With friends. Do not worry. We'll talk tomorrow."

By a subtle signal to the child, Terri must have told Cassie that he wished to leave, for the four of us started off the porch and down toward the street. Cassie walked slowly and surely as Terri stepped lightly in her wake. Annie and I followed their ancient progress down to the kapok tree where our strange party paused. "This was the quality I much admired in your father, his sense of honor. It took him a dozen trips to the island, but he finally found the peace he was seeking." Terri turned to me and spoke in a voice of great sadness. "On his instructions, I cleaned this house and left only the photographs and the simple fragments of his final stays here. He knew that that trip would be his last, that he was going to die. I asked him before he left if he was at peace about what had happened so long ago. He said that he at last felt in balance with the past. I believe that he left this island the final time at peace with himself."

"Thank you for telling me these things." I think that I saw a slight, sad smile flicker across his face. "I know that my father must have valued your friendship," I told Terri.

"Thank you. I believe that he did."

The four of us stood together at the street's edge.

"Can you tell us about the name *Byblos*?" Annie asked to break the awkward silence.

"It is just a name from the past, a name your father happened to like the sound of," Terri said, but I had a feeling that there was more to the name than just a sound.

Annie and I stood at the end of the path, next to the huge slab of wood carved with the number 65 and watched as the two of them, the little blond figure in the yellow t-shirt and the old, gaunt figure in leather and denim, moved unhurriedly up the edge of the street toward the center of town. From the movements of her head and hands, we could tell that Cassie was chattering away. They would pause occasionally, and I could imagine Terri's thin voice carefully explaining some point of telling another piece of the island's story. Mrs. Prime was right; Cassie's association with Teni could be a real advantage in her life.

"What were the papers?" Annie asked. "Something from your father?"

"I don't know. Let's see," I said and headed up to the house after the two distant figures turned a distant corner.

"Cassie said something interesting," Annie offered as we stepped up onto the porch. "She said that Terri sent her home by taxi on a few of their visits here, and that she would send the taxi back the next day to pick her up, so Cassie could walk Terri back downtown."

"Meaning that Terri used to spend the night here?"

"I guess."

"Well, Terri's an adult," I said, not yet ready to share details of Terri's and my dad's intimacy. "Here it is," I said as I picked up one of the papers Terri had given me. "A trust deed. And there's a pair of tickets to something called The Revue at Delmonico's. Looks like fun. For all his mystery, he's turning out to be something of a tour guide."

By mid-afternoon, I had a working copy of the story about

the 93 boat getting hit and what happened afterwards. Walking up to Truman Street, I found a Cuban offset printer with a copier I could use. Looking the story over as I walked back to the house before giving it to Annie to read, I tried to come to terms with how scared I'd felt coming back into the rivers after being hit. I thought maybe Annie could see something obvious in the story that had been slipping past me. Trying to continue the final op story after finishing this one, I had discovered again that that well was dry. I couldn't even remember what I was feeling that last night. Some of the facts were clear as day, while some seemed to fade in and out of focus. Just as I'd begin to remember something from that night, my mind would skip ahead or back, leaving me lost in the story, the thread broken.

Annie had put on a light blue tank suit and was sitting on a pillow on the downstairs porch when I got back. Her figure was emphasized by the thin fabric of the suit, and she must have watched my eyes as I tried to toss her a copy of the story. The stapled pile of papers fell in a heap a foot out of her reach.

"Nice look, Ned," she said as she reached forward to gather in the papers. "All the parts in the right places?"

I must have blushed. "I'm sorry, but you caught me by surprise," I managed to sputter. "It's just... I haven't seen you... like that."

"Didn't anybody feed you today?" Annie asked as she pushed her glasses up on her nose and started to read my story. "You're drooling."

I disappeared inside and decided to stay out of her way until she was well into the story. Whether I was getting the come-on or was being warned off, I couldn't tell, but I felt like I was in college on those interminable Freshman weekends. I was somehow back at square one with an exciting date, and I couldn't tell if she liked me or not.

Later that afternoon, Annie told me that she liked the story, especially the parts explaining my fear. She also told me that she had discovered in one of my father's books, the Egyptian one, what the word Byblos meant.

"It was the name of the city where the last part of Osiris'

dismembered body washed ashore and was found by his sister, Isis."

"What part?" I asked.

"I bet you can guess," Annie said with a smile.

CHAPTER TWENTY-FOUR

Cua Lon River, 9 November 1230 hours

Usually, a mission out to the west mouth of the Cua Lon from *Sea Float* was a milk run. The river was at its widest from Old Nam Can to the coast and the south bank back about a hundred yards had been hit with defoliant. The boat crews could see some of the tumbled-in charcoal ovens on the south bank and one or two cemeteries. That's all that was left after Tet of 1968 when the Viet Cong took the cities of the Ca Mau peninsula, and the fighting to get them back pretty well destroyed them and the villages all around. It must have been a hell of a fight, most of the old timers agreed.

The 127 boat and Ned's boat, the 93, were going to set up for a psy-ops run. One of the boats was supposed to play a tape from the psychological operations people called *The Wandering Soul* while running dead slow, but the boats had to make sure they were in the middle of the river, or they'd take fire from whichever bank they were closest to. It was a weird tape, complete with sound effects and an echo chamber voice telling the enemy soldiers from the North to go home quickly before they were killed down here in the South. If a North Vietnamese was killed in the South and couldn't get the proper kind of burial, his soul would wander forever, looking for peace or rest or whatever.

One of the voices on the tape was supposed to be an NVA soldier who had been killed down on the peninsula. The Jg from psy-ops, a tall kid from Newark with a birth mark on his face with bright blue eyes, read a translation of the soldier's part in a New Jersey accent. "I cannot rest. I must wander these forests all time. Never again can I sleep next to my sweet wife or watch my children play. I cannot walk behind the slow ox in my rice field or fish the small rach for food." Seemed to work, the psy-ops people thought, but Ned had his doubts.

The two boats were heading out the river to wait offshore, and Chase asked Ned's permission to fire one of the LAWs they had been issued the week before. The boat crews were all like kids and loved blowing things up and shooting the heavy weapons. The LAW was an anti- tank weapon, a fiberglass tube with a sight and a trigger housing. Inside the tube was a rocket with a shaped charge supposed to be able to knock out a tank. The whole thing was disposable, so you'd only use it once and then throw the tube away. Usually, Charlie would find the old tube and discover some way to fire it back at you. Charlie was amazing that way.

Ned said Chase could fire at an ammo box once they got offshore because there was a SEAL team operating somewhere west of Sea Float and Ned didn't want to fire into the tree line and take a chance hitting near the SEALs or screwing up their op.

Chase said OK. They were running out the river at full bore with Chase up in the gun tub, Tracy back aft on the piggyback .50, CB just standing somewhere 'midships, not really manning a gun but ready to use one of the M-60s they used as waist guns. The Kid was on the other M-60 and Tom, as usual, was driving. Ned was standing where he usually stood, half in and half out of the pilot house door on the port side. All the radios were there and so was the chart table. It was a hot afternoon, so they didn't have their flak jackets zipped shut. There were some tall thunderheads offshore that Ned could see out over the Gulf of Siam, but it didn't look like rain inland where they were. They were a little to the right of the middle of the river, the 127 boat about fifty yards astern and a little to port. The

Cua Lon was beginning to run a bit more south than west, just below where the Rach Tra Loi comes in, where the 84 boat had had a shootout with a rocket team.

Then there was a loud *blam* and Ned felt a gust of hot gas in his face.

"Dammit, Chase. I told you not to fire that LAW!" Ned yelled up to the gun tub.

"I didn't fire, Boss," Chase answered. "That wasn't me."

Ned looked up and Chase had both his hands up in the air like a little kid showing he hadn't done it.

"I think we're hit, Boss," yelled CB who was kneeling, bent over the rail looking at the hull. "Something hit us right at the waterline." Ned saw some splashes in the river ahead of them and to the left.

"Taking small arms fire from the south bank," Chase yelled and hunkered down between his twin-.50s. The barrels were at full depression, so the first ten rounds he fired made splashes close to the boat. He got his arms in the handles and started walking the fire toward the south bank of the river. The tracers arced and disappeared into the bank of the river. Ned could hear the ring and clatter of Chase's expended brass casings and empty links as they hit the bottom of the gun tub.

Ned pulled the mic from its clip. "One two seven, this is nine three. I'm taking fire from the south bank, over." Ned heard two clicks from the other boat.

"We're taking on water," Tom who was driving said behind him. "Bilge alarms are going off. Ammo storage bins." He said it very calmly, but Ned could tell he was nervous. His left hand gripped the wheel so tightly his knuckles were white, even with his tan. He had both Morse controls in his right hand.

Ned stuck his head out through the pilothouse door. The 127 boat's twin-.50s were firing at the south bank and his single .50 aft was hitting the north bank. Just in case. Sometimes Charlie tried to sucker you by firing a couple of rounds from one bank and then hitting you really hard from the other bank when you moved over closer to it.

"Sea Float, this is Abbey November nine three, over," Ned spoke into the mic calmly, trying to keep his voice from breaking or showing any excitement. Ned couldn't do it as well as the Black Pony or Sea Wolf pilots yet, but he was working on it.

"Abbey November nine three, this is Sea Float. Request you stand by, over."

Stand by, my ass. "Negative, Sea Float We're taking fire at location four niner six, eight six five. I say again, we are taking fire from the south bank, location four niner six, eight six five, over. "

"Nine three. This is Sea Float. I roger your location. Help is on the way, over," came the voice and this time it was calm and professional. It sounded to Ned like a doctor trying to soothe a worried patient.

"This is nine three. Roger, out," Ned answered. Professional. Calm. Ned didn't see any more enemy fire, just the splashes from their own .50s.

"I'm losing revs, Boss," said Tom. Professional. Calm.

That meant they had taken on a hell of a lot of water. "Put her on the beach. Starboard bank," Ned said to Tom and thumped Chase on the boot through the open bottom of the gun tub. Chase stopped firing. "We're going into the north bank. Hose down a good place to park," Ned yelled up to him and Chase swung his twins around and started shooting again.

"We're going to park for a while," Ned said into the mic to the 127-boat, not identifying himself. Professional. Calm. Very scared, Ned realized.

"Roger. I'll cover from here," the 127 answered. He'd wait around in the middle, just keeping an eye out for another ambush.

Chase softened up a place to beach the boat. Up and down the bank he raked the fire from his .50s for a width of maybe fifty yards. It would have taken someone pretty well dug in to survive that kind of direct fire, but you never knew. Just before they put their nose ashore, Chase stopped firing and Tom swung their starboard side toward the bank. Tracy let off a flechette round right into the bush, a dense lot of creepers and nipa palms. You could see the leaves shiver as the tiny steel arrows from the flechette peppered the area. Tom then gunned the engines, put the wheel over hard to starboard, rammed the 93's nose about five feet up on the beach, and put both engines into neutral. At least they wouldn't sink.

"Check your engines, CB," Ned yelled. "Tracy, go below into the cabin and see if you can find where we were hit. Keep an eye out upstream and down," Ned reminded Chase.

"Everybody OK?" Ned remembered to ask as he stared into the thick green jungle just twenty feet from their bow. The tide was ebbing. Brown mud pocked with crab holes filled the distance between their bow and the start of the low, stunted mangrove trees, their roots creating a tangle that Ned always thought was better hidden under the waters of the river at high tide. Mangrove roots reminded him of spiders. Behind the mangroves, another twenty feet up the bank, grew a thick screen of short, four to five feet high nipa palms. Anything could be hidden only two feet into the palms. A pair of mud brown crabs the size of baseballs scuttled from right to left and disappeared down two adjoining holes. The mud made sucking sounds as the brown water receded.

"I think I got hit, Boss," came the Kid's voice and Ned swung around. The Kid wore a sleeveless camouflaged shirt, regular fatigues, jungle boots, and a helmet he could barely see out from under. He was holding his left arm with his right hand, at a point just above the elbow. There was blood. A lot of it. The blood looked brown and had chunks in it.

I'm going to be sick, Ned thought, but he grabbed a field dressing from the catch-all in front of the chart table. Ned was ripping the paper package open as he moved slowly back toward the Kid. He had light brown hair and looked about fourteen years old. Everything he wore was a size or more too big for him, so he always looked like a little boy playing dress-up. He took a lot of ribbing for this, but he was quiet and a hard worker. Ned saw the Kid take his trigger finger and dip it into the mess on his arm. He then put his finger into his mouth.

"Beans," the Kid said and made a face.

"What?" asked Ned, not understanding.

"The c-rats can got hit," the Kid said.

Ned looked at the Kid's M-60 and there it was, the blown open olive drab can of beans and hot dogs, clipped to the side. The gunners did it all the time, clipping c-ration cans to the sides of their machine guns to give a smoother feed for the ammo belt.

The Kid took the offered battle dressing from Ned and was wiping the mess from his arm when CB and the radio both started at once. The engines looked OK, no oil spray, and the batteries still had a full charge to get them going again. The *Appomattox*, a one-hundred-and-twenty-foot PG assigned to *Sea Float* would be coming out to help them. Ned thought through this information slowly.

"You OK, Kid?" Ned asked. Ned was listening to Tom talk to *Sea Float*.

"No Purple Heart, huh?" the Kid said as he tossed the jagged, empty can of beans and hot dogs into the river.

"Sorry, Kid, but not for c-rats. Better luck next time," Ned told him. The Kid knew that a wound in battle meant a pay increase, so a small wound was a benefit. It also helped your statistics. If one out of five were wounded, and your wound was a small one, the odds were that you wouldn't be wounded again in a worse way. At least that's what the odds said.

Ned gave the Kid a thumbs up and turned to CB. "Go ahead and check the engines, CB."

"Strainers?" CB asked, only his head bobbing before Ned from the space between the engines. The engineman never disabled the main engines without checking first to see if they would need them right away.

"Sure. Clean them and let me know if the generator's sucking mud."

CB nodded, disappeared, and then the two engines ran light, rattled, and shut down. Aside from the soft hiss and purr of the heavily muffled generator, their landing site was quiet. "*Appomattox's* going to come straight through on a firing run, hitting the tree line with 40 mike- mike cannon fire. If it's OK with us," said Tom from the pilothouse.

"Sure. Tell them it's fine," Ned answered. "Tracy?" Ned called down into the cabin. "How's it look down there?"

Tracy's voice answered, "Got the wiring harness, Boss. Blown all to hell in half. About two feet of water in the bilge." Tracy's Texas accent was heavier than usual, a sign that he was nervous.

"Keep an eye out, OK, Chase?" Ned said up to the gun tub. "And... sorry I thought you'd fired off the LAW."

"No sweat, Boss," Chase answered. He was looking at the opposite bank through his binoculars, keeping a good watch.

"I'll be in the cabin if you need me," Ned said to Tom and went below. All the deck panels were up and stacked against the galley cabinets and reefer. On the centerline of the boat were two ammunition bins, one forward of the other. They measured three feet deep and four feet long and wide. Tracy was kneeling in the aft one on top of the boxes of ammo peering down between the two with a flashlight.

"There!" he said triumphantly and reached down with his right arm.

Ned watched as Tracy removed his arm from between the bins and held up a small piece of dull metal. "The brass slug," Tracy said with a grin, "from the rocket. Guys back at *Sea Float* in UDT said it's good luck to find one." Tracy's accent was losing some of its Texas flavor, so Ned knew he was OK. He was right about the good luck, too. The RPG-7 anti-tank rocket uses a shaped charge. If it had hit us six inches farther forward or aft, Ned realized, the ammo bins would have been in the way and Inshore Patrol Craft 93 would have been blown out of the water.

The *Appomattox's* firing run impressed the crews of both Swifts. Ned stood on the stern of his beached boat as the PG came around the bend in the river to their east. She must have been doing thirty knots when she went by, her wake sucking the river three feet from the banks and the backwash creating a wave that would have drowned anyone foolish enough to still be in a spider hole along the river. Her 40-millimeter cannon, developed for service during World War II, pumped out two rounds per second as she slid quickly by, her turbine just audible as a high whine. Puffs of white, black, and gray smoke along the tree line on the south bank sprouted every ten feet. Ned could see trees shiver and then fall toward the river, their two-foot-thick trunks shattered by the anti-aircraft shells from the twin barreled Bofors on the *Appomattox's* fantail.

Ned was startled by a noise behind him. The entire crew of the 93 boat was applauding and cheering. Ned joined in as the *Appomattox*, her firing run complete, disappeared around the next bend of the river to their west, her high-pitched turbine whine fading.

"We'll stand by here," the *Appomattox* said over the radio, "until you're underway, over."

"Roger, Pine Tree. Bravo Zulu on that run. We're impressed. Must be nice to be the toughest kid on the block, over," Ned answered, wondering about *Appomattox's* call sign.

"Thank you, nine three, but being a tough guy is a hard reputation to keep up. Pine Tree, out," the skipper of the PG said.

Hit in two separate ambushes in the next week, the *Appomattox* was withdrawn from the river. An RPG-7 rocket exploded on her bridge in the second ambush, killing her skipper.

CHAPTER TWENTY-FIVE

Key West, late afternoon

"Good story, Ned."

"Thank you," I said from the canvas chair where I had returned to work on the second part of the story, "but that's only the first part. I'm just finishing up the end."

"Ned doesn't seem all that scared, though."

"It's not until the shooting stops that the fear seeps in. You want to hear?"

"Can I stand up and get some iced tea first without being mentally undressed?" Annie asked, but she was smiling when she said it.

"I'll keep my testosterone to myself. Promise."

"Meat."

"What?" I asked as Annie disappeared up the stairs.

"When you looked at me, I felt like meat," she yelled down the stairs. She held the pause until she came back out on the porch with her iced tea and resumed her position on the pillow. Her body still danced in front of me, but I managed to look to either side, around, or through her without staring. I met her eyes as she spoke again. "You know. Meat on a hook. At a butcher's," Annie explained, looking at me seriously over her glasses.

I was confused, especially after last night, but I didn't want to bring that up. "When does a girl want to be looked at?"

"She'll let you know. And she doesn't mind being looked at. It is being stared at, ogled, or gawked at that makes her uneasy." Annie pushed her glasses up again and smiled. "It's OK. You got the point. I'11 show you sometime and do it to you."

"I can hardly wait," I said and knew that she was serious.

I began to read the end of the story aloud to Annie.

Two weeks later, on a Saturday, the 93 boat sat at the mouth of the river waiting for an escort back in to Sea Float. *The hole in her side had been welded shut and the wiring harness spliced at the repair facility at An Thoi on Phu Quoc Island in the Gulf of Siam.*

CB had stuffed a mattress in the hole after the ambush, and they had left the river that afternoon, in company with the 127 boat, and headed for An Thoi. The 127 had returned to Sea Float *the next day, leaving the 93 to the tender mercies of the repair crews and bartenders of An Thoi. The crew's unscheduled R&R had been a welcome break from being on call twenty-four hours a day. Back at the mouth of the Cua Lon, Ned sat in the pilothouse and looked at the river.*

The mouth of most of the rivers in Vietnam extend well beyond the land mass because of the gradual slope of the seabed. The 93 boat sat tied to a sun-bleached pole in a forest of similar poles about a mile offshore, nothing between them and the thin line on the horizon that would be the tip of the Ca Man peninsula. Before Tet of 1968, a concentration of small fishing shanties perched on poles driven into the deep mud at the mouth of the river supported life for about two dozen families from the nearby villages of Cay Me and Ong Trang on the south bank of the river's mouth.

Now only the poles remained, the rest of the shanties having been dashed into the sea by typhoons or washed ashore during two years of monsoon rains. The villages, too, were gone, machine gunned and burned in the fighting to retake the Ca Mau peninsula and the southernmost city of Nam Can overrun by the Viet Cong during Tet. The mouth of the river, like the mouth of a corpse, was dead.

A single small island covered with stunted, salt rusted bushes, about an acre in size, sat like a beacon guiding Ned's gaze to the actual mouth of the river, the rest of the eastern horizon a thin smudge of brownish green sameness. To enter the river, you headed for the center of the tiny island, ran almost up to its westernmost tip, turned hard to starboard, skirting its tide and current cleansed sides by maybe three feet, and steered a magnetic course of 110° for about a hundred yards. You were now in the Cua Lon river itself. All of this was a tricky bit of coastal piloting and seamanship because it had to be performed at high speed.

Charlie chose river mouths as one of his favorite ambush points. Because few fishermen had permission to work the fish traps in the area, the mouth of the Cua Lon was not a free fire zone. The 93 boat couldn't prep fire the river's mouth to discourage an ambush. They just had to run the gauntlet.

Ned stared at the island through his binoculars wondering how difficult it would be for Charlie to rig some rockets or a mine on the south shore of the island. The boats passing so close would be perfect targets. A barrel-bottom claymore at point-blank range would devastate the crew of a Swift, riding bow-high, all eyes straining to see into the foliage of the river ahead. A low thump followed immediately by a hollow clang all in an instant in the yellow flash of the explosion as bits of glass, metal, and even jagged rocks hurl across the ten feet between the low, hiding scrub and the rushing aluminum boat. Ned remembered how Killian, the bow gunner, his neck punctured by a piece of metal from a mine, had bled to death and how it had taken him hours to die. Killian kept saying that it was cold, so cold, as the life drained from him onto Ned and onto the grey deck of the bow of the Swift.

Ned remembered standing in the pilot house door on the starboard side during the Arapaho mission. The launch-bomb hit just below him and could have exploded. Both of his legs would have been shattered, like Gillies on the 47 boat, as his legs were driven up by the explosion, his body not yet reacting to the blast. Ned had seen the body of a Viet Cong killed in a bunker by a 105 round, the same charge used in the launch-bombs. Charlie's torso, arms, and head were all that was recognizable, the rest of him from the waist down having been turned to pulp by the blast. Would a rocket or mine at close quarters do the same? Do they sew you back together or just send the collection home in a bag? Who does the sewing? The Army at Da Nang or your family undertaker at home? Do they let your people at home look at you? What would they say at home, only getting part of you back?

"Hello, nine three. Welcome home."

What's left of me to send home won't even have a name, just a number. Ned looked up from his daydream and saw the twin bow waves of a pair of Swifts exiting the river mouth and heading their way.

The radio spoke again. *"Welcome home, nine three."*

"This is nine three. Can't say it's good to be back, but here we are, over," answered Tom and handed the mic to Ned. Tom went out on the bow and checked the slipknot attaching them to the pole.

"Let's go trombones," said the speaker. Ned switched the indicator on the radio to 76, a seldom used frequency, so that all three boats could communicate more freely away from the prying ears of Sea Float and probably Charlie.

"Is that you, Nash?" Ned asked. Through the glasses Ned thought he could pick out the tiny pink plastic doll Nash's gunner had attached to the front of the 127 boat's gun tub like a figurehead. The doll was male and over-endowed with everything a gunner thought a boy-doll might need to prosper in both a firefight and a brothel. Nash's gunner even had a small piece of camouflage cloth he would wrap around the doll when the 127 boat was on ambush.

"You got it, Ned. Ready for a little action on the way home?"

"I can hardly wait. Surfs up?" Ned asked. Nash liked to tell stories of his days surfing the beaches of Southern California. It kept him in shape for his triumphant return to Seal Beach, Nash told the other Swift drivers. Ned knew Nash did it for the same reason they all told those stories.

"Yeah. I'll tell you when we tie up with you. Five-eight here's going up for a week alongside the green apple," Nash explained. The green apple was the floating barracks ship at An Thoi, where they had just spent the past two weeks.

"Adios, Billy. Have one or two for me," Ned said to the 58 boat's skipper, a quiet, married Swede from Minnesota who just wanted to go back to school when he went home and get his Masters in Agricultural Business.

"Take care, nine three," answered Billy.

The 58 boat roared by, her twin exhausts steaming in the late afternoon sun, as the 127 cut her speed, set her fenders to port, and drifted up to their starboard side, tying off with a single breast line with a slipknot for a quick breakaway.

Nash was in the pilothouse of the 93 before the two boats had settled *down from 58's wake. His blond hair, always longer than regulations allowed, was tied back from his face with a red headband. He wore no helmet and his mirrored aviator glasses flashed Ned's reflection back at him. On the left lapel of his fatigue shirt a camouflaged button read* PEACE THROUGH WAR.

Ned pointed to the button as they shook hands. "Things getting a little nasty at the Float?"

"It's been a bitch, man. Charlie's sending swimmer sappers to mine the barges." Nash settled himself in the helmsman's seat. Even in the relative dimness of the pilothouse Nash wouldn't take off his shades. Ned couldn't see Nash's eyes, but the rest of his face was smiling. "We're on perimeter patrol every other night for four hours" Doing roundy-rounds and dropping grenades in the river. A real bitch. No more poker nights. Too much like the real Navy."

"It's sooo nice to come home, eh?" Ned said. "Heard from the Z lady?"

"The Z's a total." Nash's face lost its smile. "Dawn parked it next to a fire hydrant and there was a fire. I guess they tried to use a ladder truck to bulldoze it out of the way. When that didn't work, they hooked up the hoses anyway and ran them through the car. Busted every God damned window."

"Uh." Ned didn't know what to say. "How's the lady taking it?"

"I guess she's pretty upset about it," said Nash and looked out through the windshield. "Her sister wrote me to get my insurance info. Something's screwed up with hers. She and Tiffany are doing OK, though. Dawn might even get back with her old man, which would be good for the kid."

Nash paused and then tapped the psy-ops amplifier bolted to the overhead of the pilot house. "Got an op for tonight. Should be bitchin'. Get to do a little Wandering Soul *on our way into the Float." Nash's smile was back, but Ned guessed he was hiding a lot behind his mirrored glasses.*

"I've got a neat twist for the run. Even cleared it with Frederick." Nash was known for adding some grace notes to standard operations, just to give them his signature. Like the time he had everybody aboard his boat hide and just let the boat drift downstream in the river, hoping that Charlie would break cover and try to capture it. Some Vietnamese did try to board the Swift near where the Cua Lon runs into the Bo De. It

took a week for Don Cherry, Sea Float's *Intel type*, to establish that they were just village fisherman trying to help a fellow sailor. The fishermen became the guests of the intelligence community up in Can Tho for that week, so they got a round-trip ride in a helicopter and lost their catch for their trouble.

"What's your neat twist this time?" Ned asked, not really wanting to join Nash on one of his crazy missions.

"Going to use the .50s during the run. Fire off about a thousand rounds and then play Wandering Soul. Should shake them up pretty good, huh?"

"I'm not so sure there's anybody out there to shake up," Ned said. "This whole area's been defoliated and blown to hell so many times that anybody out there has got to be hard core. A few minutes Wandering Soul's not going to convince them."

Nash was adamant. "The .50s will make them listen better. Maybe they'll get the message if we do a good-cop, bad-cop. Besides, it'll be fun."

"Ok. You're the boss," agreed Ned. Nash would be in charge of any operation the two of them were on together because he was senior to Ned by about six months. Seniority in the Navy went by date of commission. Ned became an officer in late December 1967, and Nash was commissioned when he graduated from college the previous spring.

"What time do we start the run? I'm still a little antsy about being back in the river," Ned said, looking through his charts in the slot under the chart table.

"Antsy?" asked Nash.

"Well, you know..." Ned hesitated and then thought, What the hell! "I'm scared, Nash. For the first time. I've just spent two weeks thinking about how close we all came to being blown out of the water. It's so bad right now that I can almost feel my legs blown off."

By the set of Nash's mouth Ned could tell that behind his mirrored glasses Nash was listening to what he was saying. Ned hoped Nash was hearing all the things Ned wasn't saying, the things he wasn't able to put in words yet. "I never should have left the damned river. It was that time off relaxing and drinking each night and then going down to the repair shed, looking at the hole in the boat. I think the crew's the same way, but we don't really talk about it, you know."

"Whoa, man," Nash said and took off his glasses. He took out a bright red handkerchief and started to polish the mirrored lenses. Nash's *eyes had dark rings, and he blinked a lot. "It's the way you look at what you do here in the river. If you're just reacting to what Charlie does to you, of course you are going to be scared all the time. Because Charlie's calling the shots. Get on the offense. Play your own game and make your own rules. Stay on the edge of the blade. There was a group down near Seal Beach used to say that surfing. Stay on the blade." Nash smiled a funny smile, thinking about something far away. "It keeps your adrenalin flowing. It gets rid of the willies." Nash had become even more gung-ho than Ned had remembered him.*

"Willies?"

"The cold, dead feeling down here." He put his palm just above his crotch. "The butterflies tickling the inside of your stomach. What's left when the hard-on's gone. It's kind of like after getting laid. Empty. You know?"

I stopped reading and looked up at Annie. Her expression hadn't changed, but I knew I should say something. "It gets a little raunchy here. I hope you don't mind."

"It's OK. Go on. It makes sense," Annie said, so I continued.

Ned knew. Being in the rivers right now was a lot like after getting laid. But it wasn't like getting laid for real. It was like what his crew called steam and cream. The release was there, all right, but it was artificial, a put-up job. When you were getting a massage, the girl would tease you and get you all tightened up inside the same way. You'd be lying there on the table with it sticking up like a tent pole under your towel and then, after you'd paid her the extra five bucks, she'd reach under the towel...

Afterwards, you always felt the same. Hollow. But at least the tension was gone. It relieved the pressure.

"The willies, yeah, Nash. That's what I've got, all right," Ned admitted, glad that someone else felt the same way. "But I can't be going after Charlie all the time. Most of the time he's not even around."

"Oh, he's around," Nash said and put his glasses back on. "I can smell him."

Ned looked out across the water where the mouth of the river lay hiding in the fading light of day. The sun would be down soon. Nash carefully adjusted the wire frames around his ears under his long hair. He looked bizarre standing there, the flat water of the mouth of the Cua Lon and the straight poles of the old fishing village reflected as curves in the lenses of his sunglasses. Everything was distorted. But Nash was able to describe to Ned the way he saw things, and, in that way, Ned was able to see it too, distortions and all.

"OK. Charlie's always there," Ned said. "But what if he doesn't start anything?"

"Then you start it yourself""

"How? Give me for instance."

"Go into some small canals that run between the rivers. Really small ones. Ones you can't turn around in. You go busting in one end and out the other. Maybe you'll catch him with his pajamas down. If you go out looking for him," Nash said, "you'll find him."

"So that's why your boat is so shot up," Ned said. "I always thought it was because you were a surfer and just trying to get lucky."

"Luck doesn't count, man. It's adrenalin. Keep it flowing and you don't get the willies," Nash promised. "And another thing." He paused They had both been looking out at where the river met the sea in a straight unbroken line. The silver light of day was turning orange. The sun was setting behind them. It would be dark soon. Nash turned and looked directly at Ned. "Don't ever leave the river. Never. It's like sex. Once you're in, you're in for good."

He was smiling, but Ned knew he was serious.

"Or like crossing the street at rush hour," Ned added.

"You got it." Nash turned away again to look out at the river, lost in thought. Ned had never seen him this way before.

"Hey, listen to this," Nash said as he reached into his fatigue pants front pocket. He produced a small, red flannel pouch with a gold draw string. He placed it on the chart table. It was the size of a pack of cigarettes. Nash poked the pouch with his index finger of his right hand and a nasal laugh issued from the pouch.

"Haa... haa... haa," said the pouch.

"It's teeth," Nash said.

"Haa... haa... haa," continued the pouch.

"Teeth? " Ned questioned.

"Haa.. haa.. haa."

Nash opened the pouch and shook a pair of plastic false teeth with bright red gums out into his left hand.

"Haa.. haa.. haa," continued the teeth.

"They're sick," Ned said.

"Haa.. haa.. haa."

"Yeah," agreed Nash with a grin.

"Haa.. haa.. haa."

"Yeah, really." The sound reminded Ned of a kid he'd known in elementary school. Peter Cooper. He was deaf and brought an amplifier with him to class. It looked like a shoe box, and it had earphones that plugged in. He always got to sit in the best seat, at the desk nearest the teacher.

Peter used to laugh like that, nasal and all one note. Ned and his friends used to play tricks on the deaf boy, like disconnecting the battery of his amplifier. We were cruel, Ned thought, looking back on it. The laughter seemed to mock their cruelty. "Turn it off, Nash, OK?"

"Haa.. haa.. haa."

"Sure," said Nash and he pressed the teeth again. The nasal monotone stopped in mid laugh.

"Can I hang onto them for tonight?" Ned asked, the shadow of an idea forming. "I want to show them to the crew. I'll give them back to you tomorrow morning at the Float." Nash put the teeth back into the red pouch and the pouch into Ned's hand. "Stay on the blade," he said and gave one of his funny, faraway smiles.

I paused and Annie smiled.
"Got it," was all she said.

At dark they started the engines and moved into the river slowly in single file, Nash's 127 boat leading. The defoliated south bank of the Cua Lon appeared as a thin, smooth line behind each green sweep of the radar scope. Ned could dimly make out the soft black of the north bank trees silhouetted against the glossy black sky. Nash opened up first, pouring thirty seconds of tracer-punctuated fire from his .50s into the far tree line of the south bank, beginning his firing run at what was left of the village of Cay Me.

Tom stopped the 93 boat in mid-stream and they waited, their engines and generator shut down. When Nash had fired for perhaps thirty seconds, the 127 boat cut her engines and generator and drifted. Ned put the cassette in the small black box mounted on the overhead and the tortured voices and sounds of the Wandering Soul whispered and boomed from the psy-ops speakers mounted on their utility mast. Ned had used the tape a dozen times before, but this time was different. In the black night of the quiet, waiting river, the eerie voice of the dead North Vietnamese soldier searching for rest made him uneasy.

Ned listened and thought of his grandmother in St. Louis sitting in front of the big sunroom window in her green chair, chain-smoking Kents without inhaling and watching Lawrence Welk on the console TV. Ned thought of Denny and himself in Denny's driveway with his TR3's dashboard pulled out as they tried to fix the tachometer. Ned remembered going back to college the next morning after spending all night talking and being teased by Margot at her boyfriend's apartment. He also remembered the envious handshakes of the old men in the Timetable Bar in Crockett, California across from the train station when the old men hadn't let them pay for their drinks the night Ned's friends and he had left San Francisco for Seattle and the long flight to Vietnam

Ned thought of his father listening to Ned's tapes and not answering them, Ned thought of all of these things and wanted to be home.

He felt angry at being caught in someone else's river, bringing them his ghost sounds and his bullets. Ned stepped out on deck and looked at his crew in the dark as the 93 boat drifted, and he listened to the voice, mesmerized. After five minutes, the voice stopped speaking with a terrible sigh. A single whispered curse from one of Ned's crew, he couldn't tell which one, fell into the silence like a coin on a table. Tom turned the speakers off from the pilothouse so the hiss of the amplifier wouldn't give away their position. Ned felt hollow, but it wasn't like after sex; it was more like the morning after he had spent the night on the boat in Can Tho with Lee.

And he remembered what Nash had told him about getting rid of the ache of the willies. Ned returned to the pilot house and picked up the starlight scope and, in the ghost green shadows of the amplified light, he could barely make out Nash's 127 boat about a thousand yards up the river.

Ned took the mic from its clip. "One two seven, this is nine three. Over," Ned said quietly, his voice sounding strange in the silent dark. He felt ready to answer his anger and his fear, to do something about the ache.

"Nine three, one two seven. Go," answered Nash.

"OK if I try something?"

"Roger, nine three. Go for it. We'll be standing by," Nash said, and Ned could hear the smile in his voice.

Ned put the mic back in its clip and pulled the red pouch from his pocket. He put it on the chart table. He unclipped the mic for the psy-ops system and held it in his hand next to the pouch.

"We're going to lay down some .50 fire," Ned said just loudly enough for everyone on board the 93 to hear. "Put some random fire into the south bank, Chase. About a minute's worth."

"You got it, Boss," answered Chase. Ned heard him jack a round into each chamber.

"When he starts firing, Tom," Ned said to the shadow next to him, "go ahead and start the engines."

Tom gave him the thumbs up. "What are we going to do?" Tom asked.

Ned's answer was cut short by the hammer of the twin-.50s above them. The whole boat shook, and the pilothouse was lit by the ruby tracers arcing out from above them into the swallowing blackness. Tom's face glowed red in the reflected light. He was grinning as he started the two diesels and the generator. Ned thought that his own face must look the same as Ned turned the psy-ops speakers up to full volume. A moment before the .50s stopped their slamming, Ned poked the pouch with his finger and keyed the psy-ops system mic.

Through the mechanical distortions of the speaker system the nasal monotone of the laugh sounded like a child's, twisted and self-consciously willful. The helmsman looked at Ned in the instrument panel's dull glow. Tom had lost his grin. Between the laughs Ned could hear the other crew members in hoarse whispers talking to each other.

"Do we just sit here?" Tom asked Ned. Tom's voice was unsure.

"Yeah. I want it to soak in."

"You sure, Boss? That laughing thing is weird."

"Chase," Ned called up to the gun tub. "Hose down the south bank for another fifteen seconds or so."

"Yah, hoo!" Chase laughed in response and began to fire.

"OK if Tracy and I fire some too?" CB's voice at Ned's elbow asked.

"Sure. Join in," Ned answered, feeling his fear of being back in the river diminish. "Tell Tracy to drop a Willie-Pete into the tree line. Just to add a touch of realism" A white phosphorous round would give off an eerie glow as it burned. Ned was beginning to enjoy being on the blade.

"Nice show," Nash's voice whispered from the radio speaker. Ned keyed the radio mic twice in answer.

Tom did his part by keeping the boat positioned so that the speakers always pointed to the south bank of the river. Ned told the Kid to join in for the final five minutes, giving him the psy-ops mic after the battery in the laughing teeth died. The Kid's high young laugh changed to a giggle when he heard himself over the speakers. The sound of his giggling coupled with the .50 fire made Ned shiver, but the whole crew seemed to be working as a team again, and Ned was finally rid of the emptiness that had haunted him since waiting to come back into the river. Laughter's healing effects, he mused.

I put the story down on the floor beside me and waited.

"Good story, Ned," Annie said. "I liked the way the Kid gets caught up in it at the end. Shows how God damned far it can drive you."

"Yeah," I agreed. "He was still innocent, even after nearly a year over there."

"The military calls it becoming a man. What a waste... Let me see it when you've got it copied, OK? I'd like to read it by myself, too."

Annie stretched and stood up. Shadows stood in pools on the porch. I watched her move slowly in front of the screen, backlit by the trees set afire by the golden reddish glow from the sunlight slanting in from the west. "Let's go eat and visit that place Terri got us tickets for, the Delmonico," she suggested. Her profile against the light made my heart race.

I'm done for, I thought. She has me feeling guilty watching her, and all it does is turn me on even more. If only I could feel that same energy in writing about that last op.

"Yeah, I'm ready for some shrimp." I stood up and followed Annie in through the window. "Thanks for listening."

CHAPTER TWENTY-SIX

Key West, night

Delmonico's was housed in the empty shell of the old Odéon vaudeville and movie house in the center of the busiest section of Duval Street. The marquis promised a semi-pro production of the music from *Cabaret*. True to its name in lights, we sat at small tables in the great, black cavern and were served drinks by the cast as the abbreviated story of Sally Bowles and her life in pre-war Berlin told itself through a series of songs and dances. The cast was excellent, the music from the four-piece ensemble plenty for the production, and Annie and I were soon both lost in the glitter and magic of live theater.

During the break between acts, some of the cast members joined friends or made friends and sat with the audience. The two of us were surprised when the surprisingly small girl who played Sally came up to our table and introduced herself.

"Hi. I'm Raven," she said. Her black hair was cut in jagged bangs, her eyes peered out from deep pits mascara and eye shadow pits, and her rust red lipstick gave her a carnivorous aspect. She was singing the lead role well with a strong, resonant voice, and I could tell why when she sat down at our table. She had a classical singer's upper body, broad and full bosomed. For the role of Sally, she had bound herself tightly into a bright red satin flapper costume which had given me the impression of a small size. Annie in her denim skirt and white peasant blouse and me in khakis and a blue oxford shirt looked dowdy in comparison.

"Terri told me to introduce myself to you two," she said with obvious warmth. "Do you like it so far?"

"It's great," Annie answered immediately. "I've always wanted to be able to dance like that, but I've never been able to keep my energy up past the first two minutes of a number. You were terrific!"

"Thank you, but the gang I work with makes it look easy. You want some more of that panther piss they call wine?" Raven looked quickly around the cabaret and called out to a thin, black girl with a tight Afro and a slinky mauve satin dress slit up to her tiny waist "Toni? Can we have another specimen over here, please? Eighty-six."

Toni disappeared into the gloom behind the stage.

"Our treat," explained Raven. "Friends of the house."

"Is Terri here?" I asked.

"No. He's gone by now. Just helps us dress for the show."

"We just met him ourselves," explained Annie.

"That's what I thought. I hadn't seen you," and she looked across at me, "here on the island before, but I thought I'd seen you on the beach," she finished, looking at Annie.

"My first trip," I said.

"I've been to Key West before, collecting marine specimens. This is my fifth trip. I come once a year about this time."

"Sure. I remember now. The crab lady. You stay at The Chimneys. Robin's mom works backstage sometimes, and Robin's going to be in *Hansel and Gretel* this fall," Raven said.

I listened as the two women talked shop about dance training. Raven seemed brash and self-confident while Annie, in contrast, seemed eager and naive.

"Can I ask you how you do that flip at the end of the scene with the businessmen? Do you have a trampoline back there," Annie asked Raven.

"Oh, that. Toni does it. When your wine comes, check out

the muscles," Raven said, standing up. "I've got to get changed for the next scene; I get to flash a little skin for the tourists in the cheap seats. How about a drink down on the beach later? I always take a quick dip after the show, and Terri said you might have some questions."

"Questions?" I asked.

"That's what Terri said. I thought it was a little strange, but I stopped worrying about 'strange' with Terri a long time ago."

"We'll see you there," promised Annie. "What time and where?"

"About eleven down at the Pier House beach. You can get a decent drink at the bar and take it down to the beach. Ciao," said Raven and headed backstage.

"Terri's right at the center of this island, isn't he?" I remarked.

"Sure is but check this out." Annie was referring to Toni who arrived with our carafe of white wine. As she placed it in the center of the table, she leaned over me, and I saw what Raven had meant. She was a bit flat chested, but her upper arms were sinewed and beautifully muscled. Her back, too, had muscles clearly defined where I expected to see smooth skin. As I looked at her body, I began to see that it wasn't smooth and soft in the classic female style but was hard and supple as a male athlete's.

As she retreated, tucking the bills of my tip with a big smile into a silver lamé garter high on her exposed leg, Annie touched my hand with hers.

"You've made a hit with Toni," Annie observed coyly.

"You mean the tip did. I can see, now, how she was able to flip Raven like that. Quite a body."

"Do you ever wish I had a body like that, Ned?"

"I really hadn't spent much time putting other bodies on you," I said as I poured us each another glass of wine.

"But Toni's is pretty nice, huh?" I could see a gleam of something in Annie's eye.

"Pretty nice, yeah, I guess. Why?"

"Can you imagine going to bed with Toni?" Annie asked, her eyes big, in innocence.

"I can imagine myself in bed with her, I guess, but she's really not my type. She's.sexy enough, if that's what you mean,"

"Because she's black?"

"No. Not that. That doesn't bother me," and I remembered the two young black women Nash and I had gone home with in Oakland and how I stared at the posters of Huey Newton and Ché Guevara I'd seen in the bedroom of their small frame house. I remembered how white I'd felt and how insecure. "I don't mind that she's black. It's just... I don't know."

"I'm going home tomorrow, Ned," Annie said. "You OK with that?"

"You helped get me to where I need to be, Annie. Thank you. I'll miss you. A lot."

"Want to meet down here a year from now?" Annie asked. "You're going to keep the house?"

"Sure! I'll let Terri move back into his old room. He can be the majordomo. OK if I bring a date?"

"I'd love it. Who's it going to be?"

"Oh, just a girl I met when I was in the Navy."

CHAPTER TWENTY-SEVEN

Vung Tau, 4 December, 2115 hours

"Saw Morgan up at the O Club. She just got back from Saigon," announced Dog as he stepped through the pilot house door of the 93 boat. The 70 boat was rafted alongside.

"Did you tell her?" asked Ned.

"Didn't have to," said Dog as he began to rummage through Ned's charts. "O'Connor spilled the beans. Telling the whole goddamned base."

"She pissed?" asked Ned.

"Not too damned happy about it, as far as I could tell, but she doesn't like much of anything we do, I guess," Dog said with a laugh. Lee and Dog reserved their most outrageous arguments for each other, providing entertainment for all who gathered at the O Club. Dog teased her at every turn, even stitching an olive drab and black peace sign on the right breast pocket of his uniform. To pay him back, Lee had put Dog's name on three mailing lists promising a new world of peace and sharing.

"I like the hippy beads they wear in the brochures they send," Dog had told Lee one night in the O Club, waving a handful of glossy fact sheets, "but I had at least hoped to see a little bare mammary, Morgan. Come on, get me on a good list. Like nudist peaceniks maybe."

"She'll be down here to the dock as soon as she checks in at the hospital," Dog said as he pulled out a South China Sea chart and spread it smooth. "Let's set up some freqs for this game. Any favorites, Ned?"

Ned didn't answer right away. He wondered for a moment why he had volunteered. The rest of the base was dark and silent. Only the thrum and hiss of the two generators broke the silence of the Navy base. A full moon hid behind a low overcast, making the low huts and rickety wooden docks glow peacefully in the dark. One last good op, he thought. Something a little more like the real Navy. Something with ships and the sea and no brown water and jungle rivers.

Ned looked around the pilot house, all of its red lights dimmed. "My built-in's got a bum circuit," he said slowly, "so I'm using a portable. I'd like the low end for our private chat and we can let Division monitor channel 77."

Dog consulted his small notebook and looked up. "How about 10? Usually only SEALs use that one, and I don't think there are any teams in the area."

"Good. I'll send the Kid up and he can tell Frederick." Ned turned from the chart table and spoke into the dim cabin, lit only by a single red night light. "Kid? You down there?"

"Yeah, Boss," came the young voice. "What you need?" In a moment the Kid's shaggy head popped up into the pilot house. He was grinning. The Kid was always grinning, Ned thought.

"Run up to division and tell them we'll be on 77 for this op, OK?"

"You got it," said the Kid and started to duck back into the cabin below. "Back in a flash."

Ned touched him on the shoulder. "Hey, Kid. Wait a sec. Get what call signs they want us to use. OK? Ask them for ones that don't use our numbers."

The Kid's head was swallowed by the dim redness below. "I'm gone!" said the voice.

"He's like a kid at a carnival, isn't he?" observed Dog as they heard him clang out through the aft cabin door and take the steps up to the dock in one noisy leap. "Full of piss and vinegar and willing to do anything to please." Dog looked out into the night across the silent base. The moon tried to shine out through a thinness in the low clouds but it's light was again dimmed to an eerie glow. Dog slowly put his notebook away in its package and the package in his breast pocket. "Must be nice, huh? To be that turned on by everything."

"Yeah," admitted Ned. "Wish I could get the same jolt out of it I used to. When we first got here, it was like being on a constant high. You know, a real rush all the time we were in the rivers. But now it's like it takes a fire fight or some hellatious storm to even get me interested."

"What about being scared?" Dog spoke in a quiet voice Ned hadn't heard before. "Davis was scared, you know. So were the others."

Ned just stared at Dog.

"Did you get scared those last weeks in the river, Ned?"

"Yeah," Ned said quietly, so none of the crew could hear him down in the cabin. He didn't face Dog but was looking out at the huts and docks silhouetted against the glow. "Coming back into the rivers after I got hit, I was real scared. But it wasn't like it used to be, though. "

"How did it used to be?" The question was direct, unemotional, almost clinical.

"It's more like the fear was deep inside, down in the bones, just sitting there and oozing out sometimes when we were just waiting around to go out. When we first went into the rivers, being scared kept me excited and made me feel... kind of alive." Ned paused. "You know what I mean about being alive, Dog?"

"Yeah. I used to feel that way, too, in the beginning. Now... it's like it's just the being afraid. Like the adrenalin has been all used up. No more rush. No more high." Dog's hair looked thin in the red pilot house light. He had gained ten pounds in the last two weeks, thought Ned.

Ned looked at him for a moment, tapping a pencil on the plastic chart table cover. "Maybe it's because we're pretty damned good at what we do and don't need the rush anymore. Maybe only the virgins need the rush, the high."

"Wish to hell I was still a virgin," laughed Dog.

"Me too." They both heard the clatter of his boots as the Kid came back aboard and stepped into the pilot house.

"Division's got the freq. They wanted to remind us not to pass a lot of stuff in the clear. They're going to be Decatur. 93's supposed to be John Paul and Mr. Barns's boat's going to be Jones. The Viets are supposed to be Barbary," the Kid said all in one breath. "And the freighter is Tripoli. What's all the queer names about, Boss?"

"Silly bastards," said Dog. "Sounds like a screwed up naval history course." He took out the notebook, unwrapped it, and wrote in it.

"John Paul Jones was one of our early naval heroes, and the Americans put a lot of pirates out of business in a place called Tripoli, Kid," explained Ned. "Somebody at Division's playing call sign games."

"Yeah, OK. Thanks. You officers sure know a lot of shit... I mean a lot of stuff like that. " The Kid was still breathing hard.

"It's what gets us the extra pay, Kid. That and a painless operation they give all skippers before coming over here."

"What's that, Mr. Barns?" asked the Kid, his eyes big in the red light of the pilot house.

"Forget it, Kid," said Ned. "Tell CB and Chase to let me know when they're ready to go." The Kid's head disappeared.

"OK, Boss."

"Dog?"

"Uh. "

"We need call signs for our private line," reminded Ned.

"I'11 be Walter Shi-mama-fu, OK?" said Dog, patting his bald forehead.

"Sounds good, Walter. I'11 be... Fellini. The guy that did *8 ½*." Ned thought about the circus scene at the end of the film. Tonight's op will probably be just like it, a grand finale, Ned thought. He offered Dog the helmsman's seat and he stood with his back to the chart table.

Dog slipped into the seat and tapped on the deck twice with his toes. "Good. Now that we've each got a plausible nom de guerre, we can get down to it."

"Yeah," said Ned. "What did you and Frederick decide after I left the briefing? I could tell he wanted to pass something on but didn't want it official."

Dog looked over his shoulder toward the opening to the cabin below. Ned turned the squelch on the single sideband radio off and an eerie hiss filled the pilot house.

"Nobody can hear you when that sucker's on. Go ahead," said Ned.

"Pretty straightforward. I asked him what we should do if the Viet Swift started to get nasty. He didn't want to talk about at first."

"And then?" pursued Ned.

"He said that we'd just have to handle it on our own."

"Uh. "

"So, I've got an idea," said Dog.

I hope so, thought Ned. "Let's hear it."

Dog's voice was flat and unemotional. "I'll carry a flechette round in my tube and you carry a Willy-Pete. Both on trigger fire. Armor piercing, incendiary, but no tracers in the .50s. We call the Viets over. Something like, 'Hey, Nguyen. Come on alongside and we'll let you have some steaks or something.' I'll hit them with the flechette from about twenty yards and you get them in the main cabin with the phosphorous." He paused and seemed to consider what he had just said. "Then we sink their asses," he said with a smile.

Ned felt a tingling in his hands, across his thighs, in the small of his back. "Just like that," Ned said, the words not quite a question.

"Just like that." They were silent, listening to the hiss of the generators.

"Anybody home?" said a girlish voice from the dock.

"The phrase is 'Ahoy, there, 'you silly woman," boomed Dog in his best deep voice, the one he reserved for new crew members and intelligence officers. "I'll leave you two to it," he added quietly to Ned. "I'11 be ready to go whenever you are." He disappeared into the darkness outside of the port pilot house door as Lee stepped in through the starboard door.

"Hi, sailor," she said. "Buy a girl a cup of coffee?"

"Sure. Dog said you've already heard about the op." Ned stepped down into the main cabin and switched on the hot water kettle.

"Yeah. O'Connor's spouting off about it and everything else up at the Club," Lee said, taking off her cloth cap and running her fingers through her hair.

Ned came back up to the pilot house, drawing the curtain shut behind him. "Sounds like a clean one, though," he said, watching her face for the reaction. "A good, clean op."

She looked into his eyes, no smile on her face.

"Sounds like bullshit to me, Ned."

"Bullshit? How's that?" Ned didn't expect that reaction.

"You don't want to leave, do you?" she spoke slowly, as though to a foreigner or a child or someone retarded.

"Leave? This place, you mean? Come on," Ned smiled as he spoke. The mournful horn of a tugboat on the main river echoed softly across the harbor. The two Swift boats, the 93 and the 70, creaked against the dock.

"You don't. Not really, Ned." Lee was looking down at the gray deck of the pilot house. The red night light glowed softly around them. Ned wanted to touch her hair. "That's why you're going on this stupid operation. Just so you don't have to grow up and leave. If you were in your right mind, you'd roll up your...things..." She gestured at the chart table.

"Charts," he prompted.

"Your whatever you call them and get on that big silver bird and fly." There were tears now in her voice.

"But I'm still in the..." he started to say. A thin, high whistle started to come from the main cabin. "Coffee! I'll be right back." He disappeared through the curtain.

"You're still a little kid, playing soldier or sailor or whatever it's called," she called after him, her voice thick, anger beginning to give it force. She waited quietly in the red lit pilot house. "And you're afraid to go home," she said at last.

Ned came through the curtain with a white mug that steamed in the red light. "Afraid of what?" He put the cup down on the chart table.

She put her two hands around the cup, cradling it. "Afraid of what you'll find or not find when you get there. " She looked across into his eyes.

"Would you like to explain that theory, Doctor?" he said, trying to smile. She looked down at the mug in her hands.

"You don't want to hear it."

"No. Go ahead," Ned said, feeling his own anger start. "Tell it to me straight. Why am I afraid to go home?"

She took a breath, almost sighing before she spoke, not raising her eyes to his. "Nobody's left. All your old friends have either gotten married or divorced. Your dad is drinking himself into a stupor. Your mom is gone. Your grandmother is gone. What's there for you when you get back?"

"Ok," he interrupted. "I get the point."

"And you don't even have a girl friend to go back to," she continued and looked up at him, almost in triumph.

"I don't need one. I have you," he answered simply.

"No, you don't." She was speaking slowly again, patiently explaining. "You have an over- sexed sister-substitute who lets you play with her."

"Oh, come on, Lee. There's a hell of a lot more here between the two of us than that." Ned couldn't believe what he was hearing, what she was saying to him.

"Oh, Ned. You are a silly bastard, aren't you. You don't see it, do you?"

"See what?" What is going on here? he thought to himself.

"How I'm using you," she answered. Her arms were now at her sides, and she was staring at him. Her back was straight. A siren out on the river hooted once, twice, three times.

"We use each other, then," he agreed. "Is that a crime all of a sudden? We're both grown up and know what we're doing." Ned looked out through the pilot house door, across the harbor to the lights along the river a mile away. "I find you attractive and you seem to find me the same."

Lee didn't say anything for a moment. Ned turned and looked at her. She simply stared at him, and he watched as a tear glinted on her cheek in the red light's glow. "No," she said in a whisper. "I'm just trying to be normal by spending time with you...by fooling around with you." A second tear joined the first. "I like you alright, Ned, but it's not more than that. I'm just doing it to convince myself I'm not queer."

"But you're not. We've proved it," he said, his voice urging her to stop what she was doing to them.

"Bullshit," she said, wiping her eyes with the back of her hand. "I'm just a very horny lady sometimes..." She paused and reached out her right hand and placed it on his shoulder, both holding him and keeping him away with the same gesture. "Don't go on this op. You leave this hell in two days."

He could think of nothing sensible to say. "I've got to go," he finally said. "It's what I do." A stupid reason, he thought, but true.

"You have to stop doing it sooner or later. Stop doing it now. Wake up from your dream, little boy. Go home," she said, her voice loud now. "Grow up!" Her face was no longer pretty in the red light.

"Not yet. It's still too real over here," Ned spoke quietly.

"Then fuck you, Taylor," Lee snapped and was gone into the darkness outside of the pilot house.

"You should be so lucky, sweetheart," Ned said half aloud in his best Bogart voice. His hand came down against the warm mug, spilling coffee across the chart table. "Shit," he muttered and listened to the coffee splatter down onto the deck. When it had slowed to a series of distinct drips, Ned heard the clump of boots on his side deck.

"Tally ho?" Dog's voice said in the darkness.

"Yoiks," answered Ned and began to mop up the coffee, and, like the beginning of the denouement in the third act, his crew began to take their stations for getting underway for their final op.

Cua Soi Rap Channel, early morning

By 0230 the two boats were anchored twenty yards away from each other in the shallows near the skeletal wreck of a tanker in the moon's shadow of Nui Vung Tau, a 170-foot hill, almost as wide as it was tall. The imposing rock made a natural landmark, marking the eastern limit of the Cua Soi Rap channel of the Saigon River. Only the most careful radar operator could have distinguished the Swifts from the wreck, and the hulk of Nui Vung Tau formed a natural backdrop making the two boats invisible.

Ten Taiwanese agents in black or dark grey pants and white short sleeved shirts worn outside to hide their .38s sat in the cabin of the 93 boat. The Kid and then Ned himself offered the men coffee and then soda and finally hot water. Each time the same thin faced man with tiny eyes had said, "Nothing. Thank you. We will wait. " The other men just stared and looked uncomfortable, so Ned had told his crew to stay on deck and leave them alone. Even when left alone, they didn't talk among themselves.

Ten minutes after anchoring, Ned called CB forward to the pilot house. Tom sat at the helm and CB stood in the doorway.

"Let's shut down the main engines but keep the generator going. I'd like you, Tom, to take a couple sweeps with the radar every five minutes or so."

CB shifted his weight onto his toes. "Can I clean strainers, Boss?"

Ned thought for a moment and then said, "Better not. We might have to get underway in a hurry." He nodded and CB went back to the after steering station and the port and then starboard engines fell silent.

Tom bent over the black rubber hood of the radar scope, its green glow reflecting on his face, making his eyes seem black hollows. "What are we looking for again? A freighter?" he asked, his voice hushed.

"And a Swift," reminded Ned. "The freighter will be coming in from the east. The Swift's out of Saigon, so if she shows it'll be from the northwest, on a southeasterly course. Division's figured their rendezvous for a point about ten miles from here, on a bearing of about 255 degrees."

Tom grunted assent and continued to hover over the scope. "Scope's clean," he said at last and looked up.

"Thanks, Tom," said Ned. He could hear the 93 boat's

313

generator seem to grow louder as the 70 boat shut down her engines.

"John Paul, this is Jones. Radio check, over," broke the rumbling silence.

"Roger, Jones. This is John Paul," said Ned into the mic. "Read you loud and clear. How me? Over." Dog was doing it by the book. Establishing clean comms early in the mission, dotting the i's and crossing the t's. A good man to have on your wing. Bets or no bets.

"Read you the same. Break. Decatur, this is John Paul and Jones, over." Dog's voice continued.

After a minute and two more tries, Division answered with, "John Paul and Jones, this is Decatur, over."

"Roger, Decatur. This is Jones. Any information on Tripoli or Barbary, over?"

"Stand by, Jones, and we'll have numbers... " There was silence for half a minute. The voice that came back was Frederick's. "Figures follow. Tripoli bears 280 degrees, twenty-three thousand yards from you. Delta. India. Whiskey. Break... Barbary bears 140 degrees, twenty thousand, speed 10, course 255. Break... Barbary has been told by the higher authority to alter course to 345 degrees at time 0300. When she bears 220, range six thousand yards, you can go alongside and unload your cargo, over."

"Roger, Decatur. We have that," said Dog, and Ned smiled, knowing Dog had it all down in his little notebook. "Trust you'll keep us in the big picture, over. "

"Affirmative, Jones. This is Decatur, out. "

Division sounded a little up tight, thought Ned. He started to plot the ranges and bearings he had written in grease pencil on the edge of the plexiglas chart table cover.

"You get that, Fellini?" Ned grabbed the mic from the overhead clip. "I got it, Walter. Just plotting it now. Did the old man seems a little nervous to you?"

"Maybe he's just pissed he's got to be up all night at a damned circus like this," suggested Dog.

"Yeah, I guess," said Ned. "Stay on the line a sec." He drew a line from the mouth of a small river called the Dong Tran to where they were to put the Taiwanese aboard the freighter. "Walter?"

"Go."

"You know, when we're supposed to be stopping this big boy, we're going to be blind to our little cousin from Tripoli." Ned paused and then continued. "I don't really like those odds, Walter."

"I hear you."

Across the flat silver of the shallow waters of the South China Sea came first a high, ringing clink, a rattle and then the splash of the anchor, followed by the rumble and rush of the fathoms of heavy chain.

The Taiwanese freighter had been told to anchor just inside the three-mile limit and wait for her pilot. Commander Frederick had told the two Swifts that the freighter was expected to comply. So far, so good, thought Ned, and he began to look forward again to the mission.

He nodded to Tom and both diesels roared to life. The Kid, leaning out of the peak tank, hauled the last of the nylon anchor rode and the #8 Danforth anchor onto the small foredeck of the Swift and pulled both anchor and rode into the peak tank with him. He waved his hand over his head. He then jacked a round into the chamber of his M-60, checking that the ammunition belt fed cleanly from the box to his right to the weapon. The bow of the 93 boat started to rise as she picked up speed.

Tom, the helmsman, noticed out of the port pilot house door that the 70 boat was already on plane heading for the freighter lying dead in the water a thousand yards away. He watched as the indistinct silhouette of the Swift sharpened and became a definite boat shape as their running lights winked on and the moonlight intensified as the clouds thinned for a moment. Two red lights, one over the other, shone from the utility mast amidships. "Red over red: pilot ahead," Tom recited under his breath as he switched on their own running and signal lights.

"Tai Pet Garden, Tai Pei Garden, this is Customs Unit Three, over." The thin faced agent's eyes sparkled in the light reflected from the flashlight Ned held for him as he read from a small paper copybook he pulled from his back pants pocket. The agent held the mic like a live grenade, thought Ned.

"Vessel Tai Pei Garden, Vessel Tai Pei Garden, this is Customs Unit Three, over," he repeated.

Ned could hear a transmitter key once, twice, three times, but no voice broke the hiss of the radio's carrier wave. They were tuned to the international calling and distress frequency, Channel 16 FM. Ned nodded to the agent, who gave the mic to Ned.

"Vessel Tai Pei Garden, this is Customs Unit Three, aboard the pilot boat Tran Hung Dao, over," Ned spoke slowly, trying to neutralize his American accent by shaping each syllable carefully before he spoke it.

He was rewarded by a foreign voice acknowledging, "Customs Unit Three, this is the Tai Pei Garden, of Tai Pei, the Republic of China, over. Are you our pilot?"

The agent did not smile but took the mic from Ned with a curt nod of thanks. He spoke slowly, referring to characters which Ned could not decipher written in the copybook. "Tai Pei Garden, request you rig a ladder your starboard side. I am coming alongside, over."

A new voice, softer than the first voice from the Tai Pei Garden, spoke in rapid Vietnamese. "...Tran Hung Dao... " was all Ned could recognize.

Ned grabbed the mic for the secure radio but heard Dog's voice speaking calmly. "Decatur, Decatur, do you have a translation of that for us, over?"

"Affirmative. Wait one...He wants you to give your position, over," returned the voice of Frederick, and, in the background, Ned could hear an excited voice speaking Vietnamese.

No way will we give our position, thought Ned, and he poked twice at the paper in the agent's hand. "Say it again," Ned said.

"...Tran Hung Dao..." spoke the voice in Vietnamese again.

"Tai Pei Garden, this is Customs Unit Three. Request you rig a ladder your starboard side. I am coming alongside," the agent said. He started to put the mic down and then raised it to his lips and added, "We are a half mile astern of you and want your ladder over when we get there. Is that clear, over?"

Ned let out a breath and glared at the agent, who returned an equally angry look. "These civilians will obey...but only if you speak to them with authority," the thin man said. "You will see."

"This is Tai Pei Garden. Come along our starboard side, over."

The agent went below into the cabin.

"My man just blew it, Walter," Ned said quietly into the mic for the private channel between the 93 and the 70 boats.

"I heard, I heard, Fellini," said Dog. "I might just hold back a bit and keep an eye out. I don't want to get in too close until I know where the pirates are. I'm going to black out and just float for a while. Whistle if you need anything."

"I'll let you know when we're alongside," promised Ned. Through the port door he could see the 70 boat's bow wave diminish to a thin streak of white and saw her navigation lights go dark. In a moment she had disappeared into the darkness and the weak moonlight faded again.

Tom had the black rubber hood off the radar scope and the range set to 2,000 yards, one nautical mile. He looked up at the stern light of the anchored freighter and then down at the radar scope as the first two ruby tracers arced across the flat water from ahead of the Tai Pei Garden and left two spumes of water to port and ahead of the path of their speeding boat. Tom cut hard to port toward the splashes to narrow their target angle. "I've got a second target on radar just behind the ship. It just came out of the shadow of the freighter," said Tom.

Chase, up in the twin-.50s called down, "We're taking rounds, Boss! And it looks like it's from near the freighter."

"Hold your fire and tell the others," Ned started to say up

into the gun tub when he lost his voice and felt first a shove and then a hot, damp scalding in his bowels. Ned tried to turn to Tom, but his legs collapsed under him and he started to fall, the back of the helmsman's seat snapping his jaw shut. "Where's the 70 boat?" he heard a voice say.

"... port quarter, range 1,000 yards," Tom said after a moment. "Chase," Tom said slowly. "The Boss is down."

"Keep me posted."

"Walter, this is...shit, what is it? Feeling? Boss's taken a hit, over."

"Good man, Tom," Ned tried to say, "but you don't have to speak so slowly."

"Fellini, this is Walter. I want you to break off and head for home. I'll call ahead so they'll meet you at the dock. Everyone else OK?"

i must hurt like hell Dog but its like i don't feel it

"The rest of us are all OK, but the Boss's pretty bad."

"Don't use the radio, Fellini, except this channel. I want to finish up out here."

hes ok   tom is   he will do

"Hey, Boss," said CB, "you going to be all right. Just lean here back against me. Just relax, Boss."

if i relax i let go it all

"Relax, Boss," said CB.

Vung Tau, early morning

Sharp points of light and hands inside of him smoothing tugging little bits of him to one side or away from the long bones and he could feel the rip of things but not the expected pain. He rocked twice and felt his lungs flush and fill and flush again with the soft push and pull of the machine that took the nothing he was and was filling it slowly and warmly, swelling him to life size and easily stopping there but not really and starting like a mortar round to fall back again toward the earth and continuing at a slow pulse beat to empty him of all... that was in him.

And as the tugging went on but under him this time he felt himself swelling again like a balloon but this time with water and not air. He rose higher and higher as they pumped him full and heard better the noises clink clink swish as he felt first warmth and then heat where he thought his crotch used to be. When he could hold it inside no longer, he knew that all he had to do was to let go but he could not and still it filled in him.

Jesus, he thought. Jesus, and I don't really believe except maybe in what you felt up there like me now here but that isn't enough to believe in as something let go and they took part of me out and he heard the clank of it striking the metal tray. Something pulled loose inside and he felt himself empty in two long seconds *and now I can relax*

there is a flag down on the play

you are not playing the game, lieutenant

will they throw the parts away I cannot use again

"Play the game, Ned," the girl voice said, "and squeeze my hand."

He let go again and could relax. "Tell me," he thought, "what happened with the pirates?"

"What pirates? How long have you been awake?" a woman's voice said, a Florida panhandle voice that he knew.

"I only just got here," he thought.

"You had us scared, Ned. You really did," Lee whispered, and he could feel a slight pressure as she touched his forehead.

"How long have I been here like this?" he said.

"It's been almost two days. Dog just left. Tom from your crew will be back a little later." She squeezed his hand and asked, "Can you open your eyes?"

"I like it like this," he thought.

"Ned," Lee said again. "Can you open your eyes?"

"Let's just lie here like this, OK," he thought. "I'll play the game. Promise."

"Ned, can you hear me?" she said, her voice loud and impatient. A bell rang.

"I hear you and I'll be good. We can just fool around and don't have to go all the way. But answer me a question, OK?

Did you ever do this with Willie? I just want to know..."

"..awake for a little and now he's gone again," the panhandle voice said.

"Try his soles. Any reaction? Toe curl?"

jesus that feels good and it tingles all over keep it up and your eyes are bright and dancing things and your hands so cool all over me and

"Nothing. Pulse is weak. Respiration shallow."

"Losing him?"

am I as good as she

"Morgan, are you all right?"

"I'm fine. I thought for a second we'd lost him."

and it has never been like this before

"He's steady, now. We've got him. Just."

"...and he's going to have a hell of scar."

oh, jesus, that's so good

CHAPTER TWENTY-EIGHT

Key West, early morning

Ned looked down at the paper on the table in front of him. He smoothed it out and read it again. The words told him something he knew, but he couldn't figure out what. He felt empty sitting here, the morning light just starting to define the roofs of the buildings across the patio.

The citation read, *On 5 December, Lieutenant (junior grade) TAYLOR was serving as Officer in Charge of Inshore Patrol Craft Nine Three in company with Inshore Patrol Craft Seven Zero operating in support of an offshore interdiction operation off the southern coast of Cap Sainte Jacques. The two Navy units involved had completed an extensive surveillance of the area and were about to put friendly foreign forces aboard a merchant ship when enemy forces began a waterborne attack on the three vessels. Reacting immediately, he directed his craft to close the enemy forces. After receiving a wound in the lower abdomen and being ordered by the Senior Officer Present Afloat to clear the area, he continued to direct his craft and was able to provide essential radio communication between Coastal Division One and Inshore Patrol Craft Seven Zero, leading to the speedy neutralization and total destruction of the enemy force. Lieutenant (junior grade) TAYLOR's devotion to duty and professionalism reflected great credit upon himself and were in keeping with the highest traditions of the United States Naval Service.*

He stood up, letting the serape drop to the floor behind

him. Sitting on the arm of the couch, he picked up the telephone receiver and started to dial a long-distance number. He had dialed the number many times before in the past month, but this time he let it ring without hanging up. The number rang seven times before it was answered.

"Good morning," he said. "It's Ned Taylor. I'd really like to finish that conversation we started that last night before the op."

Her answer must have amused him because he smiled and then laughed.

September, 1989 – October, 2024
West Windsor, Vermont
Bushberg, Missouri

ABOUT THE AUTHOR

Bill Stanard was born at the end of World War Two, served in the Navy in the rivers in Vietnam, spent fifty years teaching English and Computer Science and building boats. He lives and works in St. Louis, Missouri.

Made in the USA
Middletown, DE
30 April 2025

74950621R00181